ONE

LAST

WAR

By C.G. Buswell

Copyright © C.G. Buswell 2020

All Rights Reserved

.

This is a work of fiction and any characters that bear a resemblance to anyone living or dead is a coincidence. The events are imagined by the author and bear no similarities to actual events.

Cover design and typesetting by letsgetbooked.com

Also by C.G. Buswell

Novels

The Grey Lady Ghost of the Cambridge Military Hospital: Grey and Scarlet 1

The Drummer Boy: Grey and Scarlet 2

Buried in Grief

Short Stories

Christmas at Erskine

Halloween Treat

Angelic Gift

Burnt Vengeance

The Release

Christmas Presence

Torturous Grief

For Fiona, Lorraine, Kate and Bravehound Lynne who have changed my life and saved me from stepping over the edge. And to my dear wife, Karla, who stopped me from leaping, thank you.

Chapter One

He paced his lounge like a veteran soldier from the First World War, defending his territory from an enemy attack. His windowsill was his sandbagged trench protection from his attacking foes. The net curtains were his cover from vigilant eyes, he thought that he was unseen from the outside. The carpet was well worn in the area beneath his tall windows from his constant fretting and patrolling to and fro. No furniture was permitted to be there. His defensive arcs of fire were the adjoining property grass and path. His new enemy would be coming, he sensed it as soon as the estate agents For Sale board went up, close to his four-foot walled border, by his lock-blocked front garden. No sole weed dared to intrude upon his domain, no flower of joy allowed to bloom, just as no visitor dared to open his heavy gate without prior approval. His cast iron driveway double gates were bolted and padlocked shut to keep out unwanted guests. His boundary to the council pavement had been carefully measured and was within a millimetre precision of his kingdom. His property. No-one and nothing could enter his realm without him knowing, his eight CCTV cameras strategically placed around his brick-built semi-detached house ensured that. But no amount of screen watching, seen from his bedroom and lounge monitors, could give him the assurance he so badly craved that he would be left alone and in peace; except for the infernal click-click of his wife's knitting needles and the distracting unrolling of her ball of wool as she created yet another jumper for him to wear.

'Come away from the window Simon, you'll wear that carpet out. Stop looking out and being nosey. Come over here so that I can measure your back.'

'Away with you Millie, don't bother me now woman, I need to see them. I want to watch out for their arrival.'

Millie rose from her rocking chair with a creak. The wooden furniture made a snapping noise like brittle bones cracking with her movement. She groaned as she stood up, her arthritic knees causing her pain. She edged carefully to him, hoping that today she would not anger or annoy him, that he would not hit her. She approached him tentatively with the knitted rectangular offering held aloft as if it were a shield against his blows. She carefully placed it against his shoulders as if gently laying a blanket over a sleeping baby to ward off the cold. Millie then quickly let her unfinished knitted jumper droop beyond his back and towards his waist and mentally calculated how many more rows she needed to complete this garment that would stave off the coming winter. She knew she should have knitted her own first because she felt the chill of the unheated home more, but as always, she had to put his needs first. 'If only he would allow me to turn the heating on more often during the cold nights and days,' she thought, 'or go outside to enjoy this fine summer's day and stock up on some heat. It is so stuffy and oppressive in here.'

'Get off me woman!' shouted Simon as he shrugged off the lovingly made garment. He quickly turned around and made to push her violently back to her rocking chair. But she was too fast for him, this time. Years of abuse at his hands had taught her to be quick on her feet, despite the pain from her joints. 'Can't you see I'm busy, stupid cow! Just leave me be and get back to your infernal clicking away.' He coughed and grunted as he breathed heavily away, the exertion had been too much for his obese torso that smothered his lungs, making them work faster as if they were pumping whilst being held in a vice.

She backed away from him, all the time keeping her eyes lowered in submission, fearfully expecting the blow that would inevitably come. Never to the face. No. He was far too clever to allow the bruises, scratches, and marks to show. Outward appearances were everything to him. His reputation in the village had to be upheld. She put down her knitting work into her basket, sat down slowly and picked up her cigarette packet and lighter and lit her fifth fag of the day. It was only 11am and he was already riled. She caught a whiff of his body odour before she inhaled the reassuring smell and savoured the taste of her favourite tobacco. How she wished he would wash and maybe even put on some antiperspirant to disguise his sweat. It was almost as if he was marking his territory with his scent like a tom cat soiling in neighbouring flowerbeds. She puffed clouds of smoke and watched them drift up to the yellowing ceiling and thought ironically that they soon disappeared as if reminiscent of her life draining away, being leached by him.

Tilly turned slowly into the terrace and smoothly changed gears whilst admiring how pretty the rows of red-bricked houses looked as the late summer sun bounced off them. She caught sight of a zebra and what looked like a hedgehog on a nearby front door as she drove her family past a green and white for sale sign planted firmly in the grass. 'Ha, ha, did you see the zebra kids?' she laughed out whilst squinting ahead for the route to the harbour.

'Nooo,' yawned Gordon and Annabelle in sibling unison. They were hoping against hope that their parents weren't taking them to another stately home to look around boring paintings and vases. Or other more ancient buildings with far too many stairs for their weary little legs to climb.

'It was on the door of that house for sale that we just passed. It was on the top glass. It looked really beautiful and made a nice change from the standard flowery patterns of most front doors,' explained their mum.

Carl turned to his wife but could see no sense of mischief in her gorgeous hazel eyes. They didn't twinkle and dance with light like they did when she was pulling their legs. 'Perhaps we'll stop on the drive back kids and you can go out and feed the zebra but watch out for the needles on the hedgehog!'

His dad joke was awarded with laughter from the back seats as Tilly sighed and tutted. She followed through with an 'Och,' learnt from her Scottish grandfather years ago and retained as a nod to her Scots heritage.

'Yes, we will. Then I will be proved right. It's a bit random though, having a zebra on a front door. I wonder what that story is.'

'Mmm,' replied Carl absentmindedly, 'I can feel one of your mum's adventures coming on kids.' A low moan of disapproval grew louder from the back seats as their mum ignored her children and husband and continued to drive.

'Is it another castle?' asked six-year-old Annabelle hesitantly, whilst playing with her blonde bobbed hair and kicking her feet against the fabric of the seat support. 'My legs are still tired from climbing all the stairs of the last one. There were hundreds of them.'

'Don't exaggerate sis,' said know-it-all Gordon. 'Dad and I counted them and there were only ninety-two steps.'

Annabelle turned to her brother and quickly stuck her tongue out at him before her mother could see her in the rear-view mirror and tell her off. He was one year older than his sister and thought he had the knowledge of seniority. Annabelle thought him more of a show-off than a know-it-all.

Tilly gave an exclamation of 'Ah ha!' as she slowed for another turn. 'Can anyone guess where we are going yet?'

Carl, in on the secret trip, stayed quiet, allowing their children to play the guessing game.

Annabelle jumped up from her seat only to be stopped by her seatbelt. As her bottom landed back onto the safety of her car seat, she gave out an excited, 'I can see the sea mummy, look, down the hill, there is a huge blue boat going up and down on the waves.'

'It's a trawler cupcake,' said Carl using his special nickname for his beloved daughter. 'They'll have just left the safety of the harbour and will be going out for a few days fishing using their big nets.' He pressed a button on his left armrest and unwound the window and gave a huge and overexaggerated sniff. 'Can you smell the seaside kids?'

'Yuck!' howled Gordon, 'it smells like grandma's kitchen on a Friday night.'

Tilly and Carl laughed out loud. 'It's the fish that has been landed by the other boats. The crew slice them open and throw the fish guts back into the sea. Usually the seagulls catch them and if you are lucky you might even see a seal swimming in the harbour lazily waiting for an easy snack.'

'Yewww', screamed out the children in unison. 'I don't want to see fish guts mummy,' cried Annabelle in protest.

Tilly reached out with her left hand and gave Carl a quick, but light playful slap across his thigh with the back of her hand. 'Stop it you, or she won't want to eat her sandwiches. Or sleep tonight.'

Carl laughed, reached behind him and gently stroked Annabelle's leg to reassure her. 'Don't worry love, the seagulls and seals will have eaten them all by the time mummy drives there.' He smiled in awe as he saw the behemoth structure looming ahead of them. The tall red and white painted lighthouse, bright in the glorious sunshine, stood out like a beacon of hope for their new life in this area, after years of struggle and strain trying to cope with the oddities of Tilly's family. He sighed, thankful that all those cares were many miles behind them now and grateful that Tilly had finally agreed to move to get away from her abusive parents. He had wanted to protect his children from their evil desires. He owed a lot to the counsellor who opened Tilly's eyes to the danger she was placing her children in and was in peril of unconsciously allowing history to repeat itself.

'Cor! Look at that big white building with the red stripes,' enthused Gordon, unknowingly interrupting his father's unhappy thoughts. 'Is it a giant's house?'

Carl laughed uproariously as if to match the waves that crashed against the rocks further ahead. 'No son, that's a lighthouse. Do you see the big light on top?'

'Yes, dad, I see it!' replied Gordon eagerly.

'Well, that lights up automatically to warn ships out to sea that they are near the coast and dangerous rocks. Otherwise they would run aground. In the olden days, there would have been several light-keepers. These men would have to light the lamps when it got dark, polish the lenses, and keep everything going. Right at the top of the lighthouse.'

Annabelle looked out timidly from her car seat, 'we don't have to climb all its stairs do we dad?' she asked seeking reassurance.

'Sadly not,' replied Tilly, regretfully, 'I looked it up on my phone earlier and it is shut up to the public. The old keepers' cottages are rented out as holiday homes.'

'Doesn't the light shine into their windows and keep them awake,' asked Annabelle.

'No, it's set to shine far out to sea where all the boats are. They aren't really needed anymore because most ships have radar.'

'What's radar daddy?' asked a puzzled Annabelle.

'It's a bit like the satellite navigation system we bought to stop mummy getting lost in the car,' replied Carl ignoring the withering looks from his wife who hated her driving skills being questioned. He concentrated instead on the chuckles from his children. 'So ships have a special computer like a sat nav, only it is called radar. It helps guide them safely around the sea. A bit like mummy and I taking you away from our old home and your school to somewhere safer. We steered you both away from the jagged rocks.'

'Oh,' replied Annabelle, impressed at her daddy who seemed to know everything and always looked after them all.

Tilly slowed down the car and gently allowed it to come to a rest in a layby conveniently placed before a long bridge with white railings. Whilst she got out to sort out the children, Carl was busy in the boot looking out their picnic basket.

Simon ran to his gates, in time to see the car that had slowed down to briefly look at his old neighbour's front door artwork, make its way down to the end of his terrace. He deeply cleared his throat and spat out its disgusting package onto the pavement as if showing his disregard for the family of four. He was oblivious to the young mother and her small son who were walking to the local Post Office and who both had to quickly dart out of the way from his phlegmatic projection with a disapproving tut and a brave scowl. He looked up to his CCTV cameras and security lights, checking that they were still firmly attached to their respective walls and grunted his approval at his own handiwork. He gave one last glowering look at the car that had dared to enter his village and returned to his house to resume his watch. As he entered his front room his wife of forty years nervously asked him, 'Would you like a cup of tea Simon?'

'Of course I bloody do woman, now get out and get me something to eat too.' He raised his arm threateningly as he approached her rocking chair. Recognising the signs, Millie jumped up, despite her painful joints, and darted through to their kitchen, only narrowly missing the punching arm that carried with it a fresh wave of offensive body odour that permeated throughout the room.

She wished that she could hang out her washing and have something to do to fill in the hours. If only he would change his clothes more than once a week, she thought, then I could have something to fill my days and he may not smell so bad, especially at bedtime when he removed his underwear and expected her to do her duty. She shuddered as she tried to expel this thought from her mind and looked out of the kitchen window as she filled the kettle from the tap. I don't even have the comfort of a garden to tend to or to watch the birds go about their colourful and serene life.

Like the front garden, the rear had also been lock-blocked, not even one inch of grass grew in their concrete garden. It was not so much a garden as a continuous pavement with a lonely rotary clothes washing-line standing in the middle like a totem to the sun gods. She silently said her own prayer to God to save her from her man. She knew that this would go unanswered and wished instead that her son,

Peter, a father himself and about to celebrate his fortieth birthday, could only see his father for what he was and take her to live with their family. No wonder their daughter, Victoria, had seen sense and married a soldier and moved with him years ago to Wales. She had enough sense to put hundreds of miles between her and Simon. She only tolerated their visits each New Year for her mother's sake. How Millie missed her children, but she was glad that they were no longer beaten by their father.

'Race you across the bridge,' yelled Carl as he pretended to start to sprint, gently swaying the picnic basket for added effect. His children took the bait and rushed past him, Annabelle lagging just slightly behind Gordon who was doing his best Hollywood run – all pumping arms and short steps.

Carl reached for his wife's hand and gently took it in his. 'I told you it was a great idea to move by the sea, it's like a great adventure for these two. They'll soon forget about their horrible grandparents.'

'I know love, but I do worry that they won't make friends and will miss their old pals. I'm so sorry I couldn't see my parents for what they were.'

'Don't worry dear,' replied Carl, stopping to give Tilly a reassuring cuddle. He broke it off and took hold of her hand again. Only he gently gave it a small squeeze this time, as if to reinforce his words. 'I won't let anyone harm us ever again. My parents aren't exactly mum and dad of the year material, but they mean well. The kids will soon make new friends when school starts after the summer holidays.'

'I'm not looking forward to that Carl.'

'What do you mean love?' asked a worried Carl.

'Well, it will be autumn soon after they go to their new school and the weather will turn. I don't fancy another year in that old draughty house we are renting. Our mean landlord just won't go to the expense of fitting a door to the lounge nor replace the draughty window. Remember how he just hammered it shut. He did a terrible job and now its stuck halfway between open and closed. It's fine for this August weather, but it'll be so cold for us all in the winter winds. Please let us use the money we made from the sale of our old house to buy somewhere nice. I've been looking online, and house prices are so much cheaper here. We could buy a three-bedroomed house and build on in a few years' time.'

Carl smiled warmly to his wife and withdrew his hands from hers and placed them on both of her cheeks. 'Whatever you want love. I only want to make you happy. Have you somewhere in mind?'

Tilly began with, 'Yes. I'm fed up living in towns, let's move to the seaside, I've always…'

Her sharing of desires was interrupted by shouts of 'I was the winner' and 'no I was, tell him mummy.'

'Hold that thought dear, we'd better sort these two out,' laughed Carl as he took his wife's hand and walked her across the tarmacked bridge to join their boisterous children.

Simon spat out his tea and threw the cup against the adjoining wall of the lounge. Fortunately, the neighbouring house was empty, he had seen to that. 'For God's sake woman, can't you even make a cup of tea the right way? It's far too sweet.'

Millie cowered before him; her hands instinctively flung in front of her face to protect her eyes from the hot liquid. She had learnt to do this habitually from previous bad experiences with the quick-tempered Simon over the decades of their marriage. 'When will this torment ever end?' she questioned to herself.

'Go on, get out and make my lunch. And be sure not to put too much pickle in my sandwich this time bitch,' he yelled as Millie obediently ran from the room despite her aching knees. He marched over to the door and slammed it shut. Then quickly opened it and slammed it several times in a row for good measure. It helped supress his anger. He then briskly turned and went back to his window, to await their approach.

'I think you both crossed the finishing line at the same time,' said Tilly appeasing both her beloved children with a reassuring smile. She looked across to a low double-gate that barred their approach to the lighthouse and the cottage buildings. A discrete sign, above a four-star sign informed her that it was private property and that the privacy of holidaymakers should be respected. 'That's a pity,' she said under her breath. Not to be outdone she said aloud, 'There's a path here to the right, shall we have a small walk around the lighthouse kids?' She included her husband in this grouping.

'Yes, please mummy!' replied Carl playfully.

Annabelle looked pleased, 'Does this mean we don't have to climb all of its steps.'

'I'm afraid so cupcake, it's out of bounds to us.'

'Hooray,' she shouted out as she found new energy and ran off down the path, getting ahead of her brother who was soon at her heels when he saw it was a new race.

Their parents laughed again, clasped each other's hands, and walked after them. As they followed their children Tilly tried to resume their previous conversation, 'As I said before, I have always wanted to live by…'

'What's that big red thing sticking out of that shed mum?' interrupted Gordon. 'It looks like one of those gramophone things we saw in one of those castles you took us to, only bigger.'

'It's a foghorn love,' replied his mother, 'it blows out a noise to alert sailors that there are rocks below. It would be switched on when it got misty or foggy. Though none are used now because of the radar your dad told you about. Besides, they used to keep folk in nearby houses awake at night with its noise so loud that it carried right out to sea.'

'Oh,' replied Gordon thoughtfully, 'how did it sound?'

'Like a cow!' replied Tilly playfully. 'My dear old grandfather used to call the one in Aberdeen the Torry Coo, after the area near the harbour and the Scottish word for cow.'

Annabelle and Carl burst out laughing, though Gordon didn't seem to get the joke.

'Moo,' went Annabelle between fits of giggles. Her father helped her out by joining in, and much louder, to the amused annoyance of Tilly, though she secretly thought they were quite funny, she wasn't about to admit it to any one of them.

'Warf, warf,' replied a voice from the rocks below, as if joining in the fun. The quartet stopped their giggles and mooing and looked over the edge of the path to the source of this new noise.

'Careful you two,' warned Carl. 'Don't get too close to the edge,' he grasped their delicate small hands into his large palms to ensure their safety.

'Look mummy and daddy, it's a seal, it's barking at us,' marvelled Annabelle. 'Isn't it beautiful.'

Her parents looked down amongst the sharp rocks to where a small inlet with a shingle beach offered the mammal shelter from the waves. Its stomach was flat on the shingle whilst its chest was raised as if trying to help its call project out to sea or below the water to encourage others of its kind to seek shelter ashore and enjoy the sunshine.

'He's gorgeous cupcake, but you and Mr Peeps here should keep a distance from him as they have a sharp bite. And they are fast, they bounce along the ground and can chase you, like Mr Peeps here used to do when he first learnt to crawl and before he could walk. He'd slither under my favourite armchair and peep out and give us his cheeky smile, wouldn't you Mr Peeps?'

'Daaad,' drawled Gordon, 'I'm seven now, you know I don't like to be called that anymore, it's embarrassing.'

Annabelle wriggled free from her dad's hand and skipped along the path, shouting out as she went, 'Mr Peeps, Mr Peeps!' This was the cue for Gordon to also slip free and run after her, their race resumed.

Tilly smiled at them, 'As I was trying to say, I've always wanted to live by the sea, let's move out of that awful hovel of a house and buy somewhere here. This village is so peaceful, and it'll be like a great playground for the children, we passed a primary school, it'll be easy for them to walk there each day.'

'Mmm,' replied Carl thoughtfully, 'I'm not sure, I've still a lot to learn about building that website and it might be a while before I see a profit. I guess I could go and get another job, only…'

'I'm much better now Carl, you don't have to worry about me, I won't try it again, I love you all too much.'

Carl took her hand and when she reciprocated with a gentle squeeze of reassurance her blouse sleeve rose and exposed the scars from her last suicide attempt, a sharp reminder to Carl of what was important to him. 'Okay love,' he said hesitantly, 'anything to make you happy, let's enjoy the day and then go home and do some sums and see what we can afford. I've taken enough time off since moving into the rented house, it's time I pulled my finger out and built more pages of the website and earned some money, after all, everyone loves a good recipe and a cookbook, I reckon that scottishrecipes.co.uk will turn our fortunes around. Who knew that I'd one day discover a love of cooking after years in the army and that I'd start cooking Scottish food? Your dear grandparents' old recipes will help buy you the house of your dreams. We've still got lots of the money from selling our old home, so I reckon we'll only need a small mortgage, and interest rates are so low these days.'

Tilly leaned across to him and kissed him whilst below they heard a resounding 'Warf, warf!'

'See, even the local wildlife wants us to live here,' giggled Tilly as she broke off their kiss.

Carl smiled as a dark cloud glided over and momentarily cast a shadow over his face, like a portent of doom passing through. 'Come on, we had better catch up with Tweedledee and Tweedledum and break off any fighting. Then we can have our picnic at the harbour.'

'Cooee,' shouted Dotty from the other side of the road. 'It's a fine day, lovely to see the sun out,' she continued as she crossed the road. 'How are you today Millie?'

'Not too bad Dotty,' she replied whilst casting a quick look over her shoulder and toying nervously with a small plastic bag.

Dotty sighed, this action by her friend was a familiar one and one that she hoped she wouldn't need to do anymore. It was the worst kept secret in the village. Everyone knew what a monster Simon was, but none dared to interfere, not if they wanted a peaceful life. 'Will you come across for a cup of tea?'

'Not today,' sighed Millie, 'I've to make a start on Simon's lunch, you know what he's like.' She opened the wheelie-bin lid and dropped the plastic bag in and gently closed the lid, fearful that any noise would alert her husband that she was outside. She shrugged her shoulders, sighed, and turned around and walked slowly back down her path to her front door.

'Yes,' replied Dotty, speaking to herself as she saw poor browbeaten Millie hesitantly enter her home. 'We all know what he's like,' she finished as she stared sadly into the adjoining house's lounge. No curtains in the window and no furniture in that room, or any others. Weeds had sprouted into the once carefully maintained borders and the grass needed a good cut. Guy and his wife, Finty, had unexpectedly moved out one day, taking everything with them and not saying goodbye to anyone. Whilst the removal men were loading up the large van, Simon had stood on the front step watching them with a satisfied smirk on his face. He had bounced up and down on the soles of his feet almost as if he couldn't quite contain his sense of achievement and satisfaction. He was almost childlike in his glee, but in his heart, there was no innocence. Everyone knew that Guy had loved this village and his home as much as he loved his wife. He took great care of her and their garden. But he was not strong enough to cope with what Simon had put them through after he had gone around to check on Millie one day. He had been concerned by the noises penetrating through their adjoining wall, noises that he suspected were items being thrown at Millie, and thankfully missing her.

'Where's my sandwich bitch?' escaped through the closed door that her friend had quietly shut. Dotty could imagine the dank, evilness pouring through their letterbox, spilling onto the front step, and gushing down the path. She shivered involuntary and ran back to the safety of her own home, lest her caring soul be tainted by one drop of that man's foulness.

'Have another sandwich Gordon, it's your favourite cheese and pickle,' said Tilly motherly to her son. 'And don't feed it all to the seagulls this time,' she gently reproached him as she looked from the bench at the harbour they had walked to.

'Oh, but I love feeding the birds mum, they fly ever so gracefully and when they come down it's like they are coming into land on a runway and then they tuck their wings in like a big pterodactyl. Then their jaws open wide as if they are about to swallow a monster.'

Tilly turned to Carl, 'You've been watching dinosaur films again, haven't you?'

'Only when you go for your afternoon nap, it keeps them happy and quiet while I flick through the recipe books the publisher sent me. I've a delicious chocolate brownie recipe to upload onto the site.'

Tilly smiled appreciatively at them both, she knew herself to be lucky to have such a close, loving family. 'Okay, at least eat half this time,' she relented.

Gordon ran down amongst the shingle and joined his sister who was nibbling away at her sandwich whilst squatting and poking about a small rock pool with a stick. He watched as the tide gently lapped up to the shoreline and then was distracted by a bobbing head. He excitedly nudged his sister who stood back up, saw her brother's pointed hand, and looked across to what had grabbed his attention.

'It's a head! It's got whiskers, it's another seal!'

'No,' whispered Gordon mischievously, 'it's a monster! And it's coming to gobble you up and take you out to sea!' He stretched up on tippy toes for added effect and held his arms out as if to engulf and devour her.

Annabelle didn't disappoint her brother and as he had anticipated, she let out a high-pitched scream.

Tilly, with all her motherly instincts on high alert, ran down to them, the shingle sounding like broken glass churning in a spin cycle of a washing machine. And like any parent, she would have walked over a path of shattered glass to reach her distressed child.

'Mummy, mummy, the sea monster is coming for me,' shrieked out Annabelle. She was pointing at the innocent seal that was merrily bobbing up and down with the ebb and flow of the water.

Her mother let out a breath of relief. 'It's probably more scared of your banshee screaming than you are of it, you ninny. When are you going to stop believing everything your brother says to you? The seal won't bother you, he eats fish, not cheese and pickle sandwiches.'

'So, it isn't coming to gobble me up then,' asked Annabelle, seeking further reassurances from her mother.

'Ha, ha, no love, dad and I will always protect you from the monsters.'

Simon threw his plate into the metallic sink, not caring that he may have chipped or shattered it. The settling spinning movement of the china reverberated around the kitchen like the dying sounds of a trapped bee in a jar. For added measure he hurled the spoon after it and ran the back of his hand over his wet lips.

Millie had watched him eat and neither waited for a compliment for her efforts, nor expected one. All that came from Simon's mouth was a prolonged belch that seemed to her to echo around their kitchen long after he had left the room. The rancid smell from his decaying teeth and gums penetrating her gloom and despondency as she shuffled to the sink to retrieve the crockery that had been gifted from Dotty and her husband Eric. 'Now there was a gentleman,' thought Millie dreamily. He had been nothing but a gentle man to Dotty and every other soul he met. Always a good friendly word or two to say to folk as he walked to the bus stop, to the Post Office, library, or shops. It was so sad what happened to him, run over by a lorry making its way to the local quarry, speeding down a nearby street because the driver was late and was taking a shortcut. He hadn't stood a chance. Poor Dotty was inconsolable for months after. Not that Simon had allowed her much of a chance to be with her friend when she needed her the most. The only time she could nip across to Dotty was when he was out and about doing odd jobs for the widows of the village who only tolerated him because they needed his DIY skills. They soon turned back to gossiping about him after he'd left with his toolbox and a pocket full of payment. Not that she saw any of this money, the local pub was the beneficiary and she the loser as he would come home drunk and often in an ill temper. 'If only that truck had run you over,' she often thought when he let rip his temper onto her, and then crossed herself for her sinful thought. 'Eric was more than double the man you would ever be,' she mussed as she picked up the pieces of shattered crockery, being careful not to cut her hands. She groaned as she stooped down to the bottom cupboard for an old newspaper to wrap the pieces in before taking them to the dustbin, provided he allowed her out again.

'Shall we go for a walk kids?' enthused Carl jumping up from the bench.

'Aw, not more walking,' replied Annabelle and Gordon in unison, in a well-rehearsed reply, honed by months of walking around castles as mum and dad continued to inflict their hobby on them.

'Not to worry children, I'll go for a walk to the ice-cream shop all by myself, and eat four ice-creams, all alone. Don't you worry, I'll be alright. On my own, with four ice-creams.'

Four small legs sprang into action at the mention of ice-cream and scrabbled up from the shingle, small pebbles bouncing around in their frantic wake. They didn't even say goodbye to the seal who had continued to bob around in the water patiently awaiting the return of the small trawlers and their cargo of fish.

'If you get hungry you can always share the fish guts with the seals and seagulls. I'm sure they won't mind sharing, that'll make a lovely dessert for you,' continued Carl whilst Tilly was merrily chuckling away whilst tidying the remains of their picnic.

'I didn't see an ice-cream shop Carl.'

'No, you were too busy looking at the zebra love!' he cheekily replied. 'There is a corner shop along from that house you liked and there was a sign for ice-cream. I thought it would make a lovely treat and give us a chance to check out the neighbourhood.'

'I really did see a zebra. And a hedgehog glass door,' replied Tilly huffily as she pushed the picnic basket into Carl's chest.

'Of course, you did dear,' he jokily retaliated. He took the picnic basket gently from her, looked quickly inside it, and asked, 'Did you by any chance pack a carrot for the zebra?'

Tilly reached across to her husband, smiled, ran her hands lovingly to his cheek and then quickly flicked his ear.

'Ow,' shouted out Carl for the benefit of his children who were now laughing at the antics of their parents.

'Ice-cream, ice-cream,' they sang in unison to their skipping steps as they left behind their parents and walked ahead for the return journey to their car. Carl rubbed his ear and then reached out for Tilly's hand as they were led away by their eager children.

Carl looked up at the lighthouse as he closed the boot of their car. There was something reassuring about its presence, right enough, he thought lazily as he looked around him. He could see his children merrily dancing on the grass verge and their mother watching contentedly. 'Yes, time to pull my finger out, get back to work, earn some money and get his family out of that cold, draughty rented house and into a home.' He walked over to his wife, took her hand once more and gave it a gentle squeeze. 'Shall we walk to the shop? It'll give us a chance to check out our new neighbours.'

Tilly smiled back just as another cloud broke loose from the sky and ever so briefly darkened the brightness of their day.

Simon thrust and jabbed with all his might like a Cromwellian soldier lancing at an enemy soldier with his pike. He worked the weed out violently from the gaps in the cement work as if he were the attacking warrior working against defensive ribs protecting the vulnerable lungs from the sharpened pole's attack. The offending weed gave way to the hoe and was swept aside to join the others that lay in a pile that was like that of sawn-off limbs by the table of a blood-spattered field hospital surgeon. Simon had the same grim determination of a striking infantryman battling against the hordes that dared to invade his country. He looked around his property, marking out each inch visibly in his head, wary against any insurgents.

'Morning!' interrupted Carl as he walked past hand in hand with Annabelle, his wife was now ahead trying to keep abreast with Gordon who she still protectively worried about crossing any roads. 'Isn't it a lovely day. Looks a full-time job that, keeping the weeds at bay.'

Simon looked up from his endeavours to see who had the bare-faced cheek to interrupt his important work; and lean over his wall. It took all his might not to ram the hoe up this man's ar...

'We are going for ice-cream!' gushed out Annabelle, 'And we saw seals, they don't like ice-cream though, only stinky fish guts.'

Simon looked through Annabelle, seeing her as something not worthy of his time. Her father seemed to sense something was amiss and said quickly to the man, 'Well, we won't detain you from your chores, have a great day.'

He was met with a shrug of indifference as Simon took a step forward to his wall, as if to check that his perimeter had not been breached.

'C'mon Annabelle, let's see what flavours they have, look, there's the shop across this road. Best you keep a hold of my hand as I've seen lots of lorries go up and down this hill, probably on their way to the fish factory to take deliveries.'

'Okay dad,' replied Annabelle as she took another look at the grumpy old man with the hoe, she was about to stick her tongue out at him, but she was distracted by her brother shouting ahead of them, by the empty house with the long grass and big sign that had been hammered into the flower bed.

'There really is a zebra Annabelle and look dad, it's a small hedgehog by its feet, amongst the painted grass blades. That's a cool door.'

'Okay, okay, you win mummy,' said Carl. 'I'll do the dishes all week to make up for not believing you.' He looked across to the windows and saw that the house was empty. 'Shall we have a look through the window? It's for sale, so the owners won't mind.'

Tilly was already one step ahead of him and was opening the gate which gave a reluctant squeak as if protesting at their presence. She ushered their children inside the garden. They immediately ran to the grass and started spinning around, their arms outstretched, heads bent back to look to the sky. 'You two don't get too dizzy, I don't want you too sick to enjoy ice-cream.'

They both stopped immediately which caused them to bump into each other and fall onto the grass in fits of giggles. They soon ceased their merriment as they looked up and saw the old man approach the nearby wall, his hoe looked sharp to them and as if to emphasise this, it glistened as the sun's rays bounced off it and danced away any cheer they were enjoying. They backed off to the safety of their parents as the man strode with purpose across his front driveway, all thoughts of weeding forgotten.

'Look at that beautiful fireplace,' marvelled Tilly, her hands were wrapped around the outside of her eyes and her nose was pressed flat against the glass to help enhance her eager eyes. 'And those carpets look brand new. That lounge is big enough for two sofas and your favourite battered old armchair, what do you think Mr Peeps?' Tilly looked back to her son and was shocked to see that he and his sister were backing away from the old man next door who seemed to be holding his hoe out straight at them, like one of the soldiers in Dad's Army with an improvised weapon advancing across a field. She shouted out protectively, 'Kids, come here.'

Concerned at the sudden change in mood of his wife, Carl quickly turned around in time to see the old man drop the hoe a few inches and start to rub it along the inside of his wall.

'God damned moss, it keeps growing back,' he muttered to himself over and over again as he stabbed furiously at the brickwork.

'I think we'd better go and get that ice-cream now kids.' He led them away from the empty house and noticed that they were no longer singing or skipping and that his wife was rubbing at the scars on her wrists.

Chapter Two

'Can I have a strawberry one please daddy?' asked Annabelle.

'Course you can cupcake,' replied her father as the shopkeeper looked on and smiled at the fatherly nickname. 'What about you Mr Peeps?'

'Daaaad,' moaned Gordon, 'I'm seven, not a toddler.'

The shopkeeper's smile broadened. 'You're too old for nicknames, aren't you? Can I recommend the mint flavoured one, it is a grown-up ice-cream, is it not?'

Gordon smiled, at last an adult who could see how mature he was. 'Yes please, that sounds tasty.'

'And for mum and dad?'

'Could we both have vanilla flavour please.'

The shopkeeper got busy for a few minutes with his metallic scoop and cones and first handed the ice-creams to the parents and then with a flourish handed the children theirs, complete with a chocolate flake and a conspiratorial wink. 'Only responsible children get the chocolate treat for free. I presume daddy is paying.'

Carl smiled and handed over a ten-pound note and juggled the proffered change along with his ice-cream and wallet. 'It's a lovely village, have you been here long?'

'I inherited the business from my dad, so quite a few years, it's a quiet village, give or take a few moments. Like most places you have your oddballs and people that you cross the road to avoid. But most are friendly, and the amenities are enough to keep some people from needing to go to the big city.'

'Yes,' replied Carl as he thought back to a few minutes ago. 'We love the zebra door that we just passed, what's the story?'

'Ah, I'm afraid they moved out a few months ago, well nearer six or seven months. The house has been sitting empty since.'

Carl's mind started to think, 'So nobody's shown any interest in the house then?'

'Sadly not, and Guy, the owner, lovely chap he was, well he was one of my best customers, believed in shopping locally. He bought the door as a gift for his wife who loved Africa and who had a thing for collecting zebras. Their home was full of zebra ornaments. He commissioned a local artist to create the glasswork scene and a nearby joiner fitted the door for him whilst his wife was out with friends. Hedgehogs were his thing. He had a wild one that he'd feed every night in his garden and watch with night goggles so as not to disturb it. A gentle soul. His wife loved the door, I think that upset her more than anything about having to move.'

'Having to?' questioned Carl.

The door to the shop buzzed and in walked the man who they had seen earlier. 'Whisky,' he shouted as he slammed a twenty-pound note onto the counter, oblivious that he had interrupted a conversation and had caused Carl to move quickly aside as he strode to the counter. 'That one,' he rudely pointed and then clicked his fingers several times as if to hurry the shopkeeper along.

The shopkeeper gently placed the bottle on the counter and in sharp contrast it was roughly grabbed by the old man. He outstretched his other hand palm upwards for his change and once offered he meticulously counted out the change, scrunched up his fist around it and stuffed it into his dirty jean's pocket and marched out of the shop without a thank you or goodbye.

'Yes, poor Guy and his wife had to leave,' he continued the previous conversation all the while watching the departing figure. Once the door buzzed again to signal that the old man had left his shop he snapped out of his revere and totally changed back into the happy shopkeeper, 'But please, enjoy your ice-cream before it melts. It really is a glorious day today, isn't it? Let me get the door for you all.'

'Aren't you driving later Simon?' questioned Millie as she ran her duster over their television screen and around the cabinet shelves.

'Yes, what of it?'

'Shouldn't you slow down; with the drinking I mean?'

Simon looked at her and then back to the bottle and back again, more contemptuously at his wife this time, and then let his stare linger. He liked to unsettle her. He took a slow, deliberate gulp from the bottle as if to goad her.

She could hear him part his lips slowly, his hand rasped against his unshaven chin as he drew it and the bottle to his mouth and there was the click of glass against enamel as he parted his stained teeth. He allowed his tongue to glide out and then he took a sharp pull from the bottle like a hungry baby on a mother's nipple. Only to Millie this looked like it was more like the frantic gulp of a drowning man coming up for a short intake of air before being dragged back to the depths of oblivion by a mysterious creature of the deep sea. 'Shall I get you a glass Simon?' she nervously asked.

'Don't bother,' he replied whilst screwing back on the cap. 'I'll finish this off later.' He rose from his armchair and threw down the bottle onto his vacated seat, as if securing his spot for later.

She cowered more, to his delight, and she wondered if perhaps he would mercifully get drunk tonight and not make demands upon her. She was sixty now and had hoped that he would slow down with age, but at nine years her senior, he still acted like a rampant teenager, unless he had the drink inside of him. But then his impotent rages frightened her more, and hurt the most, physically, and mentally. At least her children could no longer hear her screams or his shouting and were safely leading their own lives, though she did wish they would come and visit more. Her son only seemed to stay long enough to clean his car, as obsessed with its shine as his father was with the bodywork of his old Fiat. Like two peas in a pod. She prayed that the apple had fallen far from the cart and that her son, Peter, was not violent to his wife Sienna. She deserved better, all women did, surely this cannot be normal she often thought as she cried silent tears into her pillow each night.

Tilly reached into her pocket with her free hand and pulled out a tissue and handed it to Gordon. His mouth had turned chocolatey-green and was smudged along his cheeks. Blobs of ice-cream were working their way down his chin like a slowly melting icicle. Gordon took it and rubbed it across his face, further spreading the sticky mess.

'That's my boy!' exclaimed Carl proudly.

Tilly tutted and reached back into her pocket for another tissue and pushed it into Carl's face. 'Wipe your face too, you're a mucky puppy!'

The children started laughing again at the comical misfortunes of their dad who lapped up the attention and pulled various faces as he cleaned his face. 'Do you think the zebra wants a bit of ice-cream to cool himself down?'

As they walked slowly back to their car, they found themselves outside the squeaky gate of the house they'd previously peered into. Tilly's eyes were drawn to the zebra artwork once more. She looked at the bright yellow and orange strips of glass that the artist had cleverly used to create the impression of the sun's rays shining down upon the mammal. 'It really is a beautiful work of art and I really like the house. Shall we go to the estate agent's office on Monday and get the details?'

Carl pulled out his phone with one hand and expertly pushed at the screen whilst eating his ice-cream. He had wrapped the tissue around the base of the cone to help catch any more drips. 'No need,' he boasted as he wiggled his mobile phone in the air. He looked down upon the freshly loaded page and exclaimed, 'No, that can't be right, it's a really low price, about twenty thousand below what I'd expect the asking price to be.'

'Really,' said a surprised Tilly. 'What's wrong with it.' She looked up to the roof, expecting there to be missing tiles. She cast her eyes over the solid looking guttering and down-pipes and even scrutinised the brickwork pointing and the state of the windows. It all seemed in good order, it was just the garden that seemed to need attention, and that would only take half a day to get tidy. 'It seems in good nick, even the décor looked tasteful inside when we peeped in a few minutes ago. Do let's buy it, I think it would be perfect for the children.'

'And what about laughing boy next door?'

'Oh, he's a pussy cat really, he'll be putty in my hands once he gets to know me and I turn on the charm, you'll see.'

'Okay, you're the boss, let's arrange a viewing.'

Unseen by them, at the window next door, and through the net curtains, Simon was doing a viewing of his own. He did not like what he was seeing.

Guy stood by his patio window, admiring his doves as they gently glided and hopped from perch to perch and then followed each other into the shed part of his aviary. Through the glass he could just make out their soothing cooing. He carefully slid open the door and the heat from the July sunshine basked his face as he stealthily stepped out, trying not to spill his morning coffee. He gingerly walked over to the garden chairs and tables and sat in the one nearest to his prized birds. He leant back and relaxed into the chair and gave a sigh of contentment.

'I don't know why you are creeping about, they are used to you now,' interrupted Finty, his wife, as she came out to join him. She passed him a plate with a freshly buttered hot croissant.

Guy rolled his eyes heavenwards, as if to look for his doves in flight, 'I'm trying to keep them calm, so that they settle in.'

'Relax! It's been over six months since we all moved. I think they will have homed in by now. No-one is going to hurt them here, have a look around you, they are perfectly safe.' She waited for him to turn his head fully around, ensuring that he took in all his surroundings. 'There is not a sausage in sight, well, except for those sheep, way in the distance.' Obligingly the ewes and their ever-growing lambs gave a few echoing bleats and then continued to munch on their lush grass. 'He's not around, your birds are safe now.'

'I know, I know, but I keep expecting to see him squatting in the bushes, watching, and waiting. When I saw him with that air rifle, aiming at my girls, I was so shocked. And no-one believed me. I saw him. He was going to shoot my birds.' He took a bite of his breakfast treat; flakes of delicate pastry fell off as his hand trembled at the memory.

'I believed you. I know the police didn't, but I did. I know only too well what that monster is capable of,' she shuddered at the recent memories. 'He was so crafty and devious. He didn't give either of us any peace. All that noise, night and day.' She looked across to Guy, worried that his nerves were still getting the better of him. She smiled, 'But just imagine, if he hadn't been the way he was, we'd never have moved, and we'd never have found this charming place.' She looked around her, enjoying the look of the freshly mown lawn and the blooms of the borders. She too drew in a contented breath and sighed blissfully. 'It's so peaceful today, not a bit of wind and the sun is out. Can it be today?' She nodded encouragingly.

Guy smiled, 'Oh Finty love, you know how to make things alright. Yes, they are safe now, no madman is going to object to a few doves flying high and wage a one-man war to move us,' he couldn't help a look around him. His shoulders relaxed, he took another bite from his croissant, nothing dropped this time, his hands were rock-steady, Finty always knew how to reach in and soothe his soul. He leaned into his chair and munched away, allowing the buttery goodness to fill his belly. Months of stress had taken its toll and had seen his weight plummet.

Finty smiled back and sipped her coffee, soon Simon would be a distant memory and they could move forward with their lives, perhaps any day now Guy would regain his libido and they would make carefree love and could plan to start a family. Her radiant face broke into a huge grin at this thought and at the sight of her husband moving to the aviary shed door. She smiled and nodded her encouragement.

Simon nodded, smiled, and asked, with a twinkle in his eye, 'Are you ready love?'

'Oh yes!' replied Finty, knowing that her reply had a double meaning, though that part was lost on Guy.

He grinned back and unlocked the door and gently opened it wide and fastened it so that any rogue breeze wouldn't cause it to fall back. As he did so there was a flurry of white feathers as one by one his prized pets fluttered and flapped and flew out and soared high into the air. About eight started to fly in formation in wide circles around their bungalow. They were soon joined by several more of their flock as stray members eased themselves into the group configuration and effortlessly moved as one around the neighbourhood of fields and hedgerows. They were largely ignored by the sheep.

Finty laughed long and carefree. Her merriment finally yielded into a contented grin. She looked across to her often-troubled husband and was pleased to see that he was watching his flock with almost child-like admiration and happiness. He was at peace.

As he walked back to their patio, the mobile phone in Guy's pocket interrupted the silence around them. He delved in, looked at the caller ID and turned to his wife, crestfallen. His peaceful face was shattered, and a frown broke onto his features and a worried furrow delved deep into his forehead; it was the estate agent. They looked at each other for several seconds, neither wanting to decide on what to do.

Guy broke the deadlock and, ignoring the insistent caller, he said to Finty, 'Let's not go back. As much as I miss Dotty over the road, she was a kind soul, I don't have the mental energy to cope with him again. Let's not go back, let's move forward with our lives and put that house firmly behind us. I'll tell the estate agent to manage the viewings themselves and to just let us know when they get a reasonable price and a quick sale.' He looked to his wife and was relieved to see her smiling, nodding, and reaching across the table to take his hand.

Carl typed away, his fingers dancing merrily across the keyboard with resounding taps as new words, characters and sentences moved across his split monitors. A sharp photo of a plate of clapshot and haggis was on the left screen. Each ingredient of the potato and turnip meal was clear to any viewer, appearing as if fresh from the hob, almost as if a viewer could reach in with a fork and devour the dish with relish.

Tilly looked across the three screens, not understanding a word of the computer coding that her husband was entering. She did understand the recipe though. She'd cooked it often enough and it was a delicious and satisfying meal for her flock, even the children happily munched away on it. It was a simple enough dish to prepare and make, and a great way of getting some vegetables eaten by her fussy family. She did try not to think of the ingredients of the haggis that she bought from the local butcher. Happily, the kids never asked either. 'That is a lovely photo, it'll look good once you've uploaded the page. That resettlement course that you did in the army was worth going on. I don't understand all that coding, but I'm glad that you do.' She stood up and moved behind her husband and started to gently massage his shoulders. 'Don't overdo it though, you've already added two pages today.'

'It's no bother, I've created a template, so it's ever so easy to add more of your grandparents' recipes. I'm trying to get a blend of new and old, modern, and traditional recipes so that the website appeals to all ages and tastes. I'll take a break in a moment. Our savings aren't quite enough to buy that nice house you like. So, I need to start working harder, I've taken enough time off to enjoy your company and seeing the kids all day is fun. I've missed their company now that they are at school. Though they'll be off for the long summer holidays soon.'

'And after a few weeks you'll be wishing they were back at school! Six weeks is an awfully long time to keep them entertained.'

'We'll be in the new house by then, perhaps towards the end of the holidays. I think we can knock a few thousand off the asking price. It's obviously sat empty for at least six months according to the man in the shop. I think a quick sale will look attractive to the owner. Then you and the kids can start to make it homely whilst I concentrate on the website and getting some advertisers onboard to help pay for the mortgage.'

Tilly stopped her kneading and patted Carl on the shoulder, not to let him know that the massage was over, but to encourage him in his efforts. 'It is a lovely house and the village seems so quiet and peaceful, just what you need after all your adventures in the army.' She looked around her. 'This house is fine in the summer, it's nice and cool, but it's so draughty and cold in the winter and our fuel bills are astronomical. I know your parents meant well when they arranged for us to rent it, but I wish we'd seen it for ourselves. I'd have soon spotted the damp patches in our bedroom and the lack of internal doors to the lounge and kitchen. I'd probably have noticed that the lounge window was so warped that it was permanently stuck in a semi-opened position.'

Carl pointed to the screen, 'But I'm doing something about it. I'm not allowed to do any DIY whilst here, but I can make us money so that we can get away from the cold and draughts. That house looked lovely and watertight, once the heating is on I'm sure it'll be a cosy place to live in. My parents meant well, after all, we couldn't have driven all the way up here from our old house and viewed possible places to rent. It would have been too much for the children. My parents are simply happy that I'm no longer in war zones and that we've put the army behind us and are happily together and in one piece.'

Tilly leant forward, wrapped her arms around Carl and murmured, 'I'm happy that you are in one piece too. We all hated it when you went on deployment, you hear such terrible stories of the injuries, especially in your role.'

Carl took his hands from the keyboard and found and stroked Tilly's hands, careful not to venture up to her self-disfigured arms. 'I'm glad too, I'm glad that I'm here for you and the kids, nothing will change that.'

Chapter Three

Dotty paused her sweeping and leant on her brush for support. Her hip was starting to hurt, and she knew that, like her pal across the road, arthritis was settling upon her bones like an unwelcome guest, though hers was not as painful as Millie's whose body seemed stiffer each time that she saw her. She looked up from her task, hoping to catch a glimpse of her friend. She was rewarded with a wave from the upstairs front window. She cheerfully waved back and noticed a strange car pull up, outside her path. She smiled warmly to the young couple in the front seats and her smile broadened when she spied the youngsters sat patiently in the back. She gave them a friendly wave too and was pleased to see them wave back. She missed youngsters living in the area. She'd always hoped that Guy and Finty would be blessed with children. She'd loved that couple and had been trusted with a front door key to go in and through to their back garden to check on the birds, top up their water and leave out food whenever the couple went on holidays. She knew why they entrusted her, and not next door and just quietly went in once Simon had driven off. She smiled at the thought of this family moving nearby and hoped it would brighten up her future days with the sound of carefree children playing. Her own children and grandchildren didn't come around to see her that often now, not since the altercation when they parked across from Simon's driveway. He had shouted and sworn about how difficult it would be to try and swing his car out and into the road. She frowned as she watched this family go across the road and into

Guy's old house. 'Oh dear,' she sighed as she saw that Simon was at home and watching them from his front lounge window. He had a face like thunder. Dotty took her brush and ran into the house. Her hip throbbed more, pulsating pain like a warning beacon.

The estate agent drew up her car behind the couple's vehicle, allowing several feet of space between them. She had been pre-warned about where to park. She switched off the ignition, grabbed her clipboard and ran after the family who were entering the gate. 'Hello, Tilly and Carl?' she enquired.

The couple turned around whilst their children ran into the grassed area and started to play, their arms were extended, and they were making aeroplane noises. 'Oh hello, Melanie, isn't it? Thanks for seeing us at such short notice,' acknowledged Tilly.

Melanie smiled grimly, she had seen Simon at the window and had hoped to distract the couple. 'No problem, it's a well-situated house, isn't it, with the school just down the road?' She left the question hanging in the air.

'Yes, it is. And we love that there are so many facilities in the village,' replied Carl, taking a positive cue from the expertly subtle question from the well-trained estate agent. He looked down the road, pictured his two children walking happily down to the village school and smiled. His facial expression soon turned to concern when he noticed that Gordon and Annabelle had suddenly ceased their gentle playing noises. He turned towards his children to see what they were staring at.

Melanie quickly moved towards him and interrupted his thoughts with, 'You can soon add some oil to the gate, can't you?'

'Yes, that's easily fixed,' replied Carl as he turned back to her. ' I'd love to keep all this grass, but wouldn't this bit make a great driveway for my car, I'd just need to remove the fence and gate and get someone professional to lay some lock-block paving,' he stated, already imagining his family moving in.

Melanie smiled and nodded. Her shoulders relaxed a bit more as she realised that Carl hadn't seen Simon staring at them from the window. Carl was too busy looking along the roofline.

'It all seems in sound order otherwise,' he acknowledged whilst casting his gaze to the roof. 'Why has it been vacant for so long?'

'Let's go inside,' said Melanie quickly, evading the question. 'Then you can see its unique features for yourselves.'

'Okay,' replied Carl, making a mental note that he needed to ask the question again. 'He didn't bother looking behind him and neither did Tilly, as they said in unison, 'C'mon you two, go in and choose your bedrooms.' Had they done so they would have seen their children sticking out their tongues to Simon and then turn and run from the grassed area and into the front door, patting the zebra glass on the way in. None of the family saw a furious Simon thrust his middle finger at them and the rage on his face at the effrontery of the children. He left his middle finger sticking up at them, rigidly to attention like a terrifying guardsman.

'The owner had recently built this fireplace and inlaid the stonework with granite tops to safely hold entertainment systems either side. There is plenty of room for a television, DVD player and stereo.' Melanie waved her hands around the empty lounge, 'He also made these cabinets, he was very gifted,' she said as she pointed to the wooden inlaid units either side of the chimney breast.

'Yes, they seem sturdy enough,' acknowledged Carl as he ran his hands over the woodwork, admiring the craftsmanship. 'It seems odd to have done all of this himself and then up and move. Any reason?' he left the open question dangling in the air, awaiting a response this time.

'Ah, well, yes,' floundered Melanie, checking her clipboard for reassurance, before offering, 'he was fed up travelling all the way through to Aberdeen every day, his work was exhausting him, so he and his wife moved back to the city.'

'Fair enough,' replied Carl happily. 'It is a long commute, even with the new bypass.' He looked around him, at the quality carpets and matching curtains. He caught Tilly's glance and spotted her nodding, the décor met with her approval.

Tilly then went and checked the windows, reassuring herself that they opened and closed with no effort. She smiled. No winter draughts from those. 'I understand that it's been empty for some months?'

'Yes, the downturn in the oil and gas industry has not been kind to the property industry. There are so few buyers now, and sadly banks and building societies are not lending as readily as they used to, you know,' replied Melanie, now gaining in confidence. She looked out of the window, towards where the family had parked their car. She swiftly turned back and smiled warmly at the family; her concerns went unnoticed.

'Might the seller be open to negotiation?' asked Carl hopefully.

Melanie saw her chance and boldly offered, 'I'm sure he would if there was to be a quick sale?'

'Yes, that's good to hear, we could just about pay cash, without a mortgage, if he shaved five thousand off the asking price. We saved hard over the years and we sold at the right time in England. Let's see the rest of the house first.'

Melanie grinned, 'But of course, follow me through to the kitchen.' She led the couple through, switching on the lights, despite the sunny summer day, all the better to show off the fitted kitchen. She stepped back, almost hugging the wall. She wanted to create the illusion of space. 'Guy had installed this himself,' she pulled out an empty drawer and pushed it back. It silently settled itself back into position. 'Soft self-closing drawers, aren't they clever.'

Tilly nodded, 'That'll be handy for my two, they make such a racket when helping themselves to cereals, cutlery and bowls. Their dad needs a quiet life now, you know, after his army life. Is that a fridge behind those cabinets?'

Melanie nodded and opened the two large units to reveal a spacious fridge and separate freezer. 'The appliances come with the house and the kitchen was only fitted a year ago. Guy loved DIY in the evenings and weekend.'

Carl looked around him, he loved the whiteness of the units and how clean and new it all looked. 'It's been carefully installed by a true craftsman. He must have spent a fortune. It must have been a wrench to have left this house?'

Melanie left the question unanswered and stepped back into the hallway and allowed the couple to marvel at the raised oven, inset into the wall with a handy microwave above it. She heard them whisper, 'It looks almost like new; they can't have cooked many meals here.' She grinned; it was almost in the bag.

Shona looked up from her needlework, she needed to rest her eyes more and more these days. The fine threads on her cross stitching were becoming harder to thread through, even with the powerful magnifying glass and special day light that her Carl had thoughtfully bought her for Christmas. She looked across to Lewis and smiled, a little twinkle lit up in her eyes and lifted her wrinkles.

Lewis, sensing her glance, placed his newspaper in his lap and smiled back, a large cheesy grin on his face. They were both transported back to their youth, teenagers again in their imagination and outlook. They remained like that for several touching moments until Lewis broke off their joint reverie. 'Our Carl and his family will be looking around that house about now,' he stated as he looked up to the silver carriage clock, a wedding present from a long-dead favourite aunt of Shona's. It had been lovingly dusted and cared for all these years, much like she had cared for Carl and his sister, Felicity. Lewis looked back to his wife and smiled contentedly. She'd been a great wife and mother, and now grandmother. She was over the moon when Carl had told her that they would be moving back to Aberdeenshire. They'd both missed him when he'd joined the army, though they'd been as proud as punch when he came home on leave, after long absences and with a new medal each time. Though they'd worried and fretted night and day. They watched the news religiously, especially for news from Iraq and Afghanistan. They dreaded the knock on the door, and Shona had insisted that Lewis buy a phone that plugged into their bedroom and a doorbell that could be heard throughout their house. They had even relented and bought a mobile phone. They'd been so pleased when, on one leave, he'd brought back Tilly. She was a timid lass but had an inner beauty as well as being so pretty. Their romance blossomed and they were soon wed and then just as they thought their son was no longer in danger, he announced proudly that he'd passed selection and had been accepted into The Regiment. Lewis, a former military man himself, knew exactly what that meant. Many more sleepless nights for Shona and himself. They were even prouder of course, especially Lewis, he knew just how hard it must have been for Carl to earn the Special Air Service sand-coloured beret. Both father and son walked taller in those days, both proud as punch. But Lewis soon noticed a change in his son. He was unable to tell his parents much about his missions, but Lewis noticed shadowing in his eyes, a darkness in his soul that worried him. It followed him into civilian life as he saw subtle changes, like an intolerance to noise and an inability to keep laughing with others. He seemed almost to take a step back from times of heightened emotions, like at Felicity's wedding.

Lewis too had been pleased that his son had come home, with his family. He knew that it had been a rough few year for him after he'd left The Regiment. He'd struggled to fit back into civilian life and to find suitable work. And then there had been all the trouble with Tilly's family. They hadn't told them much, just that Tilly had tried to settle back home and try and make up with her family, to forgive them for things that had happened in her childhood. But when they started to look after the children, when both Carl and Tilly were at work, something happened, and Tilly had fallen out with her parents and asked to move to Scotland, away from her mum, dad and her brother. And now they were looking at a property just a few miles away, in the next village, in a lovely coastal location. Lewis hoped that it would bring Carl some much-needed peace into his life after all his traumas he'd seen and done in the military and that, in time, Tilly would patch things up with her family. He smiled again to Shona, rose from his armchair, and said, 'I'll make us a lovely cup of tea and,' he deliberately didn't finish his statement and teasingly left it for his wife to answer.

He wasn't disappointed as she smiled, laughed and said, 'Oh, go on then, have a wee bit of that Dundee cake that I made, but be sure to leave some for Gordon and Annabelle, they'll be hungry when they come over to visit.'

Melanie cast her arms over the garden, as if she were pointing out the boundary and all the features within. 'It's quite deceptive, isn't it?'

'Oh yes, isn't it,' agreed Tilly. 'How lovely, it's wonderfully large and enclosed, it'll be great for the children to play in without me worrying about them. I can keep an eye on them from the kitchen.'

Melanie moved quickly in front of her, she had listened to her briefing from her colleague back in the office and was trying to stop this couple from looking back into the kitchen window. She had already noticed Simon, standing in just his vest, at his kitchen window, staring at them, watching their every move. 'It's a south-facing garden, you'll get lots of sunshine.'

'Oh lovely, I'm hoping to recreate a kitchen garden, like I had in England. We had lots of sunshine there, though I wasn't always in the right frame of mind.' A frown passed on Tilly's face as she thought back to that awful time. 'A new start, that's what we need. The house we are renting is awful in the winter. We've only had one season, towards the tail end, but it was ever so cold. The landlord just won't put in a door to the lounge or kitchen, so the drafts chill me to the bone and I need a bit of warmth.' She broke off the conversation and looked over the grassed area and borders. Carl reached out and took her hand, giving her a small squeeze of encouragement.

'There are lots of daffodil and other bulbs under there,' said Melanie, keeping the couple's eyes away from the adjoining kitchen window. 'And the patio will be great for barbeques.' She wandered back to this area, hoping that they would quickly go indoors. She was relieved to see the couple follow her obediently like two well-trained puppies on leashes.

'It'll just need a good jet wash on there and it'll come up lovely, it looks like the previous guy had a shed here.' Carl rubbed his foot against a blackened stain that seemed to be boxed around the patio. 'Mmm, did he burn it, rather than dismantle it?'

'Er, yes, I think so,' mumbled Melanie, fudging around the question.

'Yes, it burned well,' interrupted Simon, shouting over the wall. He grinned back to the couple, 'it went up really quick and sudden,' his troublesome expression changed from glee to crestfallen. 'He managed to open the doors of the adjoining caged aviary and let his birds out though.'

'Oh bless, how brave of him,' replied a worried Tilly. 'Did they all survive?'

Simon nodded gravely, 'Yes, and roosted on my roof for several weeks, until he caught them.'

Tilly, misjudging his angry expression for one of pity for his neighbour's misfortune, replied, 'Oh, that's good, poor things, I'm glad your neighbour and his pets weren't hurt, we love our birds, don't we Carl.'

Her husband nodded, not taking his eyes from this neighbour, trying to judge his ever-changing expressions. 'Yes, I like to feed the wild birds and watch them, it's so peaceful.'

Simon folded his arms across his stained vest, inadvertently covering gravy stains. He then pointed across the four-foot wall that he'd been shouting across. 'This is my property and my wall. All along here, and this is my garden.'

Tilly and Carl looked across his cemented and patio laid area. They looked at each other as if to say, 'some garden, not even an inch of grass or one plant.' Their thoughts were interrupted as they were drawn to an elderly lady struggling to get down the adjoining back steps. She slowly reached the last step and with a weary sigh, paused, and then turned and made her way to the couple.

'You've met Simon already, er, yes, hello, I'm Millie, pleased to meet you. It's a lovely house isn't it,' she said nodding encouragingly to the couple whilst passing worried glances at her husband.

'Oh yes, we've just been admiring the garden. It gets lots of sunshine then?'

'Yes,' stated Simon, choosing to answer for Millie. 'And I like to sit out, on that seat there. And I like peace and quiet,' he looked across to the children who were gently blowing a dandelion and watching wisps of it glide off like a passing gentle cloud teasing its way across a sunny sky. He challenged them to make some noise. He then turned his back to them and walked back into his house.

'Lovely to have met you, er, Mr…' shouted Carl, still watching the figure with growing interest.

'You'll have to excuse my Simon and his funny ways. I'm afraid he's ninety percent deaf you know. He was a mechanic in the shipyards. It made him deaf, but he has digital hearing aids, though he doesn't always wear them. He won't hear you when he has his back to you. Once, when I was out shopping, two youths came into the house. Simon didn't even hear them. They'd managed to get into the lounge and were going through our cabinets. Simon came in from the kitchen and chased them down the street. He gave them such a thumping,' she absently rubbed at her belly. 'Yes, he's quick with his fists.'

Carl looked hard at the disappearing shape of Simon and then to this frail pensioner. He nodded, 'Yes, I can imagine, though not all men are like that,' he reached across and took his wife's hand. He then looked up towards Simon's outside walls. 'Is that why he has so many camera's? I noticed the CCTV. He's certainly got some good security there.'

'Ah, you spotted them then. Yes, he likes to…' began Millie. Her reply was halted by some tapping on her kitchen window. 'I'd better get along, I've housework to do. It was lovely to meet you, perhaps we'll be neighbours one day.' She smiled and then waved cheerfully to Gordon and Annabelle. The children returned the gesture and went running off, towards the grass.

Carl and Tilly returned the smile and wished her a good day as they watched her struggle up the back steps, her pain so evident in her facial expressions. Their smiles turned to frowns as they empathised with her evident discomfort. They turned away in unison and watching with pleasure their children playing carefree on the lawn. 'And what are the other neighbours like?' enquired Tilly.

'Oh, I'm led to believe it's a lovely quiet area. Your immediate neighbours, on the other side, are a lovely couple, but they work long hours, so you'll rarely see them.' Melanie hoped that her embellishment wouldn't be unearthed.

'Do you know their names?'

'Yes, as it happens, they work with my mum, at the local oil company. They are ever so sweet, Brodie and Lee, they take their West Highland Terrier, Daisy, to work with them,' she couldn't help but look across to Simon's house. 'You'll rarely hear barking, it's a beautiful dog, with a lovely white coat that seems to glow.'

'Aw, that sounds lovely, we've often thought of a dog, haven't we Carl.'

'Yes, maybe one day, it's been an uneasy few years and I don't think I'd have been able to cope with a dog as well, though the long walks would have been nice.'

Tilly pulled down the hems of her sleeve, trying to hide her scars, ever conscious of their revealing torment.

Carl, realising what he'd said, smiled to his wife as if in silent apology, and said, for the benefit of Melanie, 'Things are on the up now, so let's go inside and talk figures and have a look at the bedrooms. C'mon away in you two,' he said to his children. 'Come and show me which bedroom you've chosen.'

'Me first,' shouted Gordon as he chased after Annabelle who was quicker off her mark. 'I'm the eldest, I get to show daddy first.'

'Not if I get there before you, slow coach,' baited his sister, 'I'm definitely having the room with the biggest windows so that I can watch the birds with daddy.'

Carl laughed, he looked up to the back-bedroom windows and he hadn't the heart to tell his daughter that the windows were the same size and that the measurements on the estate agent's website had shown him that both rooms were exactly the same dimensions too.

Lewis placed the cup and saucer onto the small table by Shona's armchair. He then slid across a plate of biscuits and went back into the kitchen and came through with his own mug of tea. He preferred a larger volume of drink, whilst his wife, ever fearful of too many trips to the toilet, or of wetting herself, preferred a smaller cup. He placed his mug on his coaster and before sitting down, he reached across and helped himself to a shortbread biscuit.

As he munched down on it, Shona enquired, 'And what's wrong with my Dundee cake?'

'Nothing dear,' confessed Lewis, a crumb of biscuit went flying from his mouth and into his mug in his haste to answer. 'I just thought that our Carl and Tilly would like a big wedge of it after looking around their potential new house. I've refilled the kettle and put it back on the boil ready for them.'

Shona smiled and returned to her needlecraft, content that her husband was always thinking of others and putting her children's needs first. She knew herself to be blessed.

Melanie reached across to the rope that dangled from the former ship's bell, an antique that one of her colleagues had bought from a nearby auction house. They used it whenever a house sale had gone through.

'You never have!' exclaimed Saajan as he tried to rise from his chair. He'd caught his tie up in the flyers on his desk and the pile of papers went flying onto the floor.

'With that old bugger next door!' shrieked Olivia, 'We've been trying for months to sell number three.' She watched intently to see if her colleague and rival for sales, rang the bell. No way could she have completed a sale without her knowing, she thought. She prided herself in getting the best bonuses in the office.

'Ha, ha, no, but I think I've reeled them in and caught them.' Melanie let go of the bell and mimicked casting off from a rod and then reeling in a large and heavy fish. She beamed across to her nemesis and smiled. 'Don't you worry, I'll be ringing that bell any minute now, when I sell the house that none of you could shift. Any moment now, that phone will be ringing for me,' she nodded towards her desk and walked over with a smug expression on her face.

Dotty walked along the pavement with a copy of the local newspaper folded in her hand. In the other she carefully held a small carton of milk. She missed buying larger amounts of milk, it showed that she had a husband and large family to make teas and coffees for. Now all she needed was this small half pint. Just enough for her now that she had been widowed all these years. The sight of this small carton always made her sad. She looked up from her trance and into the smiling eyes of Brodie as he was about to cross the road, from his car, and enter his gate. She gave him a smile and was pleased to see that he waited for her to walk up the short way towards her house and past his gate before she crossed over. She so rarely chatted to folk these days and poor Millie was rarely permitted peace from Simon. 'Hello Brodie, no Daisy with you today?'

'Sadly, no, it's Lee's turn to take her to the office, he's working in the Aberdeen branch today. I fair miss her though. She brightens up the workplace and my colleagues love having her around. She gets lots of cuddles from them.'

Dotty laughed, 'She's such a beautiful dog, I can't resist stroking her whenever I see her.'

Brodie looked down at her small carton of milk and knew that she'd not have any family visiting her for a few days. 'You're about to put the kettle on then?' he left the invitation hanging in the air.

Dotty snatched up the subtle invitation, eagerly nodded, and as if reading Brodie's mind, she subconsciously moved the pint of milk to her other hand and juggled it and her newspaper and said hopefully, 'Oh yes. Care to join me?'

'That'll be lovely Dotty, though I can't give good cuddles like our Daisy!' he joked.

Dotty tapped him playfully on his shoulder, 'I'm over old for anything like that, though I do miss my Eric, such a lovely husband he was,' she said wistfully. She broke off her reverie after a few seconds and said, 'I've lots to tell you, especially about the lovely young family that have been looking around number three. They seemed really nice.'

'Oh!' exclaimed Brodie. 'I'm surprised. Do they know about him?'

'Let's go away inside and I'll make you a nice cup of tea, I've some fresh millionaire shortbread made too, a young lad like you needs feeding up, I bet you are hungry after a busy day at the office.'

Brodie smiled in anticipation of his favourite chocolate-caramel biscuit treat and fresh gossip too. He hoped that Lee would be working another hour or two more.

Chapter Four

'My room is so much bigger grandad, and it looks over the garden. When it snows, I'm going to build a great big snowman, and I can wave to it from my window and watch to see if he flies, just like that Irn-Bru advert, though I shan't go flying with him because he drops children out of the air,' declared Annabelle, now pausing for breath.

Lewis patted her legs as he tried to catch up with what his granddaughter had just said. He then cuddled her tight and was rewarded with a reciprocal hug as she continued to sit on his lap. 'How about, when it's next snowing, I'll watch the proper snowman films with you. He's much friendlier to children and great fun to see.'

She wiggled out of the embrace and threw her hands in the air, 'Yes please grandad, though I think I'd much prefer to bring my Frozen DVDs with me, I'm going to be a princess one day, just like Princess Anna and her sister Elsa. I'm going to be a good princess with magical powers.'

'That sounds lovely, and you are beautiful already, just like a princess should be. And what magical powers will you have?'

Annabelle dropped her arms, placed them in her lap, and then raised her head in the air, regal like, as she pondered this important question. She beamed as she drew inspiration, mulled it over, and said confidently, 'I'd make mummy happy again.'

'Ah,' replied Lewis, 'now that is a very magical and important power. Do you know why your mummy isn't happy?'

'I think she's worried about the draughty house and she keeps cursing the landlord and saying "tight sod" under her breath, whatever that means, but I think it's more to do with my other grandpappy and grandmammy, they did something wrong, but I don't know what. It was when we saw our uncle with them and then we spent an afternoon with the three of them.'

'I see,' said Lewis wisely, 'I'm sure that one day your mum will tell us all what makes her unhappy, but I'm sure that with your magical hugs and kisses you can make her all better.'

'I love you grandad, you're the best grandad and I'm so glad we moved to Scotland to live nearby,' she threw her arms around him again and hugged him all the tighter.

Shona walked in with a tray of cakes and smiled at the sight of her granddaughter having a cuddle with Lewis. She knew that it was going to be fun having youngsters around the house again and having her boy safe and happy.

'Have another piece Brodie, don't be shy, you are so thin, are you and Lee eating properly, do you cook homemade meals after your busy work?'

Brodie leaned across and took up another piece of his favourite home bake and smiled, 'Oh yes, Lee loves to cook, we've a vegetarian curry for tea tonight. He's going to buy some fresh aubergine on his way home, it gives it a chunky texture.' He took a satisfying crunch of his biscuit and gave a delightful 'Mmm,' as it melted in his mouth.

'All vegetables, that won't fill you up,' she rose from her chair, took up the plate of millionaire shortbread and carried it over to the small table by the side of Brodie's chair. 'You make sure to have these before you go home.' She gave him a cheeky wink and whispered, 'I won't tell Lee if you don't!'

Brodie laughed, grateful to have been between mouthfuls, he didn't want to have spluttered biscuit over Dotty's immaculately clean carpet. 'Super! It'll be our naughty little secret!' he declared mischievously, slapping his hands on his thighs for added comical effect.

Dotty smiled, happy to be feeding up her friend. But then her delight was soured as she thought of the young couple. 'He was a big muscular man, he walked upright, almost like a military stature. He doesn't look like he'll back down in a fight.'

'That sounds hopeful, perhaps he'll stop Simon in his tracks and not stand for any of his nonsense.'

'I doubt it, what happened to poor Guy and Finty was awful. They were lovely neighbours and he drove them out of the village. What he did to his poor birds was terrible, thank goodness none were burned.'

Dotty shivered involuntary. She loved Guy's doves and thought them to be graceful and elegant. She used to love seeing them fly around Guy's house on their morning flight, in formation, like the Red Arrows, she used to joke with Finty. 'I know that we've no proof, but that Simon is a sly one, he always looks around him to make sure that there are no passers-by or anyone at windows before he does anything. I once saw him lean right across to Guy's flowerbed and spray it with some weed killer, from that Ghostbusters backpack and spray gun that he wears.'

Brodie wanted to clap his hands in glee but contented himself with another laugh. He did like a bit of gossip, and chatting to Dotty was such fun, she came out with some howlers and usually didn't even know she was doing it. He composed himself and said, 'That'll be why the shrubs there are all barren and just deadwood then.'

'Yes, poor Guy, I had to tell him of course, though it just added to his burden, poor man. He'd put up with Simon's interference for too long and almost losing his prized doves was the last straw, it broke the poor man.'

Brodie looked serious, 'It really was the last straw for him. Do you hear how he is now?'

'Yes, Finty calls me sometimes and we have a good blether. She is so much happier too, each time she calls, she sounds brighter and much cheerier. She tells me that her Guy is almost like his old self again, thankfully, but what lengths that Simon went to, hounding them out like that, there should be a law against it.'

'Well, we both know what a sly one he is, it's poor Millie that I feel for, what he must do to that poor woman behind closed doors and out of earshot, you can't imagine.'

Dotty shivered as she could well envisage what he did to her.

'So, that's settled then, we make a bid with this reduced price?' asked Carl turning on the garden bench so that he faced his wife directly. He wanted to make sure that she was fully committed to the house purchase. They had made a large profit from the sale of their home in England and he wanted to invest it wisely.

'Definitely. We've both studied the local market and looked at loads of homes, but this one feels right. House prices are so much cheaper here, and I think if we offer all the savings we have, we can soon be earning again. That way we might be in with a chance of securing a new family home.'

'Mmm,' offered Carl, considering her answer. He looked around his parent's garden and admired how green and colourful it was. His father had put a lot of hours and love into it and he'd like something similar for his family, an oasis of calm, that's what they all needed. 'But I haven't work, and I'm guessing you don't want a job just yet?'

'No, I'd like to stay at home, just for a bit longer, you know, to enjoy the kids' company,' she pulled down the sleeves of her sweatshirt. 'And to help you with your website, I'm sure that'll soon be making us money,' she added as an afterthought.

Carl pretended to look across to the fledgling starlings feeding off the fat-balls hung from his father's neighbour's shed. Though they did catch his eye and he found himself admiring their soft brown feathers which looked so much nicer than the dark mottled shades of the older birds. He knew why Tilly didn't want to work just yet, she needed to gather her strength and process what she'd been through. Her months of counselling and having to face and relive what she'd been through as a child had taken its toll, but she'd come through it a better, stronger person and was once more the loving mother he knew her to be. He took hold of Tilly's hands and gave them a comforting stroke, then he reached up to her face, stroked it and leant in for a kiss.

'Yewwwwhhh!' shouted Gordon and Annabelle in unison as their parents' lips made contact.

Carl and Tilly laughed as they gently broke off the kiss. Then their eyes twinkled like winking stars on a peaceful quiet night and they leaned in for a fuller kiss to tease their children.

'Nana said that there is her Dundee cake and you've to come in before grandad eats it all. She said that it's your favourite. So that's enough of that you two, come away in now,' ordered their son with authority. He adopted a folded arms and toe tapping stance as he waited patiently on the back doorstep.

Tilly burst out laughing, in mid-kiss, spraying her husband with spittle. Carl made a big show of wiping his mouth dry and poking out his tongue and making yuck noises. 'When did you get so bossy young man?' she gently quipped.

'You two are always snogging!' said Annabelle indignantly, 'You're far too old to be doing that!'

'I'm not too old to be chasing you up the stairs young lady!' shouted Tilly, breaking off the embrace and running along the patio and up the stairs to catch her children who went scuttling off. 'Nor you, young man!'

Carl laughed, reached into his pocket for his mobile phone and knew that it was the right decision. He only hoped that there would still be some Dundee cake left after his conversation.

Brodie licked his finger and used its moistness to gather up the crumbs from his favourite treat. He then popped his finger in his mouth and quickly licked it clean. He put down his plate with a satisfied sigh, smiled, and retrieved his mug of tea. All the while Dotty continued reciting the gossip that she'd overheard in the Post Office that morning. Brodie's smile broadened as he heard a particularly tasty morsel.

'Well, I didn't know where to look!' Mrs McBride, her with the lazy eye that always looks like she is looking down at the pavement for a stray dog, well, she started talking about her husband's incontinence and how his, you know, his thingy, is so retracted that she can't get the sheath to stick to him, even though she'd shaved him bald. Well! I didn't know where to look! I'd never have talked about my Eric's thingy in public, let alone to Eric.'

Brodie choked on his tea but was quick enough with his paper napkin. He was glad of it, as he didn't want to ruin Dotty's chair and not be invited back. He loved these conversations and loved village gossip even more. Dotty was a hoot! 'She never did!' he jokingly retorted.

'And in a loud voice, for all to hear! No shame at all, but that's Mrs McBride for you. Over the years I've heard her talk about all sorts, her poor son, when he was a teenager, well, I tell you, we heard all sorts about his antics in the solitary bedroom department.'

Brodie spluttered into the napkin again and was only too glad that his mother hadn't discussed his private life in front of the neighbours, especially when he started to bring boyfriends home.

'But listen, here's me keeping you from your Lee, O! That's him now, just drawing up in his car. I expect you'll be eager to see Daisy too.' She drew aside the net curtain and gave Lee an eager wave as he was unclipping Daisy from the special harness and was lifting his dog down from the backseat. 'Oh, look at her wee tail wagging ten to the dozen.' She laughed, 'Just like my tongue, I'm worse than that gossip Mrs McGinty.'

Brodie placed his mug on the table, sat up and walked over to the window and placed his arms around Dotty in an affectionate hug. 'No, you're not, we've just been having a lovely chat and catch-up, that's all. Come and say hello to my boy and girl, then I'd better go in and help Lee with dinner, though you've fed me well enough.'

'Och, that's alright, you need fattening up, you're all skin and bone,' she chuckled as she enjoyed the hug. They both hugged tighter, gave a little dance on the spot, and broke off the embrace. 'Let's go out and see them then.'

Melanie strode up to the bell, grasped the rope firmly and swung it confidently from side to side so that the inner clapper struck the brass casing and made the 'DING, DING, DING,' sound to alert her colleagues to a sale.

'Shut the back door!' exclaimed Olivia, stopping her typing in mid-flow, her surprise masking her envy that her co-worker had made her second sale of the week.

'Oh yes! You'd better believe it! I've only gone and sold number three!'

'No way! I've been trying for months and now you've sold it within a week of taking it over, unbelievable!'

Saajan reached into his drawer and took out some party poppers. He was smiling as he walked over and with a sudden 'POP,' let one go over the head of his friend. 'Very well done, you deserve it, you've worked hard over that one. You did well to divert their attention from that nasty man.'

'It was a close one, I can tell you. He even came to the back wall to gloat about the aviary fire. You could just tell that it was him that set fire to it, nasty old bast…'

'Drinks on you then honey,' declared Olivia, never one to miss an opportunity to party, especially at someone else's expense.

Saajan and Melanie nodded approval to each other, they liked each other's company more than that of Olivia. Melanie took the lead, 'Wine o'clock at The Drummer Boy's Inn then. The first few drinks on me, I might even stretch to a few sandwiches.'

Saajan gave a, 'Woop, woop!' and then let off another party popper, already getting into the spirit of things. He smiled again at Melanie as the paper streamers cascaded gently down and rested on her hair, giving the impression of having colourful highlights. He wondered if tonight would be the night that he'd summon up the courage to tell her how he truly felt.

'There's my girl, how's my girl, have you missed your daddy?' fussed Brodie as he made his way up to his husband and dog.

'Here first, I'm supposed to be the love of your life,' retorted Lee as he puckered his lips up and pointed to them.

Brodie gave him a long lingering kiss and finished with a husky, 'Of course you are, you know that.'

Dotty was walking down her path to them; she was much slower than her friend and this gave her a chance to look across to see if her other pal was about. She wasn't, but she was quick enough to see Simon at the window watching the married couple. He was scowling and shaking his head furiously. Dotty looked away, saw Daisy wagging her tail and straining at the leash to get to her. They met on the pavement and Dotty crouched down as best as she could and made a fuss of her favourite dog, 'Who's a good girl. Yes! My Daisy is. Aren't you beautiful, aren't you gorgeous!'

The men looked on like proud parents at a christening. 'Dotty and I have been having a cup of tea and a catch up,' declared Brodie guiltily, though secretly he couldn't wait to share his newly heard gossip with his husband.

'So I see,' challenged Lee half-jokingly as he unconsciously looked down at his husband's stomach and then to his mouth.

Brodie quickly cleaned up the rogue tell-tale spots of chocolate toffee stains at the corner of his mouth with the back of his hand.

'Never mind, you'll soon work off whatever you've been snacking on later.' Lee winked to his husband and Brodie, grinning from ear to ear, returned a knowing look.

This was innocently lost on Dotty who said to Daisy, 'Do you hear that love, your dads are going to take you for a nice long walk later tonight.'

'You alright there son? That big wedge of Dundee cake is for you, be quick before these two snaffle it up,' laughed Lewis as he pointed to the coffee table in the centre of the room.

Carl's eyes lit up as he walked into the lounge and saw his mum's cake. He pushed out both of his hands and made the stop sign with his upturned palms. 'Step away from the cake children, we have a situation here!'

Gordon groaned whilst his sister put her hands up in the air to show her surrender. 'You're not in the army now dad,' sighed Gordon.

'Step away from the cake, that's your last warning, I'm heavily armed,' warned their father as he pulled out a fork from behind his back.

Annabelle, still having fun playing this familiar game took an exaggerated step back, giggling as she moved. Her arms were wobbling with her mirth and it looked like she was waving to her father.

'Careful now, I've got a fork and I'm not afraid to use it!'

Lewis and Shona joined in with the giggling, they'd never seen this game before.

Gordon sighed, though was secretly smiling, he then relented and took a step towards the cake.

His father shouted, 'OK buster, don't say I didn't warn you.' He then quickly darted forward and with his free hand he started tickling his son into submission.

Shona and Lewis looked across to each other, smiled and without saying a word, knew what the other was thinking, 'Yes, it's going to be fun having grandchildren closer to home now.'

Chapter Five

Lee chopped the aubergine with deft movements of the kitchen knife, all the while smiling at Brodie with a knowing look. 'You two looked as thick as thieves, as always.'

Brodie laughed, 'Och, Dotty's great fun and company, you know that,' he picked up Daisy and ruffled her ear. 'And Daddy pops over for a gossip and cakes too, doesn't he Daisy!'

Lee, laughing, reached over and took an onion and several carrots and potatoes and started to prepare them for the curry dish. 'She does miss her Eric, doesn't she? What a shame that ogre two doors up didn't die instead. That poor woman, how does she put up with him?'

'I guess a beaten dog always returns to its master,' he hugged Daisy to his chest as he said it and the West Highland Terrier snuggled into him in return, sniffing out the scent of toffee and chocolate. 'I guess that she doesn't have anywhere to go and no money of her own. I bet he keeps a good eye on the purse strings.'

Lee reached over and tickled Daisy's ear, glad that their dog was lavished with tender loving care, he wished that poor Millie could have someone to love her. He returned his attention back to cooking and furiously chopped away at an onion, secretly wishing that he could stick this knife into Simon. He was then ashamed at these dark thoughts, put down the knife, walked over to the cooker and scooped in the chopped vegetables into his dish and calmed himself by slowly stirring the pot contents. 'Big guy, was he?' he asked absently.

'Hmmm?' replied a puzzled Brodie.

'The family that Dotty saw going into number three, was the dad a big guy?'

'Oh yes, big guns on him and walked with intent, Dotty thought he might be a former soldier.'

Lee settled his wooden spoon on the side of the cooker, added some cumin, and absently replied, 'That's good. If he buys that house, he'll have a fight on his hands when he gets on the wrong side of Simon, it'll happen one day.' He watched his pot bubble away gently, nodded, satisfied with his creation, and then walked over to Daisy and Brodie and wrapped his hands around them both and was rewarded with a neck nuzzle from both of his loves. He gave a satisfied sigh.

Carl's phone pinged just as he finished the last mouthfuls of his tea. He put down his mug on the table and reached into his pocket and pulled it out. He read the screen and exclaimed, 'Blimey! That was quick.' He turned to Tilly and smiled, 'Our offer has been accepted. We'll be moving into number three before the winter.' He reached over and took her hand and was rewarded with a warm, gentle, and affectionate squeeze.

'Hurray!' shouted out Gordon and Annabelle in unison.

'No more of the tight sod then!' exclaimed Annabelle.

The adults in the room burst out laughing, for they knew that she didn't know the meaning of the words she'd heard her mum previously use to describe their landlord who wouldn't spend any money on the house they were renting.

Lewis rose from his armchair and put an arm on his son's shoulder, 'That's great news son, you'll be able to make another home for yourselves again.' He turned to look at his daughter-in-law, 'We'll all look after you now, I know it's been a rough few years, but you're amongst family now, and things will be alright again.'

Tilly smiled up at him and nodded, 'I know dad, thank you both.' She turned to Shona, 'It's such great news and such a lovely house and not too far for us to visit.'

Carl looked back to his phone, 'I think we should pop over to Felicity and let her know in person.'

'Hurray!' shouted out Gordon as he bounded out from his chair like an uncoiled spring, 'We're off to see Auntie Fizzy and Uncle Geoff, I'm glad I put my favourite football in the boot.' He went running off for his coat, eager to rush his family into getting a move on.

Carl tapped away on the screen, 'I'll text them and warn them!'

Tilly rose and crossed the room and leant down to give Shona a cuddle, 'Don't get up, you look lovely and comfy there.' She hugged her as gently as she could.

'You'd better get a move on,' chided Shona as she reciprocated the cuddle, 'someone is eager to leave us!'

Tilly broke off the embrace and looked at the tray of empty mugs and plates, 'Shall I quickly rinse them out?' she offered.

'Don't you worry about those,' said Lewis, 'I'll do them later when I listen to the next episode of The Archers. Eddie Grundy is in deep water with Clarrie and I want to know how he'll wriggle out of it. Besides, I might learn something for the next time I'm in trouble with my wife.' He turned and winked to his grandchildren. 'It'll keep me out of mischief!'

Gordon and Annabelle started to sing the theme tune from the radio programme they sometimes listened to with grandad and soon the whole family were humming away to it as shoes and summer coats were slipped on in the hallway.

Simon took another slug from the whisky bottle and grimaced as it burned down his throat and put fire into the pits of his belly. He let out a foul-smelling belch and pointed at his wife with an accusing finger. 'Those, those,' he struggled to articulate and find meaning to what he'd seen this morning. 'Those kids were noisy and that fella, why that man, looking at me that way. And you,' he made as if to stab at Millie with his condemning finger. 'Why you were an interfering old cow, you should leave folk like that well alone. It's none of your damn business. Leave them to me.'

Millie cowered deeper into her armchair; the softness of the fabric was in sharp contrast to the hard words shouted at her. All the while she was praying that Simon would calm down, that he would leave her be. She hoped, against all hope, that her son would visit and distract his father, that he might pacify his anger by getting him to help him wash his car. She sometimes felt that their son only ever came to wash his car. Though sometimes this suited her as Simon was such a clean freak that he would help by furiously scrubbing off dirt and then spend great care in rubbing the same spot with his cherished chamois leather. Though she knew he often did this so that he could watch the young lady around the corner, and a few doors down, who seemed to fascinate him in a way that no old man should be captivated by. That's why he often put his car down the side of the garage, squeezing it into that small lock-blocked area, with just enough room to open his door and squeeze his fat gut out.

'Are you even listening to me bitch,' bellowed Simon as he threw the whisky bottle at his wife.

It hit her full on the stomach, knocking the breath out of her. Even in her pain, as she doubled over, she was thankful that he'd screwed the cap on and that its contents hadn't spread out onto the carpet during its trajectory to her. Though that might have made the impact a touch lighter. She involuntary gave out a sharp cry, both in mental anguish and physical agony.

'Stop your whining and go and start making me my dinner,' he commanded.

Millie nodded furiously to appease him, fretful at causing him more reason to be angry with her. She quickly took the bottle from her lap and placed it on her coffee table. It was out of Simon's reach, but within his eyesight. She knew from bitter years of experience that she mustn't separate her husband from his alcohol. As she rose, she gave another involuntary cry of pain, despite her need to try and regulate her breathing. The bottle had knocked the breath from her, as well as knocking off more of her self-respect and worth. She tried standing up but the agony in her belly prevented her and she shuffled through to the kitchen, where her regular supply of painkillers would at least numb her aching but they would do nothing for this mental torture that she had to endure for the sake of appearances.

Gordon bounced his ball all the way from the car to his uncle's door whilst his sister followed behind, sighing, and rolling her eyes, 'Why did boys have to make so much noise,' she wondered to herself. She smiled as she skipped the last few paces and made it to the doorbell first. She rang it with great aplomb, turning back to grin at her brother. He usually beat her to press buttons at road crossings and to answer the house phone. But today, victory was hers!

A tall woman with long flowing blonde hair, the same jet-blue piercing eyes as her father, and a dazzling smile answered the door. She had one hand twisted around her back, out of eyeshot.

'Aunty Fizzy!' exclaimed the children as they greeted their favourite aunt.

'Ah, ah, children, say it properly please.'

Gordon stopped bouncing his ball, looked seriously, and attempted with, 'Aunty Felizzy, aunty Felity,'

'Ha, away with you, aunty Fizzy will have to do. Why change now, I know full well that you can say Felicity.' She removed her arm from behind her with a flourish and a 'Ta Da!' like a stage magician and produced two lollipops.

Both the children took one with glee and rattled off a 'Thank you,' as they tore open the wrappings like eager tomb raiders upon a newly discovered Egyptian mummy.

'Away round the back, Uncle Geoff is securing the goalposts. The recent winds took them off into the flowerbeds. Proof that it's not okay to move the goalposts in business!' She looked down to her puzzled nephew and niece. 'No, Uncle Geoff didn't see the funny side either. But then he is an accountant.'

The children ran off around the side of the house, past a pretty cornflower blue painted shed and into the large expanse of lawn, lovingly nurtured by Geoff every weekend and weeknight during the summer.

'Hello, you two ruffians!' he declared as he stretched out his arms and gathered them in for a group hug as they came running to him, mouths already sticky from their sweets. 'Now remember the rules, no sliding tackles, otherwise?'

'We'll ruin your lovely lawn,' they shouted in accord, a well-rehearsed catchphrase, even though they'd only seen this aunty and uncle a few times since moving up to Scotland. Though to the children that counted as a habitual pattern that they hoped would continue forever. Gordon broke off from what he considered a girly thing to do and reasserted his masculinity by booting the ball into the goal that Geoff always chose as his to defend.

'Oh my,' he exclaimed as he brushed aside his foppish hair, 'I'm losing already!'

The children giggled and ran off after the ball as their uncle looked on avuncularly.

The rice steamer chimed and interrupted the kissing of Lee and Brodie. Daisy gave a small growl as she was released from this three-way passionate embrace that she'd found herself to be privy too. Brodie patted her head, ruffled her neck, and placed her back on the floor. She went trotting off through the open doorway, in search of her favourite toy.

Lee turned to the cooker, picked up the wooden spoon and gave his favourite curry pot another stir. He spooned out a small amount of the sauce, blew down upon the mixture, causing more steam and heat to rise from it and risked scalding his mouth by supping upon it. He grinned. It was perfect. He smiled to Brodie and he saw him come over with two Pyrex dishes with lids. 'You need even more gossip!'

'She looks so alone. Let's put the rice and curry into these and take them over to Dotty's. She doesn't cook properly for herself. She'll love this and you two can catch up on all the tittle tattle of the village.'

Lee laughed, 'You are so thoughtful, I know you worry about her. Okay, but we'll not outstay our welcome. We'll take Daisy too. She'll be cross if we don't take her. And bring some cutlery and plates. I don't want Dotty having to do the washing up when we go home. We'll take everything back here for the dishwasher.'

Brodie whistled through to Daisy, 'We're off to see aunty Dotty.' Daisy came running through, her squeaky toy long forgotten.

Felicity put the teapot down onto the kitchen table, 'Help yourselves you two,' she nodded to the milk jug and sugar bowl, 'I can never remember who takes what, but I do have your favourite biscuits Tilly, I remembered that.' She walked over to one of her cupboards, opened it and withdrew a packet. She turned back to the kitchen table and wrapped her arms around her brother, 'And these are just for you Carl, my favourite brother, we've got to feed those big muscles of yours.' She passed him the packet and put her arms around his biceps and made a show of feeling around for something lost.

Carl grinned. 'I'm your only brother.' He looked at the packet, squinting to read the small print.

'Don't worry, there is no added sugar, it's pure beefy content, just like you!'

Tilly laughed and reached over to the plate of chocolate biscuits and helped herself, 'You don't know what you are missing,' she teased as she sucked down on the thick chocolate layer.

'He was the same as a child. I'd be getting high on sugar, but he'd be on the lookout for savoury snacks. Then when he decided on an army career, mum was always having to cook chicken and broccoli and he'd be munching on them every few hours, like an eating machine.' She rolled her eyes in mock exasperation. 'Anyway, it's lovely to see you all looking so happy, Geoff sounds like he's loving the children's company. He'd have made a great dad,' she sighed wistfully.

'No joy with the recent treatment?' probed Tilly carefully.

Felicity looked crest-fallen, 'I'm afraid not, but we live in hope. The doctors at the fertility clinic say that I have to rest my body, so that's that, for the time being.' She smiled up at Tilly again, 'But having your two around is a breath of fresh air. I haven't seen mum and dad so animated in such a long time. We're all happy that you moved up, and, remember to ask anytime that you'd like me to babysit, or have them for sleepovers again.'

'That's so kind Felicity, thank you. They love coming over, they enjoy playing football with Geoff.'

Felicity looked out of the kitchen window and spent several minutes watching her niece and nephew run rings around her husband. She then broke off her reverie, took a sip of her tea, reached for a biscuit, and enquired, 'So what brings you over?'

Carl, wrestling orally with his beef jerky, took a determined bite down and motioned, in a familiar gesture borne from years of marriage, to his wife to answer the question.

Tilly obliged with, 'We've finally found a house we like. We came upon it by chance, whilst visiting the nearby lighthouse. We put in an offer and it got accepted,' she took out her mobile phone and tapped away before presenting it to Felicity. 'What do you think?'

Felicity took the offered phone, looked at the estate agent's photos on the screen and used her fingers to zoom in on the images. 'It looks lovely. I confess that I've not been into the village, I usually drive past it on the way to Peterhead for my old school friends Symposium café catch up at their Lido coffee shop. I've not read much about that village in the Buchan Observer newspaper, I've always thought it a nice quiet place. That's a good price for that size of house, especially being a semi-detached, why is it so cheap.'

'We wondered that too,' said Carl, his bout with the beef jerky was over, he'd won and was full again, even though he'd had that big wedge of Dundee cake earlier. 'Apparently, the previous owner wanted a quick sale, he'd got fed up having to drive to Aberdeen each day for his work.'

'Fair dues, it is a long drive. I prefer to take the Buchan Xpress bus, their Wi Fi is so much better now, so I stream a telly program whilst I let the coach driver worry about the traffic. But then I can get on at the end of my street here and the Aberdeen office is a stone's throw from the Union Square bus station. Those that have offices in Altens or say work at the university or hospital, well, they need to catch another bus, or walk. That can make for a long day. Besides, village life isn't for everybody, some folk prefer the convenience of living in the city. There is a wider range of pubs and restaurants and a more vibrant nightlife.'

'We're after a quiet life, aren't we Carl,' said Tilly, biting down on another chocolate biscuit.

Carl nodded, 'Too right, no dramas for me from now on, no boss man giving me mission orders, I just want to do a bit of the website work, then go for a coastal walk and lift a few weights.'

Felicity laughed, sprang forward and rubbed his hair playfully and grabbed at his biceps again, 'Ohhh, my kid brother with all his big muscles, you're like the incredible hulk now! Me smash things,' she playfully grunted.

'Geroff!' Carl good-humouredly growled. He helped himself to another piece of protein, inadvertently emphasising his sister's banter.

The kitchen door opened, and the noise of the football being passed between the children was momentarily heightened until Geoff closed it. 'I haven't missed a cup of tea, have I?' he breathlessly asked between the trio. 'It's thirsty work keeping up with those two. They always seem to put me in the goals, and they are relentless.' He had a huge grin on his face to demonstrate that he wouldn't want it any other way. He spotted the biscuits and took two, he needed to recharge before the next game.

Carl poured him a mug from the teapot, giving him an opportunity to admire the floral pattern. He wondered when, during his busy army career, his sister got so domesticated. He spooned two sugars from the matching bowl and stirred the mug's contents. He looked forward to being in the same place, settled and putting down more permanent roots. He turned the mug around, so that the handle faced Geoff, 'Here you are mate, NATO standard.'

'Cheers, I know this one! Milk and two sugars, fantastic. Though bear with me, I don't always know your army phrases, sorry,' he pushed his glasses further back up his nose before accepting the hot brew.

'White and two, NATO brew,' sang brother and sister in unison, before reaching across the table and high fiving with a friendly slap of palms.

Felicity took it a stage further with a, 'Get with the programme Geoff!' She caught her husband's embarrassed look, 'Mission successful!' she thought and catching her brother's look, knew that he was thinking the same. They still had their own shorthand way of thinking and had always delighted in teasing her boyfriends and continued the tradition from day one of her marriage to Geoff. Carl had found a wig that closely matched Felicities hair colour and bought a second-hand bridal dress and veil from eBay and had run down the aisle screaming several minutes before her arrival, pretending to be her. Poor Geoff was a bag of nerves all through the wedding and she'd only learnt about her brother's antics later, at the wedding speeches, and tried to give him a thick ear. But Carl was too quick for her and dived under the top table. She repaid him later though, with her own devilish trick at his wedding. She'd gotten a replica wedding cake made from thin cardboard and had it iced to match their requirements for the real one with the baker. Tilly had been in on the joke and when Carl and she, using an army bayonet, made the first cut, the icing flaked off and the cake crumpled to reveal its hollow interior. The wedding photographer had been pre-warned and alerted to take a series of snaps. Felicity smiled up at her wall, where Carl's startled look was captured for family posterity. The picture was always guaranteed to make her cheerful and the siblings had been trying to out-prank each other ever since. 'Carl and Tilly have bought a house love.'

'That's great news,' Geoff reached across and shook Carl's hand, inwardly wincing at just how strong a grip was naturally returned. He happily broke off and went for a contrasting gentle embrace with Tilly. 'You'll have to watch out for the new land and buildings transaction tax, how much is the property valued at, you'll have to keep the offer under it.'

The trio laughed and Carl broke with a, 'I remember our last chat, it's handy you are an accountant, so we put in an offer of a pound under the £145,000. The house is worth far more than that, the owners wanted a quick sale with no offer due date, so we chanced our luck with a low offer. We've to appoint a solicitor pronto, get our own survey done and all the other formalities.'

Geoff reached into one of the drawers, took out an ornate silver rectangular object, gently pulled it apart, and from this business card holder, a wedding gift from his colleagues at the office, took out a card. 'A pal of mine from my university days, tell him that you are my brother-in-law and he'll give you a huge discount from his normal fees. They'll be a fraction of what the local firms will offer. But do ask him about Morris first, it'll break the ice.'

Carl's forehead creased in apparent confusion and Geoff helped him out with, 'He runs an old beige Morris Minor, it belonged to his dear old grandmother, it's his pride and joy. He's well-known in the area for it. His secretaries must allow him to double the journey time between appointments when they manage his office diary and book seeing clients at their place of work. He chugs along at thirty, even in a seventy zone. Poor Morris is held together by prayer and positivity, but he won't part with it, he says he feels closer to his long-dead grandmother in it. He spends a fortune in genuine spare parts and mechanic fees.' Geoff shook his head, appalled at the waste of money by someone who should know better.

'Cheers mate,' thanked Carl as he clinked mugs with Geoff. 'I'm all for a bit of saving money.'

Felicity reached up and rubbed Carl's stomach playfully, 'Him got more money for mammoth meat,' she grunted in her best caveman impression. She was rewarded with howls of laughter from her sister-in-law and husband just as her niece and nephew came in from outside. They simultaneously spotted the biscuit plate, noticed that there was just one chocolate biscuit left, and both bolted, hoping to outrun the other to the solitary treat. Felicity laughed, heartened to see that their sibling rivalry was as friendly, but as strong as hers and Carl's remained. She stood up and walked back to the treat cupboard, smiling all the way.

The doorbell chimed and a patter of feet could be heard within as the trio waited patiently outside. An eye was placed on the spyhole and the beam of her smile radiated through her wooden door and was glimmered full-on as Dotty opened her home to Brodie, Lee, and Daisy. 'Hello, you three, what a lovely surprise.' She looked to the trays they were carrying and spied the light steam they were emitting into the late summer evening. 'Oh, that smells lovely.'

'We thought we could eat together, perhaps at yours, or maybe you could pop over to ours?' Lee lifted his tray higher, hoping to entice their friend with his home-cooking, whilst being careful not to extend Daisy's leash, wrapped loosely over his wrist. She was blissfully unaware of this and was patiently sitting down, her tail wagging away like a street cleaner's broom, awaiting a clap from her pal.

'Oh, how lovely!' exclaimed a delighted Dotty. 'You are two of the most thoughtful boys I know.' She reached down and petted Daisy behind her ear then stood straight and ushered her friends in, 'Come away in, I see that you have everything we need for a fine feast. It's so great to have friends like you, looking out for me.' She smiled as they carried their delicious smelling wares past her. She looked up and across to her other pal, Millie. Shadows were dancing across her shut blinds and the artificial lights shone a spotlight on their movements. Dotty squinted in puzzlement as to why her friend would have her blinds drawn and her lounge lights on when it was such a bright evening with the sun not yet set. Her eyes narrowed as she strained to look across and then, despite the warm evening, she shivered as she realised that she knew what those movements were. It was of a heavy hand and arm swooshing down upon an innocent sat, trapped, upon her armchair. Reluctantly, Dotty turned towards her door and entered to the warmth and happiness within, in sharp contrast to the evening of wretchedness that her chum was enduring. She felt a pang of guilt and a gloom of impotence wash over her as she closed her door.

Chapter Six

Carl smiled at the removal men as between them, they carried the family's main television from their van and into their new home. He was pleased to see them wearing their poppies with pride, though it was only the day after Halloween. He had hoped to be in their new home for that event, so that his children could welcome in trick or treaters and make new friends. Instead, they'd said a farewell to the village that had been their home for two cold winters. They'd all loved that village but hated the cold house. The last few months, waiting for the slow, legal handover of their purchase to go through, had seemed to stretch forever. Especially for Tilly. He'd felt powerless to change anything, given that it was rented, and that the landlord stipulated in their contract that no DIY home improvements could take place. All it had needed were some replacement window frames to keep out the drafts and an internal door to the lounge to retain heat. Otherwise it was perfect, especially as it was so near to the golden-sanded beach which they all enjoyed walking along. Yet the landlord would not employ a tradesman or use his own skills to carry out the necessary repairs. So now he found himself a homeowner once more, in the next village, though with rugged hills and a picturesque harbour, rather than with a beach. Though he knew his family would be happy here, he did worry that they'd spent all their money paying for it outright and he was uncertain about the financial future. He turned from his morose thoughts, put a smile back on his face, and called out to the men as they left his new home's front door and were walking back to their van, 'Would you like a brew, lads?'

'Oh yes please mate, ta, teas with two sugars please, that'd be lovely,' replied Grant, the foreman of the duo. Ross, the younger of the pair, nodded eagerly.

'Come into the kitchen in a few minutes and I'll have them ready with a few biscuits too,' smiled Carl. He was glad for something to do. The removals men had made it quite clear to him that he wasn't to go into their van and lift anything. Their insurance policy would not cover Carl if he injured himself. He reluctantly accepted this, though he hated having to watch others doing the hard work. He swung himself off the adjoining wall from his neighbour with ease and from the corner of his eye spotted Simon staring at him from his lounge window. Carl gave him a friendly wave, turned, and walked into his new home. He did not see that Simon scowled back at him and did not return his friendly gesture.

'Just feel how warm this house is, even with the front door open for the men,' rejoiced Tilly with glee from their new lounge. 'Come in and sit on your chair a moment and feel it.'

Carl walked through from the lobby, pleased to see his wife so animated and happy. 'Feel what?'

'Come and sit down a moment,' she insisted.

Carl humoured her and sat in his favourite armchair, it was one of the first pieces of furniture to be offloaded and put into their new home. He swivelled absently about and then reclined deep into its plush fabric.

Tilly closed the lounge door, walked seductively over to him, and gently sat down on his knees. 'Can you feel it?'

Carl hugged her close and whispered, 'I can feel something!'

She thumped him playfully, 'Mmm, maybe later,' she teased. 'But you can't feel it, can you?'

'Nope. You've lost me. I can't feel anything, though I can hear our excited children's footsteps jumping about upstairs and running down the stairs.'

'There's no draught from the windows! It's going to be toasty warm this November, and every month. No draughty house! I can't wait for Christmas!' She leant in for a kiss.

Carl reciprocated and hugged his wife tighter, so pleased with her simple childlike delight, he knew she was well on the road to recovery.

'Yuck!' exclaimed Annabelle, who had crept in without her parents being aware. 'You two are always snogging!'

Carl wiggled out from under Tilly's embrace and patted his knees, 'There's always room for you Princess, come and give daddy a big kiss.' He puckered up and waited patiently.

'No thank you daddy, I've got toys to unpack.' She turned away and ran upstairs, leaving her father looking like a floundering trout in a fisherman's basket.

'Spurned again! Oh well. I bet she'll love me in a minute when I open the chocolate biscuits.' He stood up, ' I told the guys that I'd make them a cup of tea. It's so nice to see you looking so well and happy. I promise you that we'll be okay here. We'll finally settle and make another home for ourselves. You and the children will be safe here. I promise.'

Tilly stood up and lent in for another quick kiss. 'I know. Now go and make the men their tea, it's thirsty work lugging all our stuff in.' She rubbed his arm in encouragement.

Carl smiled and made his way into the kitchen where the removals men had left the box marked, 'REMOVE FIRST' in the middle of the floor. This was an old army trick that Carl and Tilly had learnt from many house moves over the years. It contained the kettle, mugs, teabags, coffee, sugar, and packets of biscuits. They knew that it would be needed to feed and hydrate the removals men and women who transported their goods and chattels from posting to posting. A well-fed crew took more care, and this resulted in little or no damage to homes, furniture and their cherished bits and pieces. Since doing this they had not needed to claim on their insurance for some years. Tilly always started the removals crew day off with a selection of canned fizzy and energy drinks and local bakery goods. Today it had been butteries generously smeared with butter and jam. These tasted a bit like a flattened croissant and were one of the things that Carl ate as soon as they re-entered the North-East of Scotland. She and the children took a while to get used to their high salted taste, but soon enjoyed them as an occasional breakfast treat. She'd already unpacked the box and filled the kettle whilst Carl was sat absently outside on the wall enjoying the crisp November air. He'd never been able to sit still for more than a few minutes in an enclosed room, not since that mission that had gone terribly wrong.

'Hello, hello!' chimed a cheery voice from the doorstep, breaking into the couple's thoughts.

Carl and Tilly walked through from their respective rooms, met in their lobby, and jostled gently for command position towards the sound of the greeting. Tilly won and stepped towards the old lady who was holding an old-fashioned tray with handles, its contents covered with a tea towel.

'Hello?' replied a hesitant Tilly as she reached her front porch, the door was wide open to allow the removal men easy access.

'I won't stop, I can see that you are busy, but I know that it's so easy to overlook being fed at a time like this. Welcome to the neighbourhood, I'm Dotty from right across the road, I thought you'd like some freshly baked scones and some of my homemade jam for you and your children and the workmen. They look ever so tired, carrying all those boxes and furniture.'

'Aw, that's so sweet of you Dotty, thank you. 'I'm Tilly and this big lump is my husband Carl.'

'Hello Dotty, those smell so tasty, let me take them from you.' Carl squeezed past Tilly and took the tray from his new neighbour. 'I'll shout the kids down, then they can thank you too. They are enjoying their last day of the school holiday.'

'Oh, no need for any fuss,' replied Dotty, pleased that her heavy burden was lifted from her aching arms. 'Just you all concentrate on getting fed and settling into your new home. Did you manage the front door okay? Guy and Finty, who owned the house before you, they were worried that it was still a bit stiff. They didn't want to come back and fix it.' She glanced nervously towards Millie's house.

Her agitation was lost on the couple as Tilly replied, 'No. It was fine, they left the house in great condition, and so clean and well-decorated too.' She gently put her arms out and embraced Dotty. 'You're so thoughtful, thank you. We'll be unpacked by tonight, would you like to pop over for some supper, perhaps at about eight o'clock? You can meet Gordon and Annabelle then.'

'Oh, what lovely names, that would be splendid,' beamed Dotty. 'I've some leftover beef, would you allow me to make some stovies for you all?'

'No, really, you've been too kind already,' protested Carl.

'No, you've enough to be doing, and I bet those two scamps are a handful, I'll pop over with a pot of stovies, some oatcakes and beetroot, to welcome you into the neighbourhood.'

'No, you can't be carrying all that over, it'll be ever so heavy,' though Carl was salivating at the thought of his favourite meal that his mum still cooked every week. He loved Tilly, but she just couldn't cook Scottish food the way his mum did. He'd bet that his new neighbour cooked his favourite beef, onion, and potato meal as well as his mother did. With any luck she'd also cook some skirlie stuffing, his favourite oatmeal and onion treat.

As if reading his mind Dotty insisted with, 'Don't you worry about that, I've two big lads who'll lend a helping hand. That's settled then, I'll see you this evening and you just leave all the cooking to me.' She gave a cheery goodbye and left the couple smiling on their doorstep, watching her chat away with the removal men as she walked back to her home.

Millie sat fretfully on her chair. Her knitting was sitting idly on her lap. She just couldn't settle upon it. Her body was stiff with tension, in anticipation of Simon being in a foul mood. He'd been unhappy at seeing the young man sat on the adjoining wall, idling the time of day. He'd paced around the lounge impotently muttering under his breath. She knew his rage would boil over like a pot just on the boil and that she would bear the brunt of it when it finally spilt over its threshold and erupted. She always did. Like a silent punchbag. She secretly yearned for his death. She envied her pal's widowed status. She wished that Dotty's Eric were still with her and that she was the widow. Simon's death would free her from a great deal of physical pain at his hands. She saw, with relief, that the young man had taken himself off the wall. Though that didn't stop the electrically charged fury emanating from Simon like an approaching storm. She so wanted to rise from her chair when she saw her pal cross the street with a tray that she knew would be fresh bakes to welcome the new family. She yearned to greet them too, as any friendly neighbour would, but felt powerless to whilst this storm was raging within her husband, all because someone had dared to sit on his wall. She sunk lower into her chair, awaiting the inevitable blows, hoping that the children next door would not be distressed by her cries of pain.

Annabelle opened the box that sat in the middle of her room and unpacked her Princess Anna pillow. She threw it up to her unmade bed and then carefully took out her CD player with almost reverential awe. She then reached across to the wall and plugged in the cable, grinned, and pressed the play button. She danced gaily to the Frozen theme tune and was soon shouting out, 'Let it go!' at the top of her voice. She didn't hear her brother walk into her bedroom. He stood there laughing at her antics until she twirled round in her dance moves and opened her eyes. 'Get out!' she yelled, cross at her untrained dance moves being discovered.

'Okay sis, but I only came to tell you that a nice old lady brought over some cakes. More for me to eat!' He ran quickly away and flew down the stairs and into the kitchen.

Annabelle swiftly followed, though she took the time to hit the pause button on her favourite song. She didn't want to miss the next track, she loved dancing to Taylor Swift's Shake It Off equally as much. She too took the stairs at a leaping bounce down and narrowly made it into the kitchen behind her brother. They both joined the grown-ups as mugs were handed around.

'There you go mate, a NATO brew to warm you up, help yourself to cakes and biscuits,' said Carl to Grant. He reached back to the kitchen worktop and handed another mug to Ross.

'I knew it. You are ex-forces too?' replied Grant as he took the mug gratefully and then picked up the plate of biscuits and offered them to the children with a cheeky wink.

'Daddy was a soldier and he's got lots of medals,' proudly interrupted Gordon as he helped himself to several biscuits. 'I took them to school once for show and tell. My friends thought they were ever so shiny.'

'Afghanistan?' enquired Ross quietly.

'Daddy went there three times, he chased bad guys,' answered Annobelle proudly. 'He was a special soldier. Though we did miss him when he was away.'

'Ah,' said Grant knowingly. 'Tough gig. We were out there with the local regiment, just the one tour, that was enough for us, wasn't it Ross?'

Ross nodded. His thoughts were lost to a land many miles away. He broke his reverie, sighed, and stated, 'Grant was our sergeant, we lost a few good lads and one lass, our medic. We did our time and then decided to go into business together, a nice quiet and peaceful job.'

'Ross and I love meeting new folk and the physical side keeps the agitation at bay, you know? Getting out and about.'

'Yes,' replied Carl, 'I know, only too well.' He looked at his children, pleased to see them munching down on a handful of biscuits and now busy at the other side of the kitchen, out of earshot, pulling aside the tea towel from the tray, their eyes widening at the baked delights revealed. 'I've seen too many pals go down too, it really affects you, the sudden, violent loss. It's difficult to stay in after that. I left a few years after my final tour. I still had some missions left in me that I wanted to see through, you know, for personal satisfaction.

Mostly here in the UK and a few quick jobs overseas. I feel that I've now done my bit.'

'Have you moved here to be nearer your family?' asked Ross to Tilly.

'No, nearer to Carl's,' she unconsciously pulled down her hoodie sleeve from her wrists down over her fingers, as if feeling the cold.

'That's good, it's great to be nearer to family. We've always lived near here and knew many of the lads' families that we served with. We've an extended family now. We sometimes get one or two of them in when we've a big job on.'

Grant walked over to the children, who, having demolished their biscuits, were now busy munching down on cakes, their faces were smothered in red jam. 'Any left for me? I need to fuel up after lifting your heavy beds up all those stairs. Did you count them?'

Annabelle nodded innocently, 'Thirteen!'

Grant smiled, reached over for a buttered scone, and said, 'Unlucky for some!'

Simon threw down some coins to Amber, the young shop assistant who took a pace back from the counter as though it afforded her a physical barrier and protection from her least favourite customer. She knew better than to ask him to wait for her to count out the silver and bronze that spun and settled upon her workspace. He wouldn't have waited, nor would he offer up a thank you or some small talk about the weather or the headlines on the newspaper that he'd bought. He folded it in half, turned around, glared at the customer behind him, and made his way out of the shop, shouldering aside another customer who had entered the doorway just before him.

A collective sigh was exhaled by all three after his exit and their tension release was evident as their shoulders sagged and they nervously started a conversation about the recent theft of a poppy collection tin from the local pub.

Outside the shop Simon opened his newspaper, took out the glossy adverting leaflets that had been inserted within the middle pages, and threw them on the pavement. He walked on past the public bin and crossed the road, not bothering to check the traffic. As he passed Brodie's and Lee's house, he gathered up some phlegm with a vile look on his face and spat across to their gate. It struck the wood, just to the left of their numbered plate with the picture of a white dog on it. He grinned in satisfaction as he saw his former bodily fluids slide down the panel, leaving a slime trail in its wake, like that of a fat, lazy slug. He walked on, towards his home and looked in disgust at the removals van that had dared to park across the front of his house, just so that their ramp would be by the gate of his new neighbours. He retched once more at the back of his throat and was trying to gather more phlegm when he was interrupted and had to swallow hard the foulness as he investigated the back of the van.

'We'll not be long sir,' smiled Grant reassuringly. 'Just a few more pieces to offload and then we'll be gone.'

'You're blocking out my light,' growled Simon.

Grant, looking puzzled, glanced up to the sky.

'From my lounge window you daft cu..'

'Hi new neighbour,' smiled Carl as he walked up his garden path. 'I hope my two aren't making too much noise?' He nodded to his upstairs window.

Simon looked at him with disdain in his eyes and slowly tapped at his ears.

'Ah, sorry, I hadn't noticed those,' offered Carl as he saw two small hearing aids poking out from under Simon's woolly hat.

'I hear nothing when I take these out, nobody can bother me that way,' Simon snarled as he continued his way.

'Charming man, that neighbour of yours.'

'Mmm,' was all that Carl could bring himself to say.

'I'll just turn the heating up a little bit dear,' announced Lewis as he rose from his armchair, 'You look a bit cold. I'll make another cup of tea whilst I'm up.'

'Thank you, and yes, you can have a piece of my sponge cake. Just a small slice for me.'

Lewis's eyes twinkled in recognition of his reward. He loved his wife's Victoria sponge cake the best and had been looking forward to it all day long.

'You've ants in your pants today. They'll be perfectly fine without you, they have moved to a new house before, you know. There was no way that you could have picked up and carried boxes, not with your bad back and sore hip.'

In acknowledgment Lewis rubbed his left hip, then conscious of what he was doing, clapped his hands and said with glee, 'Isn't it great having our boy back again! His Tilly is such a beautiful girl and they've given us two cracking grandkids.' And like a child in a sweet shop he said, 'I can't wait to watch The Snowman with them.'

Shona grinned back at him, 'I think Frozen Two might be competing with that old cartoon. Tilly reckons that they'll be dragging us to the cinema several times to watch it. They had to take her to see the first one six times and buy the DVD on the day it was released. You'd better get the popcorn on standby!'

Lewis laughed, 'It'll be worth it. Besides, we'll get our pensioner discount. Every penny is worth it to have our Carl safe and well. No more dangerous jobs for him. He's all in one piece and that's what counts. Of course, you'll have to alter your recipes. Your cakes will need to be at least three times bigger to feed his appetite and those of the children, though Tilly eats so sparingly, I do worry about her.'

'Ha! You only want me to bake more cakes so that you can have a larger wedge. I know you only too well, you're crafty! Remember, you need to lose a few pounds before the surgeon will give you a new hip.'

He rubbed at the side of his leg again at the reminder of his dull ache. 'There's plenty of time to do that, I've a feeling that running around after Annabelle and Gordon will keep me thin. And young! They've knocked years off me! Ah, if only our Felicity had been able to have children of her own, she'd have been a cracking mum, just like Tilly. I had hoped that the money we gifted them would have helped her at the fertility clinic. If only she'd accept a bit more.'

'I know, I know,' she sighed. 'But she'll maybe feel strong enough for more treatment in a few months. She brightened with, 'But her and Geoff are loving being such an active aunty and uncle. Our Carl is going to be fine here, in the loving embrace of his family once more.'

Grant offered his hand and pumped up and down as Carl reciprocated with a firm handshake. 'Thanks so much for your business mate, you enjoy that house with your lovely family, you deserve it. It's nice to see you settle down after your active service. Perhaps we'll see each other again? Ross and I are always looking for teammates to join our crew on the bigger jobs. You look like you're no stranger to heavy lifting.'

'Cheers mate, I've your card, I might just do that. Here, this is for you both to have a drink on us.' He handed him an envelope that contained one of Tilly's homemade thank you cards along with some banknotes.

'Cool, thanks ever so much, a bit of beer money is always welcome. We'll drink to your family's good health tonight. We enjoy a pint or three after a heavy day of lifting. It helps us sleep too,' he laughed. 'Laughing boy next door should try it, perhaps it'll make him friendlier!'

'Don't worry about him, my Tilly usually charms the men into submission. He'll be like putty in her hands in no time. Safe journey home lads.' He reached over and shook Ross's hand and watched them settle into the front of their truck and drive off with a farewell gentle toot of the horn. He turned and walked back into his front garden, nodding a friendly greeting to Simon who was walking around his shut and padlocked gates with a sullen scowl on his face.

Chapter Seven

Tilly finished slotting up the last of the curtain hooks on their lounge window and brushed down the plush fabric as she stepped off the small step-ladder. She took a step back and admired her choice of colour which complimented the floral wallpaper. Though the previous owners had left their curtains, Tilly felt that her theme went better. It was her way of adding her own touch to their new home. Other than that, it was all ready to move into. She still couldn't believe their luck in finding a house that included such well-maintained carpets, oak flooring and a fully fitted kitchen and even up-to-date décor.

The doorbell chimed its uplifting tune and she turned to answer it, quickly looking at the time on the mobile phone in her pocket. Time had flown by as they unpacked box after box and made this house into their own home. She suddenly felt hungry and knew who this would be. She looked through the ornate glasswork of her front door and above the zebra head she could make out two tall figures. 'Ah, not Dotty then,' she said aloud for the benefit of Carl who was walking down the stairs. Pity, she thought, as she heard her stomach rumble and she realised that she hadn't eaten since her morning muesli.

She opened the door and was greeted enthusiastically by two grinning men carrying a large pot each. 'Hiya, I'm Brodie,' said the thinner of the two, 'and this is my husband Lee. It's a pleasure to meet you. We live next door, at number one. We'd shake your hands, but Dotty has loaded us up with your dinner.'

Dotty squeezed out from behind and went between them and ushered them into the house with, 'Follow me you two, straight into the kitchen, you know the way, Guy and Finty had us around often enough.' She carried a jar of beetroot and several packets of oatcakes in her favourite bag for life. 'C'mon,' she commanded, 'you are letting all these good folks heat out. We'll not stay long, just time enough to drop these off.'

Brodie led the way and winked up to Carl who was on the stairs, 'Oh my, Lee said you were a hunk!'

Carl laughed good-naturedly, 'And it looks like my muscles are about to get a good feed.' He sniffed for effect, 'And if I'm not deceived, that's skirlie!' he declared. 'My, but you are already friends for life, what a feast. You will stay, won't you?'

'Only if our little friend can stay too, she's fully house trained.'

Carl spied the dog leash held loosely by Lee at the back of the trio. Before he could say yes, Annabelle let out a loud, 'Awwhh! Can I stroke her please? Awwh, look at the beautiful pink bow-tie that she's wearing. Like a Princess dog!' She ran forward, knelt, and made a fuss of Daisy. They were soon joined by Gordon.

'I think that the decision has been made, I'll get some more plates warmed up in the oven. I've a lovely wine chilling in the fridge for just this occasion.'

Brodie, who had been precariously balancing his pot with one hand, withdrew his other from around his back and produced a bottle of champagne. 'We thought that you'd like to toast your first night in your new home with this. I've chilled it to the correct temperature.'

Tilly, overcome with emotion, dried her eyes with a tissue from up her sleeve. As she had fumbled for it, her hoodie sleeve had ridden up her arm and with practised care, she quickly pulled it down.

Lee, the more observant of the couple, had a quick glimpse of her fragile state when he saw the raised welts slashed across her wrists. From years of self-harm and two suicide attempts. He smiled weakly, 'A fresh, bright start for both of you and your lovely children.' Though it came out as more of a question than a statement. 'I'm sure that you'll all be happy here, it's a lovely neighbourhood, on the whole.' He looked down lovingly at Daisy who was enjoying being made a fuss of by the youngsters. 'Er, have you any pets?'

'No, we've never settled long enough to commit to them.'

Lee let out a sigh and said in a low voice 'That's just as well then.' It was lost to the couple above the noise of the cooing and appreciative noises that Annabelle and Gordon were making.

'You two boys pop those heavy pots on the table there and sit yourselves down, you're in the way now,' commanded Dotty. 'Now then Carl, make yourself useful and get some glasses. My stovies and skirlie are fresh from my stove and will keep hot for a while yet. Let's have a good Scottish toast to welcome you to the village.'

Carl beamed, she hadn't disappointed him, she'd made his favourite side dish too. He was going to like this trio and their dog fine. He smiled across to Tilly and looked to his children who were leading the beautiful dog by its leash into their kitchen. They were going to be happy here, after the traumas of his military life and Tilly's upbringing, they'd finally found their sanctuary.

Millie winced as she stepped over the edge of the bath and concentrated on balancing herself as she part dragged her other leg over. She used the edge of the nearby sink to steady herself as she stood up straight with some effort. She yearned for higher grab rails on the wall. Her arthritis made it painful to step into the bath as a normal person would and there was no way that she could lower herself down into a warm, relaxing bath, and guarantee that she'd be able to pull herself up. Her stiffness and lack of muscle power prevented that. Instead, she turned on the shower and let the hot water soothe away some of her aches and pains. As she rinsed her body, she once more wished that Simon would spend some of their considerable savings on a walk-in shower. She sighed. She'd heard of some couples of her age who had employed a joiner and plumber and had raised the height of a toilet seat and had installed a wet room for their easy hygiene needs. But she knew better than to ask Simon to spend any money. She didn't know what he was saving for, nor how much money that they, or rather he, had squirrelled away. This was their rainy-day need, or rather hers, for he didn't have any aches or pains and didn't seem to care about her constant soreness. She sighed as she turned slowly round, being careful not to slip, and allowed the cascading water to rinse her back thoroughly.

Minutes earlier, she'd enjoyed hearing the laughter of the adults and children come through the adjoining house walls and had felt envious. She'd wished that she could join in the fun and welcome the family into the area like any normal neighbour. But she knew that it wouldn't be worth the beating that would follow. Besides, Simon liked them to be in bed by nine, a habit that he'd got into when the neighbourly disputes had started. Soon, very soon, these neighbours would feel the wrath of Simon, just like poor Finty and Guy, the lovely couple who always had a kind word for her. They were great neighbours, until that aviary was built. And such beautiful birds they were too with their gentle cooing noises. Not that she could show her enjoyment of them. It wasn't right what her Simon did. Mind you, she thought, it isn't right what he does to her each night. She sighed, reached for her flannel, soaped it up and reached down below and cleaned herself, ready for Simon.

'Can we have a dog daddy and mummy, please,' begged Annabelle, allowing the last word to linger and echo around the kitchen. She looked up to her parents with wide pleading seal-like eyes.

'That would be great, can we! I'll teach it to play football,' joined in Gordon enthusiastically. He too was beseeching his parents with his innocent face held high.

'Maybe one day, soon,' replied Carl, looking to Tilly for confirmation. He'd enjoy getting out of the house and taking it for long walks, perhaps even runs.

Tilly smiled as she watched her two tickle Daisy on her tummy whilst making appreciative noises. Daisy was flat on her back, legs akimbo, relishing the attention from her two new best friends. She kicked her legs playfully in the air with each new stroke. 'Let me think about it for a while, perhaps after you've settled into your new school.'

'It's a lovely school, my children went there, years ago. The building hasn't changed much, it's ever so old-fashioned looking, but the teachers and headmistress are so enthusiastic and get great reports. My friend volunteers there, and she so loves the children, I'll ask her to keep an eye out for you both. Not that you'll need it, the children, she tells me, are so well-behaved. I'm sure you'll make friends in no time,' declared Dotty.

The children, caught in the moment of enjoying rubbing the soft fur of their best friend forever, hadn't heard her. Their mother answered for them, 'Thank you Dotty, that's really thoughtful. They've got their new school uniforms already looked out and ironed and Carl's polished their shoes so that you can see their faces in them!'

'We thought that you might have been a military man Carl, especially with your physique?' enquired Lee.

'You'll have to excuse my Lee, he's always liked buff men, I don't know what he saw in me though!' joked Brodie.

'Yes, though I left about two years ago. I haven't settled on a new career that I like and then I couldn't work for a bit, you know, caring for the youngsters here.'

'Oh, were you working then Tilly? That's a very modern way, isn't it, having a house-husband to look after the home and children. Hard work though Carl, I'd imagine?' empathised Lee.

'No, I was in the hospital for a bit, but Carl looked after us all. He did a great job, but that's why we moved here. To be closer to his family, you know, for a bit more support.'

'Ah, I see, yes, I know it's not the same, but we'd be lost without our parents looking after Daisy whenever we go out or away abroad. She gets spoilt rotten and has to go on a diet.'

Brodie patted Lee's belly, 'And so do we, especially if we've been to an all-inclusive resort.'

'We could look after Daisy, couldn't we dad?' asked Annabelle. She knew to always ask her father first; she'd learnt from a young age that he was the softer of her parents and wouldn't deny her most things.

'That sounds like a most sensible alternative to getting a dog. You can learn how it needs looking after and see if you are up to the job. That's if you lads don't mind, perhaps they could take Daisy for the odd walk, or stay here if you go away?' Carl could see the two men tense up as he said the last sentence and was worried that he'd overstepped the mark.

'Er, yes, maybe. Perhaps you could take Daisy to the playing field now and again. Walk towards the shop though, not that way.' Lee pointed towards the adjoining kitchen wall.

Carl, having had training in interpreting body language, noticed that his hand was shaking as he'd quickly pointed and that his shoulders had tensed up . He frowned and chose his next words carefully. 'I think Daisy might have had a bit too much excitement for one night and needs the company of her parents for a little while. It's time you two were ready for bed and got a good night's sleep for school tomorrow. I'll walk you down whilst mum has a lie-in.'

Tilly looked abashed and explained, 'I'm on strong medicines that makes me ever so drowsy and makes me so sleepy and groggy in the morning.'

Their visitors nodded, not really understanding, but having a slight clue upon her fragile state. They smiled as the children took turns, in what seemed to be a well-rehearsed nightly ritual, to kiss their mother on both cheeks with a loud smattering of lips, and gave her a big hug whilst saying, 'Ahhh!' as they held her tight.

The children then repeated their actions to their father and then Annabelle walked over to Dotty and gave her a cuddle. 'I really liked your cooking, can we come over for tea sometime?'

Dotty, enjoying the embrace, laughed and looked over to Tilly, 'You are all welcome at any time. I've always got cakes in my special tin for my favourite guests. I do enjoy a good cuppa and a chinwag.' She broke off the embrace and winked at Brodie.

Shona looked across to Lewis and watched with amusement as his head nodded down towards his chest and was absorbed by his ample chin. It seemed to rebound softly and rise in the air, hold itself aloft like a gently floating balloon, and then allow gravity to return it to the safety of his jumper where it nestled and snuggled in, as if bedding down for the night.

Lewis gave an involuntary snort, a half snore and half inhalation which stirred him and surprised himself awake. His lips smattered several times and he looked around the room, seeming to be surprised to find himself in his living room with Shona for company. He tried to wing it and pointed to the television, 'Aren't you glad that our Carl doesn't have to go to war-torn countries like that?'

Shona laughed, 'That news clip was about the floods in Yorkshire. You've slept through the last ten minutes of the bedtime news. You've been doing a great impression of a nodding dog, too frightened to miss out on a treat, but desperate for an afternoon nap!'

'Missed out on a treat, me, never!' he declared and looked down to their empty mugs and plates. He then nodded to the larger plate which had the last of her Victoria sponge, a small, neglected slice with several broken crumbs scattered around it.

'It would be a shame to put that into a clean Tupperware pot. Why don't you finish it off? I'll be making Tilly's favourite coffee and walnut cake tomorrow and then I'm going to attempt my first courgette and potato cake. Vegetable cakes seem to be the new thing now, and my magazine has an interesting recipe.'

He smiled and reached across and helped himself to his favourite treat, though he hoped that Carl and his family would finish off the vegetable cakes, he didn't like the sound of them. Between mouthfuls and appreciative noises, he said, 'But it is nice to have him home and safe, no more dangerous situations for our lad.'

'Yes,' she sighed. 'He has been a worry over the years, but he did seem to like those jobs in the army. The new village he's in seems lovely and quiet, just what he needs now.'

'Amen to that mother. You get yourself to bed. I'll rinse through these things and lock up and join you in a minute.' He munched down on the last of the cake, full-bellied and content with life.

Amber sighed, picked up her mobile phone from the armrest of the sofa, turned it over in her palm absently, as if deciding, and began tapping at the screen.

'You okay love?' enquired her mother, sat at the other end of the sofa, feet up on the recliner part, her slippers cast casually below on the carpet. 'Are you wishing Jason goodnight? You've only just said goodbye to him. You'll see him again tomorrow afternoon, after your shift at the shop.'

Amber chewed the inside of her lip, 'I'm phoning in sick. I'm just texting now.'

'But you look okay, what's wrong with you?'

'Nothing, I just can't face him again, he's so horrible.'

'You mean that nasty old man up the road?'

Amber nodded, face cast down, like a young child caught in the sweet jar. 'Why does he have to be so horrible? Why does he even have to come in the minute we open? Some days he doesn't even wait for me to turn the open sign and unlock the doors. He hammers away, until I open early, before I've even had a chance to make my checks and restock. I must open straight away because he'll keep banging away and I can't concentrate otherwise. He knocks loudly; he really thumps the door. Bang after bang. Even then, he won't give me a second or two to get out of the way. I'm forced to jump back as he forces the door open and just barges in. Last week I jarred my back on the aisle with the new offers. The edge of the shelving really hurt.'

Her mum reached over and gently pulled her daughter in for a hug and embraced her and stroked her hair. 'He's known throughout the village as a nasty piece of work. I wish that I could say that you should stay away from him, but you need that job and you can't let Harris down, not at the last minute. He'll not get anyone else to cover your shift at this late hour. He's got his orders and collections to make and deliveries to oversee. He needs you. That old man is just a bully. He's well-known for it. He gets up so early so that he can have an excuse to slam his front door and wake his old neighbours. That's one of the reasons why poor Finty left the village. They were bullied out of leaving. Bless them. They'd be woken up at five o'clock every morning with an almighty bang, and then another when he returned from the shop with his morning rolls. He'd just blame the wind, even on the calmest of days. You just have to smile at him, serve him and let him get out of the shop quickly, just don't get on the wrong side of him.'

Amber nodded reluctantly, then wiggled out of the embrace and deleted her text, the message unsent.

Millie bit into her pillow, stifling her cries as she recoiled at yet another night at the hands of Simon. He had pulled out from her, wiped himself off, threw the tissue in her direction, taken out his hearing aids, and then turned over and fell asleep. As always, she had been left bruised and sore, physically, and emotionally, externally, and internally. There had been no love, no intimacy, just animalistic release, as if he were ridding himself of all his pent-up rage and frustration into her. She was just his plaything, his purge, for over forty years it had been this way. If only she had known what he was like before they were married, but she had been virginal on the day they were wed, and he didn't reveal his true colours until the wedding night. By then it was too late. Theirs was the generation who held their vows as sacred and she couldn't go running back to her parents, not to such a violent father. She had unconsciously made the same mistake as her mother and had married someone just like her father, which is probably why he and Simon had got on so well.

She tried to get into a comfortable position and forget about her woes, but the pain from her arthritis dug deeply into her, reaching within her bones, almost to the marrow, and kept her awake, despite the medicines from her doctor. Though she knew that it was the emotional turmoil that kept her awake. She only hoped that the children next door did not hear her cries as they resonated out from her pillow and around the room, whilst her deaf and oblivious husband snored on.

'Well, I think it's time we bade you good folk goodnight and went home to bed,' announced Brodie as he rose, stretched, and clucked for Daisy to join him.

'It's been so nice to have you round, we'll have to do this again sometime,' said Tilly as she began to gather Dotty's empty pots. 'Shall I keep these and put them through my dishwasher?'

'No, don't you worry about these. I'll steep them overnight in some hot water and Fairy Liquid. Besides, your man has emptied them clean!'

Carl looked abashed, 'Don't tell my mum, but that's the best stovies and skirlie that I've ever had, you can come for tea more often.'

'High praise indeed.' Dotty gave him a quick cuddle, needing to reach up to get a tight embrace. As the hug was returned, she felt cocooned within the safety of his muscular arms and liked the snug feeling, like a boat returned to the safety of a harbour after a choppy sea voyage. She nodded to her canvas bag, 'They should all fit in there and be so much lighter to carry home.'

'We'll have to do this soon, and invite Millie and Simon round too,' announced Carl.

A dark gloomy cloud seemed to descend on the visiting trio and their joyful farewells were cut short. Even Daisy's tail seemed to droop and wither at the mention of the other neighbours. The visitors had thought they'd done ever so well to not mention the others and had carefully manipulated conversation away from Simon and Millie and the middle-aged couple who lived around the corner from them.

Chapter Eight

Carl took a step back, put his finger to his lips and made a shushing noise. 'Okay troops, let's be having you, line up for parade.'

Annabelle, in her pretty blue-checked dress, blue cardigan, white socks and black shoes made silent marching movements around the kitchen whilst her elder brother rolled his eyes and slouched over to the kitchen wall. He stood stationary next to his sister.

'Okay, and smile, say cheese,' encouraged Carl as he pointed his mobile phone at them and snapped a photo. He looked at the screen and nodded his approval, 'Okay, mum is still sleepy, so at teatime we'll show her this photo and she can see how beautiful and handsome you look in your new uniforms.'

Gordon put his hand through his hair and adjusted his tie so that it was not so tight. He was putting his own brand upon his uniform. He rolled up his jumper's sleeve, dragging the awkward white shirt cuffs upwards as far as they would stretch. He gave up, pulled the white sleeves down and undid the button. He repeated his earlier movement and was satisfied to see that all his sleeves journeyed upwards this time.

Carl laughed, he waved his phone in the air and pointed to it with his free hand, 'Well, I think that we can convince your mother that you looked immaculate, even if it was for just one minute. Okay troops, pop your jackets and gloves on, and then let's move out in silent order.'

Annabelle started marching again, towards the lobby and the coat rack, whilst Gordon stayed still and pulled a face, 'Dad,' he drawled, 'I'm too old to be walked to school. All the other kids will tease me.'

'Don't you worry son, once we get out of here, you can break ranks and scout on ahead. I just want to see your school again and go for a stroll around the village. Besides, I promised your mum that I'd see you safely there, otherwise she wouldn't have taken her bedtime pills.'

'And they make her better, don't they dad,' acknowledged Annabelle as she walked back towards them, wiggling into her jacket.

'That's right Princess, they really do. Mum's so much better, and if we nag hard enough, I think she'll let us get a pet.'

The children's eyes lit up and they said in unison, 'A dog!'

'Shhh, not too loud remember. But not for several months mind. Let me save up some money first. We'll keep this our top-secret mission. We'll surround your mum in love and happiness first and then when her defences are down, we'll pounce and make our movement swiftly and surely, like ninjas. Then she can't say no. Okay, let's mount up and move out troops.'

This time Gordon joined Annabelle in marching silently to the front door and grabbed his jacket on the way. Gordon, taking point position, reached the front door and quietly opened it and walked out into the crisp morning air. He spied his new best friend, Dotty, across the road, at her window, polishing the glass. He cheerfully waved across as he walked up the garden path and joined the back of a group of youngsters walking to school. He soon joined in their chattering about their favourite football players.

Annabelle waited patiently at the front door whilst her father locked the door and pocketed his key, the task made more difficult with his clumsy gloves. She turned to face the adjoining neighbour and smiled at the old lady who was sweeping her path. She continued to smile at her, and the pair walked out of their path and turned towards the adjoining house. Annabelle finally caught the eye of their other neighbour and her smile broadened. 'It's my first day of school,' she declared proudly, as if needing a replacement mother figure to acknowledge her beauty.

Millie stopped sweeping her already immaculate path and leaned on the broomstick for support, 'And don't you look pretty.' She quickly looked behind her, towards her lounge window, and then reached into her jacket pocket. She pulled out a chocolate bar and looked to Carl. 'I hoped to have given her this yesterday, a sort of moving in present, do you mind?'

Carl, puzzled by her nervousness, smiled as warmly as he could, he wanted to put this poor woman at ease. 'That's so lovely and thoughtful, yes, they soon burn off the sugar. My two are always on the go.'

Millie beamed at Annabelle and a small twinkle entered her eye, as if a rainbow had burst from the skies, down upon her. She passed the chocolate bar to Annabelle and as the delighted child took it from her with a gentleness that matched her sweet character, Millie reached back into her pocket. 'Could you please give this other one to your brother, Gordon, isn't it?'

Annabelle nodded eagerly. 'We can eat them at playtime. Thank you.'

Millie smiled as she handed over another goodie bar. 'I expect my friend Dotty filled your tummy yesterday.'

Annabelle nodded vigorously this time, 'She's a great cook, we had lots of cake and then later she made dad his favourite meal.'

Millie laughed, 'That sounds like Dotty, she does love to feed people up.'

Annabelle popped her treats in her pocket, making a mental note to seek out her brother later that morning.

'You'll have to come over one night, Tilly or I can cook you and Simon something,'

Millie's shoulders stiffened at the sound of her husband's name and she clenched her brush a bit tighter. Her cold fingers turned even whiter as they clasped the wood. She wasn't allowed money to buy some gloves and they stung that little bit more as the frost nipped at her skin like a biting dog, eagerly nibbling at a favourite treat from its master's hand. She looked behind her and back at the innocent child. 'Er, yes, that sounds lovely, I'll have to check to see what Simon is doing first though,' she said apprehensively.

'Or perhaps we can bring a bottle and some snacks round? It'll save you the walk in the cold air, I can see you are having trouble with your hip, or is it your knees?'

Millie's eyelids raised and widened at the thought and her pupils dilated, as if caught in an enemy's searchlight. She became flustered once more, 'Oh no, I don't think he'd like that,' she let slip. Then she corrected herself, 'Yes, it's my knees, old age, I'm afraid.' She rubbed her stomach and then flinched. She had a big bruise from the hurled whisky bottle and it still smarted, a lot.

Carl could see that she was becoming more agitated and he thought he could tell why, though he kept these thoughts to himself, for now. 'Well, perhaps you could have a chat with Tilly when you see her, perhaps you'll make some arrangements then.' He left this thought hanging in the air between them.

Millie leaned on her broom for support and tried to smile, despite her pain. 'Yes, that sounds like a good idea. You'll need to get off to your work I expect, after you've helped this little one along to her new school.' She reached up and rubbed Annabelle's hair, traced it down to her shoulders, and then patted her twice, relishing the warmth from the youngster's body. She missed having children in her life.

'No, I work from home now.'

'Oh! So, you'll be about a lot then?'

'Yes, I'll work in the back room, on a computer, you'll hardly know I'm there.'

'Ah,' she sounded off, in relief, letting go of the breath that she had involuntarily held. 'That's just as well then. He likes it peaceful here,' she muttered, just loud enough for Carl to have heard, almost as a forewarning.

It was lost to Carl as a group of chattering girls walked briskly past, talking excitingly about something they'd watched on YouTube. Annabelle grasped his hand and pulled him away from Millie. 'We'd best be off then, otherwise she'll be late for her first day. Thank you for the chocolates, that was most thoughtful.'

His voice tailed off as they walked away from Millie. She looked after them, already missing their company. She leaned the broom against her gate, blew on her hands and then rubbed them against her jacket, trying desperately to bring life and warmth to them. She reluctantly reached back for her brush and despite her pain, recommenced brushing her already spotless path. None of the passing schoolchildren had discarded their empty wrappers onto the driveway or their front garden, such as it was, with all its concrete-like appearance, they knew better. She looked up and gulped as she saw her husband watching from their bedroom window. Her gut tightened in anticipation of what was to come and in worry at how much he had seen.

Dotty looked up at the clear skies, the sun beamed down a false ray of sunshine that did little to warm this winter morning. She felt snug in her new season's jacket, a thoughtful gift from her son, though she knew that his girlfriend had bought it and had ensured that it was the correct size. She then shivered as she saw Simon staring down at her pal and knew that a storm was brewing. This tempest had nothing to do with the weather and she knew that soon, very soon, the inevitable squall would burst, and that once more their idyllic village would have to batten down the hatches.

'Okay sweetie, off you go and have a great day, your school looks like a fun place to learn. Don't forget to find Gordon and give him his treat.'

Annabelle hugged her father, wrapping her arms around his thighs and burying her face into his stomach. 'I love you daddy!' She quickly broke off, skipped away, and was soon lost in the crowd of children, slipping easily into conversation with a girl of her own age who looked a bit lost in the sea of faces.

'I love you too Princess!' laughed Carl good-naturedly as he marvelled at how easily his girl left him behind. He hoped he'd always be the apple of her eye, for he knew that she'd always be his beloved, the best of Tilly and himself. Both his children were.

'First day?' enquired a young woman by his side who was waving off her child.

'Can you tell? I guess that I'm more nervous than she is.'

She laughed, remembering her child's first day here. 'She'll be fine, it's a lovely school.'

'Yes, I've heard that. It's a peaceful village, it has a nice stillness about it, that's what attracted us to live here. We only moved in yesterday.'

'Gosh, you'll be busy then. I was about to ask you if you'd like to join the parents committee, but I think you've enough on your plate.' She reached out her hand, 'I'm Sue.' She appraised him carefully and, liking what she saw, she proffered, 'And I will ask you later though.'

Carl returned the handshake, grateful that she wasn't one of those women that insisted on hugging everyone she met, he really didn't like being forced to cuddle folk other than his family. 'Carl. You live nearby then?'

'Yes, just a few doors away from the library. She's great as well, the librarian I mean. The children love going there and messing about on the computers. They've even got a Lego club which I was surprised that my Leonora loves. She's never shown any interest in it before. Still, it keeps them out of mischief for a while. Off their tablets, phones and laptops and playing properly, like children should. So, where have you moved into? I can't remember seeing any for sale or sold signs.'

'Just two streets away, the house with the zebra door,' replied Carl helpfully. He was already warming to the unusual glass panel that he'd inherited with his new house and had decided to use it as a landmark.

Sue's jaw dropped and she looked startled, a look that Carl was suddenly seeing a lot of today. Though he'd seen this look many times in his past, normally just before he got the drop on an enemy. He had hoped that he'd put all that behind him. He tried smiling, but with his puzzlement, it came out as a frown. Sue realised that she hadn't said anything, looked up at the clock on the school wall and stuttered, 'Well, I'd best be off then. Pleasure to meet you Carl, good luck in your new house.' She turned and made her way home and muttered to herself, 'Because you are going to need it mate.'

Carl shrugged off her unusual behaviour and looked through the playground and was rewarded with a last glimpse of his children as they made their way patiently through the double doors. He was rewarded with a cheery wave from them both and waved happily back. He turned briskly, almost like he was back on the parade square and doing an about turn, and set off at a rapid stride to enjoy the crisp morning.

Within two streets he was able to see the lighthouse, its whitewashed walls dazzled in the sunshine as he marched towards it and the sea seemed to shimmer as it gently lapped against the rocks below the grassed area. He bade a dogwalker a cheerful good morning and envied him his jet-black Labrador whose muscles rippled as he trotted faithfully by his master's side. 'Yup,' he whispered to himself, 'a family pet would be great, maybe some time soon.' He felt his grip on the grass soften as he slid momentarily upon what he had thought to be dry turf. Then he smelt that pungent vile aroma that was released underfoot as his reward for not looking where he was going and being distracted by pleasant aspirations of the future. He looked down and saw the deposit that the Labrador had left in its wake and that its owner had failed to scoop up. He tutted, took a step aside, by the neglected dog poop bin, and rubbed his foot on the grass, determined that nothing would put a dampener on his morning exercise before he hit his home gym. He stepped back onto the path, hoping that a brisk walk would soon see the muck drop from his shoes before he got home. He set off at a determined pace and was soon dreaming about the future and his plans for an advertising revenue stream from his newly created website. Nothing was going to upset the first week in his family's new life.

Chapter Nine

After being away for an hour, Carl was pleased to see, from a distance, Tilly in their front garden as he walked up their street. She was busy pruning the rambling roses at the corner of the walled border. It would be a shame to have this flower bed and the grass dug up when they created a driveway, he thought absently. He'd see how the street parking went first. There didn't seem to be a problem with graffiti in the neighbourhood, so he doubted that there would be much in the way of vandalism or perhaps even crime. It was shaping up to be a lovely village. His stomach rumbled, reminding him that he needed his smashed avocado or poached eggs late morning breakfast with Tilly. He smiled at the thought of telling her how sweet the lady next door was in bringing out a playtime treat for their children.

As he watched Tilly determinedly tackle the thorny overgrown bush, he caught sight of a figure dart towards her, raising his arms in angry protest. He could hear a roaring shouting din and quickened his pace. He broke into a run and sprinted back to Tilly.

'You are dropping those mouldy old petals onto my property. Now I'll have to pick them up,' shouted Simon, standing there with his fists in the air, waving his disapproval. He'd not even taken the time to don a jacket, such was his haste to get out to Tilly. The winter sunshine beamed down onto his bald head and made it shine bright, his face was red with anger and the colour rose and flushed around his barren pate.

Tilly took several steps back, her pair of secateurs hung limply at her side, as if she were trying to hide their part in this innocent act of gardening.

Carl ran through their gate, bounded up the grass, and reached for her free hand. He gripped it tight to offer up his reassurance. 'You okay love?'

She took another step back, away from Simon, 'I was only trimming the bush, it'll encourage new growth in the spring. That's all. I didn't do anything wrong.'

'She's made a mess of my garden, that's what she's done. Your rubbish has fallen into my property,' insisted Simon, ignoring Carl.

'I didn't mean to,' cowered Tilly, 'they just dropped over, I tried to catch everything and put it into the bucket for the compost bin.' She pointed to her gardening bin that was laid on the soil, by the rambling rose bush.

'We can soon tidy up Simon,' offered Carl placatingly. 'How about I pop over and pick up the bits and pieces.'

'Stay out of my property,' bellowed Simon. 'This is my property,' he repeated whilst waving his arms around his domain in a sweeping gesture.

Tilly sidestepped into Carl's reassuring frame. She handed him the secateurs, as if passing the blame to her husband.

He accepted them, as if taking ownership of the situation, checked that the closed lock was on them, and slipped them into his pocket. 'You go inside love, and I'll tidy up, go on into the house and warm up. I'll be in soon to make our breakfast.'

She left him, relieved to be away.

Carl walked purposefully over to Simon, He subconsciously rose to his full height and puffed out his chest, ready to meet the situation head on. He remembered his own temper, often quick to burst in hostile situations and remembered his special forces mantra, 'Breathe, breathe, recalibrate and deliver.' He needed and wanted to de-escalate the situation whilst keeping a lid on his own simmering rage. He didn't want his pot to boil over. He just wanted a quiet life.

His breathing steadied and his pulse rate lowered and with it his temper slackened and vanished. He put a smile on his face as he reassessed the situation, a simple domestic difference that so easily could have escalated out of control. He walked over calmly to the flower bed, carefully placed one foot onto the soil, found a firm footing and leaned over the adjoining granite-brick wall. He stared down in disbelief. There were two small faded yellow petals sat pathetically on a carefully raked and levelled gravel type area of what once could have been a front garden with a proud lawn. 'Is that it?' he asked incredulously.

'Yes,' shouted Simon, taking a step back from the wall at the approach from his tall new neighbour who shadowed over him. He seemed to shrivel in height as he drew back another step. 'It's making a mess of my property,' he bleated pathetically.

Carl looked to the neatly pruned rose bush and then to the large compost caddy with its side handles for easy carriage to the main compost bin at the rear of the garden that Tilly had installed straight from the removals van yesterday. It was half full of neatly chopped up dead wood from the rose bush along with withering petals. Their lengths were exactly equal and measured out, a visible sign that her OCD was not lying dormant as he had hoped. She still needed order and measurement to keep her demons at bay, despite lengthy counselling. She'd made a neat job of pruning the dying areas and cut close to the soil to encourage new growth in the spring. It really would be a shame to lose this lovely border garden that would bring colourful cheer in the next season and through into the summer and beyond, he thought. He looked to Simon and said, 'Are you really making all this fuss, and upsetting my wife, Tilly, over two small petals that could be easily picked up in a second?' To prove his point he leaned over, reached out, and scooped up the petals. His gloved hands reinforced their size, making them appear larger and the petals looked like fragile origami works of art that might crumble at the most delicate of touches. He then leaned back to his own garden and slowly, but deliberately, dropped them into the compost container. They fluttered down like small wisps of gossamer-thin fabric into a laundry basket. They crumpled as they hit the thorns of the dead wooden stems and wrapped themselves around their length like a shroud onto a corpse. All the while Carl looked neutrally at Simon, albeit with the merest hint of a mocking smile, daring him to make more fuss.

 Carl deliberately stayed silent for a second or two whilst Simon took another step back. His eyes narrowed and a terrifying snarl momentarily exuded from his face, like a dogged terrier guarding a cherished bone from another canine competitor, washing terror across the wall that forced Simon another step back towards his front door. 'I don't like it when Tilly cries, or when she gets upset. It makes me cross.' He smiled broadly. 'And I'm sure that you won't upset her ever again, will you?'

Simon turned away without a word and scurried back into his house, closing the door ever so gently behind him. He didn't see Millie watching silently from their bedroom window with a wry smile passing swiftly through her lips as she nodded her head in satisfaction.

Carl picked up the bucket and wandered through to his back garden, admiring the large quarried granite blocks that made up the main part of the walls of his new house, before giving way to the more man-made brick walls of the rear extension, his mancave where he hoped to find inspiration at self-employment. He effortlessly carried it past the patio area, with the soot-like darkened patches on some of the paving blocks and walked down a ramped path and into their back lawn. As he made his way to the large compost bin at the foot of the grassed area, he thought absently that a bird-table and perhaps even a bird-bath would look nice along the edges, by the wall. Then he could take absent breaks from being hunched over the keyboard and watch his wild feathered friends bathe and feed. He hoped to have his garden resounding with the chitter chatter of starlings and the rapid darting in and out of sparrows, blue tits and even a territorial robin if he was lucky. He did miss their uplifting possessive calls as they chanted out, in warning, their boundaries to other robins. In his last garden, down in England, not in the hovel that they had rented nearby recently, he was even rewarded with daily sightings of wrens and blackbirds scampering amongst their undergrowth, seeking out the dried mealworms that he would scatter each day. He smiled at these memories, and of those to come, and they warmed him up. He then emptied out the bucket and replaced the lid of the main compost bin, to keep its contents warm enough to break down and to help keep out any passing vermin. Soon its contents would rot and crumble and form deeply rich compost. He looked forward to the exercise that spreading it around his border beds would bring.

He walked over to the shed that the previous owners had thoughtfully left, a double length one that had been part shelved and he tidied away the small bucket and the secateurs. As he made his way out and locked up the shed, he looked through to the empty back section and was already mentally arranging places for his sit-up bench and dumbbells. The removals men had left them in his new study, the rear extension that served as a conservatory. Carl knew that the space they occupied would be better served with a recliner chair for him to absently have a think in, or for Tilly to have an afternoon nap. Doing some of his exercise routines out in the open would help keep the sweats off him. He seemed to swelter a lot these days, even on a cold day like today. He sprayed far more anti-perspirant around his body than he really needed, he just didn't want to reek like that guy that everyone avoided in basic training, in his infantryman days. Man, but he stunk. Like a festering rat decaying under floorboards. He then recalled his encounter moments earlier and remembered smelling the same heavily-rank smell. He wondered why he was subliminally thinking back to when he was seventeen and a young soldier. Now he knew, it was the same unwashed and neglected smell. The corporals had to teach this man how to wash, going into intimate details. It had turned into a company teaching session, taking each of them back to basic hygiene care, taking care of the body of what would later become a fighting machine. He wondered why this old man didn't have someone to point out his basic hygiene errors. Surely his wife, or his children, should have tactfully said something. He made his way back into his house, into the warmth of the building and his wife.

Millie made her way to the bathroom, feigning being on the toilet. She wanted to be away from Simon, even if it was just for a few minutes whitst his temper receded and before she became the focus for his rage. She'd never seen someone stand up to him so subtly and effortlessly before, and get away with it, for now. She couldn't quite hear what was said from her vantage point at the window. But she did have the satisfaction of seeing him scurry away like an old wounded lion whose pride had been hurt at the recent conquest from a young cub challenging his authority in the pack. She knew that later, much later, he would exact his revenge. Just like he had always done. She still recalled the shame at having the police at their door, enquiring just that little bit longer than at their other neighbours, about the scratch marks along the side of a car parked across from his driveway gates. They knew alright, but just did not have the proof. Simon had refused them entry to the house and access to his CCTV recordings from the camera that stretched out its all-seeing eye to across the road. She'd seen him watching the footage, day after day, for weeks after the event, with a wicked glee upon his face, relishing in his nefarious deed. She sat on the closed toilet lid, grateful for the softness of the fabric cover. She listened intently for his footsteps and wondered if she was shivering because of the cold, or through fear.

'You okay love,' shouted Carl as he loosened off his gloves and shrugged out of his jacket. He placed them on the coat rack, just inside the lobby and underneath the stairs. He looked at the empty alcove along the floor, wondering what they would fill this empty space with, perhaps some sort of storage system, he thought. Or perhaps a dog basket. He smiled at this new idea and could just imagine a large dog curled contentedly amongst some fluffy blankets, a toy or two safely stored within a paw's reach. He heard his wife blow her nose. He knew that she had been drying off the last of her tears and gave her a few seconds to compose herself. He knew she might not want him making a fuss, not just yet. He put a wider smile on his face and walked through and gave her a hug anyway. 'He's daft, isn't he, making all that fuss about nothing. I soon put him right and squared everything away. You did a tidy job love, that'll be a lovely blooming rose bush in a few months time, and the soil looked lovely and rich. That border bed has been well taken care of over the years, though I think it's barely been looked at in the last gardening season. Your green fingers will soon see it as pretty as you and Annabelle.'

She squeezed him tightly. 'He scared me, running up to me like that and then waving his hands close to me. He reminded me of my dad when he found out that I'd gone to the police, you know.'

'Yes, I know only too well. I remember how I couldn't console you that night, and that's when you told me everything. I just didn't know what to say or what to do. I always thought that you'd had an idyllic childhood and a perfect family. How wrong was I and I always thought that I was a good judge of character? Your parents and brother pulled the wool over my eyes.'

'They were particularly good at manipulating people and presenting themselves well in other people's eyes. My dad really valued his position in society as a retired doctor, even though it was in a village surgery much smaller than this village. That's why he blew his top at me reporting Finn to the police. But I had to, I mean what if he'd done it to other girls. I shouldn't have waited all those years. Mum used to childmind for many young girls of my age and younger and Finn was always hanging around. This was before he was made to join the army, to get him away from me and other children.' She shuddered at the memory and sighed deeply, glad that she'd finally found a counsellor that she could trust and open her feelings to. She had expertly healed her mind and helped put these wicked memories finally behind her. She could now embrace motherhood and even be the type of wife that Carl yearned for.

Carl, never knowing what to say when Tilly gave him glimpses of her abusive childhood, hugged her a bit tighter and murmured,

'You're safe now. I won't let anything bad happen to you or the children, not ever.'

She snuggled into him and enjoyed being encompassed by his tight muscles, it was like being cocooned within the safety of a warm womb. The couple kept the embrace for a few more seconds then broke off. Tilly reached up and stroked Carl's face lovingly, 'The kids get off to school okay?'

'Yes, I think they'd prefer it if they walked to and fro themselves. Gordon will look after Annabelle and I know that he thinks he's too old to be escorted by his mum and dad. He's at that age where he's worried what the other children will think of him. They are safe here, there's no worry about your parents being around.'

'I know,' she removed her hands from his face and then took hold of his hands.

'I'd better get to work then. I'll type out another recipe today and then we'll pop out and buy some ingredients and I'll cook it for tea tonight and take a photo for the website. When you have your rest in a few hours, I'll take my weights down to the shed and have a workout. There is plenty of room down there and that'll clear a bit more space in the house. I'll unpack a few more boxes tonight. The kids can help me move things around and get our stuff into their correct places. This'll look homely soon enough.' He nodded to the cooker, 'I'm going to have a snack, shall I cook you something?'

Tilly's eyes twinkled as she let go of his hands and lightly traced her way up his arms and reached up on tiptoes to his neck with the delicate tips of her fingers. 'I've a better idea!' she said seductively in a low voice, 'They won't be home for several hours and we have the house to ourselves, so let's go upstairs.' She winked at her husband.

Carl grinned, enveloped his wife with both his hands, lifted her off her feet and cradled her. Their lips met in an infusion of happiness and love as they kissed delicately at first and then with much vigour and enthusiasm, each hungry for the other. He carried her up the stairs, all thoughts of the encounter with the neighbour now long forgotten as their bodies became one and clothing was shed in their haste to reach the marital bed.

Chapter Ten

The sound of the bugle broke the silence of the congregation and echoed around the church as each man, woman and child stood silently, lost in their own thoughts and prayers. Carl wiped away a tear as the last post was played out and remembered those who didn't beat the clock. On the parade ground of the Special Air Service, the fallen troopers were remembered, their names etched on the edifice of a memorial, though their bodies had fallen in lands many miles away.

Tilly reached for his hand and gave it a little squeeze. She knew that he would be thinking of his fallen friends, and especially of Gavin. He'd gladly give back all the medals that adorned his left chest to have his mates back by his side. He rarely talked about them with her, but she knew that he still felt guilt over those he had lost. Though none of his missions had technically failed, all thanks to meticulous planning, they could not always second guess their enemy. It only took one lucky blade or bullet to instantly destroy a life.

Carl stood stoically to attention and allowed his wife to keep hold of his hand. He drew comfort from its warmth and petite softness. Remembrance Day was always difficult for him and he appreciated her loving gesture. From the corner of his eye he glanced down and was proud to see Gordon and Annabelle also stood to attention. That's why we do it, he thought, for the children and their freedom and safety.

As the bugler ceased his sounds, the congregation, as one, looked across to the Minister. Carl smiled, glad to be back in the less formal service of the Church of Scotland. He had warmed to this clergyman the moment he had spied the operational service medal for Afghanistan beneath the flowing black and white robes. He knew that this padre would have served his country too and would empathise with Carl's emotional pain. He too would have known the fallen, he may even have been with those injured and about to pass over. Even the best efforts of the doctors and nurses, often helicoptered into fierce combat zones, could not always save the wounded. A padre was always sought wherever possible, no matter what the beliefs of the soldier.

The Minister continued his service by asking those gathered to join him in one final hymn as they paid tribute to those who had given the ultimate sacrifice in the name of their country. It was only then that Carl glimpsed what had really kept their children so attentive during the service. The man seated two rows ahead had a large golden retriever sat faithfully by his feet. Whenever he sat down the dog would gently rest its muzzle onto his left thigh and wait patiently for its owner to gently stroke its ears in a well-practiced rhythmic pattern. Carl could not make out the writing printed on its special mauve-coloured bib and had wondered if it was a guide dog. But the owner was able to read the order of service and opened and followed each hymn from the large books that were spread out on each pew. Carl sang along as he continued to watch how attentive the dog was to its owner and how captivated his children were by the furry animal that sat by the standing owner who was belting out the words to the hymn. He looked to his wife whose sweet voice seemed to lift the spirits of the dead and rejoice in their salvation. It gladdened his heart to hear her sing so upliftingly and soon his thoughts went far from his dead friend, and that last fatal mission in Afghanistan. Though it was a cold November day, with overnight frost still splayed, like a spider's web, on the stained-glass windows, he felt himself sweat despite the chill that always seemed to be present in churches with antiquated boilers. He took his hand from his wife's grip, in pretence that he needed to hold the hymn book all the better, and discretely wiped his damp palm against his trouser leg.

Tilly noted this and saw the beads of sweat that burst out on Carl's forehead and remembered what the wives had said at the support group set up for them at Credenhill. She had made a mental note of the signs to watch for. She looked quickly away from her husband and tried to concentrate on the words to sing, but her notes faltered. She only hoped that being home and near his parents and sister would be enough to keep his demons at bay. She remained standing with her family as the last note was played on the church organ and the organists fingers came to a grateful rest.

The Minister smiled at the congregation, sweeping his eyes warmly throughout his flock and said, 'Please join us for teas and coffee in the church hall after the service.' He looked across to the rows of scouts and guides, splendid in their uniforms, and continued with a conspiratorial wink, 'And biscuits and cakes for all the children who were so well-behaved today.'

Annabelle and Gordon looked to each other and smiled in eager anticipation.

Lewis watched with pride as the columns of veterans marched proudly past the Cenotaph. He rubbed his knees absently as he thought back to the years he had flown down to London and met up with the lads for a few beers the night before and how proud he was to take part and be near to his Queen. He looked over to Shona and passed her another tissue from the box he had placed by their lounge table. 'Her Majesty was magnificent, wasn't she? She still comes every year, despite her age. She knows how our country suffered during the last World War. I just hope that America and Iran don't make it a third. I'm glad that our boy is well out of it.'

Shona blew her nose and whispered, 'And is in one piece and unaffected by all he had to see and do.'

Lewis nodded vigorously, 'He did us proud.'

'As did you love, I know that Ireland wasn't easy for you and your friends and that you didn't write home to me about some of the things that went on.'

Lewis looked down at his feet, 'Aye, well, yes, let's not go there love, not today.' He stood up and walked to the kitchen, hoping that she didn't see the tears that fell onto his tartan slippers. 'I'll just check on the roast lamb, it's going to be nice to have our Felicity and Carl with their families all round the table this afternoon.'

Shona left him be, she knew what would be on his mind today.

Carl pumped the hand of the man in front of him as he carefully balanced his coffee cup in the other hand. His medals chinked as they vibrated against each other on their mounts. 'Wonderful service Padre, nice to meet you. I'm Carl.'

'Thank you young man,' beamed the Minister as he returned the handshake, his own medal jutted out from his flowing robes. He nodded to Carl's chest, 'I see that you've been busy.'

Carl looked down, 'Yes, I'm afraid my wife is always keen for me to wear them, otherwise, I don't like to make a fuss, you know?'

The Minister gently removed his hand from the firm handshake that was in sharp contrast to his usual elderly and fragile handshakes from his regular congregation. 'Yes, I'm afraid that I do, Afghanistan was not an easy posting, not for any of us.'

Carl nodded in agreement, 'We've just moved into the village, it's so peaceful.'

'Yes, that's what attracted me to it as well, I've only been here a few months myself, I'm still getting to know folk and finding my own feet. Are you a regular churchgoer?'

Tilly spluttered her coffee and quickly pulled out a tissue from her pocket and wiped her face.

'That'll be the wife, Tilly.'

The Minister waited for her to compose herself before offering his hand. He smiled indulgently as she took it and nodded to him.

'We go every year, on Remembrance, you know to, well, remember.'

The Minister nodded. He was used to seeing servicemen and women attend his congregations just once a year. He was glad to be with them again and always tried to say hello to them all before they made their way home. He was so pleased to see so many chatting away to his regulars over drinks and snacks.

'Well, our doors are always open, and we have a regular Sunday School for the children. You are all very welcome at any time. You might like our Christingle service next month, it's always popular with the schoolchildren, I think they like the dolly mixtures on the oranges the best.'

Tilly laughed, 'Yes, that sounds just like my two. Yes, we'll be there, won't we dear.'

Carl nodded absently, his thoughts were back to foreign lands once more and he hadn't followed the conversation very well. He wasn't entirely sure what he had just agreed to.

The Minister smiled, 'Great stuff, well I'd better mingle. It was lovely to meet you, perhaps once you've settled into the village, I may pop round to your house and get to know you better?'

'Oh, that would be lovely, how nice,' agreed Tilly.

Carl nodded too, he knew that Padres loved a good laugh and looked forward to it.

The Minister smiled and said, 'Great, I'll be in touch.' He took out a notepad and paper from beneath his robes and a lime green, red, white, and blue medal was now visible to Carl. It was the Ebola Medal, awarded to those who had seen service in West Africa during the 2014 outbreak. Carl knew that the Minister would have seen many deaths during those awful few years. His esteem for this clergyman rose even higher and he looked forward to getting to know him a bit better. 'What's your phone number?'

Tilly rattled off the recently learned numbers.

'Super,' said the Minister. 'I'll give you a ring soon, my name's Colin, none of this Minister lark, just down to earth Colin. See you soon.' With a flourish of his robes, like a departing superhero swishing his cape, he turned and looked out for the next serviceman or woman to chat to.

Tilly turned to Carl, 'Weren't our two so well-behaved during the service. I'm so pleased at their behaviour.'

Carl laughed, 'You didn't see it, did you?'

'Eh?' she replied quizzically.

'No, I didn't think you did. There was a dog, I'm guessing an assistance dog of some kind, sat two rows in front of them. It was sat patiently by its owner, but our two couldn't take their eyes off it.' He looked around the packed hall, 'Over there, its owner is in the corner sat on his own, petting it. I'm surprised our two haven't gone over and made a fuss of it.'

'I'm not, there are plenty of chocolate biscuits on the table.' Tilly had spied their children eagerly munching down on Chocolate Digestives.

'Ha, that's our kids alright. I'm going over to say hello, he looks a bit lonely there.' As he walked over, he noted that the man had much the same medals as himself. He was very thin, almost emaciated, and he was continually nodding his head in small, discrete movements, almost in time to an unspoken tempo. As Carl drew closer, he instinctively held out his right arm for a handshake, 'Hello,

I'm Carl, I noticed your veteran's badge, I was in the army. What about you?'

The man took a step back, almost in surprise. His dog went with him and stayed by his side, sitting down once more. In a fluster he stuttered, 'Oliver, Ollie.' He hesitated, then returned the handshake.

Carl noticed a distinct tremor in his hand and altered his usual firm grip and gave a quick handshake. He had judged correctly; Ollie's clasp was very delicate, and his hand felt hot and clammy from sweat. Poor chap, he thought, he's a bag of nerves. 'Beautiful dog.' He'd hoped his compliment would put him at ease.

Ollie smiled and Carl could see his shoulders visibly sag as some of the nervous tension released its grip. 'Thank you, she's been a saviour. She's from the Bravehound charity, she helps with my Post Traumatic Stress Disorder. I was in the infantry, it caught up with me,' he nodded to Carl's medals, 'you know?'

'Yes, I can well imagine. I saw your medals, it looks like we were in many campaigns together, perhaps our wars overlapped.' He could see Ollie stepping back again and quickly changed the subject, 'My two children were captivated by her during the service. It kept them well-behaved.'

'I get that a lot. She does draw a crowd. She's a working dog with full assistance status, but that doesn't stop people trying to pet her or clucking to get her attention. I even had one guy do it from across the road recently. Fortunately, she ignores most people and keeps her eyes on me.'

Carl laughed, 'I see that, she can't take her eyes off you. What's the secret?'

Ollie opened his other palm, the one with his dog's leash wrapped around his wrist. 'Meatballs!'

'Ah, that's a clever tip.'

'Yes, she goes mad for them, she knows that if she keeps obeying me, she'll get the treat eventually. It took me ages to find out what treat she sees as a high-end reward. She turns her nose up at chicken and even roast beef. So, I cook pork meatballs and spaghetti twice a week and save some for her. She likes the Italian flavoured ones the best, it must be one of the herbs she loves.'

'That's brilliant, so what's Bravehound? I've never heard of them.'

'They are based in the Glasgow area, but they offer assistance or companion dogs to military veterans with mental health problems throughout Scotland. She keeps me calm in crowded places, amongst other things.'

'I know what you mean, I hate crowds too. Are there many of you with dogs up here?'

'I only know of one lass. I don't live here anymore, I've a house at Erskine, I'm up visiting my friend. He's not a churchgoer and not from a military background, so doesn't understand the need to go to church on Remembrance Day. But I like to go, you know, to pay my respects to those who didn't come home. Well not alive anyway.' His head-nodding became more pronounced.

'Yes, I'm the same. The Padre served too, it's nice to have a service with someone who understands.'

'Yes,' he simply replied.

'So is your dog, sorry, what's her name?'

'Mandy.'

'How beautiful. Does Mandy get to go everywhere with you, like guide dogs?'

'Yes, I put this special bib on,' he pointed to the mauve coat Carl had spotted earlier, 'and it stops most people challenging me. Though I've also a special identity card to show those who don't understand about Bravehound. So far, I've never been told no, though if that were to happen, the folk in the charity office would contact them and explain about Bravehound. It's like having a buddy by my side when I'm out and about.'

'That is so brilliant, and such a great idea. I've pals who had PTSD. I wish they had a Mandy to look over them, then perhaps they'd still be, well, you know, they took their own lives. None of us could talk them round to seeing just how much they'd be missed. We tried to take turns watching over them, but my Regiment is trained in escape and evasion and sadly they took themselves off when we dropped our guard.'

'Ah, that is so sad. I've lost a few mates that way too. I've been close to the edge a few times myself. I just wish the charity had more finances to help others. They've lots of great fundraisers and people are so generous, not just with money, but with their time, puppy walking and socialising the dogs. We don't get them until they are toilet trained and can perform simple commands.'

'So, no messy puddles to clean up until they learn. That's great.'

'Yes, she's been brilliant for me. I then had a dog trainer help me learn to teach her things specific for me, like picking up dropped objects. I've a bad back you see, so stooping is painful.'

'She's so clever.'

Ollie smiled proudly. 'I'm guessing you were The Regiment then?'

'Yes, for a few years.'

'Tough job, what do you do now?'

Carl laughed. 'You'd never be able to guess! I can hardly believe that I stumbled into this line of work myself. I did try overseas security work for a while, offshore guarding ships against pirate attacks, and onshore with some of the high targets, you know, chief executives who could get kidnapped, but my temper got the better of me and I lost that gig. So now I'm creating a website with Scottish recipes. Can you believe it!'

Ollie nodded, 'A nice peaceful job. I get that. You are your own boss. And the temper?'

'Yes, I have to work really hard on that, otherwise poor Tilly, my wife,' he pointed over to the table with barren plates, save for a few crumbs, 'that's her over there with the children, they're probably responsible for polishing off the biscuits. Yes, otherwise she gets the brunt of it, and I know it's not fair on her. Do you work? Does Mandy get to go along?'

'No, I too lost my jobs. I'm quick to rise and my temper got the better of me on a few occasions. I'm now permanently off sick. But Mandy fills my day up. We go around our local park and she goes off leash exploring. Her favourite is chasing the squirrels. I don't think she'd know what to do if she caught one!'

'That sounds fun! Here come my two.'

Annabelle and Gordon came up and stood by their father shyly, Annabelle clung to his leg whilst Gordon stood by his sister. Both were spellbound to Mandy. Carl laughed, 'I've never seen them so quiet. Perhaps Mandy should come home with us.'

'Yes please!' they replied in unison.

'I'm afraid I'd miss her too much, but you can say hello to her.'

'But be gentle,' warned their father as they almost tripped over each other to be the first to pet the dog. They knelt and began stroking her. Mandy, with tail swishing on the floor like an energetic broom, relished the attention. 'It doesn't bother her, you know, put her off focus from you?'

'No, I'm used to it now, and so is she. I used to get het up about it in the beginning, when I was trying to train her to my needs. The old grannies are the worst. They come up from behind and start making a fuss of her without saying anything to me. So long as I know what's about to happen and have control, I'm fine. Mandy soon gets her focus back on me and my meatball.'

'Meatballs? Are you talking about recipes again?' asked Tilly as she ambled up and joined in the conversation.

'Not this time, it's Bravehound Mandy's favourite treat.'

'Oh, how gorgeous, I've heard about Bravehound, a lady came down from Glasgow with a puppy under training and gave a talk to our wives and partners group. We fundraised for them the month after. You gave thirty quid darling, though I didn't tell you!'

'Glad to be of help!' quipped Carl who was used to his wife giving away his hard-earned money on his behalf.

'She gave us a talk about PTSD and the signs to look out for in our other halves,' She looked knowingly at Carl who had stripped down to his shirt, even though the others in the hall were still in their winter coats and some were still wearing gloves and hats.

'That's good. Spouses can often not understand the way their partners are behaving and why. My girlfriend left me after my drinking got out of hand. I'm off the booze now though, I'm highly medicated instead.'

'I'm Tilly by the way.'

'Ollie, it's lovely to meet you.' He didn't offer his hand and Tilly hadn't expected him to shake hers and instead pointed to his dog.

'You are lucky, she is so adorable. I bet she gives great cuddles.'

Ollie looked down to her with pride. 'Yes, one of the puppy trainers taught her to do so on that command. When I say the C word, she'll hug me real tight. Her paws wrap around my neck and she'll snuggle into my neck.'

'That's so sweet,' stated Carl, somewhat enviously.

'It's for flashbacks isn't it? Sorry, I don't mean to be so intrusive,' flustered Tilly.

'Not at all. I love talking about Mandy, especially to other veterans and their families. I think all veterans should have a Bravehound, many of us have hidden mental health problems.' He looked at Carl and then his wife.

Tilly nodded vigorously, 'Yes, they should,' she stated whilst looking to Carl knowingly.

'Yes, the warm presence of Mandy against me soon soothes away my flashbacks and calms me. It's as if she chases them away. Her coat is so gloriously silky and soft.'

'I can see that, my two can't stop stroking her.' She turned to her children, 'Right, that's enough you two, Say goodbye to Mandy.'

They finished by patting Mandy on the head, each repeating the action after their sibling, wanting to be the last to have said goodbye.

Ollie fished inside his pocket for his gloves and inadvertently dropped one.

'I'll get it,' declared Annabelle helpfully.

'No, no, not to worry. Leave it and watch this,' said Ollie. He waited until the children were attentive and then said to Mandy, 'Pick up.' She stood up and walked around him and gently took his glove in her mouth and lifted her head until her muzzle was by his hand and then released it into his grip without any damage to its fibres.

'WOW!' exclaimed the children. 'That's so clever. Can we get a dog? We can teach it tricks. Please,' they dragged out the last word until their mother answered their plea.

'Maybe one day.'

'Aw, why can't daddy get a Bravehound. He was a soldier.'

'I don't qualify, they are needed to help soldiers and those who served in the air force and navy.'

Ollie looked from Carl and then to Tilly and his nodding became more pronounced. She discretely nodded back.

Chapter Eleven

Lee glanced up to the lamppost outside his home and grinned. He was looking forward to seeing the recently installed face of Father Christmas lit up tonight. He chuckled as he remembered the fuss that was made by villagers after the council workers had inadvertently hung this festive light upside down the year before. It was a week before they returned to put Santa Claus the right way up. His poor hat had drooped forlornly down, and his cheery smile had looked like a deep frown.

'What's so funny?' enquired Brodie as he walked over to his husband. Daisy trotted proudly beside him, her leash held slack by her owner, allowing her the choice to have a sniff around the pavement.

Lee nodded upwards, 'He's not upside down this year.'

'Ha, I don't think the poor council workers would have dared, not after the stooshie the village committee made last year, though that was a fun time. It was the talk of the shop and social media!'

Lee reached out and the couple fell into an easy embrace. Daisy sat down patiently between their feet. 'I do love this time of year. Daisy is so going to love her present. I've hidden it in the shed, it doesn't half stink! Who knew that you could get deep fried chicken legs! They smell worse than those deer ears we gave her last year. She's going to enjoy munching down on those during Christmas lunch. I've also got her a new fun outfit. When she sits down at the kitchen table it'll look like she is wearing a Princess dress.'

'That sounds so sweet, I can't wait to see it. I bet Annabelle next door will get all excited when she sees her in it.'

Lee frowned, 'Ah, yes, about them, you'll never guess what they've bought their father as a gift. I've had to store them in our shed so that they are a surprise. They are heavy and bulky. It took Tilly and I two trips to the car and back whilst Carl was at the gym. They are going to bring Carl round on Christmas day for them. I'll bet that he will be able to put each under one arm and carry them home effortlessly. I'd better show you.'

'Okay, but give us a kiss first, I haven't seen you all day.'

Lee's frown vanished as the couple locked lips and enjoyed the warmth of their closeness, despite the late December chill.

'FILTHY,' shouted Simon as he walked towards them. 'Can't a man even walk to the shop without having to see that. You shouldn't be allowed to do that in public. Do it indoors and get out of my way.'

The shocked couple broke off their kiss and embrace and Lee took a step towards the walking figure. He felt a hand on his shoulder.

'Best not,' advised Brodie as he gently pulled his partner towards their open gate. 'Let's just get out of his way.'

Reluctantly Lee walked away from Simon, and Brodie followed, gently pulling on Daisy's leash to encourage her to follow them out of harm's way.

Daisy hesitated at the gate to smell the scent left by passing dogs' urine. Pee-mail their dog trainer had called it. Other dogs were letting Daisy know they were in the neighbourhood and Daisy had taken the time, as was her habit, to check in for their messages. It was irresistible to her and she strained on the leash so that she could remain sniffing.

'Get that pampered mutt out of my way,' bellowed Simon as he came closer and aimed a passing kick.

Lee reached out and grabbed Daisy's leash and both of her owners tugged and got her to move forward and into their path just in time.

Simon scowled as he walked past. He snorted deeply and spat towards Daisy as he marched on. It fell short and splattered onto the path, just by the gate.

'Foul old man,' derided Lee. 'There's no need for that. We've every right to kiss in public and you'd better not try and kick my dog either.'

Simon smirked, he'd gotten the rise he was after, 'You are both unnatural,' he shouted as he made his way to the shop for his tobacco and whisky.

'Leave it Lee, you know what happens if we get on the wrong side of him.' He nodded to their cars.

'Okay, alright. It's just not fair on Daisy. What would have happened if he'd have kicked her?'

'I think he aimed deliberately to miss.'

'It didn't look like it to me. He's such a horrible man, and yet Millie is the loveliest lady, that is when we get a chance to chat to her. He's always nodding his head at her to get back in the house, or to get back to sweeping. He has that poor woman cleaning all day long, despite her pain. What an awful man.'

'I know love, I know. But what can we do? It's easy to say that it's none of our business. But we've no proof that he hits her. He doesn't lay a finger to her when they are outside. I know that poor Guy and Finty heard all sorts, but Carl and Tilly haven't heard anything yet, have they?'

'Not yet,' replied Lee ominously.

Annabelle's eyes twinkled in the dark as she looked around her in the candlelit church. The dull sheen off the pews helped highlight the orange decorations held aloft by the other children and some of the adults. Small hands fumbled with the red ribbons wrapped around the fruit and broke the solemn silence. Many of the girls and boys joined Annabelle with their gleeful exclamations as they carefully held aloft their oranges with a lit candle securely wedged in by the Sunday School teachers the night before. They had also placed cocktail sticks with a mixture of dolly mixtures, sultanas, and jelly tots around the small white candles.

Gordon was silent, save for the occasional chew as he tried to discretely munch down on the dried fruit and sweets. He had enjoyed the carol singing, but with it being late afternoon, and the night before Christmas, he had become hungry and easily bored. He thought back to their earlier visit to the Garden Centre whilst their dad went off to the local gym. He'd been as pleased as punch to be able to choose his gifts from there this year. Last Christmas Annabelle had spied the remote-controlled car that drove on walls and ceilings first and had proudly bragged about being the one that chose dad's gift. He was determined that he'd be the one to choose this year. He smiled at the thought.

Carl nudged Tilly gently to attract her attention and then nodded to Gordon. They both smiled and were glad to see him enjoying the Christingle service. They were both relishing the next day and being able to enjoy their peaceful home. They reached out, found each other's fingers, and gave an appreciative, loving squeeze of happiness.

'Oh Boy!' exclaimed Brodie, whistling through his teeth. A shocked look spread through his face as he looked in their shed. He was pointing his mobile phone and using its torch. Darkness had fallen and even had he chosen to go back to the pavement, the brightly lit-up Santa Claus illumination would not have changed his troubled countenance.

'I know, right!' replied an equally worried Lee. He too had shone his phone torch into the entrance of their shed, though the extra light was not needed. Tilly had carefully festooned Christmas wrapping paper and ribbons around the gifts from the children and had followed the contours with neat precision.

'It's a bird-table and that looks like a bird-bath.'

'Yes, I helped her wrap them here. The children were so excited. They know how much their father is going to love having them, he's become a keen birdwatcher since leaving the army.'

'They don't know about Simon, do they?'

The question remained unanswered and instead the couple looked around protectively for Daisy and were reassured to see her sitting on their back doorstep, waiting patiently to be taken in and given her evening meal.

Brodie sucked air through his teeth as he thought. 'Should we tell them? We can't spoil their Christmas. It is a thoughtful present, but they have a right to know.'

Lee shook his head vehemently. 'We can't. It would totally ruin the gift. Perhaps Simon will be different. Poor Guy was a quiet man and I think Simon saw this as weakness and exploited that to get his own way. Perhaps Carl will be stronger. Remember that I told you that Dotty saw him stand his ground when Simon was shouting at his wife. She didn't hear him shout back, she described Simon as slinking back to his house.'

'I know, but remember what he put Guy through, nothing could be proved, it was all internal and against that adjoining wall, and there was no evidence about the fire.' He nodded to Daisy, 'I think that we'd better go in and get Daisy her tea and have a think about this. Let's not let it spoil our Christmas, I'm really looking forward to having fun tomorrow.'

Brodie turned around and walked back to their house, deep in thought. He left Lee to lock up their shed.

From the CCTV in their lounge, Millie watched Simon pull out of their driveway and cut across a car. She heard the blaring of angry horns from her armchair. She rarely watched the cameras, but today she wanted to be sure that he had left and to know when he came back. She rose painfully from her armchair and made her way slowly through to their kitchen.

She stooped down to the back recess of the kitchen cabinet under the chopping area and carefully withdrew her stainless-steel fish poacher. She'd scrubbed it thoroughly several days ago. She smugly opened the lid, and from this secret hiding place, took out two packages that had been wrapped with pictures of cartoon reindeer with a jolly Santa on a sleigh. She'd bought two chocolate stockings from the Post Office when she had collected her pension payment on Monday. She'd handed over the cash, as usual, to Simon, who, as normal, would count each pound and penny carefully, like Ebenezer Scrooge, before handing her back her housekeeping money. Since the family next door had moved in last month she had carefully saved up for these gifts and was so looking forward to giving them to the two sweet children who had brightened up her days. Millie replaced the fish poacher and shuffled back to the warmth of their lounge, the only room that Simon allowed to be heated. His chair was by the radiator.

She sighed with relief as she eased herself back down on the welcoming cushions and sat transfixed to the CCTV screen, its eight camera angles giving her a full view around their path, driveway, and those of her neighbours. Simon's spying ways would come in handy this evening. Despite it being Christmas Eve, he had gone to tour around the supermarkets hoping to pick up some late near their sell by date food offers. He did this to give himself more money for his alcohol, rather than to help their housekeeping go a little further.

He had come back from the village shop chuckling to himself, a sure sign that he had upset someone and was relishing the after-effects. He'd spent the afternoon drinking, so much so that she doubted that he was safe to drive. She used to secretly wish that he'd get pulled over by the police and breathalysed. But then she realised that he may eventually get a driving ban and would be at home all the time. At least she could have time to heal and for herself when he was out. He wasn't at home laying into her, physically and verbally. She rubbed the top of her arms as she recalled her last punishment, the day that he had lost his temper with the nice young woman next door. Now, when he drove with the drink in him, she silently prayed that he wouldn't run some innocent over or plough into another car. She wouldn't be able to live with that on her conscience.

She reached to her table and pulled over her blanket. The heating was never enough to keep the chill from her bones, and she draped the tartan fabric over her legs. The wrapped selection boxes were grasped tightly to her as she kept her lonely vigil.

Tilly led her family in a rendition of their favourite Christmas songs during their walk back from the church. Annabelle joined in hoping to be as good a singer as their mother one day. Carl fumbled along, never as confident at public singing unless a mighty organ, like at church, could be guaranteed to drown out his deep tones. Gordon looked intently at all the Christmas lights as they walked home, hoping that none of his newly made pals were seeing and hearing this.

They passed Simon and Millie's house, a fortress of darkness compared to the other houses who each bore a selection of lit trees and signs in their windows. Annabelle had remarked upon each of her favourites and as they passed each house, she selected another favourite, only to declare, between bouts of singing, the next window display was her new adored choice.

Carl smiled as he opened their gate and held it for his family to pass through. Tilly had placed a huge "Santa Stop Here!" sign in the flower bed. No passing sleigh could fail to see it. A dazzle of whiteness sparkled from their open lounge curtains. Tilly had created another beautiful display of seasonal peace around their home.

He closed their gate and as he walked down their path, to join his gathered family on the doorstep whilst Tilly found her keys, the security light next door came on, like a searchlight within a prison, searching out an escapee. Millie tentatively emerged from her house and carefully stepped down the steps and made her way across the lock-block towards the adjoining wall. 'Hello dears,' she called over.

'Oh, hello Millie, how are you?' enquired a concerned Tilly. She hadn't seen her neighbour for a few days and had wondered if she'd caught the awful flu that had swept through the village, just as the children had broken up for the school holidays.

Before Millie had a chance to reply, Annabelle cut in innocently with, 'We've been to a church service, do you like my Christingle? Would you like one of my dolly mixtures?' She proudly held out her orange and turned to nod at her brother, 'I've still got all of mine left.'

Gordon rolled his eyes, though he then decided to put his barren orange, save for the candle, into his jacket pocket.

'That's so kind dear, but you save it for later. Though I have something for you both.' She glanced quickly to the road and then held out the wrapped presents. 'These are for you to open tomorrow.'

The children took them eagerly and immediately felt around the packaging, trying to work out what they contained. They were rewarded with rustling noises. Millie smiled down at them, content to see them so happy with her gifts.

'That's so kind, what do you say children?'

'Thank you, Millie!' they chorused.

Millie beamed and a little warmth settled upon her, though her eyes kept darting to the road, so much so that Carl kept looking around, trying to see what she was looking out for.

'You'll never guess what we've got daddy and mummy as presents?' asked Annabelle conspiratorially.

'Sshh!' interrupted Gordon in a low voice, not giving Millie an opportunity to take part in this fun game. 'You'll ruin their surprises.'

In a quiet voice, hoping to be out of earshot of her father, Annabelle continued anyway, 'Daddies gift is so big, we've had to ask Lee and Brodie to store it in their shed. It'll give me another chance to see Daisy when we go around to collect it. I'm thinking that we should blindfold daddy when he walks over.'

Millie chuckled. 'That sounds like fun, but you must make sure that you both hold his hands so that he doesn't trip over, especially if it's icy.'

Both the children nodded seriously.

'How are you spending tomorrow Millie?' asked Tilly.

Millie's smile widened, 'At my son's house, with his wife and children, it'll be nice not to have to do the cooking for a change.'

'That sounds lovely. Does he live local?'

'Yes, in town, just ten minutes away. I don't see him as often as I'd like. He's busy with his work and his own family.'

'Ah, what's his name?'

'Peter,' she replied absently as she looked to the road once more. 'I'd better go!' she exclaimed as a car drew alongside.

Carl could make out Simon in the gloom of the car, though from what little light the dashboard instruments shone up towards his face, he didn't look happy. 'Have a great Christmas,' he said as he watched her retreating back go shuffling into her home. He looked around Simon's lounge window and could see no evidence of any decoration or illumination that would have pointed towards that expectation.

Chapter Twelve

Gordon burst into his sister's room and shouted gleefully, 'I'm up first! Race you to the presents!' He ran off without waiting for an answer.

Annabelle, deep in sleep seconds ago, came instantly awake and threw back her princess-decorated duvet and rushed for her door, neglecting to put on her dressing-gown and slippers. Her bare feet trod on some Lego and she gave a startled cry of pain, but heroically raced on to see what Santa had left her under the tree.

In the next room a reluctant hand removed itself from the warmth of her duvet and reached out for her mobile phone. Its screen told her that it was six o'clock in the morning.

A chuckle broke from the figure lying beside her and as he swung out of bed, he looked at his own mobile, read the time and remarked, 'Well, that's a lie-in compared to last year!'

Tilly groaned and tried to snuggle back to bed.

'C'mon sleepyhead, the children will be so disappointed if you aren't there to see them open their gifts. Please get up and come and watch them. I'll make us a cup of coffee.'

'Extra strength for me please,' she implored. 'I'll just have five more minutes.'

Carl listened out for the running footsteps that were bounding up the stairs, 'I don't think so!' he teased. He stood back and theatrically counted down from five.

On three, their bedroom door flew open and their excited children rushed in, each carrying a large, carefully wrapped present, the biggest they could find from the pile under the tree. 'Mummy, Daddy, look what Santa left us,' shrieked an excited Annabelle.

Gordon, equally as excited, had bounded onto the bed. He knew that Santa was really his mum and dad. He shook his mum awake.

Tilly let off a few snoring noises and shouted, 'I'm asleep!'

Annabelle joined her brother on the bed and took part in the shaking. Soon the bed was moving about like a wobbling car on a rollercoaster. 'Okay, okay,' relented their mother, 'I'm awake!' She had gone to bed the same time as her children last night and her medication was wearing off anyway. Carl had stayed up for a few hours to ensure the children had finally gone to bed and that their trips up and down the stairs for glasses of water and toilet visits had eventually ended. He had enjoyed the silence of the house and the absence of a TV or music spouting out and had read his book, though he was disturbed by some feminine crying out which didn't seem to sound like Annabelle or Tilly having another bad dream. It had soon stopped, and he then retrieved all the children's presents that he'd hidden in his study and placed them in neat piles under the tree. He doubted that they would be tidy now! Before coming to bed, he had enjoyed the dram of whisky and mince pie that their children had thoughtfully left for Santa and had put away the carrot for Rudolph. He made sure to leave the empty glass and a few crumbs on the table to make it look like Santa had enjoyed his treats.

'You said we could open one present before breakfast,' Annabelle reminded her mother. She watched her intently, making sure that she didn't go back to sleep.

Her mother sat up and rubbed her eyes, 'Okay, let's see what Father Christmas has got you. I guess that he must have thought that you were good children, because those are mighty big presents. She smiled indulgently at them and at Carl who was standing patiently at the foot of their bed. There wasn't room for him on the mattress. 'Squeeze up, make some room for your poor old dad.'

The children obediently shuffled along and were sat at their mother's feet. Carl dutifully walked back to his side of the bed and flopped down and leant back on the headboard, ready to watch the show.

Like two eagerly waiting pups for a command from their master, the children waited until their mother nodded. They then ripped open their presents, shredding the carefully wrapped gifts until the paper fell to the floor.

'WOW!' exclaimed Gordon as he turned the large box over and then from side to side. 'I can't wait to build this,' he held aloft his new Lego kit, like a gold medal winner on a podium.

'A glitter make-up set! Now I'm going to look even more like a princess. I'm going to wear my favourite dress all day long. Can you help me with the glitter mummy?'

'That sounds fun, we'll do that after breakfast. Dad has some special bacon rolls he is going to make us because lunch isn't until one o'clock. We can have you looking like the prettiest princess before we go to nana and grandad. There will even be time for dad to help you build that Lego robot.'

Gordon nodded eagerly; he couldn't wait to make a start.

'Why don't you both put your slippers and dressing-gowns on before you catch a cold, and then go downstairs and check out your other presents. Don't unwrap them yet, see if you can guess what they are.'

The pair scampered off eagerly and Tilly leant over and closed the bedroom door. She turned back to her husband and purred as she said seductively, 'And in the meantime, come here and get your Christmas present!'

Millie flipped the bacon over and the fat in the frying pan sizzled in angry protest. She smarted as a droplet of the hot, melted lard landed on her hand. She checked the time on the kitchen clock and realised that she wouldn't have even one spare moment to run her hand under the cold tap in relief against the burn. Simon would be through for his breakfast and he wouldn't accept it being one second late, not even on Christmas Day. It would be another miserable morning of cleaning for her, broken up by a few hours respite, having lunch with their son and family. If only she could tell them how lonely and awful her marriage was, though they must have suspected, or perhaps she had done too good a job shielding them from the reality. Or maybe they had come to see the way she was treated as being the normal way a wife was treated. She hoped that Peter did not treat his wife this way. She sighed as she rolled the sausage in the fat, checking that it was adequately cooked, then removed it and placed it on the warmed plate. She then placed a cut up piece of bread in the hot fat to fry and harden to just the right crispness that Simon liked. She hoped for a day off from his fists, just this once. She shuddered as she heard him come in from his check around their property, his morning routine of ensuring that no-one had tampered with the locks around his driveway gates and their sheds and garage. She quickly warmed through the baked beans and began plating up his morning fry-up, ready to place in front of him as he sat down. A silent prayer was said that it would be to his satisfaction and not thrown at her in disgust and made to cook again. It seemed such a waste and extravagance when he would be enjoying a large Christmas lunch with their family in just a few hours. She sighed again and wondered if the couple next door was enjoying the start of their first Christmas in their new home. She smiled at the thought of them opening and enjoying the chocolates that were in the stockings that she had managed to discretely give them. Though she tried, she could not remember the last time that Simon had bought her a present. She waited obediently for his return to the kitchen, plate held aloft, like an obedient waiter at a stately function, about to serve Her Majesty. Millie's smile soon disappeared as she wondered, jealously, how Eric would have treated her friend across the street, if he had still been alive. She couldn't wait for the forthcoming week when she would be staying at her daughter's in Cornwall for their Hogmanay celebrations. Simon would be on his best behaviour then, and there would be no violence upon her, not in Victoria's presence. She looked forward to driving down first thing on Boxing Day and hoped that Simon would stay off the drink the night before so that his driving was safe and his mood less dark.

Simon entered the kitchen, a scowl on his face, she did not expect, nor received a Merry Christmas greeting from him as he sat down and nodded to the plate. She obediently placed it down in front of him and took a cowering step back.

Dotty reached out and switched on her bedside lamp. For the past few minutes, she had listened absently to the reassuring hiss and splutter of her teasmade alarm clock as it gently poured her out a steaming cup of tea. She smiled at the silver edged photo frame with her favourite picture of her Eric, beaming up at her. It had been taken by a professional photographer at their son's wedding, two years before her dear husband had died. 'Merry Christmas love!' she fondly said, 'I do miss you.'

He had been such a thoughtful man, always bringing her a cup of tea in the morning, even when he worked fulltime, he wouldn't go to work until he'd taken her up a cup and saucer of tea. She'd remarked about this to her daughter-in-law one day, a few months after Eric had died. She'd said how much she missed the tea and the thoughtfulness of her husband. The next time her son and his wife came to visit, she had been presented with a wrapped present, even though her birthday and Christmas was a long way off. As she unwrapped it and saw that it was a teasmade, she was so overcome with emotion, that she cried and kept saying how kind they were. Her son had ensured that they installed it and showed her how to work it before they left and that she was to think that his dad had left her the tea to help her face the day.

Dotty sat up, plumped up her pillows so that they formed a backrest upon her headboard, reached out contentedly for her hot cup of tea, and relaxed into her pillows and began to talk aloud to Eric's photo, pausing to enjoy her freshly brewed cuppa. She spoke about how she would be collected later in the morning and taken to their son's house and have Christmas lunch with his family and how she would stay the night and the first thing that she would pack would be his photo so that they'd have Christmas Day and Night together.

Brodie reached over to cuddle Lee and instead felt the soft warmth that radiated from Daisy who was cradled in front of his husband. As their automatic alarm light gently revealed its true brightness, like a blossoming flower, he could see her head poking out between his husband's arms. She was in doggie heaven, snuggled in, content and fast asleep. Lee's face was almost cherubic, and he looked serene and at peace. He had not spent the night worrying about the gifts for Carl in their shed and what they should say to him. Brodie had decided that their best course of action was to say nothing and hope that history would not repeat itself and play out for all the neighbourhood to see. He tried to put these thoughts out of his mind as he quietly slid open his bedside cabinet and took out his gift for his husband, the latest designer watch that he'd hinted at all November and for most of December. 'Merry Christmas darling!'

Lee grinned as he relinquished his hold on Daisy, yawned, stretched, and asked, 'Are you talking to me or the dog?'

Daisy sneezed in protest at being moved, rolled onto her back, gave a yawn that ended in a cute yelp, and stretched out. This effort proved too much, and she rolled onto her side and promptly fell asleep again with her head resting peacefully on Lee's pillows.

'Both of you, I love you both equally as much.'

'Listen to him Daisy, he doesn't love you as much as I do. I'd have said that I love you more!'

Brodie laughed, he knew that, and if he was honest, he loved Daisy that little bit more too. She was much better looking and gave the best cuddles. All thought of what Simon's reaction to Carl's gifts would be were now long forgotten as he spied Lee reaching out towards his own bedside cabinet and bringing out his own gift. He'd given no hints and he had all he desired here in front of him, his two greatest loves. He looked forward to the surprise that the gift would bring.

Carl followed the sound of gentle rattling and rustling as he made his way down the stairs and into the kitchen. Along the way he'd casually looked into the lounge and smiled contentedly as he had seen the joy in his children's faces as they carefully cradled each wrapped present, weighing it up in their small hands and then turning it over on all sides, trying to guess what delights lay inside. He made his way to their coffee machine, he had a feeling that he and Tilly were going to need plenty of caffeine today to keep up with their children, he only hoped that his mum and dad, and Felicity and Geoff were equally ready for the excitable energy that was about to explode upon their day. He switched the machine on and waited patiently for his morning stimulant.

Tilly, still glowing from their bedroom activity, rubbed moisturiser onto her hands and spread it over her wrists and forearm. No matter how hard she rubbed at it, her self-harm marks would not disappear. The deeper and redder welts from her suicide attempts would remain with her and as she pulled on her Christmas jumper, she made sure that the cuffs reached below her wrists and hid her, in her own mind, shame. She looked back at the dishevelled bed and reached for the bottom sheet and straightened it taut all the way around the bed until it was as tight as a boxing ring canvas. She did the same with the heavy duvet, ensuring that the pillows were plump, and the openings of the cases faced away from the centre. Only then did she open the curtains, ready to face the world. As she exited the room, she made a mental effort to resist turning on and off the light switch eight times. Her therapist could never discover the secret of why eight times but had worked hard at desensitising her over light switches. It was her need for light and control when the darkness had come and brought him to her childhood bed. But not today, she thought, he would not spoil another Christmas. Now and the future were times to be enjoyed. She scooped up a tiny sliver of wrapping paper that Carl had neglected to pick up from the floor after the enthusiasm of their children and popped it into their bedroom bin. She watched it flutter down from her palm, like a Christmas fairy gently returning to rest after a busy night of spreading seasonal joy. She ensured it settled deeply into the basket before exiting the room and being assailed by the enticing aroma of cooked bacon and freshly ground coffee that tempted her down the stairs and into the reassuring and loving bosom of her family, one that was filled with affection and not fear. She was determined to enjoy this and many more Christmases with those that mattered and not with those that hurt.

Two small hands clasped hers and interrupted her morose thoughts and dragged her into the lounge. Her children led her to their piles of presents with cries of delight, each mustering her attention and drawing her eyes to what Santa had generously left them.

Tilly giggled like a nervous teenager on her first date and gave appreciative noises of 'Oh my,' and 'Wow!' She knelt by the tree, between the piles of presents, with one child to each side of her. She reached across and flicked on the tree's lights and as they flashed on and shone intermittently, they caught the sparkle of her husband's eyes as he watched with amusement from the doorway, coffee cup in hand. There was no need to check if there was a pile of presents for her and Carl, she had all the gifts she could possibly want here in their lounge and she thought herself to be truly blessed.

Chapter Thirteen

Annabelle let out a shriek of delight as she watched Daisy run towards her and get caught up in the ruffles of her costume dress. The dog tripped and went skidding across the laminate floor towards her new best friend. Annabelle reached out for her, caught her, and scooped her up. She held her aloft, like a mother showing off her newly born baby. 'She's so adorable, she looks just like a princess.' She rubbed noses with her canine pal and was rewarded with a wet lick. 'Princess Daisy, that's what I'm going to call you from now on!' Daisy wagged her tail in appreciation of her new nickname.

'Merry Christmas lads,' rejoiced Carl as he pumped the hands of his neighbours. 'Sorry to intrude, but I was under orders to come around straight after breakfast.' He nodded to his son and wife, indicating that it was their doing.

Lee broke off the handshake and instead cuddled Carl tightly and gave an appreciative sound and then winked at Tilly, 'Oh what a beefcake, you are so lucky!'

Carl reddened, much to the amusement of his children. He shrugged and resigned himself to the affectionate embrace.

Lee then patted him on the back and said, 'Merry Christmas Carl. We've something for you, or rather Gordon and Annabelle have.' He winked to the children. 'Merry Christmas to you all.'

Seeing that Annabelle was busy with Daisy, Gordon proudly said, 'I chose it this year dad. It's in their shed. C'mon, let's show you.'

He led the way and the neighbours followed, like three wise men following the star.

"Wait!' shouted Annabelle, waving a scarf whilst balancing Daisy. 'We have to blindfold you.'

Carl laughed as the covering went over his eyes. 'It's like SAS Selection all over again,' he joked.

Lee's eyes widened and he poked his elbow into Brodie's ribs and gave an I told you so look and then gazed back at Carl with greater admiration. 'I'd better take your hand, to make sure you don't trip sweetie!'

Carl chuckled, 'Yup, just like Selection! Lead on then darling!'

Lee guided him to their shed and stood him by its entrance, ensuring that there was room for the door to open wide.

'Is it a new bike?' guessed Carl.

'No daddy, Santa didn't give us enough pocket money for that,' replied Annabelle.

Not missing an opportunity, Gordon quipped with, 'Maybe if we had a pocket money increase you could get one next year.'

Tilly laughed, 'We'll have to make an appointment with the Bank of Daddy!' She drew up beside her husband and noted that Lee still had hold of her husband's hand and wondered if she should be worried. She was relieved to then see that Lee had now let it go and was unlocking the shed and leaving the door fully opened.

'SURPRISE!' shouted the children and Tilly in carefully choreographed unison. Tilly leant forward and took off the blindfold.

Lee blinked a few times and looked in the shed; the mid-morning light was strong enough for him to make out its contents. His eyes were instantly drawn to the two carefully wrapped items with bows and tinsel stuck around them. He made a few surprised noises and then said, 'Oh, I wonder what those could be? I can guess though and that's so lovely children, thank you.'

Gordon beamed with pride whilst Annabelle was juggling Daisy whilst pointed to her dad's gifts so that the dog would look at them.

Carl leant in and picked up the heavy wooden bird-table, he didn't need to unwrap it to know what it was. Though he ripped into the wrapping paper for the benefit of his children and then made a pretence of looking amazed. He ran his fingers over the contours of the wood and gave a whistle, 'That's such craftsmanship. The birds are going to love feeding from this. It's high enough to keep the cats from jumping up. Thank you, Gordon and Annabelle, you are the best children ever.' He put down the bird-table and checked its base for a wobble, it stood firm against his efforts. He nodded in appreciation.

The children beamed at their father and Gordon nodded to the other wrapped object. 'That's yours too daddy.'

Carl walked into the shed and picked up the object, 'That's a little bit heavy. Mmm, I wonder what it could be?' He tapped it with his knuckles. 'It's made from stone. I hope it's what I think it is!' he said gleefully, like a child choosing his favourite treats in a sweet shop. He ripped open the wrapping paper and revealed an ornate bird-bath with an intricately chiselled frog in the bottom. 'That's brilliant! Just what I wanted. I'll be able to look up from my work and see the birds splashing about and bathing themselves.'

As if in anticipation a group of starlings flew low in a spectacular murmuration display and cavorted across the sky in search of a mid-morning snack. A lonely robin fluttered in and rested upon the nearby wall and stood watching the group. Tilly walked into the shed and began picking up the dropped wrapping paper, discarded bows, and the tinsel.

Brodie looked across to Lee and gave him a knowing stare. They had carefully rehearsed what they would say to Carl in encouragement to try and keep these objects away from Simon. Brodie spoke first, 'Perhaps you could put them along our shared fence. We'd enjoy hearing the birds feeding and bathing.'

Lee nodded in encouragement, 'And Daisy does such a good job of keeping the cats away, that'll be the safest place for them.'

Carl considered this thoughtfully for a moment and then rejected their advice with a firm, 'No, I won't be able to see them from my desk there. I'll put them along the low wall we share with Simon. I'll have a better view from there.'

Lee and Brodie looked aghast for a moment and then, not wanting to spoil the children's moment, looked happy, despite the approaching storm they knew would inevitably come.

'Shall we help you move them to your garden?' asked Brodie.

'Och, no need lads, I'll soon lift these and then we'll be on our way. That is if I can drag Annabelle away from Daisy.'

The group looked across to see Daisy happily being rocked in Annabelle's arms. She looked up and said, 'I wish Santa had bought me a dog as cute as Princess Daisy.'

Carl looked across to Tilly, but she was lost in her own thoughts, so he heaved up the bird-bath and placed it across his left shoulder and then scooped up the bird-table in his right arm and walked home, whistling a Christmas tune.

Lee looked on in admiration and it was Brodie's turn to elbow him in the ribs for taking too long a stare at the departing figure.

'Thank you so much boys for lending us the use of your shed. That was a lovely surprise for Carl, and the children enjoyed keeping them a secret.'

'That's alright, anytime, you have yourselves a great Christmas, off to the in-laws?'

'Yes, Carl's dad is doing the cooking, so it's a restful day for me, what about you two?'

'We are having a relaxing day off with just us two and Daisy, it's going to be great,' replied Brodie as he took Lee's hand.

'Well enjoy the day, and thanks again.' She gave them both a quick kiss on the cheek and turned to her children. 'Right you two, let's catch up with your dad and get the bird seed we bought out of the car boot. He'll want to make a start in feeding the birds and encouraging them into the garden.'

Annabelle kissed her best friend and reluctantly put her down. 'Goodbye Princess Daisy, I'll miss you. Have a lovely Christmas.' She turned around and skipped after her father.

Gordon and Tilly followed her, leaving the couple to lock up their shed and contemplate that they had done their best.

Lewis hummed along to the Christmas carols playing on the CD player in the kitchen as he reached across for another couple of potatoes. He started to peel them as his wife came through from their lounge.

'Blimey! Are you feeding the five thousand?' She nodded to the mound of peeled and quartered potatoes in the large saucepan.

'Now then mother, just you get yourself back into the lounge. You are having a rest from all the festive cooking, we agreed. You go back in there and leave this to me.' He frowned as he mentally went through his checklist and wondered if maybe he'd taken on too much. He'd never cooked a roast dinner before. He smiled at his wife, he'd have to learn to take more responsibility as her condition worsened, and she'd have to learn to relinquish the ropes and let him do things for her. 'I've got that jar of goose fat, some fresh rosemary and those recipes Carl printed off for me, so don't you worry about a thing, it's all in hand.' A bead of sweat broke on his forehead as he pointed to the lounge and gestured for her to leave. He really did hope that this would go well.

Gordon bounded after his father, having to run to keep up. He managed to reach the gate first and opened it wide. Carl stepped through, taking care not to scrape his presents on the metalwork. As he made his way down their path and towards their back garden, he noticed Simon at the adjacent window. With his arms full, he could only nod and smile and mouth the words 'Merry Christmas.' His stride didn't break, and he continued walking on his cheerful way, already picturing where he would place his proud possessions.

He failed to see Simon staring back in disbelief, his maleficent glare was centred on the objects his new neighbour was carrying. Carl also didn't see that he was hopping from side to side with angry energy that needed a vent to dissipate.

Carl walked up to the lawn, careful of where he placed his feet because the damp air had made it wet and slippery. He lowered the bird-bath first and looked up to their rear extension and where his desk was. He could see his laptop through the slatted blinds and then imagined himself sat at his desk, looking to the right as he paused typing and sat back in his chair for a rest from the screen. He moved the bird-bath a foot towards the wall, frowned and then moved it so that it was now only a few centimetres from the brickwork. The birds could rest on the wall and take turns jumping down to bathe. Satisfied, he then positioned the bird-table about a metre away. He stood back and admired his gifts then turned and smiled to his family, 'Perfect, that's just the right spot. That's the best Christmas presents ever!'

Gordon beamed with pride and was already thinking about what he should get his dad next year.

Annabelle held out a small bag of seed and offered it to her father.

'Well timed Annabelle, we can feed them straight away.' He bent down and picked her up and carried her to the bird-table. 'We hereby declare this bird-table to be well and truly opened. You feed them first love and then give some to Gordon.'

Her tiny hands dived into the bag and pulled out a mixture of seeds and nuts and spread them on the table. Several fell off and scattered around the grass.

'The blackbirds will enjoy those,' said her father, nodding downwards, 'they don't like feeding off tables, but prefer to rummage around the ground. The same with our friendly robin.' He turned around, looking to see if it was still on the other wall.

'He's over there, dad, by the compost bin,' noted Gordon.

The family turned and stared at the plucky robin that was balanced on a thin empty twig from the buddleia bush. He was bobbing his head, as if looking at each family member in turn, patiently awaiting a feed.

Tilly shivered, 'It's Baltic out here, let's go inside and open a few more presents.'

'Yah, presents!' shrieked Gordon and went running off. Annabelle struggled out of her father's grip and he obliged by letting her down and watched paternally as she chased after her brother.

Carl turned to his wife and hugged her, 'Merry Christmas love, and thank you. I know that you went to the garden centre and steered Gordon in the direction of these two gifts. That was so kind of the lads to store them, what a great surprise for me.'

Tilly kissed him and then said, 'Let's get inside and you can give me my present and then you can watch from your chair and see if any birds have used the facilities yet!'

Carl laughed, turned, and spied Simon from their kitchen window, staring at the bird-table. Carl waved and then looked to his wife and took her hand as they walked away. 'It looks like next door are going to enjoy watching the birds as much as us, Simon is already at their window looking on.' Carl had failed to see the look of hatred that had darkened Simon's face.

Chapter Fourteen

The engine ceased its quiet purr and the back doors were flung open and two small figures went running out, laden with gift-wrapped presents. They bounded up the path to their grandparent's house, racing to be the first to enter. They know them well enough now to just walk straight in and shout out their presence; and yell out they did. 'Happy Christmas nana and granddad!' they hollered for all they were worth. Their voices trailed off as they made their way through the bungalow and from the pavement their parents exited the car and went to the boot for their bags containing a few items for the table such as after dinner chocolates. 'I wonder if your parents have survived that full-on frontal attack,' mused Tilly.

'Dad's an old Gordon Highlander, he's made of stern stuff,' quipped Carl. 'I just hope they remember to be gentle with mum.'

Tilly nodded to the adjacent parked car, 'It looks like Felicity and Geoff are already here and no doubt keeping our two out of mischief.'

'Well, best we get in there and cause some more mischief of our own!' He took her hand and they walked up the path, ready to enjoy a family Christmas with those they loved.

Simon sat back in his daughter-in-law's favourite armchair and cradled a can of beer. He hadn't said much to his son and his family and had left Millie to witter on about cooking tips to Sienna. He took huge swigs whilst his son showed him his latest bottle of car wheel cleaner and explained that it so cleverly just needed spraying on and left to dry for a few minutes. Simon interrupted his son with 'A bird-table and bath, can you believe it, and he put it right next to my wall. The cheek of the man. I bet he did it deliberately. I bet those men that live together, husband and husband, I ask you! I bet they both told him to do that. Well, I'll teach them, you wait and see. They can talk about me all they like, but I'll show them. You wait and see.'

Peter nodded, knowing that it was easier to agree with his dad when he was in one of these morose moods. He put his wheel cleaner back on the table, there was no use trying to get through to his dad when his ire was up. He reached over and passed him another can of lager, hoping that it would lighten his mood and not spoil their Christmas day.

Simon snatched it greedily, like a hungry baby seeking the comfort of a mother's breast milk. With his other hand, he threw the empty can to his son, not caring that drips of lager spilt onto the immaculate cream carpet. He opened the can, foam spraying down his shirt and trousers, and drunk deeply, his scowl still spread across his face, causing alcohol to dribble down his chin. He finished, belched, and then rubbed his face dry with his other fingers and palm and then rubbed his hand dry on the chair's fabric.

'I'll just get another can from the fridge dad, you stay comfortable and I'll be back in a moment,' stuttered Peter as he backed out of the room. Though he was an adult, he still felt like a little boy in his dad's presence, a small lad who lived in fear of the back of his hand, his slipper and even his belt. He walked briskly away.

Brodie placed the turkey in the centre of the table, its bronzed skin appeared to glow with pride. Steam rose from the roast potatoes and disappeared without a care. A dish of pigs in blankets and stuffing balls sat next to the vegetable platter. Three plates were laid on the table, two large ones with ornate floral patterns and one small one with hand-painted bone shapes around the edges.

'Wow!' exclaimed Lee, 'you've surpassed yourself today. Us two will never eat all of this, it's such a pity we didn't invite our family and our friends to come for lunch.'

Brodie nodded to Daisy's small plate, 'She'll soon help us, you know how much she loves turkey and carrots. Besides, I wanted you all to myself this year.' He leant forward and kissed his husband tenderly.

Lee placed his hands onto Brodie's cheeks and tenderly caressed them and down to his neck as they kissed. He broke off the loving clinch and patted the seat between them.

Daisy dutifully hoped up to her chair and placed both front paws on the table, as if demanding prompt service. She sniffed the air, catching the tasty aromas in her nose as she took a deep breath. She licked her lips in appreciation and expectation of a good feed.

'She looks so adorable in that dress,' said Lee reaching into his pocket for his phone. 'I'll take a photo for her Instagram page while you serve.'

Brodie sighed and shook his head. Daisy had thousands of followers who couldn't wait to see her next antics.

'This'll make Annabelle scream with delight. You know that Tilly lets her see Daisy's account on the Gram. She leaves such cute comments and emojis.'

Brodie tutted and rolled his eyes in the air as he carefully carved the turkey, placing the crumbling skin onto Daisy's plate, this was her favourite part of the bird. He cut up the meat into small pieces for her. 'Give that a few minutes to cool down.'

Lee put his phone away, satisfied that he'd used the right filters to get Daisy at her best. He leant over and started to blow on Daisy's plate to cool down her food.

'I think that we may spoil that dog,' quipped Brodie.

They both looked to her, sat there patiently, her tail wagging furiously against the hem of her dress, swishing it across her chair. They laughed in unison and reached across to ruffle her ears.

Daisy did not know in which direction to lean into for a deeper ear scratch and instead looked intently at her enticing lunch.

Tilly followed her father-in-law into the kitchen carrying several empty plates and cutlery. The meal had gone well, and everyone was surprised at just how good a cook Lewis had been. He had beamed with delight at their comments and was so glad to see his family well-fed and happy and healthy. They'd had fun telling stories and hearing fond memories and making wishes for the future. Tilly placed the plates next to the sink, 'Let me wash up Lewis, you've done enough.' To demonstrate her commitment, she rolled up her sleeves.

Lewis was about to utter protestations but then, glimpsing Tilly's forearms, he stopped in his tracks.

Tilly looked down to where his troubled eyes were looking and was aghast that she had dropped her guard and had revealed her scars for the first time.

'Oh lass, we knew that you were troubled, but what caused you to do that to yourself?' he blurted out without thinking.

Tilly hastily pulled down her sleeves, stretching the fabric taut.

Lewis recovered his thoughts and placed a fatherly hand on her shoulder, 'I'll wash and maybe you can dry them?' He nodded kindly.

'No.' said Tilly firmly. 'It's about time you knew. You must have wondered? Especially with our sudden move to Scotland.'

'Aye, well, we knew you or Carl would tell us one day. When you were ready. I'm sorry, I shouldn't have said anything, but they look so sore.'

'It's a relief, a kind of purge. I would always feel better after cutting myself. It didn't really hurt. But I don't do it anymore,' she insisted.

'You've two lovely children, and our Carl dotes on you. Can you see that? Can you see how much you are loved and what a bright future you have?'

'I can. It's taken years of therapy and I had to find the right counsellor and psychiatrist. I finally found two that I could trust and be open and honest with. They helped me with my funny little ways and to explore what happened to me as a child.'

'Oh, my poor love.'

'He would come to me in the dark and,' she hesitated and looked to the door, to see if her voice were carrying to her children. She was relieved to see them chatting away to their uncle and aunt.

'Don't say anymore lass, I know it must be difficult, and that's why you needed to move away from your father, to keep your two safe as well.'

'Yes. No. It was my older brother, but mum and dad knew. They did nothing to stop it and wouldn't believe me when I told them when I was young. I kept the memories buried for years. I tried hard to compartmentalise them, but they came flooding back. I tried to live near my childhood home. I wanted our children to have family. But my brother moved back in with my parents when he had an argument with his girlfriend and our children were there staying the weekend whilst Carl and I had a spa treat. It all came flooding back when I saw them with him, and I had a breakdown.' She started to sob, and Lewis instinctively cuddled and rocked her. 'That's when I tried to take my life, that's why I've the deep marks on my wrist. I'm so sorry.'

'Oh lass, you've nothing to be sorry about. We knew that you'd had a rough time of it. When you were in hospital we stayed at your house and looked after the children and your home. That's why Carl was able to spend so much time with you, though you may not recall.'

She shook her head, 'That time was a blur. I was placed on strong medication and can't recall much of it.'

'You gave our boy quite a fright, I've never seen him cry so much. We drove straight to you all when he broke down on the phone.'

She sobbed deeper and snuggled into Lewis's shoulder for comfort. For a few minutes they stood, one gathering support from the other until Tilly said in a low voice, 'I hadn't realised.'

'We don't like to make a fuss. We left the day you were discharged, whilst the children were at school. You didn't need us old fossils hanging around.'

'I do, we all do. Thank you. I did wonder why Carl always looked well fed and cared for and how the house and garden was spotless when he was always with me at the hospital.'

'He was so worried, especially when you tried to take your life again, in the hospital. You can't blame him for not trusting the nurses. They should have been looking out for you.'

'That was my fault. I took advantage of them being busy with another patient who got violent. It was a scary place. I slipped away with my pencil case. They didn't check my art stuff. I had a small scalpel that I use for cardmaking and used that. I lost a lot of blood and came close to death. I needed emergency care and a blood transfusion.' She rubbed at the welts on her right wrist, as if trying to make them and the memories go away.

'None of that was your fault, you weren't well and what your family did to you was despicable. But please know that you will always have a loving home and family here. Our grandchildren have brightened up our lives and our boy, and all of you, are home safe and well and he's so lucky to have you, a beautiful, gifted wife and wonderful mother.' He reached into his pocket and pulled out a cotton handkerchief that was embroidered with his initials. 'Here, dry your eyes, Shona made this for me years ago. It's clean.'

She did as she was told and once she'd dried her eyes and blown her nose, she carefully folded the fabric until she could admire Shona's handiwork. 'I've made it all dirty.'

'Don't you worry about that, just pop it in the washing machine. I'll wash it tomorrow. I've plenty more. Shona loves to sew. I've a drawer full of them.'

'Let me do the washing up and you can tell me about how you looked after Carl and the kids when I was in hospital. Did you go to their sports day? I wasn't allowed out of the hospital. I was on constant watch and the drugs made me ever so dizzy.'

'Yes, we did, I even took part in the parent's race, though my old knobbly knees came last.'

Tilly laughed as she rolled up her sleeves and reached for the washing up liquid. Soon her hands and wrists were deep in suds as she washed each plate carefully with three measured passes of the cloth and then handed them to Lewis to dry.

Carl walked in, munching down on a mince pie, leaving a trail of crumbs. 'All okay?' He looked shocked to see Tilly with her sleeves rolled up.

'Couldn't be better!' rejoiced Tilly.

'You're a lucky lad Carl, you've a brave, remarkable young lady here.'

'Aye! I know.'

Chapter Fifteen

The twinkling icicle shaped lights from the roofline of Brodie's and Lee's house acted like a welcoming beacon directing the family home. They were lost to Annabelle and Gordon as they gently snored in the back seats, exhausted from their day's activities and frolics with their favourite aunty, uncle, and grandparents.

Carl pulled the family car alongside the kerb and nodded in the direction of Dotty's house. 'She's staying the night with her son and his family. I'm glad that she's not on her own. She does miss her Eric. She always talks about him when I stop to chat.'

Tilly nodded in agreement and looked across to their adjoining neighbour's house. The gates were all locked up and the house was in pitch darkness. 'Though you could be with someone and still feel lonely.' She shivered.

The throw away comment about their immediate neighbours was lost on Carl. 'We'll soon be in our toasty, cosy house. I left the central heating on timer. You'll be warm again in next to no time.'

Tilly hadn't the heart to put him right. He always saw the good in people. She hadn't shivered from the cold. She had been thinking of Millie and the noises she had been hearing over the last few weeks as she drifted off to sleep, knowing that it wasn't her imagination or drug-induced dreaming. Though she hadn't told anyone about them, nor enquired to see if Millie was alright. She reached across and grasped Carl's hands whilst he was applying the handbrake. 'I'm so lucky to have you.'

He smiled and looked in the rear-view mirror. Was there any better sight than seeing their children at peace, happy and contented, he thought. 'I am too. That was so brave of you to show dad your scars and to tell him of your childhood.'

'Sorry. It just came out. It felt like the right time to tell him. I hope that it didn't spoil Christmas?'

'Not at all. Dad thinks the world of you and our children.'

Tilly smiled. 'He said that I should tell Shona, Felicity and Geoff one day. Would that be okay?'

'Of course,' he patted her hand. 'When you are ready. It was a big part of your childhood, awful and not right, and it shaped your adult life. Most folks don't need to know. But mum and my sister will be like dad, they'll feel for you and want to make you happy. Don't worry. Just when you are ready and judge the moment to be right.' He pointed to Simon's house. 'It looks like they've stayed the night at their son's too.'

Tilly hoped that was the case and that Millie had been able to enjoy the day. 'Let's get these two to their beds and then I think an early night for us as well.'

Carl grinned, he hoped that he'd get one final Christmas present tonight. He left the car, ready to lift his two sleeping beauties out and settle them in their cosy beds.

The stars twinkled and the air was still, a silence hung over the village as peace reigned amongst the contrasting surrounds of modern estate buildings and old-fashioned and historic fisherman's cottages. A black nose snuffled around the grass, seeking the right spot to place her white furry bottom to urinate one last time on this Christmas night. Brodie, standing at the backdoor, sighed with contentment, the last cognac had infused its flavours through his body and left him all aglow and floaty as he watched on to his beloved pet. He didn't feel the cold air nipping at his bare ankles where his pyjamas stopped, and his slippers started. He waited patiently for Daisy to finish, walk around and circle back and sniff at her liquid deposit. He smiled. She certainly was a creature of habit. She finished, turned, and went bounding back to the house as if old Jack Frost were nipping his chilliness at her paws. Brodie crouched down and allowed his fingers to lightly pass her soft fur as she bounced up the steps, eagerly seeking out the comfort of her warm, fluffy blanket and her favourite bedtime marrowbone biscuit treat.

Night settled on Carl's household and the December chill crept into the house, overcoming the faint warmth coming from the radiators as they dissipated their heat now that the central heating had been switched off by the timer.

Tilly gave a low moan of satisfaction in her sleep as she nestled into Carl for love and warmth. The couple soon drifted into a deep sleep; the day's activities finally having caught up with them. Carl gathered the duvet automatically in his slumber and the couple were soon releasing low snoring noises, almost in rhythm.

BANG, BANG, BANG.

Carl leapt up from the bed, the duvet travelled with him, causing Tilly to feel the chill, and become semi-awake. Her medicines caused her to be confused and it took her several seconds to gather her wits.

'CONTACT, CONTACT!' shouted out Carl as he sprinted around the bedroom in bewilderment. 'Where did it come from,' he screamed as he rummaged around the room for an imaginary rifle.

Tilly, sensing what was happening, shrank back to the safety of the headboard and fumbled for her bedside light. As it burst its illumination into the room, she could see the look of panic spread across her husband's face as he darted about. 'Carl, can you see me, can you hear me. What are you doing?' she gently asked, almost as if speaking to a child, hoping to reach the dark, deep recesses of his mind.

He stared at her in confusion and then looked around him and down at his naked body. He ceased cradling an imaginary weapon and looked at his empty hands in puzzlement. All the while his breathing had been erratic, and his heart was pumping swiftly. He took a deep breath, and then another and exhaled slowly and deliberately. He looked across sheepishly to Tilly and gave a nervous laugh. 'Sorry love. I could have sworn that I heard three loud bangs.' He looked to the clock on the wall. It was four in the morning. 'I'll just slip my dressing-gown on and have a check around the house and see that the children are okay. Perhaps one of their new toys fell off the bed and bounced on the floor. You go back to sleep.'

Tilly yawned, her own heart had stopped pounding and she gratefully settled back into the comfort of the warm duvet, her befuddled brain was still under the effects of her bedtime medicines and she soon drifted off to sleep, all thoughts of Carl's strange behaviour forgotten for the moment.

Carl turned on his bedside light and then reached up for his robe and made himself decent for checking on their children. He switched off Tilly's light and gave her head a few reassuring strokes. As he did so, he tried not to notice that his hands were shaking. Seeing that she was now settled he quickly left the room and switched on the landing light. From its illumination he could make out the sleeping forms of both his children as he quietly opened each of their doors in turn. He resisted the urge to enter and sit on their beds and listen to their gentle sleeping noises and draw peace from their serenity in slumber.

As he walked down the stairs he loitered long enough at the other landing and drew back the curtain to see if anyone was outside. The street was dimly lit in the new energy saving lighting that the Council had recently installed. There was no movement, nor were there shadows creeping about. Their car seemed okay. Satisfied, he made his way quicker down the stairs and swiftly went from room to room, almost on instinct, as if with a military squad doing standard operating room clearance procedures. He checked all possible hiding places and opened curtains and checked windows to see if there were any cracks from a thrown object. He could find nothing on the floors, no objects had dropped of their own accord. Perhaps he had imagined those bangs, or maybe some long forgotten memory had flooded his dreams. He shrugged and made his way to the kettle, a brew would rebalance him and he'd soon go back to bed, just as soon as his heart rate settled.

Annabelle came down the stairs, bleary-eyed, rubbing at her eyes as if to dislodge grit from them. She yawned as she pitter pattered to the kitchen table, the long ears of her rabbit shaped slippers jogged up and down with each footstep. 'Did I hear you shouting at mummy, daddy?' she asked as she hopped onto the kitchen chair and looked around the table for her favourite unicorn-shaped cereal.

Carl had both his hands wrapped around another cup, strong coffee this time. He hadn't bothered going back to sleep and instead had stayed awake trying to read his new book. Dark thoughts had clouded his concentration and instead, he'd sat here waiting for his family to awaken and for his hands to stop shaking. His heart had almost stopped its excited pounding. Whatever those noises were, they had troubled him.

'That was just me having a bad dream sweetheart. I think I ate too much cheese last night at your grandma's.' He smiled at her for reassurance. It sounded like she had not heard the noises either, just his daft shouting out.

The toilet system was flushed, its low wail spread through the walls like a tired banshee, and dissipated, and then Gordon walked in from the bathroom. 'I never heard a thing. What did I miss?' He reached over for a warmed croissant, his favourite almond one.

Several pieces flaked off and dropped onto the plate that his father had placed in front of him. Carl had given up trying to teach him table manners and just did his best to mop up the mess that followed his path. Though his mother soon found other bits and pieces to pick up. Sometimes they despaired when they entered his bedroom and soon about turned and walked away. So long as he was happy, that was all that mattered.

'Nothing, just me in my sleep. You two have a big breakfast, I'm taking you for a walk around the ruined castle, while your mum has a lie in.'

The children rolled their eyes at each other, they knew what one of their dad's walks entailed, a couple of hours away from the warmth of their bedrooms and their telly and computers. 'If only Daisy had bigger legs, we could take her with us,' spluttered Annabelle as half a piece of unicorn body fell from her mouth and into her cereal bowl. It hit the milk and slowly sunk below the surface, letting out a sugary orange trail, like the ripples of a passing water skier.

Carl reached over and tussled the hairs on both of their heads, 'Dress up warm, we are moving out in ten minutes.' He drained the last of his coffee, stood up, walked over to the kitchen cupboard, and reached in and took out several trail bars to feed his troops during their manoeuvres.

Lee made encouraging noises to Daisy, wanting her to quickly pass Simon's gate. He needn't have worried as her ears pricked up and she strained at the leash, bringing her owner with her as she tried to reach the source of the shouting.

'Daisy, Daisy!' shrieked Annabelle as she spotted her best friend as she walked up her path. She ran forward, knelt, and was rewarded with a facial wash from Daisy's licks which culminated in a rummage and snuffle in and around Annabelle's ears. The dog had nudged her pal's hat up and off her head and Carl had caught it in time.

'Good catch!' admired Lee. As he drew closer, he looked shocked to see sunken dark patches under Carl's eyes. 'Too early in the morning? You look rough.' He laughed, and asked Gordon, 'Has daddy been on the sherry last night!'

'I wish,' moaned Carl tersely. 'I got woken up at four in the morning. I thought I heard three loud bangs. I couldn't get back to sleep.'

Lee looked across to Simon's house and noticed that his driveway gates were locked and bolted shut, a huge padlock barred their opening by anyone but the keyholder. All the curtains in the house were unusually drawn tightly closed, 'Ah, four in the morning you say.'

'Yes, do you know something, or did you and Brodie hear it too? No-one else in the house heard it and I wondered whether it may have been my imagination.' He subconsciously scratched his head as if demonstrating his confusion.

'Guy and Finty did describe to me that they heard bangs for the last couple of Boxing Day mornings. Simon leaves home to travel down to Cornwall with Millie to stay with their daughter each New Year. He likes to drive when the roads are quiet, and no-one can get in his way. I'm guessing that was him securing his house perhaps?'

'What a racket he made if it was. Blimey, I'd be a bit more respectful to folks sleeping if that were me.'

Lee hesitated, thought for a moment, and decided to ask anyway. 'That's the first time you've heard such bangs from him?'

'Yes, it's been peaceful otherwise. I've never known such noises, well, not since my army days. It unsettled me for a bit. Though it seemed to come from the top of the house and behind.'

Lee looked up to Simon's roof, where he'd had two skylights installed during his loft conversion. Not for use as a light source in an additional bedroom, for no-one came to stay with him, but so that he could better see around the neighbourhood, front and back. He made use of this bird's eye view to watch the coming and going of various neighbours. He could often be seen leaning right out, craning his neck for a better view. Lee didn't have the heart to tell his friend what Guy and Finty went through. He hoped these noises were a one-off and tried to veer the subject away from the noises. 'You'll not need to worry, they won't come back until the second of January, they always do.' He hesitated to ask, then ploughed on with, 'Perhaps they dropped their suitcase, or something. No other noises?'

Carl looked at Lee thoughtfully and left an uncomfortable silence hanging over them, until finally deciding to not reveal that he thought he'd heard Millie cry out, perhaps in pain, through the adjoining bedroom walls. Maybe he needed to discuss this with Tilly first. Though he knew that these were thick walls. He'd gone through several drill bits trying to secure some shelving the other week. 'No. Normally I sleep like a baby, though sometimes, well, you know.'

Lee nodded, though no, he didn't know, and Carl didn't seem to want to explain any further. But he did look troubled, not just from lack of sleep, he just didn't seem to have any Christmas spirit left about him.

'Well, we won't keep you, poor Daisy will be getting cold. I'm taking these two for a brisk Boxing Day walk. It's a bit of a family tradition, whilst their mum has a lie-in. When they were babies, I'd take them to all sorts of places in their buggies. I just need to get out and about sometimes, you know, when the walls start to close in. It's lovely that they can walk by me now.'

Lee grinned, the two children didn't seem to think it was lovely and most probably wanted to stay indoors and munch through the sweets and chocolates that kind Father Christmas had left them.

'Thanks again for storing my presents in your shed, what a great surprise they were. I was rewarded with a couple of jackdaws feeding this morning. They look like the thugs of the neighbourhood with their dark, sunken, beady eyes.

Lee smiled, though he couldn't help thinking that Carl's sleep deprived darkened eyes compared easily to those birds.

Chapter Sixteen

Carl leaned back into the plush leather of his recliner and his legs rose and nestled on the built-in footrest. He sighed with contentment as he looked out of his study window and watched as a flock of sparrows flew in bouncing waves into his garden, like a squadron of Star Wars X-Wing fighters dodging laser-cannon fire from an Imperial Destroyer. They bobbed and weaved against invisible threats, their flashes of white sidebars giving away their position, and then rested on the roof of his large shed. They then took it in turns to fly swiftly to the bird-table for a treasured seed and then return with their treat. Some ate whilst in flight whilst others had the willpower to wait until they were back on their collective den. Others made for the hanging fat-ball holder where suet infused with nuts and seed delights awaited mining by their sharp little beaks. All the while they kept up their delighted chirping and churring sounds.

After several minutes they collectively rose and flew, all the while dipping and twisting, as they made their way into Lee and Brodie's garden. The starlings had been spotted and this chattering boisterous group had them spooked and on the run. They settled on the couple's lawn, for they didn't have any bird feeders, and were soon grubbing around.

The green-blue, almost grey, with black and mottled oily appearing plumage of the starlings manifested itself as a black cloud that didn't portent gloom, instead it brought excited clattering, like the heightening screams of playful children in the school yard. Their excitement rose as they dive-bombed the bird-table, scattering bird seed as they descended and squabbled amongst themselves for a prized spot. Their ill-mannered behaviour was in sharp contrast to the gentle patience of the previous visitors and extended to pecking each other for supremacy on the feeding station. From his chair, Carl could now see that many still sported their white spots of autumn plumage as they bobbed into the water of the bird-table and ruffled their feathers during their ablutions. Their harsh calls of 'tcheerr' belied their enjoyment of getting clean and gaining an easy full belly.

Carl spied a timid Blue Tit, a bird that he'd called a yellow tit for years, until Tilly put him right and reinforced her words and opinion with a gift of an RSPB handbook of British birds so that he could learn more about native visitors to his garden and beyond. Though he would always call them a yellow tit to his wife, now he could differentiate between a coal, crested, blue and great tit. He hoped one day to see a marsh and willow tit on his long walks.

This solitary Blue Tit sat patiently on the top of the barren rambling twig-like buddleia bush at the foot of the garden. Its short trill giving away its position as it sang out its alarm call. It made rapid head movements, like that of someone with a nervous tic, constantly looking around, on the alert for danger, much like Carl would have done on missions in far off places like Afghanistan. It stayed at its post, alert to the opportunity of a free feed, once all the big birds had gone. It hoped to find a neglected sunflower seed to help it through this cold day.

It would have to wait a while longer, because several jackdaws swooped in, landing on the apex roof of the bird-table, wings enfolding like an old Harrier jump jet as their claws appeared to bounce several times before they found their footing and worked out how to get their large frames between the openings of the bird-table to feast on the remaining seed.

A pair of collared doves cooed in disapproval from the nearby branches of a tree in the garden from the adjacent street that backed into Carl's rear fencing. They ruffled their feathers against the bitter late December morning, puffed out their plump chests and allowed their heads to sink, making their necks appear to fall away. They blinked a few times and then seemed to sit and stare at the bad behaviour of the squabbling starlings.

Not wanting to miss out in creating a soundscape to the neighbourhood a lonely woodpigeon, perched on top of Simon's chimney, gave a throaty 'coo, coo' that echoed between the surrounding buildings. It was soon drowned out by the shrieking of nearby seagulls that had flocked in from the harbour and cliffs by the lighthouse and castle remains in search of excess boiled potatoes that the man down the hill liked to put out for them, despite a previous ASBO from the Council for feeding what others had complained of as pests.

Carl watched as the starlings hungrily devoured his offerings, scattering seeds onto the grass in their haste. The plucky robin that had made his back garden his territory, boldly hopped along and swept up the seed, taking his fill without a care that larger species were above him. A cautious blackbird waited below the supposed safety of the conifers, the evergreens offering him scarce shielding from the feral cats that had the freedom to roam the village and anyone's garden.

As soon as the jackdaws came into land, their huge wingspans frightened off the starlings who gave one last chitter-chatter in complaint and rose like a church congregation about to sing a hymn, and flew off, towards the nursing home to the left and down the street of Carl's backyard. He watched with delight at their clever formation, like a swiftly moving black cloud in the dull winter day. He smiled at his gentle hobby, lost in a moment of mindfulness.

He was not aware that Tilly had quietly opened his study door and was now standing in the doorway, glad to see her husband looking so happy. She had been worried about him since his nightmare several nights ago. He had none since, and his dark mood had only lasted a day. He'd subsequently slept like a baby and was more joyful with each passing day. He'd been back on form by New Year's Night, Hogmanay as they called it here. He'd made a special Black Bun cake and their bleary-eyed children had gone with them to their grandparents to first foot them with slices of it, and then to Felicity and Geoff's party which lasted well into the morning of New Year's Day.

Once home, Tilly and the children went straight to bed for a long sleep, whilst Carl snatched a few hours and then was up with the larks, making from scratch, the traditional steak pie, and roast potatoes dinner for all the family. All had said that his pastry was exceptional.

Felicity and Geoff could only have had a few hours of sleep but were on fine form when they came over to indulge in Carl's cooking along with Shona and Lewis. Carl had invited Dotty, Lee, and Brodie along with guest of honour Daisy. They'd all gotten along splendidly, especially Dotty and Shona, and then the more able of the group had a sing-along and dance to Annabelle's favourite songs, mostly Disney ones.

A conversation with a tipsy Lee had made Tilly think and she had reflected upon what he had said.

'It's great to see Carl looking so much better,' he slurred. 'He looked ever so ill after Simon had started up with you both.'

'Whatever do you mean?' she had casually enquired as she topped up his white wine.

'The bangs. That's why Guy and Finty left, didn't you know?'

Aghast, Dotty had broken up her conversation with Shona, excused herself, and went over to Lee and placed her hand over his glass, almost protectively. 'I think that this young man has had quite enough for one night.'

Tilly knew that she had looked shocked, it had momentarily puzzled her and then had embarrassed her. She had let the comment go but had now regretted it. She made up her mind to ask her friends what they had meant and were covering up.

The next afternoon the children skipped into the lounge, Annabelle, though dainty on her feet, was juggling a large pink topped birthday cake with, what seemed to her, hundreds of lit candles that illuminated the joy in her face. Gordon was laden with several wrapped presents. Their mother, a wide grin on her face, followed obediently behind and started the chorus of 'Happy Birthday!' to which the children happily, and loudly, sang.

Carl sat in his armchair, a feigned look of surprise on his face. He had heard the giggling and sniggering in the kitchen, followed by the customary mini yelps of pain as Tilly stuffed as many candles onto the homemade cake as possible. Her difficulty was always in trying to light them, without getting burnt. He'd been banned from the kitchen all day and knew that a birthday tea was on the cards. Homemade sandwiches and a variety of Tunnock's teacakes, caramel wafers, logs, and snowballs would knock out his high-protein diet for today. He didn't care, he'd forgo training and get high on sugar. He'd sneak out later and go for a stroll around the harbour and see if the heron was roosting.

'Blow out the candles dad,' ordered Gordon as soon as their rendition, at the top of their voices, of the happy birthday song had ended. He was eager for his father to open the presents he still held.

Carl leant forward, made a big show of puffing out his chest, inflating his cheeks and let out an almighty blow which extinguished all the candles.

The children sniggered, looked at each other and then at the unicorn-shaped cake, awaiting another surprise. Annabelle tipped it towards her father's face, careful, as briefed by her mother, to not let it get too close.

Carl jumped back in astonishment as several of the candles, two by the unicorn's eyes, and one by its horn, magically relit of their own accord.

The youngsters and his wife burst out laughing and soon the cake was shaking, as if the unicorn were enchantingly shaking itself free for a gallop.

'Oh, you guys!' exclaimed Carl as he clapped his hands, applauding his family for getting one over on him. He couldn't wait to see what larks Felicity would be getting up to when she popped in later with his card and gift.

'Mummy found them on the internet, they have all sorts of jokes,' boasted Gordon.

Carl nodded thoughtfully, 'So I can expect more japes in the future?'

Annabelle looked to Gordon and then to her mum, all three nodded in agreement.

'Oh well, that'll be something to look forward to,' their father muttered resignedly, eying up the cake. He blew out the joke candles and once again there was sniggering as they magically relit. 'Unicorns really are magical.'

Annabelle nodded vigorously and her mother gently took the cake from her and put it on the table. She disappeared for a moment and came back with a tray loaded with all sorts of goodies, plates, cutlery, and a big knife to cut the cake. She'd put some in a tub to take to Shona and Lewis later in the evening. She proceeded to cut the home-bake into equal and exact portions. Carl looked on, used to his wife's precision in most matters. He'd got used to her constant need for tidiness and exactness and accepted that whilst she was doing it, she wasn't cutting or harming herself. He looked around him and knew himself to be blessed.

'I really don't think it's right, not in front of the children,' cautioned Geoff as he took a step back from the kitchen table.

Felicity laughed, 'You don't know Tilly as well as I do, she's going to be in hysterics. That's the whole point, Carl will open it in front of the kids, will have to quickly hide it, and then have to explain to the children what it is and why they can't see it.'

Geoff shook his head at the bright red action figure before him. Its hands were splayed apart, proudly in the air and its legs, stood firmly on the kitchen table, leant back so that its midriff poked out and displayed a bright red, bulbous erection. Underneath this phallus was a groove for opening bottles. 'Does he even drink beer?'

'Course he does, he's an old squaddie, he doesn't drink much at home, but when he and his pals gather, I think to remember their fallen, they get paralytic. Poor Tilly gets to spend the evening with their wives and girlfriends, making polite chit-chat because they don't know each other and by the time another year passes, they have new partners. This big tool will go down a storm with his mates. I bet he'll proudly have it in his man cave, he'll start the night by showing them around, with beer in hand, before going for a pub crawl. It's about the only time he gets blind drunk. He won't admit it to us, but I think he feels guilty for coming home, when some didn't.'

Geoff nodded, took a step towards the cheeky gift, picked it up, balanced it in his hands as if weighing it, and said, 'Best we get it wrapped then.'

Carl patted his belly in exaggerated movements, 'That was the best birthday tea ever!' he exclaimed. 'The cake was magnificent.' He picked up his bird boxes, three of varying sizes. 'I'll hang these up tomorrow, along my shed.'

'Your man cave,' interrupted Gordon.

'Yes, he big man, with big muscles,' aped Tilly to the merriment of their children.

Gordon and Annabelle went over to their father and placed their hands around their dad's arms. Carl obliged by flexing them, and as they bulged, their small hands slid off. He gathered them up and gave them a cuddle and then broke off the embrace with a kiss to each of their foreheads.

Gordon wiped his away immediately whilst Annabelle looked up to her dad and said, 'The unicorn cake was my idea.' She beamed, waiting for praise. She was gladdened to find it forthcoming.

'It was ever so pretty, almost a shame to eat it. Let's do the dishes for mum, give her a rest after your busy day preparing this feast.'

'Don't even think about it. You rest, it's your special day. You did enough with the lovely New Year meal you cooked yesterday. You sit down and watch one of your DVDs, perhaps the one your dad got you for Christmas.'

Carl looked at his empty plate. As usual he had overeaten, he couldn't resist a birthday feast. 'I thought I'd pop down to the harbour. A heron likes to settle on the rocks by the wall, waiting for the tide and the fish that follow the boats in. Who wants to join me?'

The children stepped back and then chirped up with, 'We'll help mummy tidy up.' Their little legs were still tired from the castle walk.

'Okay, just lonely old me then. I'll only be about thirty minutes, I'll be home before Felicity and Geoff come over, I think she was working today. Though Geoff had the usual extra bank holiday that Scotland gets after the New Year celebrations. I wish us Scots had that when I was in the army.' He leaned forward and took another Tunnock's teacake from the table, 'Just to keep me going,' he explained. He munched down as he left the room and donned his jacket from the hallway rack.

Simon, despite the evening darkness of winter glooming his driveway, was buffing up his car, scrubbing furiously at some imaginary dirt that had defied his cleaning. He'd left Millie to unpack and put a wash on, whilst he lavished loving attention to the vehicle that to the neighbourhood, he seemed to love far more than his wife. The large outside light had given enough illumination to allow him to jet wash his car almost the minute he had returned from Devon. It now let off a radiant shine, captured brilliantly by the full moon that beamed down, almost as if proud of the polish too.

Carl, sauntering past, gave a cheery, 'Evening,' and carried on his way. He failed to hear the evil mutterings emanating from his neighbour, nor the howking drawing in of phlegm and the spitting out aimed at his direction. Further below the next road, he passed the war memorial. He read several of the names and mentally thanked them for their service and sacrifice.

Chapter Seventeen

BANG, BANG, BANG.

Carl sat bolt upright in his bed, instantly on the defensive, 'INCOMING!' he shouted to Tilly as he pushed hard on her shoulder, forcing her awake. 'GET YOUR HELMETS ON,' he commanded to his imaginary troops. He leapt from his bed and began rummaging around the room, searching for unreal personal protective equipment.

Tilly once more sought the safety of the headboard which bounced gently back against the adjoining wall with their neighbour. 'What's happening?' she slurred, as she slowly woke up from her drug-induced sleep. She rubbed her eyes and reached once more for her bedside light; these movements were almost becoming routine. Though the fear that coursed adrenaline through her and fought against her prescription medicines was not. She recoiled as she suddenly became aware of what Carl was doing, he was reliving events from his past. She tried to remember what she had been taught, now that the nightmares that she'd been forewarned about, were playing out in front of her. She looked in shock as Carl actioned putting on his helmet, cradling a rifle and clicking on an imaginary loaded magazine. He then immediately pointed it at her.

'WAKE UP!' she screamed. She dived out of bed, hit the main bedroom light and showered Carl with illumination, hoping that he'd snap out of his nightmare. She saw him jump onto the bed, aim his pretend weapon at where she was, and fire.

Tilly reeled in shock, she looked about her, picked up a cushion from the chair, and threw it at her husband. 'WAKE UP!' she repeated.

Carl, momentarily shocked at the intrusion, looked about him, as if seeing his wife for the first time. He looked about him, wondering why his wife was appearing to him during a battle. It was as if she was here. Was his number up, he wondered, had he bought it.

'WAKE UP DARLING,' she insisted. 'I'm here, you are at home. You are safe. Look around you.'

Carl, always tuned into listening to his wife, looked about him, he looked down and saw his bare hands. He felt to his chest and then his head. He had no clothing or protective gear on. He saw his nudity; he saw that he was standing on his bed. He breathed, long and hard. Two deep, slow breaths, like his special forces training mantra dictated. 'Breathe, breathe, recalibrate and deliver,' he said aloud, instinctively. 'Oh,' was all that he could deliver.

Tilly stepped forward, from behind the safety of the chair. She reached up towards him and took his hand and gently guided him off the bed and into an embrace. She made soothing noises, as if nursing a distressed baby, and rubbed up and down his shoulder and back. Gentle, warming, reassuringly soft and slow movements. 'You are safe and at home. I love you.'

Carl, unexpectedly near to tears, cried out, 'And I love you too. Sorry. I hope I didn't frighten you?'

'No, but it's not the anniversary, is it? Have I forgotten?' She was mentally chiding herself.

Carl vehemently shook his head, 'No, not for a couple of weeks, this was something else, somewhere else. I can't begin to tell you what I had to do, what happened to us, we were…' He faltered, lost for words, unable to explain the carnage he had unleashed on an enemy. How could he describe the horrors he was capable of inflicting at such close range?

Tilly made more soothing noises, 'Don't worry, you don't have to tell me everything, just know that you are safe. What brought this on, too much sugar?' she innocently asked, feeling immediately guilty that she may have been responsible for what she knew to be fresh night terrors.

'No, not at all. I heard them again. Three louds bangs, coming from behind us,' he pointed to their headboard. 'Did you hear them this time?'

'No, I'm afraid not. You know that I'm dead to the world after taking my drugs.' She yawned as if to reinforce her explanation.

'Oh,' was all that a crestfallen Carl could say. He wondered if they were in his imagination. He knew that he couldn't control his dreams, his terrors. But they usually only came on the night that Gavin died, so many years ago it seemed to him, though always so fresh in his thoughts.

There was a timid knock on the door. 'Is daddy alright?' whispered Annabelle.

'Yes, just a bad dream,' replied Tilly whilst whipping a blanket around Carl to keep his modesty. She then opened their bedroom door and squeezed out of the narrowest gap that she could allow for her movement whilst preventing her daughter looking in whilst Carl composed himself. 'He's fine sweetie, sometimes daddy gets bad dreams, like you do.'

'Does his involve big green monsters chasing him too?' she innocently asked.

'Not quite, but something similar.' She took her daughter's hands and walked her back to her bed, festooned with a unicorn duvet and her cherished cuddly toys.

Annabelle allowed herself to be led back to bed, though she gave one last look into the narrow gap of her parent's room. She could make out their dishevelled bed but couldn't see daddy. As she climbed into bed, she reached for her favourite cuddly toy, a white fluffy West Highland Terrier that looked just like Daisy. 'Give her to daddy, she'll chase away his nightmares and protect him whilst he sleeps.'

With a tear in her eye, Tilly took the toy, leant down, and kissed her daughter goodnight. She turned on her bedside lamp and turned it onto the timer mode. It would cleverly darken every few minutes and lull Annabelle back to her unicorn dreams. She wished that something similar would work for Carl.

Tilly could smell the delightful aroma of freshly baked biscuits, their sweet fragrance of lavender infused shortbread wafted up the stairs and stirred her in her sleep. She turned over to find a mug of tea and a side plate with several round homemade biscuits sitting on her bedside cabinet. She sat up, took a sip of tea, found it near boiling and too hot to drink, and then sat it back down. She picked up a biscuit, surprised to find it still warm, and took a bite. It gave a satisfying crunch in her mouth and soon she was in sugary heaven. She spied the note that was anchored under the biscuits. It read, 'Sorry about last night. The walls were closing in, so I've taken the children down to the harbour, love Carl.' She smiled. She knew that he'd be looking for the elusive heron.

The sun popped up, brightening the sky in iridescent yellows and oranges as it competed with the night sky, appeared to battle, and then won. The lamp-posts gave up their duty and allowed the natural light to safeguard its citizens. Annabelle, Gordon, and Carl walked quietly down to the harbour, bypassing the old disused harbour wall for favour of the recently built larger inlet with its walled protection against the sea's effort to claim land.

The row of deep-brown painted fisherman's huts paraded in a neat line like a row of guardsman. Their doors were shut and padlocked, though rows of neat creels and discarded rope revealed their purpose. On the grassed area, just before the block and tackle winches, wintered fishing boats nestled patiently on blocks of wood, awaiting loving cleaning and varnishing against the elements.

The trio made their way to the open-ended hut, by the shallow end of the harbour, near to the shoreline. Its tiled roof offered shelter from the rain, whilst affording a fine view. 'Okay troops, we are closing in,' warned their father. 'Let's do one final check.'

The children jumped up and down a few times, an old army trick before deployment, to check if any equipment would rattle and give away a position to the enemy. There was no clatter or jangle. Carl smiled; he'd taught them well. 'Okay, let's make for the seats and our heron should be by the shoreline, sitting patiently on the rocks. He dangled a flask and several plastic mugs. 'And then we'll have the best hot chocolate you've ever tasted.'

'Did you remember them daddy?' questioned Annabelle in a whisper.

Carl dived into his deep pocket of his jacket and pulled out the squirty cream can and then juggled about and produced a small container of sprinkles and another with mini marshmallows. He smiled as he carefully balanced everything for his daughter to inspect.

Her eyes widened, 'Best hot chocolate ever!' she declared.

Gordon patted his pocket for reassurance that the biscuit tub was still there.

They continued their silent march and were soon sat under the wooden and slate shelter, admiring the sunrise and the vista before them.

The sun glided silently upwards and twinkled onto the sea water within the harbour, making it shimmer and sparkle as if a shoal of fish were merrily swimming by. The water lapped upon the shoreline, wetting the sand and pebbles. The granite rocks at the sides glittered in the new sunshine and dried out the overnight moisture. Upon it sat the heron that Carl had been monitoring for the last few weeks. His military training had given him the skills required of a watcher, patience, and a keen eye for seeking routine and patterns. He knew that this bird liked to fish here.

'It looks funny, with its long legs and squat body,' whispered Annabelle.

'It looks like it is getting ready to have a poo!' quipped Gordon.

Carl grinned, he did like bringing them to watch wildlife and get their innocent perspective.

Suddenly its neck rose from its squat and leaned out far into the sea. It dived into its depths and flitted out its stiletto blade-like bill and plucked up a fish. Before the trio could say a word, it swallowed it whole.

'Wow!' marvelled Gordon. 'Did you see how quick it was? Wow!'

A diesel engine spluttered in the near distance and got louder as it made its way through the narrow mouth of the harbour. A yellow oilskin-clad fisherman was stood in the wheelhouse guiding his prized boat and its valuable cargo of fresh lobster to the quayside. It gently nudged the wall with a soft bounce thanks to the surrounding safety of carefully roped tyres. He expertly threw a line onto a nearby metal cast anchor point and tethered away.

This noise alerted the heron and with a shrieking 'kaark' call it spread wide its magnificent wings which seemed to stretch the width of the rocks and gracefully rose into the air, it banked towards the admiring group and with several flaps of its wings, was soon on its way to the rocks of the outlet of the nearby power station. In this warmer water it would find more fish to feast on.

'It's like one of those pterodactyls from that dinosaur film,' marvelled Gordon.

Carl grinned and nodded as the bluey black undercarriage of the bird soared overhead, momentarily shadowed the trio, and was lost to the skies. He reached for the flask and mugs and was soon busy preparing their breakfast feast.

Annabelle gave a laugh and pointed to the harbour water, just to the side of the fishing boat. A head with large whiskers and the cutest, deploring eyes was bobbing up and down to the rhythm of the gently moving tide. A seal was waiting patiently for its breakfast, the discarded heads, and guts from the nets of another fishing boat. Annabelle knew that she'd be faring better and would have a much more appetising start to the day.

'You are up early love,' remarked Carl as he entered the kitchen and saw his wife sat having breakfast. He began pulling off his gloves and hat.

'Yes, I've something I want to do, besides it's ten thirty and I figure that it is time for me to stop lazing about in bed. I'm even thinking that perhaps it is time for me to reduce some of my medicines.' Tilly looked at Carl, to judge his reaction. He was always worried that she would have another mental health relapse.

'Do you think that is wise?' he simply offered.

'Look down,' was all she said.

Carl did as he was bidden, 'Wow!' Her spoon, with a tell-tale circle of milk in its centre was sat crooked by her empty cereal bowl and fallen bran flakes were scattered on the table. 'How long have you sat there?'

'Just ten minutes. I've been having a good think during that time.'

'And no intrusive thoughts, no deep need to rush for the cleaning cloth, or to straighten and clean the spoon?'

'Nope. And I haven't felt the desire to cut myself since we moved up here. And I'm sleeping like a baby.'

'I'm glad one of is,' muttered Carl.

'Yes, I've been thinking about that too. How about I make an appointment with the doctor, for both of us? Then we can chat about reducing my drugs and perhaps what you need to see you better.'

'Okay, but see me better? I'm fighting fit.'

'No, you are not. You've been having nightmares, haven't you? It's not normal to be searching for a weapon and helmet in the middle of the night.'

'I haven't, don't be daft,' he denied vehemently.

'Yes, you have. Nightmares, and I bet other things?'

'I don't know what you mean.'

Tilly sighed, the speaker at the partners group had warned them that there would be denial. The first battle with Post Traumatic Stress Disorder was getting the veteran to acknowledge that they may have it. The second would be getting them to a health care professional, preferably to their GP initially. 'Gavin,' she simply stated.

Carl turned his back to her, an overwhelming rush of emotion threatening to engulf him. He felt the need to cry and was confused, he never cried. He dabbed at his eyes with his woollen gloves and was saved from having to face the truth when his children, having taken off their coats and shoes in the lobby, came bursting into the kitchen, eager to see their mother.

'Best hot chocolate ever!' sang Annabelle.

'And we saw a heron. It was massive,' boasted Gordon as he reached out as far as he could with his arms. 'It was this big.'

Tilly looked to Carl with a stare that said, 'This conversation isn't over.' She smiled at her children. 'I wish that I could have seen it. I shall have to get up early in the mornings from now on and join you in your walks.'

Their children nodded vigorously. 'Could you take me to school one day mummy?' beseeched Annabelle, 'That's what all the other mums do.'

Tilly patted her lap and Anabelle dutifully climbed up and sat across it and looked up to her mother with pleading eyes. 'Of course, honey. I'll make an appointment for daddy and me to see the doctor and while we are there, we shall see about cutting back some of my tablets. Especially those that make me so drowsy in the mornings, how does that sound?' Though she was saying the question to her daughter, she was really directing it at Carl.

He nodded reluctantly in agreement, though he planned to put her right about her thoughts about him. Besides, it would be good to have her less dopey. Especially at bedtime. He felt a stirring in his loins as he thought this and a smile appeared on his face and he turned back to face his wife, emotions firmly in check.

Tilly mistook this for agreement to her terms of the health centre visit and said, 'That's settled then. Now tell me about this hot chocolate, was it as good as mine?'

Annabelle looked shyly at her mum and gave a slight nod of her head, 'Daddy puts sprinkles and marshmallows in mine.'

'Oh, he does, does he! Well, let me put my thinking cap on and see how I can better daddy!'

Gordon produced a small tub and placed it on the kitchen table. Never one to miss an opportunity for a better treat, declared, 'And special biscuits.'

'Okay, it looks like mummy is going to have to look up some recipes on the internet. Are there more of those lovely biscuits stored somewhere else?'

'In the big tub by the kettle,' pointed Gordon helpfully. 'Do you want to try one?'

'Yes, I'll have some more please, daddy took some upstairs for me before you went out. But put several into your tub for me please, I've someone I want to share them with. You two go off and play now, daddy will be downstairs if you need him.'

The children obediently left the kitchen and raced each other up the stairs. Carl looked sheepishly at his wife. 'Yes, I know it's the right decision for you to cut back on taking all those medicines, but I worry that you…'

'May try again,' interrupted Tilly.

'Well, yes, you do have form.'

'I know, but that was when we lived by my parents and brother. They are well off the scene now. I'll never have them in my life again and I can't stay doped up all my life. The new doctor we have here is brilliant, she has a genuine interest in mental health and when I chat to her, she really listens. She isn't sat by a computer typing away whilst you try and talk. She's already referred me to a new psychiatrist, to monitor and advise about my drugs. I won't go back to that dark place ever again. You have my word.'

Carl reluctantly nodded his agreement, happy that she'd been deflected from talking about Gavin.

'Okay, I'll phone for two appointments later. But first, I want to share your biscuits with a friend and get some advice. Look after our two, will you, I'll only be an hour at the most.'

The doorbell chimed its uplifting lilt and echoed through the hallway and pervaded into Dotty's lounge. She looked up from her cross stitch, a West Highland Terrier playing ball, a gift for her pals across the road, looked at the time, and tutted. She was about to have her elevenses. She hoped that she could quickly deal with whoever it was, perhaps it was that new postie, the young lady who always wore shorts, even on the coldest winter's day, she thought. She carefully put down her needlework and made for the front door, smoothing down her dress as she went. She opened her door and was surprised, but delighted, to see Tilly on her doorstep. She had turned back after a quick glance across the road, onto Simon's roof.

'I come bearing gifts,' declared Tilly, carefully moving the tub from side to side to demonstrate that it contained treats.

'Ah, I've been expecting you, come away in and I'll put the kettle on.'

Millie reached up to the pane of glass and rubbed as furiously as she could, despite the pain in her shoulder.

'Hurry up woman,' barked Simon from his armchair as he read the sporting section of his morning paper. His chair was positioned near to the window so that he could watch the coming and going of his neighbours. 'I don't like the blinds being pulled to one side like that. Everyone gawks in as they are passing. And make sure to get the corners this time.'

Millie winced with pain as she polished away invisible marks, she'd only cleaned these three days ago. He doesn't like them open because folk can see what he is up to. If only they were open all the time, then he wouldn't hurt me in this room, she wished.

'What's that strumpet next door carrying to Dotty, a small tub of something. Jesus, I don't believe the nerve of her,' ranted Simon as he threw down his paper. 'She's having a good nosey at us.' He rose from his chair, making to the window, to give her his middle finger.

He pushed Millie out of the way with a nudge of his hip. She stumbled aside, managing, just, to prevent herself from falling over. She dropped her cleaning cloth and spray bottle.

'Stupid woman. Pick those up,' he commanded as he stared across the road. 'She's gone now. Into Dotty's house, what are they going to be saying about me?' He stormed out of the room, slamming the door shut behind him, leaving a shaking Millie alone.

BANG.

Carl looked up, towards the lounge wall that he shared with his neighbour, and then to the ceiling. His heart was beating so rapidly that he thought that his chest would burst open, like in the film Alien. Though his monster was kept firmly inside, he just wasn't aware of it, just yet. He stood up, all thoughts of relaxing in front of the telly with his favourite comedy DVD forgotten. He strode purposefully to the doorway, walked to the foot of the steps, and shouted up, 'You two keep the noise down.' I'll be glad when they go back to school, he thought. He returned to his comfortable armchair and picked up the control. It dropped onto the floor, bounced, and flew under his recliner. He leant forward, reached for it, and as he fumbled about and finally grabbed it, he could only then see how shaky his hands were.

'It's about what Lee said the other day,' stated Tilly as she cradled a cup of tea at Dotty's table.

'I thought it might be, about why Guy and Finty moved away?'

'Well, yes, you both looked shocked, as if Lee had given away a big secret. We've often wondered, Carl and I, about why the house was so cheap and how our low offer was so quickly accepted. We thought that perhaps there was a structural fault that the surveyor had missed, but that the previous owners knew about. It did seem strange that they didn't show us around the house. Though we believed the story that they were fed up driving to and from Aberdeen. So, can you please tell me why they really moved. I promise not to be upset with you,' implored Tilly. 'I think I know, but I'd like to hear it from you.'

'We didn't know you then and didn't think that it was our place to say anything. We thought he'd be different. We know what a coward he is and thought that your Carl was a big lad. Well he is a big lad, we thought Simon would be different around him. Guy was already a nervy type and always did what Simon wanted, to keep the peace, but the fire was the last straw.'

'Fire!' exclaimed Tilly, 'In the house?'

'No, in the back garden.'

'Ah, that would explain the black marks on the patio which I can't rub off, even with all the rain we've had recently. Was it a barbeque that got out of control?'

'No, it was his bird aviary. He kept the most beautiful white doves. I used to love seeing them fly around the area. He'd only let the poor things out for five minutes mind you. He tried to keep the peace.'

'Did a heater catch fire?' asked Tilly innocently.

'We've no proof mind, but no, he didn't use a heater because the shed attached to the aviary, where they roosted, was warm enough for them. No, everyone thinks that Simon set fire to the shed deliberately. You've only a short wall there and it would have been easy enough to pour petrol across, light it and scamper. That's just what a coward that man is. He's known in the neighbourhood for being sly and devious.'

Tilly looked aghast, 'Those poor birds, how awful, to die like that.'

'Guy managed to get them out in time. He rushed out of his back door, well, your back door now. He could see it through your kitchen window and then through the study windows. He never kept a blind there. When they had the extension built, it was part of the criteria to the planners that he could still see the back garden from the kitchen sink. He ran out as soon as he saw the smoke and flames and opened the sputnik trap. It's a side cage-like area which he used to open with a flap to allow the birds to fly out. Then he'd close it and they would pop through a special one-way system grill on the top. They couldn't fly back out you see once they hopped down. When the fire broke out, they were all cowering there you see.'

Tilly nodded, picturing the poor birds frightened into a corner. She put down her cup and saucer, her hands reached for her face, ready to dry tears that she knew would be coming.

'Guy had burns to his hands, they took months to heal. Finty had to take him to the hospital so many times for various treatments. He's been left scarred. Not just physically, but mentally too. He had a bit of a breakdown you see.' She smiled compassionately, almost motherly, and nodded to Tilly's covered arms, 'I think that perhaps you have some understanding of that?'

Tilly tried to pull down her sleeves further than the material would allow. The tears came now, a steady flow.

Dotty reached across and patted her friend's hands and then pushed across a box of tissues. 'I think your story will keep for another day, when you are ready, I make a good listener and a kind friend. And that's what you and your lovely family are, and I hope still will be. If only we had known you before, we would have advised you not to buy. But we didn't know you. I hope you can forgive me?'

Tilly nodded, not trusting her voice to declare her clemency. She wiped her eyes and blew her nose.

'You are kind. When you reach my age, you find that friendships are few and far between. Some of my friends have passed over,' she looked up to her wall and to a framed photo of her Eric, sat on his old BSA motorbike, smiling up at her. 'And of course, there is my Eric, now there was a right good husband, unlike…'

'Simon?' interrupted a now composed Tilly. 'He hits her, doesn't he?'

Dotty sighed. 'There are just some things you can't do anything about. He's known throughout the village for it, and for worse. He's a nasty drunk, but clever with it. He never hits her in public, it's always behind closed doors. The police gave up years ago, she just won't report him and go to court. So, she puts up with, well, with that and other things.'

'I hear her at night. I hear his grunting and her crying out for a long time afterwards. My tablets make me sleep, but I drift off worrying about her. It doesn't seem right.'

'No, and it isn't, but she won't leave him, she can't leave him. She has no money; Simon sees to that. Her parents are long dead, and her brother and sister are in a nursing home now, he had a bad stroke and she a poor heart. But when they were well, they begged her to leave him and stay with them instead. But she believed their children would grow up better with a father. But her son is just like Simon, the apple doesn't fall far from the tree.'

'You don't mean?'

'Yes, I'm afraid so, you watch just how timid Sienna is around Peter. A woman can always tell, don't you think?'

Tilly nodded, 'When Carl was in the army, we lived in married quarters, and we wives and partners always knew when one of the soldiers was being heavy-handed. It's so sad, Millie is such a sweet old lady.'

'She is, and he works her like a dog. She is in such pain, yet he has her waiting on him hand and foot, it's not just the hitting that hurts her. He just doesn't seem to care.'

'I had a run in with him a few weeks ago, he really scared me.'

'Yes, he likes to throw his weight around women. He might claim to have been great pals with my Eric, but my husband didn't like him. He'd have conversations with Millie whenever he could, to encourage her to live with us, their kids as well. He realised what Simon was doing and even had it out with him one day. I thought my Eric was going to thump him. I saw your fella stand up for you. Good on him, I hope he gave Simon what for?'

Tilly laughed, 'I saw from the lounge window, I thought Simon was going to wet himself.' The two women laughed; Tilly's tears were now forgotten.

Dotty patted her pal's hands, 'You are alright, you know. I'm blessed to have you as a pal. Now, what's in your tub?'

Tilly reached for her forgotten treats, 'I can't claim credit for them, it was our Carl who baked them.' She peeled back the lid and the lightly golden, freshly baked biscuits let off a delicious sweet lavender aroma that spread out around the room like angel's wings.

'A hunk, and a cook, you are a lucky girl! He's a keeper!' joked Dotty as she stood up and walked to a cabinet and took out two china plates.

Tilly nodded in agreement as she proffered the treats to share with her pal.

Carl paced the lounge. His heart was beating like the clappers and he just couldn't sit still. He eyed his armchair like it was an opponent in a boxing ring and walked warily around it several times. He gave up and went to the television and turned it off.

BANG, BANG, BANG.

He jumped and ran to the door, flew through it, and bounded up the stairs. He flung open Gordon's door and then did the same with Annabelle's and stood between their doorways and shouted, 'Who's making all that noise?'

Silence threatened to deafen him, and he could feel his heartbeat quickening, almost overpowering him as it thudded away. He suddenly felt hot, despite the coldness of the winter's day, and stripped off his jumper.

No-one came out of their respective rooms, so he popped his head in Gordon's room first and was met with his back to him. His son was oblivious to his father standing there, he was wearing his headphones and talking to his pals in an online racing car game. He leant to and fro in his chair, steering clear of hazardous obstacles such as large flaming oil drums, all the while chuckling away.

Carl walked out and leant into Annabelle's room, she was laid back in her bed, serving tea to her favourite dolls.

'Hello daddy, you are just in time for lunch. We are having Earl Grey today, want some?'

Carl, aware that his shoulders were hunched up, let out a breath and relaxed his stance, he looked around and couldn't see anything that may have dropped, his daughter always kept her room tidy, a habit she'd probably picked up from her mother. He smiled and his anger quickly dissipated at the innocence playing out in front of him. He walked over and ruffled her hair, 'Yes please sweetheart, I'll have mine like Jean-Luc Picard.'

'Eh?' she looked up in puzzlement.

'Oh, dear sweetie, I have not educated you and your brother well, have I? I'll have to dig out my Star Trek DVDs. No milk and no sugar please darling?'

Annabelle took up her teapot and poured out an imaginary cup of tea and handed it to her father.

He graciously took it, thankful that there was no liquid in the cup, for his hands were shaking again, and he wondered if the noises were also in his imagination.

'Have you heard any other noises,' asked Dotty tentatively. She scrutinised her pal's face, hoping that history was not repeating itself.

'No, not me, you see I take strong medicines just before bedtime and I'm usually fast asleep within minutes and knocked out for nine hours.'

'But?' proffered Dotty.

Tilly bit her lip whilst she pondered about sharing Carl's odd behaviour. She decided to limit what she said, 'Carl, he's always been a light sleeper, he's had to be, you know, with being in the army. He's been hearing a serious of bangs in the middle of the night.'

'Three, in a row. Quick and really loud,' stated Dotty, nodding her head like a wise old owl.

'Yes, Carl thought they came from the children's bedrooms. He's convinced the noises seem to echo around our house and aren't coming from outside. He's checked. Nothing has dropped, nothing catches in the wind and no-one is going in and out of their cars. It's a mystery.'

'I'm afraid that I can solve it for you Tilly, come away upstairs with me, you'll see better.' Dotty stood up and left the room.

A puzzled Tilly dutifully followed her from the kitchen and up a flight of stairs. With each step she looked up and smiled at the framed photos of Dotty's husband and their children taken at various celebrations such as their respective weddings, their christenings, and a double graduation from Aberdeen University. She was led into Dotty's front bedroom, about the same size as the one Tilly shared with Carl. She saw further photos of Eric on a bedside cabinet and along the walls. He had truly been loved and was missed. 'He was a handsome man, your husband.'

Dotty smiled, 'Yes, I was incredibly lucky, he treated me like a Princess and I always felt loved. Unlike my poor friend Millie.' She pointed across the road. 'Now don't stand too near the window, you don't want to be seen by Simon, he hates people watching him. Which is a bit ironic really because he likes to watch folk.'

'I've seen him. Especially when he reverses his car to the side of his house. He pretends to be polishing his car with an old chamois leather and all the while he is watching the twenty-year-old girl around the corner. It gives me the creeps, so goodness knows what it does to her. All that constant rubbing on the same spot, it's almost sexual, isn't it?'

'You've spotted that too. Yes, it's ever so sad. Bella is her name, last year she lost her brother Paul in a road traffic accident and then about a week later, her mum and dad simply vanished off the face of the earth. The local gossips say that they took their lives together as they couldn't face life without their son. But they were caring people, they were former army people too, nurses, I think. But they just wouldn't have left Bella all alone. She's got enough to cope with and doesn't need Simon perving over her. I don't think she notices though; her boyfriend takes her everywhere and he is with her constantly. He moved in to look after her, she became ever so thin and withdrawn. Like a stick she became, and now she hardly speaks to anyone. She refuses to move in with her boyfriend's parents. She sits at the window staring for hours, hoping that her parents will return one day, poor lass.'

'Oh my, how awful for her. I can see her garden from Annabelle's bedroom window, it does look a bit neglected. The poor girl, I'll try and say hello one day, if I can catch her eye.'

Dotty nodded, 'Bless you. Now stand here, but don't move the net curtain. Now look across to your roof and then Simon's. What can you see that is different?'

Tilly obliged and then declared, 'He has one of those Velux windows on his roof, the type that opens both ways, like a skylight.'

'He has one on the back roof too. He likes to stand and watch, a bird eye's lookout almost. Like I say, he likes to watch. But that's not all, he used them to make Guy and Finty leave home, they upped and sold the house to you. No-one who knew the area well would buy the house. They heard the rumours about Simon, but I'm guessing you didn't.'

'No, Carl's family live in another part of Aberdeenshire, about fifteen minutes drive away. The same with his sister.' A lightbulb moment flashed with Tilly. 'Do you mean that he is opening and then slamming those windows, several times in the middle of the night?' she asked incredulously.

'I'm afraid so,' sighed Dotty, feeling for her friend. 'I saw them opening and then quickly closing, several times in quick succession one night. I don't always sleep through the night and after Finty told me what she thought was happening, I made a point of sitting here with the curtains open, listening to the wireless. It was a summer night, so I could see Simon well enough. Guy didn't want the police involved. He was a quiet man who didn't want a fuss. So, they were forced out.'

'But why? That's just not normal to be hanging about at that hour,' Tilly fumed and her face reddened. 'He's unsettling Carl's mind. He saw heavy combat over the years and loud bangs trigger bad memories for him.'

'Simon claimed that Guy's doves would roost on his roof and that is why he banged the windows, to scare them away. But they roosted in his shed and aviary every night, well until the fire that is.'

'But we've no birds.'

'Yes, but Lee and Brodie told me what your children thoughtfully bought their father. In ordinary circumstances it would have been a touching gift.'

'Ah, the bird-table and bath. But surely the wild birds roost in the trees at night?'

'Yes, but Simon is a clean freak,' Dotty hesitated to mention this, but thought it best to be totally honest with her friend. 'It's almost obsessive with him, he needs order and cleanliness. He'll think that the wild birds are messing on his roof, window and even his garden.'

'But they aren't. His garden is so barren, they won't want to grub around all his concrete.'

'He's not a sane person, rumours bounce around the village about him. That's why no-one stops to chat with him.'

'Poor Millie, her life must be so lonely.'

'And painful, 'said Dotty wistfully. 'And there is nothing we can do about it.'

'I'm guessing that Finty and Guy didn't bang back, to keep Simon awake in return.'

'There would have been little point,' replied Dotty pointing to her ears.

'Of course, he's totally deaf without his hearing aids. It's one of the first things Simon said to us when we met.' Tilly thought for a moment, 'It's almost as if he was pre-warning us. What a horrible old man.'

'Yes, yes he is. And it sounds like you've already gotten on the wrong footing with him,' Dotty shook her head ruefully.

Chapter Eighteen

Carl smacked his lips with a loud puckering noise, put down his play cup on Annabelle's carefully arranged tray of toys and made a big show of wiping his mouth on the back of his hand. 'That was the best cup of tea I've ever had, thank you sweetie. Now, I'm off to feed the birds and top up the bird-bath so they can have a wash after eating. Do you want to help?'

Annabelle nodded vigorously, grabbed her favourite doll, and dutifully hopped off her bed and made for the door. She needn't have worried about beating her brother down the stairs, he was too busy with his online chums, berating their driving skills into his headset's microphone. Carl followed and left Gordon to it, he seemed happy enough.

Once downstairs, the duo put on their hats, gloves and jackets and walked through to the study, towards the backdoor. Along the way Carl pocketed the shed key from the long line of keys hung along the kitchen wall. They slipped on their outdoor shoes which were sitting obediently in a neat row along the side wall, the only part of the study that didn't have windows.

Annabelle made her way down the outside steps and to the storage shed. With each step she pretended that Dolly was walking bedside her and chattered away about their favourite cartoon.

Carl soon caught up with her and unlocked the shed, walked in, and scooped up a measure of mixed bird seed from a large sack. From another adjacent bag he took out another scoop, this time of nuts. He walked out and followed Annabelle to the bird-table. 'Would you and Dolly like to feed them today?'

A small hand moved behind Dolly's neck and pushed it forwards and backwards several times.

Carl handed over the container of seeds.

Annabelle took it and stretched out on tiptoes and reached up, bringing Dolly with her, and scattered the seed along the wooden base of the table.

'MOVE IT!' bellowed a voice from over the wall.

Annabelle dropped the seed container with fright and the kernels cascaded onto the grass.

'MOVE THAT BIRD-TABLE AWAY FROM MY PROPERTY GIRL!' Simon bellowed as he stepped into her view. He leant over as if to grab at her. He did a doubletake when he saw Carl. 'I, I,' he stuttered, 'I didn't see you there.'

'No, that's clear. Don't talk to my daughter like that.' He laid a protective hand on Annabelle's shoulder as she ran to the back of her dad's legs, bringing Dolly to safety with her.

'I didn't see you there. I don't want to fall out with you, but you need to move that bird stuff. They are messing in my garden.'

Carl moved to the wall. Annabelle stayed where she was. He leaned over and made a show of checking for mess. He couldn't see any. In a low voice he growled, 'I've warned you before, don't upset my family.'

'Aye, well,' blustered Simon, 'I didn't see you there.' He started to walk back to his house. When he was several feet away, he swiftly turned around and said quickly, 'Just move them. Or else.'

'Or else what?' demanded Carl, a glower swept upon his face like a sudden eclipse. His question remained unanswered as Simon scuttered away into his back door and closed it with a loud slam. Carl glared after him, surprised at the action of his neighbour. He turned back to his daughter, a reassuring smile upon his face. 'He's a strange old man, isn't he?'

Annabelle nodded, she bent over, picked up the seed container and handed it back to her father as if it were a hot potato in her delicate small hands. 'I don't want to feed the birds anymore daddy,' she timidly said.

'I'll give you an example of just how horrible that man is,' cautioned Dotty. 'He sold his old estate car to a man in the next village, well really he sold it to the local garage and then found out who bought it. He boasted about driving around the area until he found it parked in someone's driveway. He then visited the new owner and proceeded to tell him all the things that were wrong with it and how glad he was to get rid of it and for a good price. He delights in others misfortunes. He then went around the village bragging about it to anyone unlucky enough to be stopped by him, me included. Can you imagine what a fool the new owner must have felt like, knowing that he'd bought a vehicle that wasn't roadworthy and would be costing the earth to put right.'

Tilly nodded, though looked shocked. 'The poor man, how awful.' She sat up straight, 'Well, he'll have a fight on his hands with our Carl, and me.'

'But don't do anything to provoke him, try and stay on his good side. You don't want to make an enemy of him. It's best to just give him what he wants. Get Carl to move the bird-table and bath, like Lee and Brodie said, move it to the other side of the garden and keep the peace.'

'I think that it may well be too late for that, Carl chose the spot carefully so that he could see them from his desk, to enjoy seeing the birds feed and bathe when he takes a break and a stretch.'

Dotty sighed, 'It's probably too late anyway, once you've crossed his path, he doesn't forgive nor forget. But you'll always have a friend in me.' She tried to give her pal a reassuring smile, but her heart just wasn't in it as she thought back to Guy and Finty.

A groan exuded from the depths of the duvet as Lee tried to snuggle further into its depths. A fresh wave of pain bombarded his head, like a cluster bombing on an enemy target. 'Never again,' he croaked.

Brodie laughed as he gently placed a steaming mug of coffee and a packet of Nurofen onto his bedside cabinet, 'That's what you said last time. You've something worse than a hangover, do you remember what you said last night, to Tilly?'

Lee pulled the duvet over his head, hoping that his misdemeanour would go away if he covered his ears. 'Yes,' he drawled like a guilty schoolchild caught running in the corridor.

'How could you be so stupid?' berated his husband.

'I guess that our friendship with next door is now over. They'll hate us for not saying something sooner.'

Brodie patted the bed and Daisy obligingly jumped up and sniffed out her other daddy. She pawed at the duvet and Lee released his hold on it and allowed her free rein to sniff about his face and ears. He got a lick on his lips as a reward. 'At least someone still loves me,' he pathetically whimpered.

Brodie rolled his eyes, 'Stop being so theatrical and sorry for yourself. Sit up and have a drink, you need to rehydrate after your excesses at Tilly's.'

Lee groaned, 'She'll never speak to me again, not ever. And she was such a laugh. And I'll never get to cuddle up to Carl anymore. It's such a waste, he's such a hunk.'

Brodie rolled his eyes again and tutted, he decided to lay it on thick, 'I saw Tilly go across to Dotty's.'

Lee shrieked a quick high-pitched yelp which was soon silenced when his head started to throb even more. Daisy, ears pinned back, sprang off the bed and ran out of the room. 'That's it then, she'll be over here any minute now, shouting and cursing us. Don't answer the door.'

'I took Daisy for a walk and on my way back she came out of Dotty's house, so she must have been there a good hour. They cuddled on the doorstep and were smiling.'

Lee opened one eye, 'Smiling you say?'

'And having a cuddle.'

Lee opened his other eye, 'Have you brought up the extra strength Nurofen?'

Brodie lifted the packet and gave them a rattle for emphasis, 'You have me well-trained o master,' he chanted.

Lee sat up and took a long draught of his coffee and then reached for the tablets, 'All is not lost then. Dotty will have worked her magic.'

'And we did all we could to encourage Carl to keep the bird-table and bath away from the wall.'

'If Dotty has worked her magic, then perhaps it's time to say sorry to Carl, and have a make amends cuddle!' Lee sprang from the bed, headache long forgotten, and reached for his bathrobe.

Brodie rolled his eyes again, sighed, and couldn't help but smile.

Tilly walked into her lounge to find Carl giving Annabelle a cuddle. He was sat on the sofa and their daughter was on his lap. 'You two okay?'

Annabelle shook her head and kept up the embrace with her father. She buried her face deep into his neck, as if to hide her tears from her mum.

'Laughing boy next door upset her.'

'He did what!' bellowed Tilly as she made to leave the room.

Carl, knowing where his wife intended to go, caught her attention with, 'Whoa there. I've dealt with him. I've told Annabelle to stay away from him. I'll have another word with him in a day or two and let him know that he can't shout at her.'

'Why would he do that, Annabelle doesn't play loudly or throw anything over the wall. He's no right to talk to her like that. Just who does he think he is.'

'Would you believe that he got upset with her for feeding our lovely feathered friends.' Carl stroked his daughter's hair as he felt fresh tears spring up in her as she gently sobbed into his wet neck.

Tilly nodded, 'I'm afraid that I can. I've a few things I need to tell you about that muppet next door, and it's probably best to say them without Annabelle being here, I might just swear.'

Annabelle sat up and innocently said, ' But you've told us that it is wrong to swear mummy.'

Tilly laughed, 'Yes, it is sweetie, but where that idiot next door is concerned, you just have to swear. In fact, I think daddy might be saying a few naughty words in a moment too. Why don't you go upstairs and make me a nice cup of tea and I'll join you in a minute?'

Annabelle wiped her tears on her sleeve and nodded. She grabbed Dolly who had been sat beside Carl, patiently watching the conversation. 'I'm going to swear about him to Dolly,' she said determinedly as she trotted away.

Carl and Tilly managed to contain their laughter until they heard her gentle pitter patter on the top steps of the landing. Tilly then walked across to her armchair and flopped down. 'I've had rather an interesting chat with Dotty, I even got to see her bedroom, it's just like my old grandma's, tea making machine and all. There are lots of photos of her Eric, he was quite the dashing looking gentleman. Anyway, it seems there is a good reason that we got a knocked down price for this house.'

'Laughing boy next door?'

'You always were a good judge of character. Yes. He has put potential buyers off once they learn he would be their neighbour. It seems he has a reputation for beating Millie.'

Carl sucked air through his teeth, 'I thought as much. I can hear her crying, after you've gone to bed, especially if I sit down here in silence, reading a book. For a few weeks I thought that it may have been you having nightmares again, but you've been sleeping so deeply. The poor woman.'

'You've heard them too, and here was me thinking that I'd imagined them. I've been meaning to ask you if you heard them as well, but I thought my drugs were making me dream up things. I hear him grunting away as well, you know what that means? And every night too.'

'You can't mean,' asked Carl incredulously, 'at his age.'

Tilly nodded sadly, 'That poor woman. He's well-known for it, but no-one can stop him or make her leave him.'

'A beaten dog always returns to its master,' said Carl in a low, sad, voice.

'He has a thing about bird mess.'

'Yes, poor Annabelle and I found that out this morning. That's why he shouted at her, well, until he saw me. Then he scampered away, muttering to himself like a mad man.'

'I don't think the elevator goes all the way to the top floor with him,' mused Tilly.

Carl laughed and rallied with, 'The roof is short of a few slates!'

'Oh, and that's another thing! You've not been imagining the bangings. They aren't in your dreams, your nightmares. He's been opening and slamming his Velux windows to make the noises in the middle of the night.'

'The devious ba___'

Tilly cut in, 'He's causing your nightmares.'

'Well, I'll soon put a stop to that.'

'But how, if you upset him, he'll set light to something. He burnt down Guy's shed and aviary, with the birds in them.'

'No way, no wonder they wouldn't come back here to show us around. That's what those black marks on the patio are; the ones you keep scrubbing away at.'

Tilly nodded vigorously. 'He's opened up a can of worms in your head and I think that you have Post Traumatic…'

Carl cut her short with a terse, 'No I haven't, it's just lack of sleep, it's making me a bit tense, that's all. But I'll soon have it out with him and put an end to his devilment.' He jumped up from the sofa and made his way out of his house and walked determinedly to Simon's, leaving a worried Tilly trailing after him.

Millie, busy polishing the inside glass door of their lobby, heard the doorbell and instinctively went to answer it. She pocketed her cleaning cloth into the pocket of her apron and carried the polish with her to the two short steps to the front door. She unlatched the chain and opened the door and smiled when she saw Carl on her doorstep. 'Hello love, what brings you here? Are those sweet children of yours behaving themselves? You do look a bit tired.'

'That's why I'm here Millie,' replied Carl gently, he had calmed down on the short walk around to his neighbour. 'Though I don't want to cause any trouble for you.'

'Whatever do you mean?' she answered quickly, her free hand instinctively rubbing at her bruised stomach.

'We are hearing noises in the middle of the night; do you hear them too?'

Millie quickly nodded, 'I can't stop him, he'll beat…'

Simon blustered through from his lounge where he'd been sat reading his newspaper, he was dressed in an old workman style blue donkey jacket with large buttons up the front and two pockets along his abdomen. He wore a bobble hat, despite being indoors. 'What do you want?'

Carl wanted to take a step back, not from fear or intimidation, but because the man stank. His jacket was stained with the remnants of many meals and there was a pervading dank smell of body odour. How does Millie tolerate that, he thought? 'I've come about the noises.'

A smirk appeared fleetingly on Simon's face. 'Noises?' he jeered.

'The ones in the night,' helpfully replied Millie.

Simon gave her a look of contempt, 'Go and see to lunch,' he simply instructed.

Millie turned on her heels and went scurrying off to her kitchen without saying goodbye to Carl.

'Your wife is correct. You've been making deliberate noises in the night.'

Simon looked Carl up and down and gave a mocking sneer, 'Prove it.'

'I'm asking you to stop.'

'Make me,' warned Simon as he slammed the door in Carl's face with a loud thud.

Carl stared at the ornate thistle patterned windowpane of the door, uncertain as to how to proceed. He weighed up ringing the doorbell again and having it out with Simon if he answered at all. He decided that he didn't want to antagonise him which in turn may inflame his anger which he would probably take out on poor Millie. He looked above him and along the fascia where several security cameras were looking down at him and along Simon's property, and by the looks of it, along Carl's garden and front door. He looked straight at the one trained on him and shook his head.

Dotty watched from her bedroom, safely out of view from behind her net curtains. It was a familiar scene she and Eric had seen play out over the years with the succession of neighbours that had lived in the house now owned by Carl and his family. Irate neighbours walking around to Simon's and getting smirked at, then the cold shoulder and slammed door treatment. Soon after the "For Sale" sign would appear, hammered into the front garden, for a gloating Simon to watch over. None of the prospective viewers ever met with his approval and he always found something to fall out over with new neighbours. They never lasted long, hounded out of the village by a man who could simply take out his hearing aids and have no retaliatory noises affect him. Of course, he would always win, serving to reinforce his nasty behaviour.

'I can hear him laying into her from here,' exclaimed Tilly, sitting at the kitchen table in distress. 'It's not right, the poor woman, perhaps you shouldn't have gone over Carl.'

'But we can't let him get away with it. He can't keep me awake every night. It's not healthy for me. It's only been several nights, and I'm already shattered. When I was on Ops and had to keep awake, it was different, I was a lot younger.'

'Just give him what he wants, move the bird-table and bath. Think of poor Millie.' As if to highlight what she had said, a fresh wail came through the wall, followed by a roar, like that of an angry lion. More wailing pierced through the adjoining wall.

Carl reached into his pocket and dialled 101.

'What are you doing?'

'Phoning the police.' It was picked up on the third ring and Carl explained what was happening.

'I'll transfer you to 999 sir, this is classed as an emergency, please hold,' said the calm voice.

Carl looked shocked; he only wanted some advice. 'Police emergency,' stated another composed voice, 'What's the nature of your emergency?'

'Er, I don't know if it's an emergency, but I think my neighbour is hitting his wife, you see I went over to talk about…'

'His address,' interrupted the operative.

Carl gave it, feeling caught up in something he didn't want to be involved in. He could hear typing following by a sharp intake of breath. 'Officers are on route, they'll want to speak to you as well, please can you wait for them to come to your door. Please don't approach your neighbour.'

'Okay…' began Carl.

'Thank you, caller,' stated the advisor and hung up.

Carl looked at his mobile phone, hearing its harsh tone which indicated he needed to press the red phone symbol. He did so and pocketed it. He looked to Tilly, 'I think that things are out of our control now.'

She nodded and ran the tap to fill the kettle up. 'I'll make them a cup of tea; I expect they won't get a warm welcome next door.'

Chapter Nineteen

The patrol car went whizzing down the road, sirens blaring their klaxon noise as it reverberated around the sports field to the right. The local children's football teams stopped play to observe its movements, almost in reverence like veterans on Remembrance Day, they stood still until it passed, then continued play. The vehicle displayed its blue strobing lights, catching the eye of the bus driver who was about to pull out from the bus stop. He did a harsh brake and the elderly woman in the seat behind him tutted her disapproval. The police car ignored the shop to his left and did a swift turn right and pulled up alongside the semi-detached houses. A burly officer jumped out from the passenger seat, pulling his hat on as he ran to the house's gate and pounded down the pathway. He was swiftly followed by the driver, a petite woman, younger than her colleague by a good twenty years. She ran to catch up with him as he was now ringing the doorbell and quickly followed through with several bangs on the door. They waited in silence, in sharp contrast to the recent wailing of their sirens.

They stood there for about thirty seconds, listening out for signs of a struggle, or arguing. The stillness of the village hung in the air, save for the occasion cheer from the crowd of parents at the football pitch. Several of the bored parents had wandered down, following the route of the patrol car, their mobile phones at the ready in case they could film a juicy arrest. Each hoped to be the first to break the news on social media, and with the sharing of scandal, gain more likes, shares, and followers.

The officers ignored the gathering crowd, at a respectable distance, just across the road. The female officer walked over to the lounge window, cupped her hands to screen the bright winter's sun from her vision, and peered through the glass. She could make out an elderly woman, sat on her armchair, alternating between wringing her hands and cradling her stomach. She appeared to be rocking gently, as if to soothe herself.

The front door opened, and Simon growled, 'What do you lot want?'

'Hello sir, may we come in?'

'No.' Simon stood his ground, barring the officer from looking beyond the front door.

'We have had reports of a disturbance. We'd like to come in, just for peace of mind.'

Simon took a step forward, forcing the officer to take a step back, and thrust his head towards Carl's house. 'That'll be him then, poking his nose where it's not wanted.'

The officer refused to follow this line of conversation and looked to his colleague.

'She's in the lounge,' she said, turning away from the window and walking to Simon, she effortlessly climbed his two steps and put her hand on his door before he could close it. 'Like we said, we'd like to come in.' She didn't pose it as a question, but pushed his front door open a bit further and made to walk in, forcing Simon to take a few steps back. Her colleague, a brief smile of admiration and approval passing his lips, followed her, closing the door behind him, much to the chagrin of the gathering crowd. Several put their phones away and made their way back to the sports field, some stopped off at the shop to buy some snacks and share their new-found gossip with the shopkeeper and anyone that would listen.

Simon, forced to walk back to his lounge, made some blustering noises that were ignored by the duo who had invited themselves in. The female officer made straight for the lounge door, opened it, and quickly walked in. 'Hello, Millie, isn't it? My name is Yvonne. Are you alright?' She tried to close the door. Normal police practice was to try and separate the household and she knew her senior would be taking Simon into the kitchen. However, on this occasion, Bruce hadn't been quick enough. Simon stood malevolently at the doorway, watching silently.

'I, I don't know why you are here,' stammered Millie, wincing at a fresh burst of pain that shot through her stomach.

'We had reports of a disturbance,' Yvonne gently encouraged, 'Are you alright? Can you please tell me what happened?'

Millie looked to the doorway, 'I don't know why you are here. I'm fine.' She had been briefed, during the doorbell chiming and knocking on the door, by Simon, to say nothing, or else.

Simon smirked and turned to the male officer. 'I'd like you to leave now.'

Bruce pointed to the kitchen, 'Please go in there, sir, we need to take a few details.'

Simon tutted, but surprisingly did as he was told.

Bruce leant forward and gently closed the lounge door, hopefully Yvonne would get to the bottom of what's just happened, he thought. He followed Simon into the kitchen, trying to keep his loathing for him from appearing on his expression. He'd been here before, about seventeen years previously, as a young probationer. He'd been told by his mentor that they were frequent visitors to this household and that they knew he beat his wife, but they just didn't have any evidence. He thought that she'd finally left him. It had gone quiet for about five years. The poor woman must have just put up with him, he sadly thought. He took out his notebook and pen. 'May I have your name, date of birth and the town you were born in, please sir?'

Simon grudgingly rattled off the information, though Bruce knew this man before him well enough, he had been the talk of the station for many years, especially the year that he'd caused his wife to be admitted to the local hospital for several nights with a head injury. Simon had spent this time in custody, only to be released the moment Millie was discharged from hospital and asked for all charges to be dropped. She had said she'd fallen down the stairs. The laws for domestic violence then were not as stringent as they are now, though he doubted they'd get much evidence.

'Can you please tell me what happened?'

'Nosey neighbours, that's what,' yelled an indignant Simon. 'This has nothing to do with you, nor them.'

'We had reports of yelling and screaming coming from your property.'

Simon smirked and said smugly, in a carefully rehearsed speech, 'My wife has a medical condition. It causes her to get confused and she yells. It's nothing to be concerned about.'

'May I ask please, what sort of medical condition?'

Simon tapped his head a few times by way of a reply.

'I'll need you to be specific please sir, for my notes.' He wondered if the head injury and concussion may have led to a long-term health problem.

Simon sneered, 'Alzheimer's. It's the early stages, but she doesn't always know what she is doing.'

'I see,' though he doubted the truth of what was said, 'Can your GP confirm this?'

Simon nodded, easily lying.

'That doesn't explain the reports of a male bellowing in rage.'

'How very descriptive,' Simon scoffed. 'I'm afraid today has been an exceptionally bad day for Millie, I let my temper slip.'

'Do you do that a lot sir, let your temper slip?'

Simon glared at him, his anger evident across his face, the policeman had touched a nerve.

Dotty, sat on her bed, eyes glued to the drama across the road, shook her head, worry etched on her face. Her pals were in for it now, she thought, the "For Sale" signs would be erected any day now.

'Your husband won't be coming in for a few minutes, can you tell me, in your own words, what happened?' probed Yvonne tactfully.

Millie hesitated, torn between telling the truth and running with the script that Simon had placed in her head several minutes ago. She tried not to show her physical pain but winced all the same as the bruises on her abdomen gave her a physical reminder to do as bidden, or else. 'I have the early stages of Alzheimer's disease and I get confused easily. Can you bring Simon in now please? He'll tell you what happened.'

Yvonne tried not to show her disappointment, Bruce had warned her on the drive in. He'd been called to this house so many times, though not in recent years. He'd wondered aloud to her that there must have been new neighbours in number three. He'd told her of the fire in their backyard and who the suspect was and how there was no evidence for a charge. He'd also warned her of just how crafty the husband was and to expect denials from Millie.

'Of course,' she reluctantly said, 'If that's what you really want?'

Millie nodded her head slowly, half-heartedly, knowing better than to deviate from the script.

Yvonne walked to the closed door, sighing as she went. Seven times, she thought, seven times most assaulted partners go back to their other halves before leaving them. How many more times must this poor woman go through her ordeals before she saw sense? She looked back at the pitiful sight in the armchair and shook her head as she went to the kitchen.

A few stragglers remained on the pavement across the road, gossiping amongst themselves. Their vigil paid off as they were rewarded by the sight of the police officers leaving Simon's house. They were surprised to see him remain at his home, cheerfully waving them off, like they were cherished visitors who had spent an afternoon catching up. He remained waving, with a large grin on his face, though he was inwardly fuming at the audacity of the group watching him.

'Let's jump in the car a moment Bruce,' said Yvonne as they exited through the gate and were out of earshot, 'I just want to get on top of my anger for a few moments.'

Bruce nodded, 'He has that effect on folk, we'll drive around the block and park up around the corner, otherwise he'll stand on that step like the Cheshire cat, waving away like the village idiot until we've gone. It's been the same for years. She'll never leave him.' He removed his hat as he made to sit in the car once more.

The doorbell chimed and Tilly immediately went to the front door whilst Carl waited at the foot of their stairs in anticipation of their children running down the stairs to be the first to answer the door. He stopped them before they could jump the last few steps. 'I'll need you two to stay in your rooms for ten minutes,' he waved them off with a shooing motion, 'And no arguing, do as you are told.'

The duo obediently did as they were directed, but when Gordon quickly looked out of the landing window; he could see a tall policeman about to walk up the outside steps. He put his forefinger to his lips and made a shh noise to Annabelle. They loitered on the landing, out of sight of their father, but able to hear what was going on below.

Tilly met the officers on the doorstep and ushered them inside. 'Please go through to the kitchen, I've a teapot stewing.'

The officers looked to each other and then Bruce discretely looked at his watch. He gave Yvonne the thumbs up. Her eyes lit up when she walked through into the kitchen and saw the plate of biscuits.

'Please sit down and I'll pour you tea,' offered Carl. 'Sorry to have called you, but we didn't know what to do. It sounded like poor Millie was being attacked. Is she alright?'

'Yes, Mr?' questioned Yvonne.

'Carl, and this is my wife Tilly.'

Yvonne made a mental note, she'd get their full details later, after refreshments, she hoped. It had been a long day. 'Yes,' she answered, 'Your neighbour tells us that she is fine. We'll need to take statements from you, though no crime has been reported from their household. We'll need to take you in separate rooms and ask a few questions, but I can tell you that Millie tells us that she is okay,' she said it doubtfully.

Carl and Tilly nodded, catching her hidden meaning. They had supported enough friends on the army bases through domestic disputes that had escalated out of control suddenly. Especially when drink was involved.

'Grab a brew and some biscuits and I'll go in the lounge,' ordered Tilly as she went and made herself comfortable. Yvonne followed her through, quickly stirring several sugars into her mug and snaffling three biscuits onto her plate, her shift wouldn't finish for several more hours.

Carl grinned, 'It was the same in the army, we snatched a brew as often as we could when on duty.'

'Local regiment?'

'For a while, then I specialised.'

'Oh?'

Carl quickly changed the subject with, 'Sorry to get you out, it sounded serious next door. I didn't expect it to go through as an emergency call though.'

Bruce quickly swallowed his bit of biscuit, 'You did the right thing. He is well known to us.'

'Ah, I see, the poor woman.'

'Sorry, I shouldn't have said that.' Bruce, hoping to distract Carl from his slip, took out his notepad, 'I just need to take your details and a brief statement, in your own words. Can I have your full name, date of birth and where you were born.

Carl obliged the officer with the information, whilst mulling over what he had revealed. He hoped that he had not inflamed the situation and made things worse for poor Millie. He'd recalled a night on guard duty when one of the blokes on the base, a known sufferer of Post Traumatic Stress Disorder, had been woken from a nightmare by his wife. He'd beaten her badly before he came out of the combat night terror. Carl had been called to the married quarters house to assist in his arrest and had caught a glimpse of the soldier's wife as she was stretchered into the back of an ambulance. She was not a pretty sight. Though there was no excuse for the cowardly actions of his neighbour. He sighed and described why he felt he had needed to call the police to Millie's home.

Dotty exited her garden gate, resisting the strong urge to walk across the road and go to check on her pal, Millie. Instead she walked as if going to the shop on an errand, and then crossed to Lee and Brodie's house. They were at their window, both wearing a grim expression. Lee left their vigil and went to answer the quiet knock on their door.

'It's started,' blurted out Dotty as Lee opened the door and ushered her in. For once, she ignored Daisy who was sat next to Lee, eagerly awaiting being petted. 'My poor pal, what can we do? I feel so helpless. Did you seen him waving like the police were his best friends? He's pulled the wool over their eyes again. Millie will suffer tonight.'

Lee, lost for words of comfort, wrapped his arms around his friend and held her tight as he felt her shake with anger and then relent to her tears.

'Thank you both,' stated a grim looking Bruce to Carl and Tilly. 'If it happens again, please don't hesitate, dial 999 and we'll be straight there.'

The couple nodded, 'Thank you officers, I'll see you out,' said Carl.

The trio walked out of the hallway, Yvonne leading the way. She opened the front door and walked down the steps, assuming her colleague was right behind her. She walked on, past Lee and Brodie's house and around the corner to where they had parked up.

Bruce hung back on the doorstep, he turned back to Carl, hesitated, summed up his thoughts and then decided, 'Remember Carl, Simon is well-known to us, do not hesitate or feel that you are wasting our time. Think about Millie. I didn't have this conversation with you.' He then turned and walked away, taking long strides to catch up with his partner.

Carl took several steps down his path and looked in Millie's lounge window. The curtains were closed, though it was broad daylight. He shuddered as he wondered what horrors were taking place inside. He went back into his home and was met in the hallway by Tilly. They simply stared at each other.

BANG, BANG, BANG.

'What the f…' exclaimed Carl. 'That's not the kids, it's him, isn't it?' His heart was racing, and he held his breath, anticipating more noises. 'Tell me you heard that?'

Tilly was about to say yes but was interrupted with another crescendo of banging noises. The children came quietly down the stairs and stood by their parents, as if seeking protection.

'It's really loud in my room,' objected Annabelle, 'It's scaring Dolly.'

As if hearing her, three more loud booms echoed around the family home.

'Right, that's it, I'm going over to have it out with him,' fumed Carl. He went storming out and briskly walked out of his front garden and turned towards his neighbour. As he walked over, he noted that the upstairs curtains were closed. Movement on the roof caught his eye, the skylights were being opened and closed in quick succession. Carl hammered on the front door. He waited and could hear shouting from within and then the door flew open.

'What do you want, don't you think you've caused enough trouble. Getting the police out here for no reason,' protested Simon.

'How's Millie, is she okay?'

'That's none of your business. Go away.'

'What's with all the banging?'

Simon smirked, pleased that his neighbours could hear his bangs, 'What on earth are you on about?'

'Don't deny it, I saw you from the pavement. I saw your Velux windows being slammed shut, then opened, then slammed again.

Simon said smugly, 'Prove it.'

Carl, thinking quickly, pointed to his friend's house across the road. 'That's easy enough, I'm pals with Jake across the road, we train together at the gym sometimes. He'll set up a video camera in his spare room, the one in the front, straight across from your roof. We'll soon capture your deliberate attempts at keeping my family awake.'

Simon, hoping from foot to foot, didn't like being outdone. He stepped out of his house and pushed at Carl. The younger man didn't budge. Simon pushed again, 'Out, out, get out of my property!' he bellowed.

Carl moved back a step and then stood his ground. 'You might be able to bully poor Millie, but you can't me.'

'Wayne, Wayne,' he shouted pitifully.

A man suddenly appeared from the garage door around the corner from Simon. He went waddling out onto the pavement and appeared to swing each hip wide as his obese frame tried to walk swiftly. His right arm was in the air, as if to warn off Carl from his neighbour's property. Over their adjoining wall a rotund woman appeared from nowhere, her mobile phone shot out and remained at arm's length, pointed at Carl.

'What are you doing to the old man, shame on you, you should be ashamed harassing an old man, getting the police unnecessarily.'

'Unnecessary my foot,' said Carl, assessing the out of shape man as no threat, he turned back to Simon, 'You're the one who should be ashamed, hitting a lady,' he gave Simon a look of utter contempt.

The look chilled Simon to the bone, but he kept up with a cry of, 'Out, out, get out of my property. I don't want your sort here,' and pushed Carl again.

'I've got this on my camera, throwing accusations like that, it's a disgrace,' warbled the woman, reaching closer with her camera as if to prove the point. She tried to climb over the wall, but she couldn't lift her swollen leg high enough. A dog came bounding over, all the while barking, it jumped up to the wall, it's brown and white speckled paws resting on top, as if saying to its owner, 'I can easily get over if you want me to.'

Carl, seeing that the situation was escalating, gave Simon a withering look and walked away. As he passed Wayne, he gave him a look of contempt. He walked back to his house.

'That's right, get lost, and mind your own business,' shouted Simon, seeming to find his courage now that Wayne was by his side, 'Why don't you move out?' The duo watched him go, as the woman carried on filming, a smug expression upon her face.

Carl was about to go inside his house but chose instead to walk around the side and into his back garden. He'd sit outside in the arbour and calm himself down and watch the birds feeding on the table for a few minutes. As he rounded the side of his house, he saw Brodie to his left, by his flower bed. He smiled and said, 'Alright?'

'Yes, are you. I see you've met the charming Wayne; he must have dragged himself reluctantly away from his pies.'

Carl laughed at the image playing in his mind. He'd taken an immediate dislike to Wayne and his partner.

'He and Simon are good mates. Simon can't do anything wrong in his eyes. Though he must know deep down what's going on. I'm guessing that you've had to call the police to Simon?'

Carl, having calmed down now, sighed, 'It sounded like he was knocking seven bells out of Millie.'

Brodie grimaced. 'We had hoped that it had stopped, Guy and Finty must have just put up with hearing and knowing what was happening. He was a timid man. He wouldn't have liked to have called the police and made a fuss. It'll have been another reason for them to have moved. I'm sorry that this is happening to you.'

'It's not your fault, but what can we do?'

'Nothing, we've tried over the years, she just won't leave him. Come over for a chat, bring the family. I'll put the kettle on.'

'Sure, let me round them up, I'm sure they'll want to get away from the noises.'

'Ah, he's back to doing that. It nearly drove, well it did drive poor Guy mad. Though I believe his nerves are on the mend, with the good love of Finty and his beloved doves.'

'Let me take a rain check on that drink. You've just reminded me, I need to go across to Jake, I'll just pop in and get my mini tripod and camera first.

Brodie looked puzzled momentarily and then brightened up, 'What a great idea! The watcher won't like being watched; he'll soon stop slamming those windows.'

Carl grinned; he did like finding solutions to problems.

Chapter Twenty

BANG, BANG, BANG.

Carl jumped out of his bed, 'TAKE COVER, TAKE COVER!' he screamed at the top of his voice. He dived to the floor and scrabbled at the carpet, trying to get under the divan of the bed.

Tilly felt the bedstead rock and then violently lift, she snapped out of her deep slumber and shouted out, 'Carl, what are you doing?'

'TAKE COVER!' he yelled back at her.

She had no option, but to remain lying in the bed, clinging desperately to the side as it violently swayed.

Gordon burst into the room, 'What were those noises, they woke me up?' He switched on the light and was surprised to see his naked dad lifting the bed. He burst out laughing. 'What on earth are you doing?' he asked between fits of laughter. Then he saw his mum's distressed look and a scowl entered his face. 'You are frightening mum, stop messing about.' He moved forward to shake his father by the shoulders.

'NO, DON'T!' warned his mother. But she was too late.

The second that Carl felt a hand on his shoulder, he dropped the bed and grabbed at his son, lifting him off his feet and pushing him backwards, by the throat. Gordon thumped into the doorway, forcing the door closed with his back. Fortunately, his mother's thick winter dressing-gown was hanging on the door and absorbed most of her son's impact, though there was a dull thud as the door shut. Gordon's head missed the door hook by a few centimetres.

'WAKE UP CARL!' screamed Tilly, 'YOU ARE HURTING GORDON, IT'S YOUR SON.'

Carl looked aghast, first at Gordon, and then at his hands. He quickly removed them from his son's throat, as if he were holding hot coals. Gordon slid down the doorframe and Carl quickly caught him and held him tight to his chest.

'What have I done, I'm sorry mate,' he blubbered.

Tilly jumped out of bed, snatched Carl's hands away, and protectively embraced her son instead. 'Get yourself together,' she warned Carl. 'And then you and I are going to have a stern talk about your Post Traumatic Stress Disorder.'

'But I don't have PTSD,' argued Carl whilst slipping into a pair of boxer shorts.

'Yes, you do,' snarled Tilly, 'Look at what you've done to our son.' She turned back to Gordon and smoothed down his hair whilst making soothing noises. She checked out his throat, where red marks were deepening. 'How are you feeling Gordon?'

Gordon said nothing, he was too shocked to speak. Tilly gently led him to his bedroom and began settling him in his bed.

Back in the marital bedroom, Carl simply sat on the bed and looked at his hands, feeling guilty about what he could have done, knowing what he was capable of. He started to weep.

Jake readied himself for his early morning run by stretching out his legs, one was lifted at right angles upon the bed, pulling his toes towards him for all he was worth. He looked forward to this outdoor exercise which he took several times a week, he'd always have the route down to the harbour and along the coastal path, behind the fish processing factory and power station to himself. No-one else in the village was daft enough to be up this early, but he enjoyed the solitude which gave him a chance to have a think. After a few repetitions of this warming exercise, he remembered about the camera his pal had dropped off. He'd heard the rumours around the village and wasn't at all surprised when Carl had popped over last night with a tripod and camera. He'd helped him set it up and assured him that he'd have it visibly displayed in his window.

His girlfriend had remarked upon the creepy old man across the road staring at their house and he'd reassured her that he was looking at the camera and not her. She wasn't convinced. Since she'd been staying overnight, she'd always felt watched by the old pervert, as she nicknamed him. Simon seemed to just stand and stare at her, and she wasn't imagining it, Jake had seen him do it whenever her car pulled up and she made her way in with her overnight bag. She'd even gone as far as saying that she'd like them to move into a flat of their own somewhere else, a place that they could call home together and not this house that he used to share with another woman. Jake agreed and they'd been earnestly looking for somewhere nearby since.

As he checked that the camera was still recording, he hoped that his pal had had a restful night and that there were no bangs to disturb his family. He looked to Carl's and was surprised to see his lights on in his upstairs landing window, downstairs hallway, and lounge. Perhaps the camera hadn't acted as a deterrent after all.

Carl cupped his coffee mug with both hands and hoped that Tilly didn't see his hands shaking. He'd taken to only filling his mugs halfway, to prevent any spillages.

'Look at you, it's not normal for someone of your age to have shaking hands, unless they are withdrawing from drink or drugs.'

Carl looked down at his hands, willing them to stop trembling.

Tilly looked at him sternly, 'Well, are you?'

'Eh?' asked a puzzled Carl timidly.

'Have you been taking drugs or drink?'

'Of course not,' replied an indignant Carl.

'Some of the sufferers of PTSD take cannabis and worse, to try and stop the flashbacks and anxiety.'

'I told you, I don't have…'

'YOU HAD OUR SON BY THE THROAT,' she screamed at him.

Carl looked down at the floor, tears welled in his eyes, 'I'd never have hurt him,' he whimpered.

'But you almost did. What if I hadn't been there? What if I couldn't stop you.'

BANG, BANG, BANG.

Carl dropped his mug and cold coffee spilled onto the carpet and seeped into its plush material. He scrambled to scoop his mug up whilst Tilly ran out of the lounge and into the next room, grabbed some kitchen towel and ran back and placed it onto the damp patch. She absorbed as much as she could and took the empty mug from her husband and popped the damp paper into it. She got off her knees and stood over her husband. 'I'm taking you to the doctor as soon as I can get an appointment.'

'I don't have a problem,' protested Carl.

'Yes, you do,' insisted Tilly. 'I love you, but we can't go on like this. I heard the noises then too, but can't you just ignore them, like I do?'

'I can't seem to; they get my heart racing.'

Tilly thought back to the training that the wives and partners had, 'Anything else, any flashbacks?'

Carl vigorously shook his head in denial, but Tilly knew when she was being lied to. She left him to it and made her way upstairs to wake up their children and have a talk about not going near their daddy when he had nightmares.

Jake jogged slowly through his garden gate allowing his leg muscles to get used to the exercise. He crossed the road and jogged on past Simon's house, surprised to see him exit a darkened house. For once, his security light did not automatically spring on. Jake slowed his jog to watch him. For an old man, he moved surprisingly quick. He bent over at his garage door, allowed it to open fully and then he swiftly banged it shut with a reverberating echo that seemed to thunder around the nearby buildings, including Carl's. Simon then repeated the manoeuvre several times, and with each thud of the garage door, Jake could have sworn he heard an evil cackle, like that of a malevolent witch.

Carl screwed the lid of his flask tight, picked it up and went to the back door. A loud crescendo of rumbling, like that of a storm, or to Carl's mind, that of a passing jet, breaking into a sonic boom, as it dropped its payload of bombs, broke his silence and made him drop his thermos in fright. It cracked upon the tiled flooring but held its contents. Carl cursed as he saw the damage, it was a gift from his friend, the last birthday present from Gavin. He picked it up, studied the crack for a moment and then stepped outside. He made his way to the bird-table and bath, intent on restocking the seeds, nuts, and fat-balls. As he walked down his lawn, carefully walking on the ornate stepping-stones, he was shocked to see the table and bath lying on their sides. They appeared pushed towards the centre of the lawn, away from the wall. As he neared, he could see that a large chunk of the stonework had been damaged from the bath and that a deep crack was within its centre. The table's woodwork had been splintered in several places and the apex roof had been torn off and laid haphazardly further up the lawn. 'Oh!' he exclaimed in disappointment.

A bald head popped up over the wall and then a sardonic wide grin, 'Shame that!' Simon mocked in fake commiseration. 'I expect that a cat or the wind must have knocked them over.'

Carl stared at him, knowing full well that there had been no strong winds last night and that the chances of a cat overturning both of his prized possessions were minimal. This had been retribution for calling the police yesterday. This was confirmed by the cackling laughter followed by the merry whistling coming from Simon as he made his way back to his house.

Simon stood over Millie with a hammer in his hand, 'You'll do as you're damn well told woman,' he warned. 'Now get out there quick, before he goes indoors.'

'But I don't want to,' she protested, 'he's such a lovely man.'

'Fancy him, do you,' mocked Simon. 'I can think of a better use for this.' He held the hammer in front of her menacingly, with a snarl upon his lips. 'Get it done, or else,' he firmly threatened.

Millie reluctantly took it from him, rose painfully from the kitchen chair, and made her way to the back step.

Simon watched her gloatingly, hotly anticipating the reaction of Carl after Millie did his bidding. He watched from the kitchen window as she lifted the hammer and banged it against their back-step railings and then rattled the railings, hard, along their length, or as far as her arthritic limbs would stretch. She appeared to bob, almost in an apologetic courtesy, then made her way slowly and unsteadily indoors, hoping that Carl, or his family, wouldn't see that it was her.

Simon grinned as he looked through his window and towards the arbour. Through its slatted wooden structure, he could see Carl visibly stiffen in shocked reaction to the sudden, violent noises that interrupted his moment of solitude. Simon guffawed with glee, like a naughty schoolkid playing a prank on a fellow pupil, rubbed his hands together and did a little dance on the spot. 'Let's see him complain about her now,' he sneered aloud.

'No, Millie, no way,' protested Tilly as she looked on at her husband in bewilderment. 'She wouldn't do that; does she even have the strength?' She's a frail old lady.' She looked at Carl, wondering if he was imagining all this.

BANG, BANG, BANG.

'Tell me you heard that?' protested Carl.

'Yes, I did.' Tilly looked out of her window and saw Millie sweeping her path.

BANG, BANG, BANG.

'Well, that solves that little mystery. Millie can't be making those bangs, she's outside, sweeping, again.'

Carl, heart racing, jumped up from his armchair and paced the room, like a roused panther in a zoo enclosure. 'I don't think I want to be in here, listening to that lot. It sounds like he's slamming his bedroom door several times in a row. I can hear it, no matter what room I'm in.'

'Okay, we've obviously upset the man, let's not go near him for a few days and see if he'll get bored and stop. I don't think that we should be upsetting the man. He's a bit deranged if you ask me.'

Their doorbell rang before Carl could agree. He went to answer it and was puzzled to see Bruce and Yvonne, the police officers from yesterday on his doorstep.

'Can we come in please sir,' Bruce formally addressed Carl.

'Of course, is it about the bangs?'

'Bangs?' questioned Yvonne as she entered after her colleague.

'It sounds like slamming doors, in quick succession.'

Bruce nodded discretely to Yvonne as they followed Carl through to the lounge. 'Good morning Ma'am,' he said to Tilly. 'You can stay if you wish.' He turned to Carl, 'We've had a complaint that you threatened your neighbour.'

'Eh?' said a puzzled Carl.

'From your neighbour's son.'

'I've never even met the guy,' protested Carl.

'We've received an interesting video. It's been heavily cropped and jumps about in scenes. It only shows you, no-one else.'

The penny dropped with Carl, the large woman behind the wall with the barking dog. She'd been filming him on a camera.

'From your neighbour's CCTV.'

Carl had forgotten about those.

'We can't see your neighbour, that seems to be the bits that have been cropped.'

'I'm not surprised, he was pushing me, well trying to.'

'Yes, we thought as much. His son is claiming that his father is a frail ninety-year old.'

'My foot!' exclaimed Tilly. 'He's only in his late sixties, maybe early seventies.

'We aren't charging you, nor cautioning you, there isn't enough evidence. As I say, the film is heavily cropped. Your elderly neighbour doesn't appear nor speak in the bits we have seen, so we can't say who you threatened, though we have two witnesses, both of whom are closely related, so it's a bit hearsay. We shan't be taking the matter further. But we strongly advise you to stay away from your neighbour.'

Carl nodded, funny how the banging had suddenly stopped. I bet it'll restart as soon as these two left the building. 'Of course, officers, I get the picture. Will that be all?'

'For the moment sir, we'll see ourselves out.' The still standing duo, turned, and left, smiling reassuringly at the two small children coming down the stairs.

When Tilly heard the front door close, she turned to Carl and said, 'Dotty warned me that he was devious. He's edited those recordings to make you the bad guy.'

'And him the victim,' rued Carl.

Their children walked in, Gordon carefully scouted around Carl, rubbing his throat self-consciously. They sat on the sofa and looked to their mother.

BANG, BANG, BANG. echoed around their house,

'I told you that it wasn't us,' avowed Annabelle. 'Now will you stop blaming us daddy. It frightens me, all this noise.'

Carl, heart racing, paced the room and then sat by his children, his soul wrenched when he saw Gordon flinch and then rub his neck.

Tilly nodded in encouragement.

Carl, in a low voice, said, 'I'm so sorry Gordon. That was so wrong of me and will never happen again. I had a nightmare and my mind was elsewhere. You know that I'd never intentionally hurt you.'

The children nodded sagely, their mother had spoken to them earlier and described that daddy had been fighting in the army and sometimes he relived experiences and had to be left alone, to wake up gently and not be suddenly roused from his bad dreams.

'I hope it doesn't hurt too much mate?' questioned Carl gently.

Gordon rubbed his throat and shook his head.

'Friends again?' ventured Carl.

Gordon nodded again and his father held up his hand for a high-five. Gordon left him hanging

Simon handed over, begrudgingly, a twenty-pound note to Millie, along with a sheet of paper with a list of items to buy.

She dutifully took them from him, flinching in anticipation of a smack, or worse.

A smile of pleasure crossed his face as he saw the fear in her eyes. 'And I'll expect some change.' He lifted his hand, palm outstretched towards her, 'Now get going and give me some peace.'

Millie scurried off, relief on her face. She stopped at the lobby cupboard and took out her two canvas shopping bags and left her home. As she walked up her path, eyes cast downwards, shame on her face for what she had done to the nice young man next door, she didn't see her pal across the road, nor Tilly with her, deep in conversation. Millie made her way to the nearby bus stop.

'It's probably best not to give her any attention, or call across, it'll make Simon angry with her,' warned Dotty.

'The poor woman, he is so controlling,' replied Tilly pitifully. 'She has two large shopping bags; won't he give her a lift into town and help her carry them?'

'No, and with her arthritis too. It's a pitiful sight, isn't it?' Dotty didn't wait for a reply, she knew it was. She'd seen these events play out for too many years. 'You should see her struggle off the bus when those two bags are full of groceries. But that's not the half of it,' she continued with a sigh, 'Watch Simon, he'll be by the lounge window, watching her make her way to the bus stop.'

Tilly discretely looked out at the corner of her eye and sure enough a smirking Simon was by his window, staring at his wife.

'Now watch,' cautioned Dotty. 'Look out for her.'

Tilly looked at her pal with a puzzled look and then saw a woman with bobbed hair, which accentuated her round face, make her way over a wall, having to heave one oedematous leg over the brickwork with both hands, and then repeat the procedure with the other. Once over, she stopped to catch her breath and then floundered across his side driveway, along Simon's path and let herself into his house.

'Oh, I hadn't realised that they were such good friends to just let herself in like that.'

A rueful expression crossed Dotty's face, 'Watch the bedroom window.'

Tilly did as bidden, this time turning all the way around so that she could have a more comfortable look. She was shocked to see the woman at the front bedroom window, reach up and close each curtain. Just as the drapes finally shut out her view, she saw a beaming

Simon in the background. Stunned, Tilly turned back to Dotty with an incredulous look upon her face, 'You can't mean?'

'Yes, it's awful, isn't it? That's been happening for years. They are so close, well as close as folk can get. I'm sure that I don't need to paint you a picture.'

Tilly shook her head, 'Please don't. She must be half of his age.' She shuddered at the thought.

'Her husband, Wayne, he works full-time, during the week, in Aberdeen, so she knows he's away from home. She's well-known for having gentleman callers shall we say. Though for Simon, she makes house calls.'

Tilly looked appalled, 'That's awful. You hear of such things, but to actually see it going on.' She looked aghast and lost for words. After a few moments she asked, 'Does Millie know?'

'I think that she suspects, but how do you even begin to tell a friend that her husband is seeing someone with voracious appetites behind your back. That's why he sends her out on the bus, he knows that he can have an undisturbed two hours. By the time she gets back, Daniella, that's the hussy's name, climbs back over the wall.'

Tilly didn't know what else to say and merely shook her head.

'It's bad enough that he won't give her a lift into town when he has a perfectly good car, nor helps her push the trolley around the supermarket and lift the heavy bags, but he treats her like that, and for all the neighbours to see. He's no respect for her. Well, he doesn't, does he? Otherwise he wouldn't beat her every day. I'm so sorry that we didn't warn you before you bought the house.'

Tilly nodded, 'I wish we had known, but don't blame yourself, we didn't know you then.'

Chapter Twenty-One

BANG, BANG, BANG.

Carl sprang up from his bed, shouting, 'GAVIN, GAVIN, NO.' He screamed out the last word and it seemed to echo around the bedroom. He was actioning as if he was aiming a rifle at someone and shooting. He then dropped to his knees and felt around in an imaginary combat vest for some equipment. All the while he shouted, 'MEDIC, MEDIC, MAN DOWN.'

Tilly, still groggy from her medicines, forced herself awake and switched on the main light and found her husband on his knees, arms wrapped around an imaginary comrade, forcing life into a downed friend. She sighed; she didn't know how much longer she could cope with the broken nights. 'Carl, can you hear me.'

Carl looked at her, though his mind wasn't in the present. He looked puzzled and then shouted, 'Help him, he's been hit.'

'Gavin is dead Carl, you are home. Look at me, why would I be in Afghanistan?'

Carl looked at her again, and then down at the carpet and then to his hands. He was cradling thin air. 'But I can taste his blood in my mouth,' he shouted in protest.

Tilly looked aghast. Over the years her husband had saved her the knowledge of the missions he and his comrades had taken part in and he'd shared no details of Gavin's injuries, nor the event that cost him his life. She shuddered at the thought of having someone's blood in her mouth and was horror-struck at the thought of what his injuries may have been. Her imagination placed terrors in her head as Carl shouted out, 'I had to spit one of his teeth out.'

At that fresh revelation, Carl sat with his hands to his eyes, trying desperately to stem the flow of tears.

Tilly reached for the phone. She didn't care that Millie may suffer more for her actions: she had her husband to protect. She dialled 101.

'Police Scotland, how may I help?' asked the brusque operator with a hint of a Glaswegian accent.

'There is a disturbance next door, it sounds like he is banging on the wall.'

'From your neighbour you say, can I have your name and address please?'

Tilly offered the information, speaking a bit louder than normal so that her voice would carry above the noise of her weeping husband. She also gave the name of Simon and his address.

'Perhaps he is doing DIY?' offered the operator helpfully.

Tilly looked at her mobile phone incredulously at the suggestion, and the time, 'It's three in the morning!' she exclaimed in bewilderment.

'Ah, yes, sorry, that was a daft suggestion. Have you tried talking to your neighbour?'

'Yes. but he shouts and pushes my husband. The police have advised us to stay away from him.'

'I see,' said the operator. He was silent for a while, as he read the screen before him. I see that you've had to call before. I'll send officers around as soon as possible. Could you please answer the door to them? They'll want to hear the noise for themselves. You could also try the local council, though I don't think your area operates a twenty-four-hour service.'

'Thank you, we'll do that.'

The operator thanked her and hung up.

Tilly put her phone down on her cabinet and slid down the bed and joined her husband on the floor. She put her hands around his neck and pressed her forehead to his. 'Are you with me now?'

Carl nodded his head, slightly bumping heads with his wife with the movements. 'I can still taste his blood.'

Tilly reached down to his shoulders and held him tight. After a while she said, 'I know you won't tell me what happened, but can you see that now is the time to see the GP.'

Carl reluctantly nodded.

'Good, it's about time. I thought that almost throttling Gordon would have been a wake-up call. You need treatment for PTSD, whether you like it or not.'

The doorbell rang. Carl sprung up and reached for his dressing-gown. 'I don't have PTSD, just nightmares when that lunatic starts his banging. That'll be the police, I'll let them in.' He left the room and swiftly went down the stairs, leaving Tilly to shake her head in despair.

Simon sat up in bed, rubbing his hands in glee as he watched the screens before him, on the adjoining wall. The large TV screen was split into eight sections, one for each camera doted around his property. On the sixth segment, trained at Carl's front door, he could see those gormless bobbies who had bothered him the other day. They were the same pair who he'd shown the video clips of Carl, daring to be in his property, that his grandson had carefully edited at work. Not that they did anything about it. He watched as they entered Carl's house.

Simon smugly looked at the hammer and piece of wood and cloth he had on his bedside table, next to his pair of hearing aids. He'd taken great delight in placing the fabric and block of wood upon his wall, to prevent damage to the wallpaper and plasterboards, and then hammered out his frustrations. He kept his vigil on the screens. He'd get busy once those constables cleared off.

'Thank you for coming out, we're sorry to disturb you,' offered Carl as the officers went through to the hallway. 'Please go into the lounge.'

'Thank you, sir, we had reports of noises. Is it arguing and fighting again?' asked Bruce.

'No. This noise has been going on for weeks. But we've had enough. It's not normal to make bangs through the night.'

Yvonne looked to her colleague knowingly, 'Loud bangs?'

'Yes, enough to wake us every night, several times a night. Always three in a row,' answered Tilly as she entered the lounge and sat down on her armchair. She ushered her hands to the sofa, 'Please get comfy.'

'I see, wouldn't your neighbours be fast asleep now. Their house is in total darkness.'

'We think that he has a prostate problem. His wife doesn't hang washing outside, but one day I saw seven pairs of what looked like nappies on the line. I'm guessing that they are reusable pads of some sort, to absorb his urine and smells if he leaks or has incontinent. He always smells awful.'

The officers looked at each in puzzlement and then back to Tilly. She answered their question when she saw the confusion on their faces. 'That's why the noises are every hour and a half, he probably makes them after he's had to nip to the toilet.'

'I see,' stated Bruce. 'But there isn't any noise now,' he declared, looking at the adjoining wall.

'That's right, it's three loud bangs followed by silence,' insisted Carl, backing up his wife's explanation.

'But surely he'd waken up his wife too?' questioned Yvonne reasonably.

Tilly made a tutting noise, 'He doesn't care about her, you've seen the way he treats her.'

The officers looked to each other knowingly but chose not to challenge the statement.

'I'm afraid that we need to hear the noises ourselves, for us to take any action. We can't wake up a sleeping household if there isn't any noise,' declared Yvonne.

'He's too crafty for that, you've seen all the cameras, it can't be right that one is pointed right at our door,' insisted Tilly.

'We really do need evidence. The cameras are legal, so long as they also point in your neighbour's own property. Have you tried the council? The environmental health department can help with nuisance noise,' offered Bruce helpfully.

'The man is insane,' stated Carl. 'He follows me around with a hammer. Then hammers whatever is nearby. His favourite is to clang against the metalwork of the bench he keeps to the side of his driveway.'

The officers looked at him incongruously, 'Really?' objected Yvonne.

Carl nodded, 'It's unsettling,'

The radio on Bruce's chest burst into life with a crackle and a coded message was garbled. He sprang to his feet and nodded to Yvonne, 'We have to go, urgently, but please speak to the council.' He ran out of the room, followed closely by Yvonne, leaving Carl and Tilly pondering what to do next. Their silence was broken several minutes later by, BANG, BANG, BANG.

Carl leapt up, paced the room, and then went to the window and pulled aside the curtain. He looked out, 'They've gone. He must be watching. Do you know what Jake's girlfriend calls next door? The local perv, that's what. He has us under constant surveillance, and there is nothing we can do.'

'Yes, there is, we'll get you an emergency appointment with the doctor in the morning, then contact the council.'

As if in agreement, a booming, BANG, BANG, BANG, reverberated around the room, seeming to call out from the ceiling, ricochet around their home and seep back into the adjoining wall like a malevolent force.

'We can't even retaliate and keep him awake with our own loud noises. He takes those hearing aids out and sleeps like a baby. Besides, it would awaken poor Millie and she has enough problems going on,' despaired Tilly.

'It would also waken up our two,' agreed Carl as he sat down

Annabelle walked into the lounge, as if hearing her father and showing her agreement. 'I can't get back to sleep, the bangs frighten me.' She hugged her teddy bear tightly.

Carl put out his hands and patted his knees. He put a smile on his face, though inside he was all het up and wished he could strangle the scrawny neck of his evil, devious neighbour.

Simon gave the street a cursory check for any passers-by, and then content that he was alone, slammed home his front door with all his strength. He grinned as he locked the door, even though Millie was busy in the kitchen, and walked up his path. He hesitated at his gate, looked around once more for any early morning walkers, and swiftly exited and then rammed home the gate with a resounding clang. He walked purposely to the other side of the road and made his way to the local shop for his morning paper and fresh rolls. He lifted out a large rusty nail from his filthy jacket pocket and grinned as he passed Lee's car, 'This'll teach him to back-chat me a few weeks ago,' he muttered under his breath as the nail made a satisfying gouge along the shiny metal panels of the driver and rear sides of the vehicle.

He passed an open drain with slanted covers and casually threw the nail down to the gutter. It bounced once and then plopped through into the collected rainwater, ready to be washed away during the next downpour.

'But he needs to be seen today, he started coughing this morning, he spat all of his cereal out. It made a right mess on the floor,' argued the irate mother.

The surgery receptionist looked down at the toddler who was happily smiling back at her from the buggy, parked right under her window. 'She seems fine enough to me,' declared the receptionist bravely, from the safety of her swivel chair.

'And how would you know?' shouted the mother questionably. 'You're not a doctor, are you?'

'No, but I am a mother, and like I said, there are no appointments left, you'll have to ring first thing tomorrow morning.'

Carl, having no option but to overhear, made to stand up, to offer his appointment to someone who truly needed it.

Tilly placed a hand on his knees and applied enough pressure to force him back in his chair, 'Don't you even think about it sunshine,' she hissed.

Carl sat back in resignation. How does she do that, he thought, she always seems to know what I'm thinking.

'Carl,' called a tall thin man with an equally slender tie, knotted tightly against his throat.

Carl stood up, 'That's me,' he declared.

'This way please, I'm Doctor MacBride.'

Carl dutifully followed him into the inevitable room with a desk, several chairs, and an examination couch. He was disappointed not to see an anatomical skeleton, but instead there was a height chart next to some scales and an ominous looking body mass index chart. The woman complaining would have tipped that chart he unkindly thought. He was about to close the door, but hadn't realised that Tilly had followed him in. She squeezed through the door, giving Carl a cheeky wink. He sighed and closed the door and took a seat next to her, and before the desk. It made Carl feel like he was at the headmaster's office with his mother and about to get another telling off.

'How can I help?'

'We were expecting to see Doctor Neal,' complained Tilly. She was her favourite GP; she took the time to listen.

'I'm afraid that she is off sick, I'm a locum, filling in for her. How can I help?' he looked to Carl as he asked the question.

Tilly opted to answer whilst Carl was fumbling for words. 'Our neighbour is keeping us awake. I get back to sleep easily enough, I'm on anti-depressants, they make me drowsy, but Carl needs something to help him sleep. Our neighbour keeps him awake. He bangs on the walls.'

'That sounds more of a social problem. Have you chatted to your neighbour to see what he is doing?'

'Yes, but he pushed Carl about.'

The GP looked at Carl and doubted that anyone would be daft enough to push someone built like him about. 'Perhaps the police, or the council.'

'We are about to see the council; the police couldn't help.'

'It's a big step, offering sedation to someone as young as you.' He flipped through the notes on the screen by nudging the computer mouse. 'I can't see any clinical indication.'

'He has PTSD,' offered Tilly. 'He was in the army.'

The GP looked to Carl and saw that he looked unshaven, but otherwise seemed in rude health. 'Has it been diagnosed? By a psychiatrist or psychologist? I can't see anything in your notes.'

'I don't have PTSD,' declared Carl, looking at his wife defiantly.

'I see,' said the doctor. 'Do you get flashbacks to events from when you were in the army.'

Carl shook his head, 'I'm all fine.'

'No, you aren't, you've been having nightmares,' insisted Tilly.

'I'm just reacting to the noises, it's what I've been trained to do.'

The doctor looked at Carl more closely, 'How have you been reacting?'

'He's been trying to shoot back at the enemy, he's been trying to put on his helmet and other protective gear, he even hurt our son,' Tilly blurted out.

'I only pushed him out of the way,' asserted Carl, hurt that Tilly had brought that up to someone else.

'YOU HAD HIM BY THE THROAT!' screamed Tilly.

Carl looked down at the green carpet, it was not the best colour to see if you were ill, he thought.

'And what about Gavin,' probed Tilly insistently.

Carl stood up, 'I'VE HAD ENOUGH OF THIS,' he shouted, knocking back the chair. It fell backwards with a dull thud. Carl looked to his wife and in one syllable words he stated, 'There, is, nothing, wrong, with, me.' He flung open the door and stormed off As he passed the receptionist, he noticed that she was still having a verbal wrestling match with the worried mother. He wished that he'd offered her his appointment as his had been a waste of time.

Tilly turned to the doctor with an apologetic look upon her face. She shrugged.

'See the council, I think that is your best answer,' advised the doctor from behind the safety of his desk.

The couple had driven home in silence. Carl had parked in their usual spot across from their home, and once the car had been locked up, he'd not bothered to walk across to their front door with Tilly. Instead he'd marched off around the back of the house and into the rear garden where he'd hoped for some peace.

Tilly left him to it and, seeing the time, walked down the road towards the school, to pick up their children and walk them home. She hoped that Carl would be in a better mood when they got home.

Carl applied the last layer of wood filler to the bird-table and took a step back. Though he could tell where the damage had been, a final sand down and several layers of paint and varnish would soon mask it, and it would look as good as new.

He walked over to the rear of the shed and sat on his workout bench. He lifted his dumbbells and powered through a few repetitions of his exercise regime. He slowed his breathing to match the flow of the weights and was soon finding his mindfulness. He also soon realised what an idiot he had been. Of course, Tilly was trying to help him. She wasn't trying to interfere, she was attempting to support him, and he'd thrown it back in her face. He put the weights down and resolved to go inside and make amends.

'Yes, I understand that,' said Tilly patiently into her phone, 'but the police advised us to call you. They said that the council should be able to help us. Specifically, they told us to ring the environmental health office.'

Carl entered the lounge and sat on the sofa. She rolled her eyes as if to say that she was dealing with a blethering idiot.

'Yes,' said an exasperated Tilly, 'please do put me through to one of your officers.' She looked at Carl and said, 'It's worse than trying to get into MI5!'

Carl laughed, it looked like he was forgiven, Tilly had someone else to complain about. He picked up his favourite 2000AD comic from the coffee table and opened it up to his much-loved Judge Dredd strip. His mum still bought him this and even posted it out to wherever he was deployed when he was in the army. Now she handed it to him every week, like a schoolboy getting tuck from a shop, and he relished each page and devoured it eagerly. His one regret was that Gordon showed no interest in reading it, he much preferred his video games.

BANG, BANG, BANG.

Carl stiffened, and the pages of his comic crumpled in his grip. He threw down the magazine, it slid across the surface of the coffee table and fell onto the carpet. He got to his feet, picked it up, looked forlornly at the comic and placed it reluctantly on the table. He wouldn't be able to concentrate on the futuristic lawman's latest adventures with that racket going on. His mind was racing, and he wasn't liking where it was going, where it was being driven to, with an old lunatic in the driving seat. Why can't he just stop. I don't have PTSD, he thought, I just need that moron to stop banging on the wall.

Tilly, ear to her phone, hearing on hold music, failed to hear these noises. She was humming away to herself and her feet were dancing out to the tune.

Annabelle walked in and sat by her father. 'Those bangs frighten me daddy, can't you make them stop?'

Carl reached out and drew her into a cuddle, 'I've tried sweetheart, I've really tried, but he won't let me talk to him. The police have advised me to stay away from him.'

Gordon walked in, munching down on a cookie, 'Can't you dispense your own justice, like Dredd?' He mimicked firing the lawgiver weapon that the Mega-City One judges carried. As he made firing noises bits of biscuit flew from his mouth and landed on the carpet.

Carl laughed, whilst keeping one eye on his wife. She saw the mess but hadn't rushed to pick up the crumbs. Perhaps her condition is getting better, he thought. He was also relieved to see that his son was having fun with him again and had given away that he secretly read Carl's comic. I'll keep leaving the new edition on the coffee table, he thought.

'Yes, hello, my name's Tilly. The police have advised us to contact you about noises coming from our neighbour,' said Tilly, turning reluctantly from the soiled carpet and giving her attention to her phone call. She described to the environmental health officer about the noises. She sighed, 'Yes, we have tried talking to him, but he pushes my husband away out of his property and shouts until he goes.'

'May I have your address and the name and number of your neighbour please?' enquired the EHO.

Tilly obliged with the information and she heard a rattle of fingers on a keyboard and then a sharp intake of breath. 'I see. I think it best that I attend your property, with a colleague, and we can try and hear the noises ourselves and then we can see how we can proceed.'

'That would be good, though our neighbour has CCTV and will know you are visiting.'

'I'm sure he won't be watching, are you sure that the camera isn't pointed at just his own property?'

'Oh, we are sure alright, he's several cameras scattered around his roofline, with one pointing right to our front door.'

'That can't be right. Have you tried the police?'

'Yes, they say that it's perfectly legal, he has them only looking at his property.'

'Well, that's okay then, we'll say tomorrow at four in the afternoon.'

'Yes, thank you, see you then.' Tilly hung up.

BANG, BANG, BANG.

Carl stiffened and his heart went racing again, he took his arm from around his daughter and placed them on his thighs and began tapping, trying to expel some energy. He felt a tiny hand on his shoulder.

'I don't like the noises either daddy,' consoled Annabelle. 'Sometimes I don't like being in my room.'

'I wish that he'd have made them when I was on the phone for the woman to hear,' moaned Tilly. 'It's almost like he has us bugged and knew the moment my phone call had ended.'

Carl nodded in agreement. 'It wouldn't surprise me if he has microphones on the cameras as well, he's devious and paranoid enough.'

Tilly sat up, 'That reminds me!' she exclaimed. She looked at the children, 'You two make yourself scarce, I need to chat to daddy.'

Carl, wondering if he was going to get a nagging for not being honest with the doctor, nodding encouragingly to the children. 'Off you go, I'll be going to work in a minute, so I'll see you two at teatime.'

The children obediently left the room, leaving their father to face the music. When they had closed the door behind them, Tilly said, 'You'll never guess what!'

Carl sat up straight, it sounded like he was off the hook, 'What?' he replied hopefully.

'You'll never believe it, but the nutter next door is only having an affair with the woman around the corner, in the house next to him.'

'What the hippo?'

The children burst in, having been listening at the hallway, 'Who's the hippo?'

All three looked at Carl. 'Well, that's what she reminds me of,' he explained. 'She pokes her eyes and nose over the fence and wall, whenever she is in the garden. That's all I can see. Just those beady eyes watching whatever I am doing. It reminds me of a hippopotamus wallowing in the mud. That and her blown up face reminds me of one. She even walks like one, wading along, her huge bulk plodding the pavement.'

'The hippo, the hippo,' sang out the children. They left the room, giggling away, wondering what an affair was.

Carl laughed, 'You can't mean that those two are at it. She's half his age.'

'That's what I said to Dotty, but I saw them with my own eyes.'

Carl shuddered at the thought, 'You can't mean you actually saw them at it?' he asked doubtfully.

It was Tilly's turn to shudder, 'No, perish the thought. But he makes Millie go shopping on her own and she takes the bus, every few days. That way she's away from home for a few hours. Then she, the hippo, climbs over the wall and goes into his house and then he and she were at the bedroom window, closing the curtain. Apparently, she's well-known in the village for entertaining the men whilst Wayne is at work.'

Carl, lost for words, kept his mouth open, it became more agape as his wife explained what she saw. 'At his age too.' He shook his head. 'Poor Millie, what an awful life that man has dealt her.'

As if he agreement there were three bangs, each in quick succession.

Carl tightened his grip until his fingernails dug into his palm. He didn't know how much more of this he could take.

Annabelle hugged Dolly tight, trying to shut out the noise. A metal ladder had been bouncing outside her window, onto the wall between her room and that of the awful man next door. When it was resting there came the clanging of a metal bar being struck against the railings below.

She put her hands to her ears to try and block the noise, but it kept coming, relentlessly. She summoned up her courage and hopped off her bed and went to the window. No-one was on the ladder, it was empty. Suddenly it moved away and then was thrown against her wall with an almighty bang. She looked below and saw a bald head and then a bright orange jacket. She stared in horror as the figure threw the ladder once more at their building with an almighty clatter.

Simon looked up and gave a maniacal grin to the youngster, relishing in her torment. He gave the ladder several more tosses at the wall, narrowly missing the window frame.

Annabelle grabbed Dolly and ran from her room, screaming for her protector, 'Daddy!' she yelped over and over as she rushed down the stairs.

'What on earth is all that banging? It sounds like someone is beating on our kitchen wall,' groaned Tilly.

Carl was up and pacing the room, not knowing what to do with himself. 'It's coming from a different area. He's not just banging on the wall this time.'

The duo then heard the distressed calls from their young daughter, their protective emotions kicking into play.

Annabelle burst into the lounge, 'Daddy, daddy, make him stop!' she yelled, above the din resonating around their home. She ran to her mother and nestled into her, seeking motherly protection. 'He's laughing at me while banging a ladder against my wall, he nearly banged it against my window,' she protested.

'Right, that's it,' declared Carl as he bolted out of the room. 'That's the last straw, I'll stop that nutjob.'

'No, don't, Carl,' protested Tilly.

It was too late. Carl had made his way through the kitchen and was flinging open the outside door from his study. During his run he was accompanied with a soundtrack of clanging and a cacophony of bangs, like the worst band trying to tune their musical instruments via loudspeakers.

'STOP YOUR NOISE YOU EVIL BAS....' screamed Carl as he leant over his railings and flung his upper torso across to Simon. He pointed his finger in accusation and phlegm spat from his mouth in protest, a snarl of deep hatred and contempt was upon his lips

Simon laughed. A deep belly laugh. He steadied the ladder with his right arm, then tucked his left arm into his chest and gave Carl the middle finger, all the while laughing. He was content in the knowledge that he could crop out his deliberate goading actions from his CCTV recordings and beautifully capture his neighbour's swearing and finger pointing. He'd soon act shocked and scared to the police when he played them this.

Tilly made it to the back step seconds later and grabbed Carl quickly. She'd never seen him so worked up and angry and thanked the stars that there was a railing dividing the two men. She dreaded to think what would have happened, of what Carl would have been capable of. She made soothing noises of encouragement as she led him away. Her eyes were drawn to the all watching cameras upon Simon's roof eaves and then to his smirking face. He looked like the cat that had gotten the cream.

Chapter Twenty-Two

The inevitable knock on the door came a week later. It had taken Simon's grandson several days to get the edited video back to his grandfather and he'd had to seek favours from the more tech savvy employees at his work. A few pints at the local watering hole after work had allayed their sceptical questions. It had been money well spent. His grandfather had put him in no doubt as to who the victim was.

During these days, Carl had spent much of it sleeping, in-between nightmares. He wouldn't tell Tilly, but his flashbacks were becoming more frequent, and intense. He could smell Afghanistan, the all-pervading smell of goat dung, human body odour, and fresh blood. That sickly-sweet, cloying tang that clawed at the back of your throat and hung in your nostrils. He replayed the death of his best friend day and night, morose in the knowledge that nothing could bring him back, not even his immense guilt.

Today had been a better day. He had managed to get dressed, though not to shave or shower. He'd masked his smells with a liberal spray of anti-perspirant. He looked up at the direction of the front door but remained in his armchair.

Tilly knew the knock well enough. They had been to the house several times now. The environmental health officers had made it clear, that after staying for two hours and hearing nothing, that their time had been wasted. They wouldn't listen to her protestations that Simon's CCTV was trained on their door and he knew of their visit.

The EHO team had told her that it was a police matter, though they questioned if the noises were imagined, they planted the seed that perhaps an old man and woman were being harassed.

They knocked again and Tilly grudgingly went to answer it. She knew that the opening of the front door would herald an ill wind for Carl.

'Hello, may we come in please?' stated Bruce. The policeman didn't make it sound like a question.

'Yes, but why are you here, we haven't called you about the noise, there doesn't seem any point since you can't stop him.'

Bruce ignored what she had said, though made a mental note of it, 'Is your husband in?'

Tilly stepped out of the way, resigned to what was about to happen. 'He's in the lounge, you know the way.'

Bruce led the way, followed by an apologetic looking Yvonne. Tilly closed the outside door and followed them in. She was in time to catch the tail end of his formal caution and heard, '…threatening and abusive behaviour.'

'He was noise-harassing our daughter, that clown was banging a ladder against a seven-year-old's window. That's threatening behaviour.'

'We have a witness who heard it all and is willing to go to court to testify,' offered Yvonne.

'Her around the corner,' hissed Tilly.

'We have also been handed a video clip which clearly shows you threatening your neighbour and using foul language,' affirmed Bruce.

'I didn't threaten him,' argued Carl, rising to his feet.

'I'd advise you to say nothing more. We'd like to take you to the station and have a chat.'

'You mean that you are going to formally interview Carl and charge him?' questioned Tilly.

The two officers looked down at their feet, neither wanting to be the one to answer. They both clearly knew who was really at fault. They'd been handed another carefully edited video clip on a memory stick with the grandson's employee's logo etched on it.

'Will I need a lift home,' asked Carl in resignation. His head was downcast, and he was already feeling thoroughly ashamed for getting into bother with the law.

'No,' stated Bruce firmly. 'We'll give you a lift home, and chat about the noises on the drive back from Fraserburgh police station. 'We've allocated time to do that.'

'Lead on then,' said Carl as he emptied his pockets of his wallet and mobile phone and gave them to Tilly. He held her hand for a moment as he passed them to her, 'Don't worry love, I'll be home soon.'

Tilly merely nodded.

As the trio left, the children came down the stairs in time to see their father led away by the two police officers. Horror filled their faces and they went running to their mother.

Carl, walking to the police car that had parked across the road from his house, looked back. Instinct had told him to, a sixth sense that had kept him alive during many dangerous missions that usually went belly-up the moment their plan was initiated. His eyes were drawn to his neighbour's house. Simon was by his window, blinds drawn right back so that he had a better view. By his side was a figure that looked like him, only younger, with hair and thinner. He assumed, rightly, that this was his son, the one that still spoke with his father. Another son had left the family fold decades ago, and never spoke to his parents again, or so Dotty had told him one day. Carl eyeballed them for a moment, until his head was firmly touched by Yvonne and he had to duck into the back of the vehicle. As Yvonne sat down next to him and he heard the rear locks being activated, he caught sight of the two grinning men, appearing to do a jubilant dance from foot to foot by the window. What he didn't see was a fretful Millie, rocking gently on her armchair, guilt twisting her innards, agonising over her part in Carl's downfall.

The police car drew alongside a bollard that housed a scanner. Bruce lowered his window and flashed a card over it and the heavy gates to the car park slowly opened with a clunk. He drove to the first parking bay and expertly reversed in and got out of the car. He opened Carl's door and ushered him out. Once exited, Yvonne left her side of the car and joined the duo. They escorted Carl to the custody sergeant.

Once inside, Bruce snapped on a pair of thin blue disposable gloves. 'I have to search you first Carl. If you could please just stand with your legs slightly apart and your arm raised.

Carl did as he was told and felt a pair of hands deftly begin to frisk him over, 'Do you have anything on you that you shouldn't? Drugs or weapons?'

Carl's mind flitted back to another failed mission, or rather a mission from which lessons had been learnt. This feeling of being a prisoner was unsettling his mind. He took two deep breaths and replied, 'Neither.'

Yvonne hovered a paddle like piece of equipment over Carl's body and nodded to the custody sergeant. She caught Carl's eye and pointed to the desk.

The middle-aged woman confirmed Carl's details with him and then asked him a surprising question, 'Have you ever served in the Armed Forces?'

'Yes,' replied a puzzled Carl instinctively, 'with the Special Air Service.' He inwardly flinched as he realised what he'd said. He didn't like revealing his service with this regiment for security reasons.

Bruce looked at Yvonne knowingly, months of working together had given them time to build up a secret code of body language, known only to them and their past conversations during long shifts.

The custody sergeant handed Carl a leaflet. 'This organisation offers support; I'd advise you to read it and take the help offered. Would you like a solicitor? If you can't afford one, we have a duty solicitor.'

'No thank you,' he turned to Bruce, 'more than just a chat then?' He left the accusing question in the air.

'I'll get us all a drink of water,' flustered Yvonne as she went through to a nearby corridor.

The custody sergeant broke the silence between the two men, 'No need to take him to a cell.' She nodded to a row of metal seats that were bolted to a wall.

Carl dutifully walked over to them, Bruce shadowing his movements.

The duo had just sat down when Yvonne poked her head in from the corridor. She held the door open and said, 'Interview room one is ready for us.'

Bruce stood and waved Carl towards Yvonne, like an usher at His Majesty's Theatre in Aberdeen.

Carl stood up, let's get the show on the road, he gloomily thought as he carried through his leaflet.

Tilly had finally consoled the children and had given them plenty of reassurances that their father would be coming home and not be going straight to prison. Though she inwardly wondered that herself. She felt her long-at-bay anxiety start to rise, that familiar heavy feeling in her chest, that it would burst open. She hadn't had this bad friend come to visit since their move to Scotland. And now she was in her bedroom, about to open the bottom drawer of her bedside cabinet and reach into the depths of it and pull out her tin. The one that she'd kept hidden from Carl and hadn't felt the need to open for many months. She rolled up her sleeves in anticipation.

The camera on the wall eyeballed Carl in a silent accusation. I can't get away from those things, he thought. Carl reflected on the charge he'd just received, 'How long will I get for this? I've never been to prison.' Carl was taken aback when the officers laughed.

'You have to do bad things to get to prison these days. I suspect you'll be asked to do community payback,' reassured Bruce.

'Or given a suspended sentence and told to behave yourself for a set time,' added Yvonne helpfully. She turned the iPad back to face herself and Bruce, the video not needing to be replayed to Carl, she'd been surprised and impressed when he admitted the crime. Few criminals did, even with overwhelming evidence. 'If you'd chosen to have a solicitor present, he or she would have given you a rough idea of what to expect. You'll have to wait for a letter from the Procurator Fiscal office, our court system. Have you anything to say in mitigation?'

'Mitigation?' queried Carl, buying himself some thinking time.

'Any extenuating circumstances?'

'Just the lunatic slamming his ladder against my daughter's wall. It made her upset and that angered me, I'm sorry.'

'We will write to the Procurator Fiscal, in our report, that your family hear the noises too. But they cope with them better?' questioned Yvonne.

'They didn't serve. Loud noises,' Carl searched for the right words, 'disturb me. You know?'

Yvonne and Bruce nodded. 'We see things that disturb us, we get it, but do you?'

'You mean that I imagine the noises?'

'No,' said Bruce firmly. 'You cope differently. We'll put your service record in our report. Take the sergeant's advice and read the leaflet carefully, and please get your wife to read it. Help is available.'

Carl nodded. He knew when to listen. He also knew when he was temporarily beaten, and that this war was far from over. He made that promise there and then.

'I bet he's in a cell somewhere, probably up in Fraserburgh or even Aberdeen, sweating cobblers, eh, father?' asked Peter in jubilation. He looked across to Simon, hopeful for some praise from his dad for a job well done, though it was his own son's video editing work.

Simon would thank neither his grandson nor his son. 'Aye, I hope he doesn't come home for a while, it would serve him right to be locked up for a few months, speaking to me like that. Just as well there were those railings between us, I'd have swung for him myself.'

Peter cringed; he knew full well what it felt like to be on the receiving end of his father's rage. 'I'd better be off then,' he said hopefully, not wanting to stay long enough to get on the wrong side of his father.

Simon ignored him, he just kept up a silent vigil at the window, waiting to see if his neighbour came home.

'You be off then son,' said Millie in a low voice, for fear of disturbing her husband. 'Will we see you soon?'

'Sunday,' nodded Peter, 'I'll park in the driveway as usual and wash my car. I can only stay for a while, you know.'

'Yes,' sighed Millie, she knew right enough, stay long enough to wash your car, and not come inside for tea and cake, because of him. She glared at her husband, only brave enough to do it because his back was turned to her and his concentration was upon the window. 'Just time to wash your car,' she said wistfully.

Carl followed Bruce along the corridor, out into the main reception room and into a room a little bit bigger than the interview room. There were no seats, nor the soundproofing along the walls. There was a large machine to the side and a table with a camera. Fingerprints and mugshot time, he thought. He looked around him but could see no ink blotter like on the television.

As if reading his mind, Bruce said, 'It's all done digitally now, with special equipment. It makes life so much easier and there is no mess. You'd be surprised at the number of folks who'd smear their fingers and thumbs over walls and anything they could lay their hands on. Out of spite, just for us doing our job and charging them. Okay, just place your first finger on this glass plate here.'

Carl pushed his digit out as requested and rested it full on the piece of equipment.

Bruce pushed a few buttons and told him, 'And roll it from side to side, nice and slow.' He checked the screen, 'Perfect, thank you. We just need to repeat the process with your thumbs and other fingers.'

Carl obliged. Shame was creeping upon him, not for himself, but at what Tilly and his children would be thinking about him. How could he tell his parents that he'd gotten into trouble with the law? They'd be ashamed for sure. He didn't feel remorse, and would probably have done the same again, or even worse, to anyone who harmed or upset his daughter. He concentrated on rolling his fingers instead. The sooner they finished here, the sooner he'd get home and reassure his family that he wasn't about to make use of the facilities at the newly opened HMP Grampian in Peterhead, even if it did have a fine coastal view.

Bruce interrupted his reverie with, 'And if you could stand over there, against the wall and with your face to the camera. Please don't smile.'

Carl knew that he didn't have anything to smile about, having a criminal record would prevent him applying for certain jobs in the future, if he couldn't get a better income from the websites.

Dotty so wanted to pop across and provide some sort of comfort to her pal. She'd seen Carl being led away in a police car. The neighbourhood knew what had happened, Simon had finally made the man snap, just like he'd done with the neighbours before Guy and Finty. Only this time he'd had CCTV installed and now it had proven its worth, unequivocal evidence against Carl. But she couldn't go to Tilly, Simon was keeping his guard over the window and she didn't want to get into his bad books, she'd seen so many times what happened to people who did that.

Instead, she got herself ready for bed by filling up the small jug with water for her teasmade. She'd pop on radio 4, she didn't want to miss the last instalment of the Book at Bedtime. The soothing tones of the actor reminded her of Eric's kind voice that used to bid her goodnight.

It was dark when they left the police station and this time Yvonne drove. Bruce settled in the back seat, and between the two burly men there was little gap. Fortunately, they had no third passenger, just enough space to comfortably chat.

As they drove along the main road leading out of the town, Carl remembered happier times when his parents took him and his sister for a stroll along this old Victorian promenade style of walkway. Small amusement rides had been installed in time for the long summer holidays and Felicity and he had been young enough to enjoy them. The memory of their laughter no longer filled his soul, just a despondent sense of injustice.

Bruce broke the silence, 'Are the noises at specific times of the day, can we catch him at it?' he whispered conspiratorially.

'The worst are at night. It's like he is banging on the adjoining wall. That's why the other neighbours don't hear those. But they must have seen him run to his gate, slam it, and run off again, whenever I'm in the front garden. Or take his hammer to the nearest object, usually his bench. At the back garden, he rattles his railings with a metal pipe, or his hammer. He also uses this to hammer on his wheelie-bin lid.'

Bruce turned to look at him and said aloud, 'You are having me on?'

'No, really,' implored Carl. 'I wish that I can show you.'

'Do you have a good mobile phone?'

'Aye,' replied Carl absently, not sure of why the question was asked. 'I left it at home. I knew that you'd search me and thought that it would save you logging it all in along with my wallet.'

'What he means is do you have a good video camera on it,' said Yvonne over her shoulder helpfully. She drove on through St Fergus, the oil refinery was lit up like a space station with all its antennas, pipes, and other metal installations.

'To record him,' suggested Bruce.

'Oh, I had thought of that, but isn't it against the law, to record someone against their will, without permission?'

'No,' explained Bruce. 'The law changed a few years ago. You can film, but whatever you do, don't put it on social media. It can bias a trial. Get us the evidence and we'll do the rest. We didn't have this…'

'Conversation!' finished Carl. He sat up in his seat, enjoying the moment an owl swooped low over the car and plunged into the nearby trees. He made a note of its colourings and size, he'd check out his book later. He grinned. Getting evidence would be like taking candy from a kid. He'd set himself up as bait in his arbour. Simon wouldn't be able to resist smashing away at his dustbin like a possessed fiend. It'll be nice to have him taken away in a police car, whilst he watched at the window.

Lee looked upon his car with utter disbelief and a sinking feeling in the pit of his stomach. Brodie stood next to him, an incredulous look upon his face. Daisy sat obediently, her leash was held loosely by Brodie, but she could sense the despair emanating from her owners and elected to wait patiently. Her tail gave periodic tentative sweeps along the path and then was stilled as Lee broke the silence with, 'Who would do such a thing, I love my car? I've been in all day and only came out to get a treat for Daisy that I'd forgotten about. I bought them yesterday, on the way home. The car was fine when I parked it. I'd have noticed something like this.'

'I know love, I know,' replied Brodie, trying to comfort his husband. He knew just how much pride he took in his car. 'It's easily fixed.'

'I'll have to use our holiday money to get it repaired. The gouge runs deep as well as long. We've saved up so hard and I was looking forward to relaxing on the beach.' He looked down at Daisy, 'Though I'd have missed you.' Her tail wagged away, hoping to cheer her owner up. 'Who'd have done such a thing?' he wailed forlornly.

The couple instinctively looked towards Simon's house and their eyes locked on his, Simon was continuing his vigil at his window for Carl's return. As a bonus, he was able to see the hurt in the couple's faces. Pain that he had inflicted earlier with his nail. Simon grinned back.

'He always finds a way to upset folk, to get in their heads. This is his retribution for the other week when you answered him back and almost swore at him. He waited for an opportunity to get the upper hand. Let's go back inside,' advised Brodie. 'There is nothing that we can do until the morning. Let's not give him the satisfaction of seeing us upset. We'll go in and phone the police and ask them to make a note on their system. In case anything else happens.'

Lee reluctantly agreed and took his husband by the hand and the trio made their way across the street and into their house. As Lee closed his front door, a police car turned the corner of their road.

Chapter Twenty-Three

The two police officers followed Carl into his house and waited patiently in the hallway whilst his children and wife made a fuss of him and welcomed him home, like a soldier returning from deployment.

'Are you okay, I've been so worried? Did you get charged? What sentence can you expect?' bombarded Tilly, not waiting for her questions to be answered. 'I hate that old man for what he is putting you through.'

Whilst the children hugged their father and asked what the police station was like and if he saw any really bad people and was he handcuffed and did he try to escape, Yvonne said to Tilly, 'We know about the noise harassment and have advised Carl to film your neighbour.'

'Oh. We thought that he'd complain to you that he was being harassed and that we'd get arrested for filming him. So, we can whip out our phones and film him in the act, if we are quick enough?'

'That's right,' confirmed Yvonne.

Bruce nodded in agreement too. 'And you should be dialling 101 whenever he makes extreme noises after eleven at night. I'll be suggesting to my sergeant that we have officers standing outside his property, ready to hear the noises themselves. Then we can charge him with harassing your family.'

'Can you do anything about his cameras, they are pointing to the pavement too. Your officers will be spotted,' protested Tilly.

'We've several unmarked cars and if the noises are as loud as you say they are, then they should hear them from across the road. Hopefully, the cameras don't stretch that far.'

Tilly ruminated for a moment, from what was just said she surmised that the police had not actually seen the CCTV screens and angles of filming for themselves and had probably just taken Simon's word for it that they weren't trained on their front and back door 'Well, if anything, Carl will get a good night's sleep on those nights. It might help settle his mind. Peterhead environmental health officers have been next to useless.' She remembered who she was talking to, 'In my opinion.'

Bruce smiled grimly. It was a difficult situation this family found themselves in, and sadly an all too common one. But they could only work on the evidence given to them.

The courier eyed the blue coloured wheelie bin as he rang the doorbell and waited a few seconds. That would be counted as a safe place to leave the parcel. Though many households across the country would differ in that opinion.

Carl opened the door, feeling refreshed, despite the early hour, seven on the dot the doorbell had rung. They were first on the route, the nearby villages' households expecting a parcel from this delivery driver would benefit from a lie-in. 'Cheers mate, that was a swift delivery, I only ordered it two days ago.'

The courier, not caring, held out an electronic keypad for Carl to sign.

Carl juggled his parcel and the piece of equipment and duly signed, his signature appearing as a random scribble on the pad.

The man eyed the pad as he received it, 'Don't worry mate, they all look like that!' Have a great day!' he cheerfully said as he ran up the path and jumped back into his van.

Carl eyed his parcel, 'Oh, I will!' He looked up and smiled at the cameras on his neighbour's roofline. He closed the door and walked back to the kitchen, where he'd left his coffee machine working its morning magic. He was surprised to see his wife up and about, pouring herself some cereal out of a cheery looking box. Chocolate orange flavoured cardboard, he thought, that won't be full of sugar and all things bad.

'You look surprised to see me up.'

Carl was astonished that she had read his mind, she could read him like a book. 'Well, you don't normally surface until after ten, is everything alright?'

'Yes, I just slept like a log. I'm guessing you did too, laughing boy next door didn't keep you awake?'

'Not a sound. I reckon Bruce was true to his word. I've slept soundly for two nights now. I bet that a police car was sat outside again.'

Tilly nodded. Dotty had remarked yesterday that she'd seen one there the night before, a nondescript grey car with two men in the front seats, wearing casual clothes. At about two in the morning. When she went for a pee, she'd peeked through her net curtains. 'If only they'd stay there every night. It seems such a waste of police resources.'

'It's that clown next door who is wasting the council and the police resources, they've better things to do than catch a bitter old man noise harassing us over birds. He's pathetic.'

'Yes, yes he is,' agreed Tilly. 'Though he shouldn't get away with it.'

Carl beamed, placed his parcel on the kitchen table and pointed to it, like a child delivering a Christmas gift to a favourite relative.

'Okay, I give up, what's in the box, you are dying to tell me,' sighed Tilly theatrically.

'Okay, I can't go into specifics, but some of the jobs I did, for The Regiment.'

'Shhh!' interposed Tilly, continuing her dramas, 'It's all very hush hush!'

Carl rolled his eyes, 'Anyway, to continue, before I was so rudely interrupted.' He cast his hands over the box with a flourish, like a magician revealing his magic trick. 'These little gadgets will record video and sound. They are motion detected, even through windows. They can be applied to most surfaces, very discretely, and they'll record next door's actions from our kitchen, study, and Annabelle's windows. I'll even put a few outside, especially from the arbour. I'm going to enjoy a mug of coffee out there as soon as I come back from dropping the children off at school. I bought seven of them.'

'Clever, let's have a look then, and how much did that set you back? Where do you even buy these from?'

'Best not to ask,' replied Carl tapping his nose. 'I've made several contacts over the years.'

'Craig,' guessed Tilly, 'you got them via Craig.'

Carl looked at Tilly in astonishment, she really did know everything. 'Yes, he knows the best suppliers from the dark web. Unsavoury characters come in handy in his line of work.' Craig, like Carl, had served for seven years in the SAS and now had set himself up as a highly regarded detective agency for celebrities and high income business men and women in need of specialised operatives, employing many of his former buddies, Carl included.

Tilly walked over to a nearby drawer and took out a pair of scissors. 'Well, let's have a look then. It's not an excessively big box.'

'That's not what you said last night,' winked Carl.

Tilly chose to ignore his innuendo, though a smile cracked her lips at the joy of seeing Carl so enthusiastic. She handed him the scissors.

Carl took them and sliced open the tape and opened the box and pulled out several tiny black objects. The lenses on them were about the size of a ballpoint pen tip.

'They are ever so small, will they work?'

'Ahem. That's what you said last night!' quipped Carl, much to Tilly's chagrin, as she saw her children race each other to the bathroom. She hoped they were out of earshot.

Gordon lost, so wandered into the kitchen, 'What are those?' he asked whilst reaching over the table for a croissant.

'Okay, this is top secret Private Gordon,' joked his father.

Gordon rolled his eyes, 'Get on with it, dad,' he ordered.

'You mustn't tell anyone, otherwise we lose the element of surprise, but these are secret cameras, to record next door. He'll not be upsetting your sister again.

'Cool!' exclaimed Gordon, reaching up to give his father a high-five.

Carl grinned as he returned the gesture with a resounding clap that noted its approval of the spy systems.

A withered hand with liver spots poked through the railings of his back step and reached for a drawstring. It tugged and the wheelie bin lid opened, like that of a coffin lid creaking open in a ham seventies horror movie. The hand snatched at it, opened it wider, and then rammed it home with a resounding slam. A pair of legs, dressed in stained denims, a wet patch at the seam of its seat, ran from the back step and into the kitchen. The door was slammed tight.

Carl, in the arbour, tried not to react, he needed his prey to reveal the depths of its wickedness to his hidden camera. He sipped at his coffee, the caffeine making his already fast-beating heart pump that little bit faster. He remembered his special forces mantra and took two deep breaths, recalibrated and waited to deliver. He didn't need to wait much longer, he'd stalked his prey and knew its routines, a schedule cast in stone and not deviated. The habit was derived from the sole focus of annoying Carl, upsetting his family and him as much as possible.

The old man did not disappoint. He went running down the stairs, almost tripping up over the last step from his kitchen door, to his rear slabbed garden. He turned left and reached his wheelie bins, withdrew a hammer from up his sleeve of his heavily soiled donkey jacket, his work uniform for over forty years and proudly never washed, and thumped on the bin lid for all he was worth. Three times. He grinned as he looked to Carl in the arbour and his face froze, his victim did not jump with fright. Instead he was laughing. He stared at him brazenly through the wooden slats, was holding up his phone between the gaps, and was laughing hard and long whilst waggling his mobile.

Carl switched off the recording and shouted, 'Gotcha!' and hit the record button again. The reaction of this lunatic was priceless. He couldn't wait to share this to his pals. He might even share it on social media. A crazed old man hammering on a dustbin lid for no apparent reason. It might even go viral, like the old woman who put the poor cat in the wheelie bin. He laughed, even louder so that his mocking tones would carry, as the old man turned on his heels and scampered up his back steps, closing his back door quietly behind him.

'Worth every penny!' chuckled Carl, racing heartbeat not subsiding. He sat down, picked up his mug and took a slow, enjoyable sip of his coffee. He pulled out a protein bar from his pocket, slowly unwrapped it and took a bite. As he slowly munched through the treat he listened to the cooing of the wood pigeons, the ooo-woo of the pair of collared doves that fluttered down to his feeders and the tcheer call of the group of starlings busy at the fat-balls. He loved this new harmonious soundtrack of his back garden. His new pal, the robin, sang out his melodious tune in approval at his actions. The birds would now also enjoy a peaceful back garden.

Now all Carl had to do was to stop the Hippo from slamming her small shed door, located at the foot of her patio, and overlooking Carl's wall, next to the arbour. Since the bird-table incident, she had taken to opening and slamming home its doors in unison with Simon's wheelie bin hammering. He had no doubt that her beady eyes would be popping over the fence and gossiping with Simon. Though Simon would of course play the wounded martyr and complain that he was spied upon. The voyeuristic watcher really did not enjoy being watched in turn. Carl pitied Wayne, to work so hard all week and not realise what his wife got up to with Simon and other men. He quivered at the thought of Simon and that woman rolling about in bed, then immediately put those thoughts out of his mind and looked back to the birds frolicking about in his garden, just as nature intended. He patted his pocket and felt his phone snuggle safely from the cold late January day. He'd take his time transferring the recording to his laptop and then onto a memory stick. He didn't want his phone taken away as evidence by the police. He'd make Simon sweat for a bit. Carl thought that he might even lie back in his study recliner and enjoy the peace and quiet for a while longer.

Lewis drove into the disabled parking bay, thankful that he and Shona had found one so near to the rheumatology unit of Aberdeen Royal Infirmary. It was housed in the old part of the hospital, built to accommodate the influx of limbless casualties of the First World War. Its boxed brickwork had stood firmly against the North East elements and provided shelter and rehabilitation to countless servicemen and then for decades had been used for innumerable clinics. The listed building could not have double glazing installed and many of the original windowpanes had been deemed too thin to provide heat for overnight patients. The old boiler would only produce enough heat to sustain warmth for the day. Instead, patients needing overnight care went down the hill, towards the main building with its hodgepodge interconnected array of buildings, ranging from concrete monstrosities to recent urban architectural aesthetically pleasing newbuilds. All famed for excellent care. And that was what Shona was about to receive, an infusion of a drug that neither she nor her husband could pronounce. All they cared about was that it took much of her rheumatic pain away.

'Do you want me to find you one of their wheelchairs?' asked Lewis helpfully.

'No, no, the leg stretch will do me the world of good. The doctor said that it was important for me to walk as much as possible, to stop my muscles wasting away.'

'I'll just see you safely in then.'

She nodded. She appreciated the escort, ever since a young lad, who looked spaced out on something, slammed into her as he ran out of the building and knocked her off her feet. Lewis hadn't managed to get a parking space that day and had driven through the one-way system and double backed to the Borg Cube, the tall multi-storey car park, just off-site. It had been nicknamed by the local Star Trek fans. He'd then spent his customary hour wait in the canteen, innocently enjoying a mug of tea and a piece of cake, unaware that his wife was being checked over by the on-call doctor before her infusion.

Lewis slipped his gloved hand into her warm mitten-covered hand and they walked over to the automatic doors like two teenagers out for a summer stroll.

BANG, BANG, BANG.

Carl leapt from his armchair and dived under his desk. 'Gav, Gav,' he shouted several times. He started to rock, hitting his head on the wood. 'There's nothing I can do,' he despaired.

Hearing his yells from the kitchen, Tilly flung open the kitchen door and strode into the study, looking for her husband. She looked startled to see him under the desk. Bits of paper were trembling, making their way off the surface with the vibrations below. She ignored them as several sheaves fell to the floor. She knelt, 'Carl, it's me, Tilly.'

He ignored her and clasped his knees as he rocked and moaned, shouting out, 'His brains, I can see his brains.'

'Oh Carl,' cried out Tilly, 'what horrors did you see?' She instinctively reached out for him.

Carl, deep in a flashback, felt a hand touch him. He snarled and pushed with all his might.

Tilly went flying across the room, her back slammed into a bookcase and her head snapped back and hit one of the shelves. She let out a yelp of pain and sat there, stunned.

Carl, understanding the reality of what was going on, came to his senses. He crawled from under his desk and, still on his knees, went to his wife, his posture looking as if seeking forgiveness. He put out his hands for a cuddle. 'I'm sorry.'

'Leave me alone,' she shouted. She rose unsteadily to her feet and ran from the room.

Carl took two deep breaths and followed her. She had run up the stairs. He followed, slowly, allowing the flashback to fully wash over him, the emotions causing him the sensation of wanting to weep for his long-dead friend. He climbed the stairs, this can't go on, he thought, I think I need help, he finally admitted to himself.

He reached the bedroom door and hesitated at the handle. He expected to hear sobs, or a nose being blown into a tissue. Instead he heard the familiar rattle of a small storage tin, like an old-fashioned pencil case, or instrument case used by mathematical students. He'd not heard this noise since they lived in England, by her parents and brother. He went straight into the room.

Tilly was poised with a thin razor blade. It hovered over her arm where angry welts rejoiced its return and yearned for her to cut a new scar to join them.

Carl reached out and gently took it from her, 'I'm sorry that I've driven you to this. I didn't mean for you to get hurt. I reacted badly to the banging against our walls.'

Tilly nodded. She relinquished her hold on her old razor blade with reluctance. Her open drawer had given away its hiding place. She stayed silent for a few minutes, enjoying the stillness with her husband and the hold of his warm hand. 'I think he's slamming home his doors, three times in a row. If only we could film him doing that.'

Carl wanted to tell her that he'd finally caught him but didn't think the time for rejoicing was now. He kept quiet.

'You need help. I want you to look at me and tell me that you know you have PTSD.'

Carl looked at her dubiously, but then saw the razor blade he had carefully put back into the tin. 'If I do, will you please allow me to throw these out.' He nodded towards the tin.

'I was going to cut myself again. For the first time in months. Because of you. Admit it and then throw them out. If you promise to get help, I'll promise to not cut myself, and you can throw out my gear.'

He looked down to the floor, shamefaced at having to admit to needing help, 'I have PTSD. I'll book an appointment with the GP, the nice one, and ask for a referral to a counsellor, or whoever she thinks I need to see.'

'Thank you,' said Tilly with a grateful sigh, her growing headache temporarily forgotten.

The rattle of their letterbox echoed up the step. Carl stiffened. He'd been dreading each day's postal delivery. He'd been awaiting the inevitable Court summons. 'I'll make us a cup of tea first, then grab the kitchen calendar and phone the GP. Do you have any more razor blades hidden around the house?'

'Only those, I promise.'

Carl reached up and gently pressed his hand on her cheek and bent down for a quick kiss. He then snapped down the lid and left the room.

Tilly reached into her pocket for her phone and dialled Lewis. She had a feeling that from the few snippets that he'd revealed about his own army career, that he'd be best placed to help his son.

Simon slammed his fist into Millie's stomach, venting his rage at getting caught by his neighbour.

Her breath failed her as she acted as a human punchbag. Waves of pain surged through her, and in her confusion, she sought to understand what was happening, why she had angered him. She crawled into a ball, still held fast in her armchair, she tried to cry out but her need for air was more pressing as she floundered like a fish out of water, desperate to survive. As she gasped away, Simon walked over to the doorway, safe in the knowledge that he'd already shut the curtains from prying eyes, and rammed home the door, three times in quick succession. Each boom vented more of his anger and he left the room, intent on rifling through her purse and going out to the shop for alcohol. He left her crying and reeling from her punishment.

Lewis heard someone's phone ring out, breaking his concentration from that morning's Press and Journal newspaper. He heard the lady, sat in a wheelchair, by a nearby table, dressed in a dressing-gown and sporting the tell-tale barcoded hospital wristband, tut at the intrusion. Lewis rolled his eyes in fellow disapproval and then went red-faced as he realised that it was his mobile phone. He shamefacedly dug it out from the depths of his jacket pocket. He only had it for emergencies and hoped that Shona was okay, and that she hadn't been assaulted again. He breathed a sigh of relief when Tilly's name flashed on the screen. He fiddled with the buttons clumsily, until he remembered that Felicity had set up facial recognition for the lock screen as a security reminder. He held it up to his face, never knowing whether to smile or wink at it, and then pressed the accept call button. In a whisper he said, 'Hello Tilly, how are you?'

'Hello Lewis, not very well. Carl's not coping with the loud bangs we told you about. Can we come and see you?'

'I've been worrying about him. He's been looking paler and paler each time we see him. His mum thinks he's even losing weight. We are at the hospital, mum's having her treatment for about an hour. Is it urgent?'

'It can wait. Can we come over for tea?'

'Yes, but we won't get home until about four this afternoon. It'll have to be something quick and easy. I'll have to go shopping first.'

'How about we bring fish and chips, from the Ashvale, our treat?'

Lewis's eyes lit up and he spoke loudly into the phone, forgetting about the other café customers, 'Oh, magic. Shona will have a small haddock supper and I'll have a haggis supper.'

Tilly grinned, she loved how quaint it sounded, the habit of calling chips with the takeaway food, supper. 'Your usual then. I'll get you a bottle of Irn Bru to share with the kids. We won't stay long, it's a school night, just long enough for you to talk sense to Carl.'

'Should we be worried? Are you and the children okay?'

'Mostly. But it's Gavin, he's been having nightmares and flashbacks about Gavin.'

'Ah,' replied Lewis, in a whisper again. He'd feared this, ever since Carl had spent a few days on leave, after the funeral, years ago. He'd never seen his son so silent. Lewis thought back to Northern Ireland, and his own demons that he'd battled so long to keep at bay, with Shona's help. 'Okay, see you soon. After we've eaten, perhaps you can keep the children and Shona busy whilst I'll take Carl down to my new wooden bench. I've been meaning to show him it. Make sure he brings a warm jacket; it's going to be a cold night.'

'Will do, thank you Lewis,' sighed Tilly as she hung up.

Lewis looked at the phone, dropped it back into his jacket pocket and pushed away his plate with the cream cake on it, he'd suddenly lost his appetite.

Chapter Twenty-Four

Tilly walked down the stairs, expecting the sound of the kettle and the clinking of mugs. Instead she was met with silence, even the idiot next door had ceased his noise.

She entered the kitchen and found Carl sat at the table, looking down at a brown envelope. 'Is that what I think it is?'

'Yes. I've been waiting for the Court date and this has the stamp of the Procurator Fiscal on it. I can't bring myself to open it.'

Tilly sat down, then patted his hand and he slid the envelope across to her. She left it in front of her, 'Want me to open and read it first?'

Carl nodded, feeling like a sixth-form student not wanting to know his exam results.

Tilly slit it open with her fingers and unfurled the letter. A small booklet fell onto the table. She ignored that and read the letter. Between sentences she peeked out and looked at Carl. First with a deep frown and then with a shake of the head. 'You call Judges Sheriffs up here?'

Carl nodded, it must be bad, he thought, to go in front of a Sheriff. He stayed silent whilst she read on.

She poked her head out again, like a librarian about to silence a talkative customer. 'The High Court,' was all she said.

Carl felt the prickly heat rise in him. He snatched off his jumper and slung it across an empty seat.

Tilly bobbed out from the letter again, 'You have fifteen on a jury up here in Scotland, is that right?'

Carl didn't know, but it sounded like he'd soon find out. Beads of perspiration dotted his forehead. He looked for a napkin on the table to wipe his head and then spied the leaflet's cover. It boasted, 'Diversion from Prosecution: Your Guide.'

'You teasing bit…' he began, only to be interrupted by peals of laughter from his wife that resounded through the walls and were wasted on the empty kitchen next door. Simon had long-gone and had left a wailing wife in their lounge whilst he shopped for booze.

'You're not off the hook just yet boyo. The Fiscal Office have stipulated that you see a GP, follow a treatment plan, and go to their offices to see a social support worker. And you'd best do everything they say, or you'll have me to answer to.'

Carl got up and hugged her, a beaming smile on his face, he'd read everything carefully, but it sounded like he wouldn't have a criminal record after all. He broke off the embrace, took out his phone, and waggled it to Tilly, almost seductively. 'I've something special for you to watch!' He placed it on the table and hit the play button, he watched with joy as her smile spread across her face and beamed as radiant as the nearby lighthouse's guiding emission.

It was Brodie's turn to look at his car despairingly. All four tyres were flat, and the car sagged to the road, like a tortoise stuck in his shell in the sand and seeking a drink. He looked around him, as if seeking the culprit. He was on his own and resisted the temptation to call Lee and share this burden. But he didn't want to worry his husband. Lee had tossed and turned all night and had risen early and had taken his car to the local garage to be assessed for repairs and respray. He'd taken Daisy along for companionable comfort. Brodie didn't have this luxury, there was no way that he could drive to work. He reached for his phone and tossed up whether to ring for a breakdown truck first, or call his work to say that he'd be late in. As he was going through his contacts list, he heard scurrying movements, like that of a runner with a limp.

'Oh dear!' rejoiced Simon, 'It looks like someone won't be getting to their work on time. That's such bad luck, having all four tyres pop like that, dear oh dear,' he mocked. 'It looks like someone took a Stanley knife to them,' he challenged.

Brodie stared at him in disbelief, and then in anger, 'Do you know anything about this?' he accused.

'Me, sir, no sir,' taunted Simon, 'I'm just going to the shops, minding my own business. Like you and your,' he searched for a derogative word, but noticed a mother and small child walking nearby, 'good friend should,' he settled with.

Brodie nodded but kept silent. He knew that this would escalate if he wasn't careful. He turned away and continued to go through his phone contacts, looking for the breakdown service that he'd joined when he bought the car. His fingers hesitated over the screen.

'There's a good boy,' jeered Simon. 'And keep your unnatural fella in check too. He wouldn't want another scratch on the other side of his car either, would he?' He laughed as he made his way to the shops, leaving a fuming Brodie behind him.

Brodie flicked his finger on the screen and went out of his phone contacts, he dialled 101 instead.

Carl, as was his custom when visiting this car park, gave an imagined salute to the war memorial that stood proudly by the pavement, acting as a talisman to the crossroads. A solitary figure of a Gordon Highlander soldier was depicted, as if ready to engage the enemy, rifle poised for action. He was kilted, booted, and carried his webbing stuffed with ammunition. He was mounted on a granite plinth that commemorated the fallen, the war dead of two World Wars and of those in conflicts, thereafter, including some who had died in action in several campaigns that Carl had been involved in.

He couldn't find a parking space, so parallel parked and kept the engine running. 'Fall out troops, I'll stay here and guard the car from enthusiastic traffic wardens.' He turned around and winked at the children and whispered, 'Mind and ask for them!'

The children took their cue and exited the vehicle and ran into the take-away which had tables at the back for those who wanted a leisurely fish and chips experience. Annabelle and Gordon waited patiently at the counter, whilst their mum finished questioning their father.

She eventually joined them, a puzzled look on her face. She took out a slip of paper and rattled off an order to the assistant, who then conveyed the order to the harried looking fryer, like a game of Chinese whispers.

'And two deep-fried Mars Bars please,' called Gordon above the counter to the fryer taking their order.

The assistant looked to Tilly and she sighed and said, 'Just this once. But you've to share them with your grandparents.'

Gordon and Annabelle looked at each other, twinkles in their eyes, they knew that their grandmother wouldn't want one and that she wouldn't allow their grandfather to have one either. He was supposed to be watching his cholesterol, whatever that was. They knew they'd have a whole one each.

They peered out of the window, thick with condensation, hoping to give their father, waiting in the car, the thumbs up. He'd wanted them to get the deep-fried treat so that he could take a photo for his Scottish Recipes social media accounts.

Gordon stepped forward, rubbed at the window with the sleeve of his jacket, making it damp, peered out and stuck his thumb in the air. A triumphant toot came from the waiting car. He stepped back to the queue, eyeing the fridge, seeking out his favourite orange fizzy drink that his grandfather had introduced him to. He grinned as he saw that the chiller was well-stocked.

The steam from the laden fryers rose like puffs of clouds and sought an escape from the take-away. Finding its exit blocked, they clung to the windows and dripped to the wooden base. Annabelle then took her turn at the condensation heavy window and drew a large smiley face for her father to see, in-between looking out for the blue striped peak hats of the traffic wardens, though they had been replaced in this area by Police Community Support Officers. Carl had missed the memo, he was just looking out for anyone carrying a handheld scanner type device, a peak hat and fluorescent jacket.

The assistant expertly shovelled the correct portion of chips into the containers holding each particular order, asked which ones needed salt and vinegar, seasoned those that needed them and swiftly parcelled up the suppers with several layers of insulating white paper that soaked up the excess fat.

Tilly helpfully placed a reusable canvas bag on the counter for the assistant to put their meals in, with two smaller white parcels on top, containing the children's cherished dessert.

The trio made good their escape from the heat of the take-away and piled back into the car. 'Any signs of the enemy sergeant-major?' interrogated Gordon.

'No, we are good to go sir!' quipped Carl, waiting for everyone to put on their seat belts before driving off, the heavy scent of vinegar and fat caused his stomach to rumble and his mouth to salivate.

Lewis placed the assorted trays around the kitchen, each with a paper napkin and cutlery. It looked like a junk shop assembly line, with its mix of colours, tin plating, wood, and plastic coatings. His favourite tray, reserved for his son, was that of the wings and daggers emblem of his Regiment's cap badge, central on the highly polished tray, with campaigns and years to either side. He'd just finished looking out some glasses and the ketchup bottle when the front door was opened and let in a tell-tale draft of cold air that let him know that his visitors had arrived. He heard the children tell their grandmother about the deep-fried Mars Bars and he kept one ear out for her reply. Sadly, he knew he wouldn't be getting a bite, and earlier, she hadn't been too pleased to hear about the high cholesterol take-away they'd all be munching down on in the living room. Though she made an exception when she learnt that Tilly needed a chat and was worried about Carl.

Tilly walked in and took out the carefully wrapped parcels and transferred them onto the plates all ready and waiting on the trays. 'Thank you for listening to me on the telephone Lewis, I'm at my wits end with Carl.'

'I've been suspecting this,' he said in a low voice so that it wouldn't travel to the other room. 'Let's get this lovely food eaten and our bellies warm, and then I'll take our lad outside for a chat. He usually listens to the wisdom of his old dad.'

Tilly smiled gratefully and piled on the food, shouting each recipient through from the lounge, having first made sure that Annabelle carried through Shona's tray. She then asked Gordon to take the brown and red sauce through and offer it to his grandmother.

Soon the family were silent and munching away, the local television news playing quietly on the background.

Lewis cast several glances to his son, recognising the distant look in his eyes, the dark shadows under his eyelids, and his sudden loss of muscle, with a slightly gaunt look in his face. Unusually, he hadn't taken the time to shave or comb his hair. He just didn't look right.

Carl pushed his tray further down his knees, away from his body, signalling that he'd had enough of his black pudding and chips. He'd only eaten half of the meat and he'd toyed with his chips, moving them around his plate idly. He used his napkin to wipe away the oily residue on his lips, crumpled up his napkin and announced, 'I'll save these left-overs to put on the bird-table tomorrow.'

'Have you seen any interesting birds, I bet you get loads with all the surrounding trees and bushes?' asked Shona.

Carl half-heartedly told her about the sole magpie he'd seen earlier.

'You might be lucky enough to get a pair nesting nearby.'

'Maybe, here's hoping. Though there are lots of crows.'

Lewis shuddered; a momentarily dark look crossed his face. He stood up and announced, 'I'll take you out to see my new bench Carl. Put your jacket on and I'll switch the outside lights on.' He made his way into the kitchen, popped his tray on the table and removed his jacket from the back of one of the chairs. As he was putting it on, he heard Tilly say, as they had rehearsed earlier, 'I'll tidy up whilst the children eat their dessert.'

Carl handed Gordon his mobile phone, 'Take lots of photos from different angles, especially of the middle, I want folk to see the caramel goodness ooze out.'

Tilly now realised why he'd let them have such a calorific laden and unhealthy treat. She'd gotten used to his odd requests for photos for his growing social media accounts. He'd tucked into potted hough and oatcakes the other day. When he'd bought it home from the butchers, Tilly thought it looked like dog food. She didn't try any after he'd taken his photographs. She caught her husband winking at the children as he left the room and joined his father in the kitchen.

'It's a bit dark and cold to being going out dad,' he thoughtfully suggested.

'Nonsense, we've warmed ourselves up with that lovely fish supper, let's have a look at my bench, I've placed it at the foot of the patio, overlooking the lawn.' He walked out, ushering his son out, and ensured he closed the door so that the children didn't follow them out.

Carl dutifully made his way to the bench and stood squinting at it, the flare from the lights attached to the back wall just about illuminated it.

Lewis sat down and patted the space next to him. 'Let's have a father son talk.'

'Ah, I see,' the penny finally dropped with Carl. 'Tilly has put you up to this.'

'Busted! As the grandchildren have taught me to say. But seriously, you aren't looking great son, you look like you've lost weight and I noticed you hardly ate anything. Tilly tells me you've been having nightmares.' He left the statement open.

'Just bad dreams really,' admitted Carl.

'More like night terrors. You've been frightening her as well.'

Carl looked down at his outstretched feet and then at the grass, noticing the little tray of cat food and small saucer of water that his dad had left out for the local hedgehog. Though he never fed the birds. He couldn't see any feeders, nor a bird-table. 'I don't mean to,' he confessed.

'Neither did I son, neither did I.'

Carl looked at him in puzzlement.

'As you know, I was in Northern Ireland, you played with my medal often enough when you were young. I know the traumas we saw, what we had to do.'

'You've never really spoken about it.'

'It was at the height of The Troubles son, and they were troubling times, especially for the mums and wives. The Provisional Irish Republican Army were devils, most as young as we were. I'd barely left my teenage years behind. We went on the usual foot patrols, getting spat at and bottles thrown at us by the young yobs. But one day I was with the Reaction Force, sent as back-up to an illegal arms cache. Two of your boys, the SAS, they'd had it under surveillance for weeks. We were tasked to provide protection whilst it was dug up and neutralised. Taking out the rifles and ammunition would prevent future deaths, we were told. Only it was booby-trapped. It blew my best mate to pieces, right in front of me. As if that wasn't traumatic enough, the IRA had been watching the SAS blokes without them knowing and had posted a sniper. He kept taking pot shots at us when we tried to move. It took us hours to find his position and kill him. I had to watch as crows ate away at bits of my pal. Then, after our sergeant shot dead the sniper, I had to pack the body bag, well, what was left of my mate, from the birds.'

Carl looked appalled, 'You never said.'

'I did try and steer your career into a civilian job, but your heart was set on the army. I just couldn't stop you. That's why we were worried so much whenever you were deployed.' He patted his son's hand, his tremble giving away his emotions, 'And that's why we gave thanks to God that you came home in one piece and found the love of a good woman and brought delightful grandchildren into our lives.' Tears fell from Lewis's eyes, 'Don't ever let them join up, don't let them have nightmares.'

Tilly switched off the light from the kitchen so that she could peer better out of the window and see how Lewis was getting on, she was shocked to see Carl reach out and comfort his father who was openly weeping, shoulders heaving and giving away his distress. Carl put his protective arms around him and held him tight. It was supposed to be the other way around, she thought. She sighed, switched back on the light, rolled her sleeves up, and reached over for the washing-up liquid.

'Sorry, that caught me unawares,' explained Lewis, drying his eyes on a handkerchief from his pocket. 'His name is on the war memorial in the town square, next to the chip shop. I put a small poppy there every year and save one to put on the anniversary of his death. I still see those crows, pecking away and gouging away at chunks of my mate. For years I watched his parents attend the Remembrance Day parade through the town. Then the father died, from a broken heart, some say. His mother died a few months later.

Such a waste. It's the crows I see in my terrors, pecking away at my pal, and then me.'

'I see Gavin,' revealed Carl.

'Your best friend, the one you took home on leave one year?'

'Yes, he was an orphan and had no family. He said that it was the best Christmas he'd ever had, he loved being made a fuss of by mum.'

Lewis smiled at the memory, 'He was a big lad, bigger than you. He almost ate us out of house and home,' he chuckled, tears now long gone.

'That's why he was made point man, he could wield the shotgun and break through any door, usually.'

'The mission went wrong?' enquired his dad softly.

Carl started to hyper-ventilate and he could feel his heart racing, 'It was supposed to be an intelligence gathering mission. The compound was supposed to be empty,' he cried out.

Lewis remained silent, waiting for his son to gather himself and to continue.

'An AK-47 doesn't shoot straight like in the films. The insurgent shot from his hip, we'd surprised him. The recoil made the rifle fire high, right through Gavin's head. It tore his mouth apart.' Carl began hyper-ventilating and rubbing at his face, he stuttered and cried out, 'I can still taste his blood, I had to spit out his teeth and brains.' He gripped his father, 'I can still see it happening,' he beseeched as his grip tightened. 'Every single night,' he wailed.

Lewis reached out and put his arms around his son. Carl thumped his head into his chest and his father instinctively cradled him, stroked down his hair, and made soothing noises, as if Carl were a child again. Carl wept and wept.

The last of the grease left the final plate and Tilly placed it on the drying rack and tipped away the dishwater. It made its way down the sink hole and into the drains outside, its gurgling noise lost to the wailing going on out there. Her heart broke as she saw her husband, reduced to a crying, shaking wreck, being cradled by his elderly father. Have I made things worse, she guiltily questioned herself?

Chapter Twenty-Five

Carl stared across at the young lady behind the desk, her eyebrows drew him in, hypnotising him as they became his focus. He couldn't work out if they were real, painted on, tattooed, or if she just looked shocked. He saw her mouth drop, a red patch appeared at her throat and she self-consciously rubbed at it, as if trying to make it disappear. Only it made it worse. Deeper red splotches sprung up along the neckline of her blouse and she fiddled with her tiger-striped scarf in an attempt at protecting herself from what she had heard.

'I, I, don't know what to say...' the Fiscal support worker stammered. 'I wasn't expecting that.' She shuffled the pieces of paper in front of her, trying to get them to align, to give some order to her surroundings. She put them into the folder, the one with Carl's name on the cover, then took them out again, leafed through them, and then tucked them away again. 'I think,' her voice croaked, and she reached for her bottle of water, a cucumber slice was inside, floating like a specimen in a test tube. Her hand shook and water was spilt onto the desk.

'Allow me,' offered Carl, reaching over for a tissue by his side of the desk. He plucked one from the box and mopped up the spilt water. He looked around him for a bin in this sparse office and couldn't find one. He shrugged and left it on the desk.

'Th, thank you,' she stuttered. 'I just need to step out for a moment, I think I need to speak to my supervisor.' She sprung up, made to leave the office, had a brief think, turned back to the almost barren desk, grabbed the folder, and ran out of the room.

I think that I may have over-shared, thought Carl laconically. He tried to swivel in the metal chair. Like at the police station, this one was bolted to the floor, as was the small desk and the other chair. There was no computer on the desk, though there was a double plug socket and adjoining telephone socket, though no phone. Probably to stop people throwing furniture and monitors about, he pondered as he waited. This was confirmed when he glanced around the white walls and saw faded posters that warned that violence would not be tolerated against staff. The thin line of electronic panic alarm strips that surrounded the room gave further credence to this thought process. The grey carpet was barren and there was no pattern for his idle eyes to follow and pass the time. He took out his mobile and started playing a game, effortlessly moving pieces of fruit about. After several minutes he gave up, the music was doing his head in and having to keep up with the ever-dropping supply of shapes was increasing his anxiety levels. He seemed to be getting stressed about the least thing these days. The stuffiness of the room and the confined space, just enough room to swing a cat, was making his skin itch, another heat attack was about to engulf his body. He leaned forward, shrugged out of his jacket and then his jumper and was busy draping them over the back of the chair when a middle-aged woman walked in, smiling reassuringly at Carl. She was followed by the young lady, holding his folder tightly. He was about to wonder what it said, but his thoughts were interrupted.

'Hello Carl, I'm Marion. I've been having a chat with Amelia.'

Carl nodded and said hello, and then as an afterthought he turned to Amelia. 'Sorry, I think that I gave you too much information, I didn't mean to speak about Gavin, it just seemed to all come out.'

Amelia looked down at her folder and placed it to her chest, as if it were body armour about to protect her from a fresh onslaught of information. She didn't trust her voice, not just yet.

Marion spoke for her. 'We are glad that you did. The Fiscal Office, based on the police reports of how many times that your neighbour has kept you and your wife awake, and that you lost your temper with him, realise that you need help.'

'I didn't mean to swear and point my finger at him, but he was upsetting my daughter.'

'We know. There is a long history of harassment over this man,' began Marion.

'He's the one harassing my family,' interrupted Carl.

Marion nodded, 'Though we need proof of that. I mean to say that he has been accused, in the past, of harassing other neighbours.'

Carl was about to reach for his mobile so that he could show her the video clip; but thought better of it. He knew that he'd need to be patient and get more video clips and build up a better case against his oddball of a neighbour. Just a few more weeks of going into the arbour should do it.

'It's a pity that the council couldn't have been more helpful,' continued Marion. 'Mind you, the environmental health officers have to send your neighbour a letter to say that they will be recording before they install microphones, which doesn't help either.'

Carl looked at her in disbelief, 'In my game, the element of surprise was always our greatest asset. We didn't go into covert operations by telling the enemy that we were watching their movements.'

'Yes,' agreed Marion. She looked at her colleague and nodded encouragingly, almost motherly.

Amelia coughed, 'We've identified that you've a lot on your plate, having to look after a vulnerable wife who suffered child abuse, trying to set up and run a new business, caring for young children and now we think that you have Post Traumatic Stress Disorder and need help, not punishment.'

Carl was about to argue that he didn't have PTSD until the, 'not punishment,' part registered in his brain. He saw his get-out clause appear in front of his eyes, in big flashing neon lights. He'd go along with it for the moment.

'So, we've devised a plan,' explained Amelia, her red rash dissipating from her neck. The more she spoke, the more she gained her strong voice and confidence. 'We'd like you to agree to see a SSAFA support worker, going back to your GP and following his or her advice and going to Combat Stress for an assessment. What do you think?'

Carl mulled it over, he'd heard of the military charity. They stood for Soldiers, Sailors, Airmen and Families Association, but thought that they were for old folk who needed those electric wheelchairs.

Marion must have seen his puzzled expression and prompted with, 'We think SSAFA can help you find sources of donations to help you with soundproofing your house. Your regimental association and other charities such as Poppy Scotland and the Royal British Legion can help, but everything must be referred through SSAFA. That should deal with the noise issues.'

It just sounds like I'm going to be referred from person to person, without anyone tackling the real issue here, that awful old man, he thought, but decided to go with the flow anyway. He nodded his head obediently.

'Great stuff,' said a delighted Amelia, thankful not to be hearing anymore about the violence that Carl had witnessed and perpetrated during his military career. 'I will need you to sign forms agreeing to us sharing your information. Once that's done, we don't see the need to see you again, unless you don't go to these appointments with Combat Stress, your GP and SSAFA. But if you do all three, the Fiscal Office will probably drop your case.'

Carl nodded, took the offered forms and pen, and dutifully signed them. Just moving me on to the next problem, he thought, just like the police and council, let me be someone else's problem. He returned the forms and smiled at Amelia. She smiled back and yes, they were tattooed on, he thought as he was ushered out of the office.

Brodie, now driving Lee's car, tooted his horn as he saw his pal come out of the revolving doors of Buchan House, the

Aberdeenshire Council Headquarters. He pulled into the side of the road and wound down his window. 'Carl, want a lift mate?'

Carl gave him the thumbs up and walked to the car, he gulped as he saw the long, deep gouge along the passengers doors, it tailed off with an upwards stroke near the petrol cap, as if the perpetrator had left a tick, a mark of approval at his handiwork. 'Cheers mate, I was going to walk home and have a bit of fresh air.'

'That's a long walk mate, a wasted walk without a dog.'

Carl put on his seat belt and looked behind him to the empty seats, 'No Daisy?'

'No, it's Lee's turn to have her at work today.' He nodded to Buchan House, 'Paying your council tax?'

'No,' replied Carl thoughtfully, 'I've had to see the Fiscal Office support worker, you know, over the swearing and shouting.'

Brodie nodded, the neighbourhood knew all about it, Simon had been telling everyone who would listen that he'd been assaulted by the man. Half of the village must have heard Carl, his voice carried through the houses as he tore verbally into Simon. 'It isn't right, what he's been putting you through. I hope they aren't going to prosecute you?'

'No, the opposite, they are getting me some help. The young lady thinks that some army charities can help with soundproofing.'

Brodie turned left, away from the new Aldi store and along some stunning views of Peterhead harbour and lido. That cheered the duo up and Brodie said happily, 'That's a brilliant idea, then you won't hear that lunatic slamming doors in the middle of the night. Have you tried earplugs?'

'Yes, hopefully it'll work. Tilly and I have tried every type of earplug online at eBay, but they are all uncomfortable.'

'I know what you mean. Daisy sleeps in our room, Lee won't have it any other way. But she doesn't half snore?'

The duo broke into laughter. Brodie continued with, 'Then I found wax mouldable earplugs, they shape around your ear and the wax sticks to your lobe, so they don't go into the ear canal. They block out loads of noises. I've slept like a baby since. You can even wear them during the day and hear the TV and conversations, but not loud noises. I'll drop off a couple of pairs tonight, or get Lee to call in, you know how much he likes seeing you!'

Carl nodded, 'Brilliant, thank you.' He hesitated, not sure of how to begin this new conversation, but ploughed on anyway, 'Er, you do know that there isn't anything going on between Lee and I?'

Brodie burst out laughing, 'You mean he won't turn you! Of course, I do, he's always like that to hunky men. I think if one truly returned the embrace and made advances, he'd run a mile.'

Carl grinned, that was another weight off his mind. 'What on earth happened to your car? It looks like someone took a screwdriver to it.'

Brodie looked grim. He went straight across the McDonalds roundabout, surprisingly clear for once. 'We have no proof, but after Lee had an altercation with your neighbour, those gouges appeared by the next morning. This is Lee's car I'm borrowing. Mine had four flat tyres when I next went out. They are getting replaced at the garage. Lee's car had been deliberately scratched overnight as well. As you know we always park with the bonnet facing towards the shop, so we can drive away out of the village and get to work that little bit quicker. We all know who did it, don't we?'

'He's a wicked man, he causes nothing but misery wherever he goes, and he's so underhand too. He's too cowardly to say anything to your face.'

'Maybe to you, but he calls Lee and I such nasty names, about our sexuality mostly.'

'That's not right, he just thinks that he's above the law.'

'Yes, and he gets away with it. He puts on that outraged old pensioner look. But really, he's sticking his finger up to the law. Do you know that he convinced the last neighbours, those before Guy and Finty, that he was a frail ninety-year-old man? He even convinced the council mediation team and the police sergeant who the family called in to help them. They moved too.'

Carl grimaced, aghast at this fresh information. He thought to the motion detector cameras he'd placed discretely throughout his home and garden. They'd be working their magic. He might even go down to the arbour and have a sit for a few minutes and draw the enemy out.

Lewis looked at his watch with worry. He hoped that his son was getting on alright. Carl had promised to phone him with news and Lewis had told him to make sure he chatted to Tilly first. The poor woman was beside herself with worry and Carl needed to reassure her that he was getting cared for. Lewis hoped that his son would have had a sympathetic support worker, someone who would make sure he got some help out of the situation he found himself in, through no fault of his own.

He rolled down his sleeve and adjusted his shirt cuff and pushed the shopping trolley obediently after his wife. She was in the Tesco electronic buggy, racing ahead, careful not to run anyone over. They were doing the big shop in Danestone and the aisles were far too much for Shona to walk up and down. Lewis was doing his best to scan each item into the special scanner he'd attached to his trolley, but he was all fingers and thumbs. He dropped a tin of beans and watched it go rolling down an aisle. As he followed it, he saw, surprisingly, that it came to rest by a pair of paws.

'I'll get that for you,' said a quiet voice, helpfully. A hand stretched down and scooped it up and held it out for Lewis. Her other hand was holding a leash.

'Thank you,' said Lewis gratefully as he received the runaway item. He nodded to the dog, an almost white retriever, with traces of golden on her flanks, 'She's gorgeous. Are you training her?'

'Sort of, she's mine now, but I need her to learn a few more commands before she's fully assistance. See you.'

Lewis watched her go and made a note of the 'Bravehound' that was written on the back of her fleece jacket, he'd go onto the internet and see what they were about.

The dustbin lid was forced down with a large push and clattered shut, breaking the silence of the surrounding gardens. A pair of collared doves rose to the air in silent protest, save for their gentle flutter of wings. They roosted on a nearby tree and bobbed their heads about as they watched Simon intently.

Simon snatched out his hammer and beat down on his bin lid three times, smirking as he saw Carl jump out of his seat in the arbour.

Two teenage girls watched from an adjoining house, their mobile phones capturing the clip. They wanted to show their mother where the source of the noises had been coming from. She'd take them to the council so that they could finally stop her peace being ruined.

Simon ran back to his house, proving that he wasn't a frail ninety-year-old at all.

Carl, heart racing, sipped his coffee, happy in the knowledge that he'd not have to play the sacrificial goat for much longer.

Chapter Twenty-Six

Carl sat in another office, behind another desk, with another young woman in front of him. This one had natural looking eyebrows, but her eyes held his throughout their conversation. He shifted in his seat at the sight of the helicopter picture in front of him. The framed photo to his left was no better, they were troops in Iraq by the look of it. Were they there to deliberately put him at unease?

As if reading his mind the psychiatric nurse before him apologised and said, 'We only rent the room from Poppy Scotland, I'm sorry that you've had to drive all the way to Inverness, we don't have any facilities in Aberdeen, I'm afraid.'

Carl tried to make light of it, 'Not to worry, we are going to visit Culloden afterwards.'

'It's so surprisingly peaceful there, despite what happened, in the battle.'

Carl looked to the pictures again, 'Yes,' he finally offered. He'd spent the last forty minutes being grilled by her. She asked such personal and probing questions and wouldn't take no for an answer. She made him talk about specifics. Despite her being dressed in a winter jumper, he had stripped down to his t-shirt and was itching to get outside. Beads of perspiration were on his forehead and he kept lifting his arms, to dry the damp, he was feeling in his armpits.

'I'm going to repeat this again, as I think that you chose not to hear me first time around,' she insisted. 'You have PTSD. Yes, your neighbour is a focal issue, and is most probably the cause of it manifesting. Though, given the amount of trauma you have witnessed, especially seeing the death of your friend, it would have manifested at some stage of your life. Frankly, I'm surprised that it hasn't manifested before, especially during your long army career.'

Carl squirmed in his seat. He was thinking back to when his pal had been taken aboard a similar helicopter. He'd placed him in the body bag, or what he could find of him. He wanted out of the room, out of the building, and into the cool, refreshing air. The urge to sprint out was so overwhelming, but he fought it and won, just.

'You need to be admitted to our treatment centre in Hollybush House, in Ayr. I'd suggest the six-week course, to begin with, as soon as possible.'

Carl looked shocked, he'd expected to come along and tick the box that he'd been and then go home again. He really didn't believe that he had PTSD and wanted to argue with her but knew that no crime goes unpunished. He wasn't going to give that old man the satisfaction of seeing him in court. He went with the flow and listened to her describe the treatments he'd receive. Then added, 'Have you anything nearer, my wife is in a fragile state, I can't leave her on her own to cope with our children, the house and herself. She might start cutting again, or something worse.'

She looked down at her notes, 'Yes, I can see that would be a problem for you. Leave it with me, I'll see what I can do for you. I have someone locally in Aberdeen who runs a support group, for veterans. That should help you, and please the Fiscal Office.'

Carl's leg was pumping up and down, in rapid beat to that of his heart, in rhythmic agitation. 'Thank you,' he muttered.

'That's us then, I'll see you out.' She stood up and ushered him, noting the damp sweat stains on his t-shirt. They halted at the inner security door and she waved her pass, it gave a beep of approval and she pointed to the outer door. 'You'll need me to clear you through there as well.' She walked him to the outer security door and watched as he briskly left, taking no time to pull on his jumper or jacket against the chilly day, nor to say goodbye to the receptionist who had looked up and smiled.

Out on the pavement, Carl briskly turned away from the Poppy Scotland offices and marched off to the nearby zebra crossing. It had just been a paper exercise, just like the SSAFA case worker who had visited a few days previously. He'd been a nice enough bloke, had told Carl about his own service, in the Air Force, fixing planes. He now worked at Aberdeen Airport. He wouldn't offer any opinions though, he just needed to see Carl's bank statements, figure out what expenses he had each month, and tick more boxes.

Carl had gone along with it all to please the courts, anything to escape punishment. He crossed the road, inadvertently stepping into the path of a motorist intent on not stopping for the approaching pedestrians. Carl ignored the blaring horn and marched on through the old Victorian indoor market, its stunning glasswork ceiling was lost on him, as were the jewellery and clothing shops he passed within. Though it was a dull day, the glass ceiling allowed what little sun there was to filter down and bounce off the trinkets and charms, making them shine enticingly, but not for this shopper. He made straight for the café, and found Tilly sat in the corner table. He flopped down.

'How did it go?' she asked.

'Not very well, everyone seems convinced that I have PTSD. She's another one.'

'What did you talk about?'

Carl kept quiet and during the silence he tried to fill the time by looking at the menu, he had to put it straight back down when he noticed that his hand was shaking, badly. He couldn't make out the words and sentences, the delights of various cakes were lost in a fog of text to his jumbled mind. He broke off with, 'Gavin.'

Tilly nodded sagely and she warded off the approaching waiter with a hurried request for another tea and a flat white coffee for Carl. She placed her hand onto Carl's, for comfort and to stop his tremor that was shaking the table.

'I had to, I had to,' he fumbled for words, yearning to share his burden with his wife, 'I had to pick him up. His helmet kept most of it in, but his brains, his brains were pouring through my hands,' he recalled in horror. 'I'd forgotten. Or kept it buried, so deep in my mind.'

Not caring where they were, Tilly stood and cradled him in comfort, wrapping her arms around his shoulders, snuggling into his neck, providing her succour in the only way she knew. She held him tight, not even letting go when the waiter quickly placed down their drinks in embarrassment; the large man was crying.

Gordon turned on his grandfather's computer. It groaned in protest as the fans whirred into life. The icons on the monitor took several moments to appear and the welcoming tune sounded distorted. Gordon looked down at the tower standing on the floor under the desk PC. He'd never seen one of these, it was an antiquated device, in his opinion, at least ten years old.

Lewis sat on the spare bed next to his grandson, he was about to declare him an apprentice, or more like an accomplice. He'd hatched a plan to find the help his son needed. A black flat-coated retriever had been his guardian angel years ago and had helped him find inner peace of sorts. After seeing the young lady at the supermarket, the other day and visiting the Bravehound website, Lewis knew that he'd found his son's guardian angels. He just had to convince him and Tilly, especially Tilly as the dog may shed hairs around the family home and he didn't want to add to her burden. She had enough to cope with. He'd run it past Gordon first.

Several days went past in a haze for Carl. Though he had been to Culloden with Tilly, and had stopped off at Loch Ness, he remembered little of it and hadn't taken any comfort from the picturesque scenes before him. He was now sat down in front of another woman, though a good decade older than the previous one. Carl was beginning to grow accustomed to being behind a desk, pouring his heart out to a stranger. This time he was in a GP surgery, being assessed by another doctor. This time she listened, really heard what he said. But he didn't like what she concluded. 'You definitely have PTSD,' she declared.

'Oh,' was all that Carl could muster in reply.

She left him to mull it over and waited for him to reply.

'I just thought that I needed a good night's sleep. I've found earplugs that are comfortable, but they don't totally block out the noise.'

'I can certainly help with that, but you need to be honest with me and yourself. Tell me about the nightmares, is it the same thing every night?'

Carl looked to the floor, finding it hard to admit his struggles, 'Yes,' he finally admitted. 'It's like a movie playing in my head, only everything feels so real.' He saw her nodding, understanding, 'I need it to stop, before I play out my actions and really hurt someone.'

The doctor nodded, 'And during the day?'

Carl sighed. He remembered the threat of court action. 'Yes,' he confessed. 'I see things that are not there. People. Dead people. My friend, Gavin.'

'There are medicines that you can take, I can prescribe them, Pregabalin, is the best one. I'll start you on a low dose and you can build up to a full dose, that way you should avoid any unpleasant side-effects.' She looked at him, 'I think you'll need it.' She jotted down a timetable of what doses to take and when. 'Have you been self-prescribing?'

Carl looked at her in puzzlement.

'Any illegal or street drugs, or alcohol?'

'No, not really. No drugs, I have young children, but I have been drinking more than normal.'

'I will need you to stop, otherwise you'll get a bad reaction. The PTSD drugs I give you will make you drowsy and floaty, so I think Tilly should drive for the next few weeks. They should help you sleep through your neighbour's noise.'

Carl brightened up at this prospect. He took out his mobile phone and played her one of his videos.

She looked aghast. 'I think there may be an element of mental unbalance with him,' she blurted out in shock. 'Have you shown these to the police?'

'I will do, I wanted a few more to show them. Those bins are placed right under our bedroom window and the internal banging noises start at midnight and continue all through the night.'

She nodded, 'I doubt that his prostate gland allows him much sleep. He'll need to visit the toilet, every hour or two. I want you to do talking therapy too. I'm going to refer you to a psychologist. I don't think that you should wait for Combat Stress.' She hesitated, 'In my experience, they don't have a good track record of caring for our veterans as well as they claim. It's important that you keep the psychologist appointments and follow through with their help.' She kept looking at him until she could see him nod his assent.

Satisfied that he'd understood everything she'd said, she tapped away at her keyboard and a printer whirred and spat out a small form, which she signed and passed over to him. 'Take this prescription in the meantime. I'd like to see you again in two weeks, to keep an eye on you until your referral to Aberdeen Royal Cornhill Hospital comes through.'

Carl nodded obediently, took the form, saw that there was a box for him to tick, and left the room, satisfied that he'd now completed all that the Fiscal Office needed from him.

Tilly paused the television when she heard Carl's phone buzz on the table between them. They had taken an afternoon off to catch up on their favourite programmes whilst the children were at school.

'Hello,' he enquired of the caller.

'Hello Carl, it's Nicki, the Combat Stress nurse, we met at Inverness. How are you?'

'Not too bad, the doctor has me on new medicines. I'm a bit drowsy, so I'm taking a few days off work and just watching telly.'

'That's good to hear. I'd like to discharge you.'

'Eh?' said a puzzled Carl.

'Well, you can't go to our treatment centre in Ayr, and I'm afraid that the service in Aberdeen has closed, just last week in fact. So, I'll discharge you from our system.'

'But I'm no better,' protested Carl whilst Tilly looked on with worry, she'd only been getting one side of the conversation as it wasn't on speaker.

'It's the computer system. I must discharge you. But you can phone me again if you'd like a referral to Ayr.'

'I see,' was all that Carl could bring himself to say. He'd heard of how ineffectual Combat Stress was from other veterans and hadn't given them much hope. It was just another box ticked and the problem moved onto someone else.

'Thank you, Carl. Goodbye,' she cheerfully said as she hung up.

Carl looked to Tilly in despair, 'I've been discharged from Combat Stress.'

'What! Over the phone?' she asked sceptically.

'Yes,' he replied simply.

'But they can't do that.'

'They just have.'

'I'm not having that, it's wrong. You aren't a well man and they need to fix you. The army got you like this, and the army had better make you well again. Give me your phone,' she demanded.

Carl, still numb with shock, obediently passed it to her and then made his way out of the lounge, through the kitchen and study and exited their house and made his way to the safety of his arbour. He sat down, hoping to watch the birds peacefully go about their day. He was rewarded with a blue tit, darting about, checking for predators before it made its way to the feeders.

BANG, BANG, BANG!

Carl startled as the dustbin lid was hit with a hammer with all the might the old man could muster. He reached into his pocket. It was empty. He'd given his phone to Tilly and couldn't record the mad antics of a bitter old man. Instead he stood up, turned around and looking through the slats to his foe asked, 'Is that all you've got?'

The railings were rattled with the hammer in reply and as Simon reached his backdoor, he gave them a almighty hammer blow that caused them to echo around the neighbourhood and have the other neighbours come to their windows, seeking out the culprit.

Carl looked to his windows and then to the top slat of his arbour where several hidden cameras were doing their duty, he smiled, despite his racing heartbeat.

Chapter Twenty-Seven

Several more weeks passed and Carl still hadn't gone to the police, but his hidden cameras had been busy recording the insane movements of his neighbour, including sound recordings of Simon threatening his wife with a further beating if she did not rattle the railings with his hammer. These made Carl mad and he had to dig deep into his inner resolve and stop himself going around to his neighbour and putting a stop to this domestic violence. Instead, he drew upon his service experience of collating evidence and movements of his enemy and transferred the recordings onto a memory stick along with a logbook of dates and times that corresponded with the number he'd saved them as. He noted that they were now in triple figures.

Today, having been driven here by Tilly, he was now in another room, again facing another woman. There was no desk between them though, just two comfortable chairs facing each other, with a small desk to the side of the lady. She looked to be in her late forties, petite in stature and build, and immaculately dressed in a floral dress and matching colour of cardigan. She had a kind face and a quiet, but firm attitude; perfect for listening to Carl and guiding his mind to a healing direction. This NHS psychologist had introduced herself as Poppy. Carl had seen the irony in her name, given that SSAFA had e-mailed him to say that none of the army charities would help him with soundproofing and advised him that he should move. He'd felt terribly let down, especially when he thought about all the twenty pound notes that he'd popped in their poppy appeal tins over the years and the direct debits he'd paid to the Royal British Legion and Army Benevolent Fund each month. He cancelled them within hours of the e-mail.

'I agree with the Combat Stress nurse, you definitely have PTSD. I've cared for many former military men and women in the area and have treated them successfully. It's saved several having to go to Combat Stress, and frankly, you'll get better treatment with me or one of my colleagues. It'll be consistent and provided you come each week,' she looked at him for confirmation and was gladdened to see his nod of the head, 'I can get you in a position where you will learn to cope better. Normally I would take your information and go to a team meeting and we'd decide which of us would treat you. But from today's assessment, I can tell that I'm best placed.' She said this with no ego attached to her words.

Carl nodded, he was glad that someone was now taking responsibility for him and that he wasn't about to be passed onto another person or organisation. 'Can you really stop the flashbacks and nightmares?' he asked hopefully, almost childlike, seeking affirmation from an adult.

'Not totally. But I can help you understand your triggers and how to avoid them and how to cope after experiencing them. I've looked after many special forces, not just here, but at your HQ. You can trust me.'

Carl sat up straighter in his chair, his attention firmly on the lady.

'I've been tasked to help settle minds after successful and aborted missions, as well as providing care for veterans like yourself. For you, I will do this through EMDR, which means Eye Movement Desensitization and Reprocessing. It's a technique which was first discovered in the treatment of Vietnam veterans in America. I think you'll respond better to the use of my fingers, rather than a light, as you seem comfortable with me sitting so close to you. I'll move my fingers from side to side, at different speeds. It'll be right in front of your eyes. I'll need you to keep your head still, and to follow them with your eyes. Then when I lower my hand, I want you to close your eyes. I'll then talk and ask you questions. Are you happy with that?'

Carl nodded sceptically. It all sounded mumbo jumbo to him, but he'd go along with it anyway, especially if it pleased the court system.

'Good. On our first session, which I'll start in a moment. I want you to go to a safe place, perhaps a beach, the woods,' she hesitated. She was about to say, 'your garden,' but thought better of it, given what he had told her about his awful neighbour. She hadn't believed him until she was shown several video clips from his phone. 'Or even out on the hills. I'll make some notes whilst you are doing this, so don't worry if you hear me scribble away. Once in your safe place, I'll then take you to the start of the event, somewhere that you felt relatively safe, then, once you've described it to me and I've asked you some questions, or given you something to think about, I'll take you back to your safe place. It's important that we always end in you going back to your safe place. Over several months,' she stopped when she heard his surprised gasp. 'Yes, I'm afraid that this is no easy fix, I think that you have complex PTSD.'

Carl interjected with, 'Complex?'

'Yes, you've been involved in several exceptional missions and wars that have left you mentally scarred.'

'Oh,' startled Carl, 'well, yes, I guess so?'

'Definitely. That's why we need several months perhaps even a year or so of treatment. And I can see that you are fully committed.' She stopped talking and waited for another nod from Carl.

He obliged with a tentative nod, unsure that he fell into this category.

'Your nightmares haven't been just about Gavin, have they?'

This time he shook his head.

'You have killed, lawfully, whilst serving your country, but this too has left its trauma on you.'

Carl nodded, marvelling at how perceptive this woman was. She was so small in contrast to his huge frame, yet she was fully in control of the room and had entered his mind shrewdly and with great care and sensitivity.

'I can help settle your mind, reduce your nightmares and flashbacks considerably, but you in turn must be fully committed and honest. There can be no secrets in this room. I in turn will always be open and honest with you as we explore your memories, reprocess them and slot them away properly, like a well-organised filing system. Shall we begin?'

Carl licked his lips and tried to remoisten his dry mouth, 'Yes please,' he managed to say through his parchedness. He made a mental note to bring a coffee from the canteen next time.

'Good, okay, I'm going to bring my chair a little bit closer, are you okay with that?'

'Yes, that's fine.'

She dragged her chair several feet closer and sat down, plumping her cushion for added lumbar support. She placed her clipboard and pen on her lap, smoothed down her dress, preparing herself for the first EMDR session. 'Get yourself comfortable, lean right back in your chair, try and sink into it.'

Carl obliged, thinking that this sounded like a hypnosis session. He went with it anyway and looked to her right hand. He'd judged correctly, this was the one that she put in front of him. He wondered absently what using a light would have been like.

'Now follow my two fingers,' ordered the therapist as she waggled her index and middle finger at such a frightening speed.

Carl followed them as best as he could, though they were jiggling back and forth so fast, like an irate mother scolding a naughty toddler.

'Good, now keep following, that's right,' reassured the psychologist in a gentle voice. She slowed her movements down whilst keeping an eye on Carl's face at all times. 'And close your eyes,' she directed as she lowered her hand in a steady, but deliberately slow movement. 'Now describe your safe place to me, what you can see, hear and smell.'

'It's the sea, a deep blue, clean ocean, lapping against some fine-grained sand. There's lots of shells scattered around and there are rocks to the side. It's my favourite bay at the airbase in Cyprus, in Akrotiri. I loved going down there with Gordon strapped to my back in a special toddler carrier. He loved bouncing up and down and seeing the sea.'

'Good, now remember that you can go back to this lovely, safe place at any time and I will guide you back there when the session finishes. But now I want you to go to somewhere near the start of your mission, the one with Gavin.'

At the mention of his friend's name, Carl began to hyperventilate, his legs started to tremor, and his hands were shaking. He clawed at his knees, attempting to cease their movements and to try and dry out his palms. The familiar whole-body sweats broke out.

Poppy, seeing this, said in a calm voice, 'Think about your body, what it is doing. I want you to take several slow deep breaths, in through your mouth and out through your nose, concentrate on this movement and flow for a few minutes.' She watched as his tremors slowly subsided and he seemed in a more relaxed state, his anxiety was much reduced. In a slow, even drawl she almost whispered, 'Throughout our time, and when at home, especially when your neighbour acts out, I want you to remember and do this exercise. Simply close your eyes and regulate your breathing and spend several minutes getting nice and relaxed and slowing your breathing right down. Okay, keep your eyes closed and think about your mission, try and think about the start.'

Carl almost rocked back in his chair as memories of Gavin came flooding back, threatening to overwhelm him. He could smell the cordite from the weapons, the blood, the brains, he acted out spitting out through his dry mouth, though nothing was expunged. In his horror he jumped up and brushed himself down, trying to wipe off the blood and brain matter from his combat uniform and equipment, but when he opened his eyes, he saw that he was wearing jeans and a t-shirt. He found himself in an office, though Gavin, or what was left of him was in front of his eyes. He yelled out, 'NO, YOU CAN'T TAKE ME BACK THERE, I WON'T LET YOU!' He towered over Poppy, pointing out his finger as he screamed each word.

Poppy looked up with a calm and serene expression, allowing Carl to offload his feelings and his anger. She wasn't surprised to see him turn and make for the door. 'Sit down,' she said firmly.

Her words were lost on Carl as he left her office, slamming home her door, not caring about the loud noise.

The school bell rang, and a cacophony of young and excited voices rose from inside the building. Parents and guardians waited patiently outside for their charges and were rewarded with a flung open double door and a barrage of children streaming down the two steps and into the yard. They swarmed out of the gates and made their way to their respective adults, or walked home in groups, eagerly chatting, and shouting away.

Gordon strode up to his grandfather and fist bumped him in greeting and then stepped back and allowed Annabelle to come running in for a cuddle. After those two exchanged a kiss on the cheek, Lewis asked the pair if they'd done their secret homework.

'Yes, we've done as you asked granddad, we dropped lots of hints. We started by asking daddy all about the dog he grew up with and what it was like having a best friend with a wagging tail,' declared Annabelle proudly.

'And then we listened and said how lucky he was and how his dog would have loved living here with the beaches, harbour and hills to go for long walks,' interjected Gordon, not wanting to be outdone by his sister.

'That's good, you are two clever children,' boasted their grandfather as he took Annabelle's hand. He knew better than to take Gordon's whilst his school friends were about. 'And what about your mummy?'

'She wanted to know about moulting, and daddy had to explain what that was to us, and then daddy jumped up, sat on the floor and shuffled along on his bum!' announced Annabelle with glee.

'He then went on all fours and sniffed the carpet where his bum was,' laughed Gordon, recalling the fun they'd had at dad's antics, mimicking his dog's habit of trying to empty its impacted anal glands.

Lewis laughed, 'We soon stopped it by adding a carrot, Weetabix and Bran Flakes to its diet.'

The children looked up, not sure what he was on about. They hadn't understood their dad's explanation either.

'I think mum would let us have one,' offered Gordon.

'Especially if it helped daddy, like the old soldier at the church on Remembrance Sunday, and the lady at the supermarket that you saw,' joined in Annabelle helpfully.

'You two have been such stars, mission complete, as your father would say,' rejoiced Lewis with more glowing pride. He pointed to his car, 'No need to go home first, I'll drive you straight to the ice-cream shop and we'll have a treat with grandma. But don't tell your mum!'

The children waved to their waiting grandma in the car whilst shouting 'Hooray!' at the thought of their upcoming sugar hit. Though their grandfather was secretly much more eager than them for his favourite treat.

Tilly looked up from the magazine she was reading in the hospital outpatients' waiting room. She was shocked to hear shouting, in what sounded like her husband's voice. She hoped that his therapy was going well and that he wasn't yelling at the therapist, she seemed such a fragile, petite looking lady. She was surprised to see, down the narrow corridor, the door of the room that Carl had gone into open so soon after his appointment. He'd only been in there for half of the hour allotted to him. She closed the magazine whilst keeping her eyes on her husband and was horrified to see him slam home the door and stride off. As he reached her, he failed to stop and speak to her, or even acknowledge her presence. Her heart broke as she saw the tears streaming down his face. She watched him dive into the gent's toilets and knew that she couldn't go in after him. Instead, she tossed her magazine onto the nearest table and walked purposefully down the corridor.

Gordon raced around his grandfather's car so that he could be the first to open grandma's door. He gently opened it all the way and then moved closer to her so that he could support her as she painfully rose out of her seat. He stood as straight as he could so that she didn't have to bend as she gratefully reached out and took his arm.

Annabelle was with her grandfather as he unlocked their front door. She noticed a letter on the doormat and helpfully picked it up.

Lewis took it from her and smiled when he saw the Glasgow postmark, 'Thank you love, I think these are the leaflets I asked for from the charity. Let's get inside and have you cleaned up from all that chocolate around your face and hands, and then we can have a look.' He handed her his keys, 'Can you lock up the car once grandma's out please?'

Annabelle's eyes widened and she had a beatific smile on her ice-cream coated face at being trusted with such a responsible job. She reached out a smeared hand and took the keys like they were a treasured relic. Her grandfather rewarded her with a cheeky wink.

Poppy heard the timid double tap knocking on her door, a noise that she'd hoped to hear, though not this quickly. Not all her patients came back after their first painful appointment. Sadly, they would continue living with their emotional pain so needlessly, when she knew that she could have helped them, given time and patience. 'Come in,' she confidently offered.

Tilly cautiously opened the door slightly and poked her head through, 'Er, hello, I'm Tilly, Carl's wife.'

'Oh,' said a surprised Poppy, 'I was expecting Carl.'

'He went storming into the gent's, I felt that I couldn't go in after him.'

'No.'

'I heard him shouting, I'm sorry about that, and the slamming door.'

'That's okay, I was hoping that it was him coming back when you knocked.'

'I'll get him back to you, is that alright?'

Poppy nodded. She looked to the wall clock, 'He has another twenty minutes left for his appointment, it would be good to see him.'

Tilly stood up straight, resolved in what she had to do, 'Leave it with me.' She immediately left and went striding after her husband, she knew exactly where he would be.

Lewis passed the leaflets to the children now that their hands had been thoroughly washed. They'd taken their ice-creams down to the river as it was such a lovely spring day, but their treats had melted, and they couldn't gobble them fast enough. He was glad that their mother hadn't seen the mess they'd gotten into.

Annabelle pointed to the most beautiful Scotty dog on the cover of her pamphlet. 'Will daddy get a doggie like her, she looks fun!'

'No,' remarked Gordon as he held out the centrefold of his leaflet. 'He'll want a big dog like this.' He was showing a handsome black Labrador around the room, holding it straight out to grandma first.

'Wouldn't it be great if he got one as gentle as our Jodie used to be? He loved that dog. He couldn't wait to get home from school each day so that he could walk her and play football with her and all his pals,' reminisced Shona.

Lewis smiled as his memories of Jodie came flooding back. He only hoped that Tilly would say yes.

Tilly opened the entrance to the enclosed garden which Carl had commented on during their walk down the main hospital corridor. She knew he'd be here. He'd remarked upon the many bird feeders, filled each day by the in-patients as part of their ongoing rehabilitation. He was sat on a bench, alone and cradling his head in his hands, stooped forward and still crying. She fought back her own tears and quietly walked over to him. Standing about a metre from him, out of reach, she gently said, 'Carl?'

He sat up, wiping his eyes, 'I don't want you to see me like this.' He turned away, fighting hard to get a check on his emotions.

Tilly sat down beside him, her hands in her lap, staring at the feeders. She gave him time to gather himself together. After a few minutes she said, 'You've visited me so many times in places like this. Thank you for not giving up on me.'

Carl turned to face her, 'I never could. I love you.'

Tilly placed her palms onto his wet cheeks, 'And I love you too. That's why I'm taking you straight back to your therapist. No arguments.' She stared straight into his moistened eyes. He tried to shake his head, but she kept a good tight hold on him. She shook her head instead, 'No arguments. We forgive you, but you've hit out at me and had Gordon by the throat. You must do it for us.'

Tears welled up in his eyes, 'I don't want to go back there again, to the compound, to see Gavin die,' he wailed out.

'She will look after you and take away your pain. You must trust her, like I've had to trust psychiatrists and counsellors over the years after what the monster did to me, after my parents turned their back on me. I'll stand by you, like you did for me, but you must go back, to the therapist and back to Afghanistan in your mind, your memories. Let her recalibrate your mind and deliver you back to Annabelle, Gordon, your mum, your dad, your sister, Geoff and I, most importantly, come back to me.' She leaned forward and kissed him, despite his tears and running nose. She then drew him tight, cuddled him and whispered, 'I love you.' She didn't wait for a reply, but stood up, taking his hand as she rose, forcing him to his feet and guiding him gently back to Poppy.

Chapter Twenty-Eight

There was a much bolder double knock on the door and Poppy called out, 'Come in Carl, and sit down.'

The door opened and a slender hand grasped the side of the door and pushed it open. There stood Carl, head bowed low, looking at his feet. This other hand drew back and pushed Carl forward and in he walked, followed by a silent Tilly. She turned him around and pushed his shoulders down until he was forced into the vacant seat. Tilly looked at him with a grim determination, turned immediately, smiled briefly at the therapist, and then left the room, closing the door firmly, but silently.

The silence in the room remained for several minutes and was finally broken by Poppy, with, 'That's a remarkable wife you have. About ten percent of my patients find the first session too painful and walk out and never return. Another five percent stay, but don't come back for their second appointment. The others, I help, given time. That's the first time that a spouse has ever marched someone back. She really loves you.'

Carl looked up and nodded, 'I'm sorry. I shouldn't have treated you like that.'

'That's okay, I've had worse, they don't nickname you lot Sadists and Psychopaths for nothing!'

Carl grinned at hearing the slang for the SAS, though he hoped that he didn't fit into either bracket.

He marvelled at the mind-reading ability of Poppy when she asked, 'Well? Which are you?'

He laughed. Wiping the last of his tears, he replied, 'Neither, I hope?'

Poppy smiled, and then challenged him with, 'And Gavin?'

The smile dropped from Carl's face as quickly as an executioner's axe. 'Neither, he was a brave man.'

'Tell me about him?' she asked and left the question open for him to talk about anything he liked.

Carl hesitated as he gathered his thoughts, 'He lived for the army. He didn't have a family, so saw us, rightly, as his brothers and sisters. He was big, even bigger than me, yet could sprint like an Olympian and had the stamina of a marathon runner. He drove a battered old MG. He could barely fit in it and his head touched the roof when he drove. He loved my mum's cooking and always had seconds. They loved him too, like another son. He was my brother and best friend.'

'Thank you, Carl. And thank you for coming back to see me. We have a lot of work to do. Not just today, but for many months ahead. I'd like to see you every week for a few months. It will be hard, harder than today. I'll need you to dig deep and continue to explore your memories and feelings about Gavin, and then we'll explore your other missions. Will you do that please?'

Carl looked behind him to the closed door, as if seeking out Tilly, 'Yes. I need you to help me stop striking out at my family, during my nightmares and flashbacks.'

Poppy nodded, not at all surprised to hear about this violence. 'We can do that together. But not today. Our appointment is almost at an end. I need you to close your eyes and think about your oasis, your calm place.' She waited until he sank into his chair and closed his eyes, 'Describe the ocean to me.'

Gordon and Annabelle were sat either side of their aunty Felicity, vying for her attention. Each was talking over the other, pointing out the various dogs in the leaflets that they were thrusting into her eyeline.

'That one looks just like Jodie!' she exclaimed.

'Dad's old dog,' affirmed Gordon.

'That's right, well, she was shared by us all, though your dad never liked me putting bows on her collar.'

Annabelle pouted.

Uncle Geoff, on the other side of the trio, perched on the edge of the sofa, reached out and ruffled her hair and then took two biscuits from the table. He handed one to his niece, 'Never mind sweetie, I'm sure your dad will make an exception for you. I'll bet he'll help you dress up his dog any way you like.'

Annabelle perked up and joined her uncle in biting down on another snack. Soon they were competing in who could crunch the loudest. They smiled at each other as they bit down with their protruding teeth.

Lewis smiled across the room, he just hoped that he was doing the right thing and that Tilly would agree.

Tilly insisted that they walked across to Victoria Gardens after Carl's appointment. She knew that he loved this park and soon its spring colour was working its magic upon her husband. Behind them, amongst the tall trees and rhododendron bushes, wood pigeons cooed out to each other and fluttered down from the branches, glided onto the lawns, and foraged for grubs and worms around the grassed area. She looked to the huge Victorian fountain, its bare cauldron-like base was empty and she was disappointed, wondering whether she would ever see it restored to its once glorious state. It would make a great paddling pool for children and even for dogs to frolic. They had sat in companionable silence and watched the local dog walkers stroll past with their dogs obediently trotting by. She noticed that Carl always seemed to linger at the sight of the larger dogs.

'Thank you for going back.'

He looked at Tilly and sighed, 'You didn't give me much choice. You can be quite scary sometimes.'

She bumped shoulders with him, 'Only sometimes!'

He laughed, 'You always have me like putty in your hands.'

'Things will get better. It did for me. You helped me through the worst times in my life, and now it's my turn to help you. Shall we get going then? The car park attendants might be out and about.'

'Yes,' said Carl absently, smiling as he watched a black dog go running after a stick. It grabbed it up in its mouth whilst still on the run, skidded around and sprinted back to its owner. Instead of giving it back, it was trotting jubilantly around its owner's legs, as if it held boastful treasure and was doing a show and tell at school.

Tilly looked up to him and was pleased to see his pleasure, she knew bringing him closer to nature was part of his recovery process. She reached out and took his hand and the two were soon walking down the park like two young lovers out for an afternoon tryst.

Carl, outside his parent's house, hesitated at the car and checked himself in the mirror to make sure his tears had all dried up. A pale-faced, red-eyed, unshaved hobo stared back. His reflection didn't seem to bother him, and he pushed back the sunshade against the car windscreen and dutifully followed his wife.

He was surprised to see Felicity and Geoff sat on the sofa; their car was not outside. They must have walked, he thought. They too must have been enjoying the mild spring day.

'Blimey, you look rough!' exclaimed Felicity upon seeing her brother. 'Are you okay bro?'

Carl nodded, though it was Tilly who answered. 'He's a bit washed out; it was his first hospital visit.'

'Ah, I hope it went well?'

'Yes,' answered Carl, reaching for the last biscuit on the plate, 'I've to see her every week.'

'That's good son,' interjected his mother whilst looking knowingly at Lewis. 'You make sure and follow the therapist's advice. Like your father did years ago.'

Carl nodded, though Felicity looked puzzled and was about to question her father, but Lewis stood up and asked Tilly, 'Come with me lass, I'll show you my new bench.'

Tilly left the lounge and followed Lewis through the kitchen and into the back garden. The sun was starting to set, but there was enough light to see his bench. 'You haven't really brought me to see it, have you? This is where you take us to have a fatherly chat.'

Lewis chuckled, 'You know me so well. But let's sit first. How was it really?'

Tilly sat by him and turned to face him, 'He walked out. Well, more stormed out. But the lady, she was good with him, she wouldn't take any of his nonsense and told him how it would be when he came back.'

Lewis sucked in his breath and had a brief think. 'I sense that you may have had a hand in fetching him back?'

'It wasn't easy. He is at rock bottom. He yelled at the woman, slammed the door at her. Then he sat in the gardens and cried his eyes out.'

Lewis fought hard against crying himself. He hated to know about the pain his son was in. 'Thank you for being there for him.'

Tilly patted his hands, 'I always will be. I promise.' It was only then that she noticed the leaflets that he was holding. 'What are those?'

'These are why I wanted to talk to you alone. Does Carl ever mention Jodie?'

'Not half!' she laughed. 'He seems to talk about nothing else with the kids. I remember when Shona got out the family album when Carl and I were first dating. Every photo of Carl seemed to have his dog in it.' She thought back to the park, 'I think he misses having one.'

Lewis handed her the leaflets. 'These are from Bravehound. It's a Scottish charity, set up to help servicemen and women, like Carl, with mental health problems, particularly PTSD. They come fully trained. Toilet trained as well. So, there shouldn't be any mess.'

'Other than dog hair, maybe?' She bit her lip nervously.

'Och, that's easily managed with your vacuum cleaner, the children have promised to do that for you each day.' It was now Lewis's turn to bite his lip, to stop himself revealing his scheming.

'I thought as much. You've all been having a plot, haven't you!' she teased.

'Yes, sorry about that. But Jodie wasn't just Carl's dog. I bought her for me really. For fourteen lovely years she kept me sane and calm. She got me through the worst of my demons, until I found the right drugs that settled me. Treatments for PTSD were quite new then and I was one of the early guinea pigs.'

'Oh,' she replied in shock. 'I knew that you served in the army, but I didn't know that you had PTSD too.'

'I did everything I could to stop Carl from joining. I rarely mentioned the army to him, but he was so adamant that he was joining up. I did try and dissuade him.'

She patted his hands, 'I'm sure you did, but you know how stubborn and set he can be. I hope you haven't suffered too much with it.'

'It's manageable, Shona looks after me well enough, that's why we are in twin beds these days, not because of her arthritis, but because I thrash around. Anyway, enough about me, these leaflets are for you to read and have a think about. Maybe even phone Bravehound, or e-mail them?'

'Yes, I promise. I'll agree to anything that'll help Carl out. Besides, our two will have an even happier childhood with a dog in their lives.' She reached across and hugged her father-in-law.

Carl walked through to the kitchen, seeking a quiet room where he could take this phone call. His mobile continued to play its ringing tune whilst he carried it into the other room. He looked to the screen as he walked and saw SSAFA flash up. 'Hello,' he tentatively said, expecting to hear more rejections from army charities, though he thought they'd gone cap in hand to all those he knew about.

'Hello Carl, it's Catriona, from SSAFA, I work in the office, at the old Bridge of Don Barracks.'

'Hello Catriona,' he said neutrally.

'I've some great news for you. Though Help for Heroes can't go to the larger expense of soundproofing, they are willing to buy you headphones, to blot out the loud bangs coming from your adjoining wall.'

'Thanks, but I've tried headphones. They don't help unless I have my music up loud. That just makes me even more anxious.'

'These are top of the range headphones. They've ordered them from John Lewis in Aberdeen, and they will be delivered by courier tomorrow. They've a two-year guarantee and connect to your mobile phone. They will give you almost soundproofing quality. We recommend that our veterans with PTSD wear them all the time.'

'That sounds good, I'll give them a try. Thank you, Catriona, and please pass on my thanks to Help for Heroes. But I'll need to take them off when I talk to my wife and children.'

'No, you shouldn't, I should have explained better. They have a clever button that you press on the headphones to switch immediately from noise cancelling to ambient sound. These really are top of the range, worth several hundred pounds and are made by Sony. You won't need to have your music on loud and the quality of the music or spoken word will be superb. One veteran spends his time listening to radio plays and comedies and another goes for long walks whilst hearing books being read out by actors. So, when your neighbour next hammers on his wheelie-bin, you will be oblivious to the noise.'

Carl was silent for a while, he was fighting back a sudden rush of emotion, from the kindness of Help for Heroes and thinking about all their generous donors and fundraisers.

'Hello, are you still there, Carl?'

He swallowed hard and managed to say, 'I'm really blown away by this help, it sounds fantastic and will be a real gamechanger, it's going to make sitting at home more peaceful, thank you.'

'You are welcome Carl. We have been trying ever so hard to secure you funding for soundproofing; but are meeting wall after wall.

It's the same for an army nurse and medic we are helping. His Association refused to pass on e-mails to charities on our behalf and wouldn't meet any of the costs themselves. Normally, each charity chips in a few hundred pounds to a thousand and between them, they raise the funds to provide total soundproofing for semi-detached and terraced houses so that the veteran can relax at home without hearing any neighbourly noises. I'll keep trying for you and him. I'll call or e-mail as soon as I hear any further news, bye for now.'

'Thanks again, and bye Catriona.' He switched off his phone and pocketed it whilst looking out of the window. Tilly and his dad were having a cuddle with huge grins on their faces, he idly wondered about what plans they were hatching. He reached over and switched on the kettle, eagerly thinking about those special headphones and what he could listen to, perhaps that new Lewis Capaldi album Gordon was raving about.

The extended family were gathered in the lounge, sipping on fresh mugs of tea, eating from a new packet of biscuits. Lewis nodded to Geoff and Felicity, indicating that now was the time to broach the subject.

Geoff gave a nervous cough to clear his throat, 'Carl, your father and mother were kind enough to give us some money for a course of IVF and it cost several thousand pounds. As you know it wasn't successful, but we worked hard and paid for another course ourselves.' Felicity reached for Geoff's hand and gave it a squeeze of encouragement. 'She has to rest for a while before we try another course. We hope one day to have children as sweet as yours.'

The group looked to Gordon and Annabelle. The children were oblivious to the chat going on, they were busy looking up breeds of dogs on Carl's phone and cooing over the photos that the search produced. They failed to see the look of adoration on the adult faces.

Geoff continued, 'Of course I'd rather have put the money we are saving into a high-yield investment, perhaps some sound shares or an ISA, but Felicity wanted the safety of Government held savings, so we opted for Premium Bonds…' he was interrupted by a dig in the ribs from his wife.

Felicity continued the topic with, 'What Geoff is trying to say is that mum and dad want to gift you the same amount of money and we want to lend you the remainder. So that you can get a local carpenter to soundproof your home, rather than wait for the army charities. We want you to live in peace.'

Carl, once more trying to get a check on his emotions, looked from parent to parent, and then to his sister and brother-in-law. 'I can't ask you to do that,' he protested.

'Yes, you can son,' said Lewis firmly. 'I've already spoken to the chippie who built our kitchen for us and he'll be round tomorrow to measure up and discuss with you what he can do. He's soundproofed many veteran's homes in this area. Each have had to pay for it themselves. So, please don't waste any more time waiting for the charities, let's get you sorted ourselves.'

Carl stumbled for his words and Tilly chipped in herself with, 'Thank you, all of you, that would be great, won't it, Carl?' She looked to him and nodded her head in encouragement.

He nodded, knowing not to argue with her. He walked over to each of his relatives and gave them a huge cuddle, only Geoff was embarrassed by this public display of emotion and simply let himself be enveloped by what seemed a bear hug. 'I'll pay you back, I promise. I'll soon start making a profit from the website.'

'We know you will son,' agreed Shona. She felt down the side of her chair and passed him a tatty looking notebook with several food stains and watermarks on the cover. Geoff looked relieved to be let out of the embrace. Once Carl had taken it from her, she continued with, 'It belonged to your gran, it's all her favourite recipes and meals from scratch. You and Tilly will have to convert the measurements from the old ones, but I'm sure you'll soon get busy with them. You can write about them on your website. I'm afraid my old hands can't do the mixing and kneading anymore.' She looked down at her painful swollen fingers, but only momentarily, because Tilly had walked over and sat on her armrest and gently embraced her.

'Thank you,' Tilly whispered in her ear. 'That's made me feel special, it's a real family heirloom which we'll cherish.'

Carl flicked through the book as he tried to deal with this new rush of emotions and nodded to each of the adults in the room, he finally found his voice, 'Of course, this means you'll have to pop over and share these meals with us.' He was met with voices of agreement.

Tilly, judging the moment right, rejoiced with, 'And we are getting a dog!' She knelt by the children and gently took the phone from her children. She quickly typed in a search term, pressed a few buttons and passed it back to Carl, 'Or rather you are, here is the Bravehound application form, I expect it to be filled out and sent before bedtime.'

The children couldn't contain their excitement any more and wildly ran around the room, shouting out their preferred choice of dog for all to hear. Lewis winked at them as they passed.

Chapter Twenty-Nine

Carl found himself warming to Neil as they went from room to room, loft and cellar crawlspace included. Neil was the local carpenter who his father had arranged to come over to his house at nine in the morning. He'd arrived punctually and even had the stereotypical small stub of a pencil tucked behind his ear. He used it to scribble his measurements down in a small notepad, his fingers had a dull orange tinge from years of smoking roll ups. 'I'm a former infantryman myself,' he revealed to Carl. 'I went out in the tail end of Afghanistan, it was a bit quieter then, but still eventful. I get why you need the soundproofing. I live in a steading, so have no neighbours. It was rundown mind, it took me years to do it up, in-between jobs. I'll soon stop that idiot from disturbing your peace. We'll build a false partition on every inch of wall between you both and pack it full of insulation which is designed to absorb sound. No need to worry about the cost, I'll do your father a good price. He's already given me a deposit, so I can start as early as next month.' He looked to Carl, making sure that he heard this bit of advice, 'It'll be noisy mind. Especially my nail gun. You may want to be away during the day.'

Carl thought about the package that arrived that morning, about an hour ago, that he hadn't quite had time to unwrap. He'd been busy getting the children ready for school. 'No need to worry, Help for Heroes sent me some noise cancelling headphones, I'll just slip them on before you get to work. Do you need me to do anything special, other than move the furniture out of the way?'

Neil grinned, 'Well, your mother always had the kettle on and baked me these wonderful biscuits!'

The gentle twittering of the sparrows as they casually sat on nearby trees or swooped down to feed on the fat-balls was lost to Carl. He was wearing his new noise cancelling headphones and was blissfully listening to the latest instalment of The Big Finish podcast and making a mental note to download their new Doctor Who release. He could listen to it when he went for a walk. He was also unaware that behind him, his neighbour had taken a hammer and thumped more dents into a battered wheelie bin lid.

Carl leaned back and relaxed into the back of the arbour, stretched out his feet and looked at the empty bench to his right, imagining a dog curled up alongside him, having its tummy rubbed. He smiled. He couldn't wait to hear from Bravehound. He had asked for a large dog on his application form.

As if reading his mind, a dialling ringtone interrupted his podcast and sounded in his ears. His headphones had cleverly paused the podcast. He remembered the instructions and gave his right headphone two taps. 'Hello,' he hesitantly said, 'Can you hear me okay? I'm using my new headphones; they have a built-in microphone.'

'Oh, that's clever!' said a saucy, cheery voice, in a thick Glaswegian accent. 'I'm Franny, from Bravehound. Is this Carl?'

'Yes, this is Carl. Lovely to hear from you Franny. Did you get my application form okay?'

'Yes, that's why I'm ringing. We've sent off the letters to your GP and psychologist to verify your condition and another to the MOD, to confirm your service, thank you for ticking the box giving us permission, that speeds up the process. We are in Aberdeen next week, visiting a Bravehound and her veteran, it's a routine check-in that we do, about twice a year. We wondered if we could drop in past while we are in your area, have a chat, meet your family and go around your home and garden, just to make sure that it is dog friendly.'

'That would be fine, I don't have a piece of paper to hand, I'm in the garden.'

'Not to worry, I'll get our administrator to send the time and date by e-mail. She manages my diary, I'm rather forgetful these days.'

'Do I need to do anything for you?'

'No, don't you worry, just as you are, we don't stand on ceremony at Bravehound. Perhaps a cup of tea and a sit down.'

'That's no problem, I look forward to seeing you.'

'Bye then Carl, I'm looking forward to meeting you and welcoming you to the Bravehound family.'

Carl grinned and looked down at the arbour bench as the phone disconnected and his headphones cleverly recommenced playing the exact clip that he'd been listening too. The Daleks were screaming 'Exterminate!' just as the railings were rattled. This deliberate goading noise was lost to Carl as he watched the birds darting between his feeders and bird-bath. A starling was dipping in and out of the water and shaking its feathers dry between baths. He was in, he had been accepted, he had not been turned away from them like the other military charities had done to him, making him feel that his long service had not been deemed worthy enough. He'd soon be getting a dog. He couldn't wait for the children to get home and share in the good news. He wondered if the local bird population would mind sharing their garden with a four-legged friend with a wagging tail.

Simon stared with venom at Carl from his kitchen window. He fumed, hopping from foot to foot, like a penguin on hot coals, in a nervous need to expunge his built-up rage. He stared at the much-hated figure sat in the arbour next door. The man hadn't jumped at any of the loud noises that he'd made, nor reacted to the booming rattle of the railings. He looked puzzled, but was determined to get a response, he had to make this man move from that house. He always got his way, in the end, always, he thought.

Carl walked back to the front garden and was about to open his front door when a furtive movement to his right caught his eye. His sixth sense, honed by years of undercover and surveillance work in the military, alerted him to the sight of his elderly neighbour, Simon, shuffling fast to his metal garden gate, opening it wide, and slamming it home. No sound penetrated Carl's protective headphones, only the reassuring sound of Nicholas Briggs talking about his The Prisoner series of audio dramas. Carl laughed, especially at the sight of Simon running back to the safety of his house, scurrying in like a naughty schoolboy. His short legs were peddling fast, like a comical cartoon character. Simon darted into his house; ramming closed his front door.

Carl walked over to the adjoining garden wall, looked up at the CCTV cameras, chose the second one along the eaves, smiled, waved, and pointed to his headphones. He then turned and strode confidently into his house, a home once more.

One week later, Simon was stood at his lounge window, staring intently at two women in a large car that had the audacity to park outside his house, just inches from the dropped kerb that led to his driveway. He ran out of his house, up his driveway and onto the pavement just as they were exiting their vehicle. He walked over, staring from the kerb and then to the two strangers.

'Hello!' said the taller of the two in a joyful Glaswegian accent, 'Isn't it a lovely morning.' She turned and followed her friend who was already halfway down Carl's path. She failed to see Simon lift his hand and throw his middle finger defiantly up in the air in an unpleasant salute.

Simon ran back to his driveway and then climbed his two concrete steps to his front door, turned and stared at the strangers, as if he were a guard of honour welcoming a visiting dignitary. Only his demeanour was anything other than hospitable.

The other woman gave him a friendly wave and was not at all puzzled as to why this old man was staring at them and watching their every move. Under her breath she said to her pal, 'That will be the awful neighbour that you told me about, from Carl's application. The poor lad has enough on his plate without that moron adding to it. Still, he looks old, maybe he'll do the world a favour and croak it soon.'

Her mate laughed, loud enough for Simon to hear. This time they both saw the raised middle finger. Rather than looking shocked, she turned to her pal and remarked in a voice that she hoped would carry across the low wall, 'That's probably the only stiffy he gets these days!'

She got the reaction she wanted, Simon looked furious, more so when the duo burst out into fresh laughter whilst staring back at him.

The taller woman turned and rang Carl's doorbell, it was answered straight away by a beefcake of a man wearing headphones. 'Carl? Hi, I am Nancy, and this is Franny, from Bravehound. Shall we come in?'

'Of course, come away in, it's lovely to meet you both.'

'You can hear us okay? Only you've headphones on.' Nancy pointed to Carl's head to emphasise her concern.

'Ah, sorry, I have to wear them,' explained Carl. 'I've an unkind neighbour who makes lots of deliberate noises. They are switched to ambient sound. Though I will take them off, he never makes any noises when we've visitors, like my parents or sister. He has us under surveillance.'

'We can see that, he followed us from the pavement and down his path and then stood on the doorstep, staring.'

'Yes, he does that, though the surveillance is also from his CCTV. When you are next out, look up to his eaves, there are more cameras there than in a supermarket.'

'We read what you wrote about him in your application form. We can believe it all now. How awful for you,' offered Franny.

'Not to worry, these new headphones have been a Godsend. I hear nothing now, more so since the GP upped my medication. Between nightmares, I sleep like a baby.' Carl pointed thorough to the lounge, 'Come away in and get comfy. Before the medicines I would be woken up by loud bangs of him slamming home doors. My heart would be racing for hours. I slept little.'

'It's an awful thing to put you through, what a horrible, bitter old man. I see from your application form that you are on the highest dose of Pregabalin, is it helping?'

Carl sat down on his favourite chair whilst Franny and Nancy sat on the sofa, a look of consternation crossed his face, 'A bit. I'm undergoing EMDR with a psychologist, so I'm all over the place, reliving things I'd rather keep in a box, hidden away in my brain.' He looked over his shoulder, making sure that Tilly had not come in early with the children from school. 'I'm getting intense flashbacks as she makes me recall events that I've buried deep in my mind.'

The duo nodded and Franny said, 'Many of our veterans find the reassuring presence of a dog breaks the patterns of flashbacks. We train them to cuddle on that command. The large dogs reach out on two legs and put their front paws on the veteran's shoulders and hold on tight. The warm feeling can be comforting.'

Carl nodded, 'I miss my cuddles with my old dog.' He fought back tears from a sudden rush of emotions and pointed to the table, 'I made you some flapjacks, with chocolate chips and dates. Help yourself. I'll bring through a pot of tea,' he managed to say.

The two women made appreciative noises and tucked in, discretely leaving Carl to get a check on his tears. They were well used to helping veterans with PTSD at extremes of emotions.

Carl left the room and returned with a tray and was soon passing mugs to them and chatting away. 'Did you both set up the charity?'

'No,' replied Nancy between mouthfuls of a flapjack. 'I'm a dog trainer and I socialise a puppy. Fiona set up the charity, she is a lovely woman, so dedicated to the care of our veterans. She's at a meeting today; but sends her good wishes.'

'I oversee the welfare of our dogs and veterans, so you'll see me quite often,' remarked Franny. 'You've joined the family of Bravehound, so you can ring me at any time with any problems or issues. Not just about the dog. For instance, I can help you with hospital appointments by coming with you if you find going places difficult or help with finances.'

Carl pointed to the blue plasterboard on the adjoining wall, 'I may take you up on the finance check help, we've had to use our savings and my parents and sister's financial help in soundproofing our house from top to bottom. There is a foot of soundproofing material on that wall and all the others from the top of the house through to the bottom.'

'The noises were that bad?' asked an incredulous Nancy.

'I'm afraid so, the carpenter even soundproofed against the cellar and loft walls. It's helped a lot but took all our money.' He pointed at the plate of lightly golden flapjacks, 'Though I've started a new venture as a recipe writer online.'

Franny helped herself to another one, 'I'm sure it'll be a success, these are rather moreish. I will just finish this, and we will get down to business. Perhaps you can tell Carl all about Ruby.'

Nancy smiled and looked to Carl, 'I've been training Ruby, a large golden retriever. She often gets mistaken for a boy because she is so big. But she is a gentle giant and we think that she will be ideal for you. Most of our veterans like a smaller dog, like the spaniels we get donated, but Ruby is ever so special. She was donated by a family who lost a wife and mother. The husband and son wanted her memory to live on in a dog that helped a fellow veteran and we all think that her characteristics live on in Ruby. We think you and she will be well-suited.'

Carl simply nodded. He was overcome with the lengths that people were going to help him and others with the debilitating condition of PTSD.

'She's been trained to block and cover, that means that she'll go in front of you or behind, depending on the command, and not let anyone near you. We tell everyone to remember the commands like this, block your balls and cover your arse!'

Carl had taken a sip of tea and almost spat it out as he laughed, especially as the words came out of this delightful lady. He recovered himself and said, 'I thought it was just me. I hate going into shops and busy places. I've become a bit of a recluse.'

'That's the joy of having a Bravehound. She will give you company, but also get you out and about. One veteran takes his to the cinema and it lies under his legs and goes to sleep. We also teach the under command and the chill command for those reasons. Another just mentions bedtime and the spaniel runs up the stairs, nudges open his bedroom door, jumps up on the bed, snuffles under the duvet and rests its head on his special pillow, ready to sleep next to his veteran. It wakes him up during the start of his nightmares by gently touching noses. It breaks the cycle. Another veteran complains that his wife won't let the dog sleep in their bed! We don't get involved in that argument!'

Carl marvelled; he had not thought of those type of commands.

'We'll go through all the commands she knows later and teach Ruby any that are specific to you. Perhaps you can have a think about that over the next few days and if you are free, we would like you to come to our training centre, to learn how to handle her. Bring your family too, Ruby will become a family pet, as well as your service dog. We will also have a benefits advisor chat to you; in case you have not claimed for something that you are entitled to. How does that sound?'

'That sounds great. I hadn't realised that things would go so quick.'

'Your GP and psychologist helped; they wrote by return post. You are very deserving of a Bravehound, you, like all our veterans, have done some remarkable things for our country.'

Carl looked down to his mug of tea, overcome once more and fighting back tears.

'Are you able to stay the night in the local Travelodge in Glasgow? We like you to have a night with the dog before it comes home to you for good. Just to make sure that she is happy with you and vice versa. Besides, it is a long way for you to travel and you will be surprised at how mentally tiring the training can be.'

'That all sounds fine, do you have a photo of Ruby? I'd love to see her and show her to the children.'

The duo smiled at each other and Nancy gleefully said, 'She's in the car, would you like to meet her?'

Carl grinned, 'That would be amazing, yes please.'

Nancy stood up, 'Great, I'll bring her in. Perhaps after she's had a sniff around you can show us all around your garden.'

Carl nodded his agreement as Nancy left the room and went to her car.

Simon was pacing his bedroom by the window, keeping vigil on the large car. He leaned into the pane, bumping his nose on the glass as he peered out when he detected movement. He cursed at the false alarm, it was just a local mother walking to the school, preparing to collect her child.

His bladder was aching and protesting its need to empty, urgently, but he did not want to leave his post. He restarted his pacing, hoping his prostate would not fail him again. The wetness he felt proved otherwise and he ran out of the room and fled down the stairs, hoping to get to the toilet quickly enough before the full flow. He failed. He soon felt the inevitable hotness in his pants that preceded the gush of humiliation.

Carl heard a delightful jingle as a dog tag clinked against the metal ring of a collar. Four paws padded along the lobby laminate flooring and then a rush of yellow and white burst enthusiastically into the room. She scampered along the carpet and its tail brushed against the plate of flapjacks, dislodging one onto the floor, in front of a sniffing wet snout.

'Leave and sit,' commanded Nancy.

Carl marvelled at the will power of this beauty before him. She left the dropped food alone and was sitting proudly, keenly awaiting a fresh command. He too ignored the discarded treat and was soon petting the fur of this adorable puppy before him. He judged, correctly, as he would later find out, that she was about eighteen months old. His fingers enjoyed the sensation of the silk-like feel of her fur and the warmth it radiated. He was eager to feel the cuddle command when the time was right. He was oblivious to the nodding and smiles from the two women and was captivated by this dog, 'Hello sweetie,' he murmured to her whilst stroking her ears.

The women's faces were beaming away, they knew they had found another perfect match.

Simon took the walk of shame upstairs, cradling his damp trousers and underwear in his hands, covering part of his lower nakedness. He went into his bedroom and threw them on the bed, making sure they fell on Millie's side of the bed. He had not bothered showering or sponging down his urine stained flesh. Instead, he had simply put on clean clothes and then gathered up the sodden mess from the bed, walked back downstairs and then flung them at Millie, 'These need a wash woman.' Then he had sat by his CCTV monitor, playing back the recordings from his many cameras to see what he had missed.

Millie, trying not to wrinkle her nose at the ammonia smell that evaded her nostrils and would cling to them all day, gathered up the wet things, trying hard not to show her disgust. She knew from bitter experience what would happen if she objected to the way these soiled garments were given to her to launder. She also knew better than to suggest that he shower or have a strip wash at the sink. She shuffled painfully to the washing machine in the kitchen, trying hard not to get any wetter than she need be, nor to have any drips on their threadbare carpet.

Carl could not resist it any longer. He had looked down at those pleading deep brown eyes and his heart melted, he gave the command he just knew Ruby was waiting for, 'Cuddle,' he gently said.

He was not prepared for the instant leap that Ruby gave. It rocked him back into his recliner and he fell back laughing. Though his peals of laughter were muffled by a warm, hairy chest. Two thick paws landed on his shoulders with a firm grip that augmented no quarrel. A wet nose was gently placed on his and he could feel hot breath on his mouth, like that of an excited lover. He fused into Ruby and their bodies became one and he found himself once more feeling down the dog's back, enjoying the sleek sensation of her warm, reassuring fur. 'That's so lovely,' he murmured into her ear. He could feel Ruby's paws inch closer around his neck, until she had an even firmer hold of him.

Nancy and Franny helped themselves to another flapjack and munched down whilst this was going on. In between bites, Nancy spoke softly to Ruby, 'Snuggle.'

The dog obliged by pressing its nose firmly into Carl's neck and pressed down its jaw, almost merging as one with Carl. He in turn cuddled back the dog, making appreciative noises of encouragement.

Franny, giggling, said, 'Okay you two, once you are quite finished, let us look at your garden.'

Carl let go of the dog, but it remained on his chest and neck until Nancy commanded, 'Off.' It then pushed back on Carl's chest with its front paws, leapt off him and sat by his feet in a proud, upright stance, like a guardsman at attention. Carl gave it a pat on the head and another ear ruffle, stood up, and said, 'The garden's this way, through my study.'

The two women followed, as did Ruby when she heard, 'Let's go!' It trotted obediently next to Carl, almost as if it sensed who its new owner would be.

Chapter Thirty

The garden gate had been opened to two newcomers and then Carl, Nancy and Franny heard excited chattering coming from the side of the house. Then they saw Annabelle and Gordon stop in their tracks in astonishment at seeing two strangers in their garden, but it was the dog beside them that captivated their attention.

Nancy gave a soft, 'Go play!' command to Ruby whilst keeping a good watch over her. She was pleased to see that she trotted over to the two children, sniffing attentively. It sat down by Annabelle and pushed its snout into her stomach, making tentative movements.

Annabelle gave a shriek of joy, dropped her school bag, knelt and cuddled Ruby whilst demanding of her father, 'Oh she's so lovely, is she ours now? What is her name? Can I take her for a walk? Can she meet Daisy?'

A short-bobbed hair and nosey features were protruding over the garden fence and a pair of beady, watchful eyes were observing the group. She was seen by Carl, but he elected to ignore Simon's lover and neighbour. 'She's called Ruby, and yes she's mine,' replied Carl and though he had said, 'mine,' he knew that he would forever be sharing her with his daughter. He did not mind, he loved seeing the joy in his children's faces, 'they deserved that, after all I have put them through,' he thought.

Franny and Nancy looked to each and once again grinned, they knew that Ruby had found her forever home, they just had to train the veteran now.

The week had dragged on, remarked Annabelle to anyone who would listen, which included her favourite dolly and her parents. She had talked about nothing else but Ruby. She had even rushed through to Lee, Brodie and of course Daisy and chattered endlessly about her new best friend. Most especially, she took great pains to explain to Daisy that she would still be her best friend too. The two husbands sat patiently and listened, pleased to hear of the family's good fortune, knowing that a dog could easily heal a fractured mind. They too looked forward to seeing their two dogs play together. Even Dotty had to sit and listen to Annabelle talk ten to the dozen about her father's dog. She too was pleased for the family, though was inwardly concerned about Simon's reaction. She prayed harder than usual that week.

'Finally,' sighed Annabelle as the family car pulled up and parked at Bravehound Headquarters. She gave a squeal of delight as she spotted Ruby and Nancy, threw open her door, and bolted out, making a beeline for her much-missed buddy. She ran towards Ruby, threw open her hands and wrapped them around the patiently waiting dog.

Gordon sauntered up beside them, trying for an air of casual nonchalance. He reached out and patted Ruby's head twice and sat down on the bench beside Nancy. 'Alright?' he enquired.

'All good here, did you have a nice trip down?'

'We stopped at McDonalds and had breakfast, I can't wait to take Ruby for a milkshake,' enthused Annabelle, all the time ruffling Ruby's chest as the two kept their embrace.

Carl and Tilly joined their children, not daring to interrupt Annabelle's long anticipated reunion with her best buddy. 'She's missed her,' remarked Carl.

Nancy laughed, 'So I see! How have things been with you?'

'Much the same, I'm afraid. I had another session with the psychologist.'

Nancy saw the far away stare from Carl and chose, wisely, not to pursue this line of questioning. 'I've set up some free play. It is like playtime for dogs. It gets them to use their brain, as they must hunt for their treats, and it burns off the excess energy. It is a useful exercise for days when you don't want to go for a walk. Shall we make a tea and then we can get started. Ruby is very food orientated, so training her has been relatively easy. I've also taught her a new command that I think will be particularly useful for when you are in crowds, Carl.' She ushered them indoors.

The training room was segregated almost like a nursery, with a small fenced and gated waiting area with chairs for spectators and waiting families. Carl and his family sat down and waited whilst Nancy made juices and teas in the kitchen to the right of the enclosed area. They looked to the main training area and saw several ramps, an area of carpet, a large, but low box which contained small plastic balls, like the sort in an indoor kid's adventure playground, a hooped tunnel and several wooden steps that led to nowhere. It was like something from Crufts.

'It looks great fun!' remarked Tilly with joy in her eye. 'It's going to be exciting having a dog in our lives.' She hugged Carl; she knew that he was in good hands for a few hours.

Millie winced as a vitriol of spite and anger was verbally hurled at her by a pacing Simon. He had been on edge ever since the family next door had left early in their car. He had watched on his screens as several holdalls had been placed in the boot. She had secretly laughed to herself when she saw Carl turn to the cameras and give a cheery wave and then a thumbs up before driving off. Sadly, she now paid the price for his cheek.

'And we will be having an early night. You had best put an extra blanket on the bed, the weather report says that there will be a frost tonight. It is April, but they expect it to be minus seven until midday. They are even reporting that some areas of Aberdeenshire will get snow.

In Glasgow, the weather shone down approvingly, despite the chill in the air, as the weary family, having had a fun, but busy day at Bravehound, pulled up to the Travelodge car park. The middle seat contained several bags. Not to separate two squabbling youngsters, but because Ruby was in their boot, eagerly awaiting her first sleepover with her veteran, Carl.

Annabelle once more jumped out of the car as soon as Carl had applied the handbrake. She had a leash in her hands, attached to it were two foot-long flashes with the warning, 'PTSD Assistance Dog in Training' in bold red letters. She waited patiently at the boot, as instructed by her father, he did not want Ruby bolting out of the boot. He would hate to have lost her on their first night.

He need not have worried as she was patiently sat to attention in the boot, awaiting her next command. Carl tentatively opened the boot, all the time saying the 'Wait!' command.

Gordon, sauntering up beside them, helpfully said, 'Nancy and Franny said that you only need to say the command once.'

Carl gave a mock salute to his son, 'Right you are sir!' He snapped his heels to attention whilst Ruby looked on patiently.

Annabelle reached up and clipped the leash onto Ruby's body harness and then smoothed down her Bravehound vest that alerted everyone that she was a service dog and must not be petted. She smiled as she saw the Scottie dog mascot emblem and hoped that one day, she would meet Gwyneth, the dog that belonged to Fiona, the founder of Bravehound. She would give them both a big cuddle for helping her daddy. She passed the leash reluctantly to her daddy and walked back to the passenger seat for her rucksack.

Carl winked to her daughter as he took control of what he knew would always be called their dog. He gave his attention to Ruby and gave her the down command.

Ruby obediently jumped from the boot, landed by Carl's feet, shook herself as if trying to shed the vest, and then stood patiently, though she gave the air a few sniffs of inquisitive exploration.

Carl gave the 'Let's go,' command and was pleased to see her trot by his left side as he went around the car and took the larger of the two holdalls. He left Tilly to take the lighter, smaller one, and to lock up now that his hands were full.

The family made their way to Reception, with Annabelle keeping step by Ruby's side.

Carl, feeling self-conscious, but reassured at having a canine pal by his side, introduced himself and gave their booking number to the beaming lady. 'That's a beautiful dog you have,' she remarked whilst reading the writing on Ruby's coat. 'Is she yours, or are you training her for someone else?'

Annabelle boasted, 'She's ours, we share her with daddy.'

Carl and Tilly exchanged delighted looks; Annabelle had set out early with how things would be. Their eyes twinkled like stars reaching across galaxies as grins widened their faces.

'Then you are a lucky girl, she is as beautiful as you are,' replied the receptionist whilst handing Tilly a card that would allow them entry through the security door and to their room. 'You are all in the family room, number 212 on the second floor, the lift is to the right of the door that way. This card slots in the machines and will open the doors. Breakfast starts at seven and finishes at eleven if you want a lie-in.'

Tilly looked from Annabelle to Ruby, 'I doubt that will happen, she has already scouted out the park around the corner.'

The receptionist laughed, 'Have a great evening and a good night's sleep.'

Carl thanked her and allowed Ruby to lead the way, clearing an easy path between the groups of people in the hallway trying to get a signal from their phones.

The hands of the clock on Simon's mantlepiece struck nine in the evening and he turned to his wife with a lecherous look on his face, 'Get yourself cleaned up below,' he slurred. He pointed a finger to her groin area, 'It's time for bed,' he snarled as he clumsily put down his whisky tumbler. It rattled on the table, neglected ice-cubes chinked from side to side as the glass bounced twice and then fell on the floor, rolling to the side of Simon's chair, spilling out the ice.

Millie ignored the glass and their spilt contents. She would have to clean them up in the morning or come down the stairs after he had his pleasure. She shuddered and she shuffled painfully to the bathroom. In that moment, the power to the house went off. The high winds that brought the icy weather had caused a blackout that affected the whole village. She fumbled her way into the kitchen and found the torch they kept for power cuts. It had taken hours to fix the last time this happened.

Carl, in the corner seat of the Travelodge bar, looked up as another couple came to a nearby table and sat down. He eyed them warily.

Tilly placed her hand on his, 'You don't have to keep watch all the time, relax. There are no madmen with hammers here. Besides, you have your buddy watching over you.' She pointed to Ruby who was sat beside Carl, her muzzle nestled on his lap, providing a warm, reassuring presence. He was stroking her neck and ears. Franny had joined them after Ruby had free play and had taught Carl the muzzle command, which Ruby picked up easily.

He sipped his orange juice and smiled at his wife and children, looking from one happy face to another. This is all that matters, he thought. They are so contented and safe, as am I now, he cheerfully thought. He gave Ruby an extra ear rub and she nestled further into his lap; she too was content.

Millie stared up at the ceiling in their darkened bedroom, allowing herself to be violated once more by this stinking man atop of her. She felt her inner soul wilt further with each violent thrust, wishing bad things upon him that she knew would never happen. Her life was over, she would have to remain his plaything, cleaner and cook for many years to come. As he yelled out at his climax she braced for his juddering and then felt his final heave from her. She reached down and pulled down her nightdress and wearily sat up whilst reaching blindly for a tissue. 'I'll just go down for another toilet, I think I drank too much tea,' she pitifully whispered in the air, grabbing the torch in haste.

Simon, not listening, rolled over, puffed up his pillow, took out his hearing aids and placed them on the commemorative plate on his bedside table. He then burrowed into his pillow and promptly fell asleep whilst his wife shuffled agonisingly out of their bedroom, silent tears streamed down her face.

Ruby had been for a final pee outside in the grassed area which had surprised Carl with being crunchy underfoot with an unusual seasonal frost. He had instructed Annabelle, not wanting to leave Ruby's side, to be careful as it would be slippery. Now the family were in their room, weary from all they had learned at Bravehound HQ. Tilly was already in bed, as was Gordon. Annabelle was busy pushing her bed towards the king-sized divan that her parents shared.

Carl watched her struggle and then resigned himself to helping her push the bed as near to Ruby as possible. The dog's blankets were by the side of Carl's part of the bed and were now between father and daughter. The family finally settled for bed.

A heavy frost shrouded the village that Millie had spent her adult life in, since marrying Simon at the tender age of eighteen. She had been an innocent then and now wished that she could have her life once more. She regretted her marriage. She sighed as she stooped over and picked up the whisky tumbler. She carried it through to the kitchen sink and placed it by the side of two washing up liquid bottles.

One was full, whilst the other was empty, awaiting being put out for the recycle bucket in the morning. She reached for this empty one and, with swollen fingers that made the task difficult, unscrewed the lid.

Several hours later, Tilly's bladder awakened her. As she crept to the adjacent bathroom, she looked over her shoulder to make sure that she had not woken her sleeping family. She grinned as she saw that Carl, surprisingly peacefully asleep and having had no nightmares so far, was sleeping on his side, with Ruby wrapped in his arms. The dog was snoring contentedly, nose almost parallel to that of her husband's. This was not just the cause of her happiness. Annabelle had also crept up into the huge bed through the night and was fast asleep beside Ruby too, with one arm wrapped possessively around the dog. Tilly sighed contentedly, the dog had already stolen the hearts of her husband and daughter, and she did not mind one bit.

Simon's eyes sprung open at five in the morning, like they did every day, not out of habit because he had always gone to work at this time of day, but because he had gotten into the habit of rising early to start tormenting his neighbours. He thrust his arm out and poked Millie in the ribs. 'I want eggs and bacon this morning,' he ordered as he sprung out of bed and ran to the bathroom before his prostate got the better of him.

Millie unusually smiled. It was still cold, she thought, good, she contemplated as she stirred her stiff joints into working.

Downstairs, Simon dribbled urine onto the toilet seat and floor as he finished urinating. He did not bother wiping it clean, nor did he wash his hands. Instead he went back upstairs to get dressed. 'The electric's back on. Get me a cup of tea,' he commanded to Millie as he threw off his pyjamas and donned his stain-ridden jeans and sweater. 'And don't bother with the heating, I don't care how cold you think it is.' He failed to see her smirk as he left the room. Millie reached over and switched on the CCTV monitor and sat back on the bed. She plumped up her pillows and put them against the headboard. She then leaned back, relaxed, and, unusually for her, was glued to the screen.

Simon reached for his hammer, from the shelf in the lobby, grasping it tight in his left hand. He was ready to start tormenting next door, he'd know if they were in by looking for their car. Either way, he'd bang and rattle bin lids and railings, just in case. He unlocked the front door and walked out of his house. His feet skidded in the frost. The top step was like an ice rink. His feet went flying and he fell on the concrete with a sickening thump. A loud crack tore through the air, like sudden lightning, as his femur shattered in several places. He started to bleed internally from this trauma, just as his head thudded against the step and bounced twice, shattering his skull. Red blood poured from his scalp, mingled with the ice, and formed a strawberry looking, spilt, slush puppy drink mixture. He'd automatically let go of his hammer. It was thrown in the air above him and landed with a squelch on his left eye, burrowing deep like a crazed mole, pushing his eye into its socket. It gave a squelch and popped, causing more fresh blood to pour from him, the warm sensation mingled with the unusually seasonal frost. He yelled out with the last of his breath, but blood flowed into his mouth, causing him to choke. He reached with his hand to the passing figure who had crossed the road just before his driveway gates.

It was Amber, the young woman in the shop, on her way to be ready to receive a fresh delivery of newspapers and morning rolls. Her ponytail bounced with each confident stride. She hadn't seen him, and probably wouldn't have gone to his aid anyway, few neighbours would have. She was wearing her new earbuds, a gift from her mother, and failed to hear the gurgling and dying choking of the man who tormented her each morning. She was listening to her favourite music, humming along as she went, unusually happy for once.

As he lay dying, Simon's last thoughts were that Carl had won, he may have lost a few battles, but that infernal man and his birds had won the war.

Millie smiled and then stuck her finger up to the monitor, despite her painful digits. She mouthed a few swear words that seemed foreign, coming from this sweet old lady's mouth. She reached over and switched off the monitor, then walked back to bed, snuggled down, and fell asleep, dreaming of all the days ahead of her. Of having the heating on whenever she wanted, of making friends and apologising to the neighbours for the noise harassment she was forced to commit. She started to think about the life insurance she would receive, of using it to get help around the house, of new carpets, a sofa for guests, and even a walk-in shower. She fell into a deep sleep dreaming of no longer having to be forced to feign dementia, ripping out the CCTV and how she had used the time of the power cut to pour water through the letterbox, using the old washing up bottle, and onto the front door step, unseen by cameras. The step had frozen overnight, thanks to her quick thinking and action.

Tilly awoke, feeling cold. She was on the edge of the bed and with no duvet wrapped around her. She felt along the bed, in the dark, and stopped her fumbling when she felt her daughter beside her, wrapped snugly in the duvet. Tilly switched on the torch function on her mobile phone and looked around the king size bed. Beside Annabelle, snoring loudly and blissfully, was Ruby. Annabelle had both arms wrapped around the dog and both were fast asleep, heads on the same pillow, noses almost touching. Beside them was Carl, sleeping soundly on his side with an arm also wrapped around the dog. He looked so peaceful. Tilly didn't recall him shouting out or having a nightmare, for the first time in months, since he developed PTSD. She smiled, reached for her dressing-gown, wrapped it around her and sat back on their bed. She switched off the torch from her phone, put it down and reached for her Kindle. Before starting the new chapter, she made a mental note to buy a bigger bed for this new chapter of their happy lives together with Ruby.

Author's Note

Thank you, dear reader, for your support and interest in my books. I do love writing them and I hope that they bring you much pleasure. If they do, please leave a review at Amazon and/or GoodReads, it'll help me in my literary career as the author scholarships and competitions I enter judge me on the 5-star ratings I receive.

I'm about to change direction, from ghost and horror stories with a twist to two shorter novels of romance. I can't wait to share them with you. Learn more about them and me at www.cgbuswell.com where there are links to my Facebook, Twitter, and Instagram pages.

It's been a joy to write about Bravehound, and an even bigger joy, to be the lucky recipient of my Bravehound, Lynne. She keeps me sane and safe, helped heal my fractured mind, and has brought pleasure back into my life. I owe a huge gratitude to Fiona, Lorraine, Lee, Kate, Gwen, Denise and many more, and especially to the family who donated her in memory of their loved one. Thank you.

Thank you to my dear friends, Ray and Katherine for your advice and expert proofreading. If you ever need remote IT support, Ray can be contacted at www.crudenbaytraining.co.uk/ or in his shop in the village Post Office.

Amanda, at Let's Get Booked, has done a fantastic job on the cover. Thank you. See more of her covers at www.letsgetbooked.com where you might find a new indie and traditionally published author to read.

Chris

Printed in Great Britain
by Amazon